MISTER MANNERS

A STORY FROM THE FILES OF ALEXANDER STRANGE

MISTER MANNERS

J.C. BRUCE

Mister Manners
A Story From the Files of Alexander Strange

Copyright © 2021 J.C. Bruce

ISBN: 978-1-7347848-8-6 (Hardback)
ISBN: 978-1-7347848-2-4 (Paperback)
ISBN: 978-1-7347848-3-1 (eBook)
Library of Congress Control Number: 2021905428

Printed by Tropic Press in the United States of America.
First printing edition 2021

Tropic Press LLC
P.O. Box 110758
Naples, Florida 34108
www.Tropic.Press

What the Reviewers are Saying:

Bruce's prose is consistently crisp and controlled, and the tension between the various characters is genuinely entertaining throughout. A charming and suspenseful page-turner punctuated by dashes of the surreal.

Kirkus Reviews

Florida Man by J.C. Bruce will take you on a pleasant ride. It is full of twists and turns. It is simultaneously mystery and comedy... It's a unique and entertaining plot. The dialogue was my favorite part of the novel...I would recommend this book to fans of mystery, murder, and mayhem... Those who do give it a try are sure to be as hooked as I am on the adventures of Alexander Strange.

Online Book Club

This story has the feel of a dark Florida river chock-full of weird creatures and bizarre surprises as it winds its way through swamps to somewhere wonderfully strange.

Florida Writers Association Judges

I went through Strange Currents like a box of fine French candy, carefully savoring each delicious piece. What a well-crafted story.

Bill Pflaum

I've read all of the "Strange" books, and this (Strange Currents) is the best! It's got the most sophisticated plot, the most-developed characters, the most memorable settings, and the best dialogue. And it is strange, which is what makes J.C. Bruce's series so unique and readable.

J.B. Tillson, author of The Dayton Book Guys

Mystery, intrigue, and laugh-out-loud moments with a noir flavor that just won't quit. Think Carl Hiaasen, Clark Kent, and a little Woodward and Bernstein…"

Bill Roorbach, author of The Smallest Color

A fast-paced mystery that resonates with wit as delightfully dry and intrigue as heated as its Arizona setting…

Jess Montgomery, author of The Widows

I have read all four books, and I'm a big fan of Alexander Strange and J.C. Bruce. Twisting engrossing plots, tear-producing humor, and wonderful characters and dialogue will leave you begging for more.

Charlie Freydberg

Bruce weaves a funny, quirky, and memorable tale involving oddball characters, voodoo (sort of) … and an off-beat, sometimes unreliable narrator into a mystery story that's also a voyage of discovery. If you're looking for a fast-paced, enjoyable read that keeps you guessing, you'd be wise to purchase Florida Man.

Marc Simon, author of The Leap Year Boy

This is what happens when you have a great writer with a wicked sense of humor and is also an experienced newspaper journalist who writes a great crime mystery. Lots of fun stuff. Action. Adventure.

Mark Wilson

The Strange Files Series

The Strange Files

Florida Man

Get Strange

Strange Currents

Mister Manners

This book is dedicated to:

Sandy Bruce

Logan Bruce

Kacey Bruce

They are my world

CHAPTER 1

Goodland, Florida

MY GIG AS a mystery writer began with a dropped call—literally—when the phone slipped through my fingers as I dove for cover.

The phone clattered beside the wheel of a pickup truck parked at the curb, followed by me, then by my pal Lester Rivers, the private detective who'd led us into this shooting gallery.

BOOM!

The F-150's windows disintegrated, and we were showered with shattered glass.

"You still there?" my caller demanded over the speakerphone, which, remarkably, was still working.

Lester nonchalantly lifted the phone off the asphalt, brushed off some dirt and glass, and handed it to me, as if taking calls in the middle of a gunfight were the most natural thing in the world. I stared at the phone for a moment, a little dazed and confused, then finally figured, what the hell, I might as well say something:

"Sorry, things have gotten a little ballistic here."

My caller was Naples author Cordelia "Kitty" Karlucci, whose bestselling series of romantic mysteries had made her and her protagonist—Penelope Peach—international household names. I'd interviewed her the day before after she became the most recent victim of Florida's notorious vigilante, Mister Manners. He'd Super Glued a grocery cart to the roof of her Lexus, and she was pissed.

Before our conversation was interrupted by gunfire, Kitty had given me an update for the column I'd written. She'd posted a fifty-thousand-dollar reward for information leading to Mister Manners' arrest and conviction.

She also had a "proposition" for me, she said, but we hadn't gotten to that.

BOOM! BOOM!

The truck rattled, and a tire blew. Specifically, the tire attached to the wheel Lester and I were huddled behind.

"What's that noise?" Kitty demanded. "Sounds like fireworks."

"Twelve-gauge, I think."

"Wait, are you shooting skeet or something? That's more important than my call?"

"I'm not shooting anything. I'm trying not to get shot."

"Is it Mister Manners?" she screeched. Guess she had him top of mind.

"No. Different lunatic."

Lester made a megaphone with his hands. "This isn't necessary, Mr. Duke," he shouted toward the white clapboard cottage, the one with the front window busted out, with the barrel of the shotgun protruding. "We're just here to take it back. We're not the police. Hand it over, and we'll be gone."

Being gone sounded like an inspired idea, but for the moment we were riveted in place. We were also in violation of social distancing rules, bunched together as we were, although we were wearing our face masks—excellent at blocking viruses, not so much for stopping buckshot.

"Are you listening to me?" the voice on the phone shouted.

"I've got this shooting pain right now, Kitty. Give me a few and I'll call back, I promise."

She hung up.

The madman firing at us had complicated identity issues, according to Lester. His real name was Horace Sniffen, but he'd abandoned that unfortunate moniker when he awoke one day in a detox center to discover the spirit of Raoul Duke had possessed him. Duke was the imaginary alter ego used by the late gonzo journalist Hunter S. Thompson.

Sniffen's reincarnation as a fictional character occurred after a lifetime of genuinely heroic levels of self-medication. And, it seemed, he also shared Thompson's affection for alley sweepers.

"You ever heard of shotgun golf?" Lester asked me. It was a quiet moment. Sniffen probably was reloading.

I shook my head.

"Hunter Thompson invented it with Bill Murray. It's like shooting trap only on a driving range, and the challenge is to shoot golf balls out of the air."

Lester reached down and began fiddling with his prosthesis—a legacy from an IED in Afghanistan that resulted in the loss of his left leg below the knee. He pushed a pin on the device's ankle, and I heard a click. I'd seen Lester do this before. He once threatened to beat a man senseless with it. I think he finds multi-purposing his artificial leg therapeutic, a way to turn a perceived weakness into a weapon.

He slipped it off and began waving it over the hood of the truck. "Goddammit, Raoul, look what you've done!"

We heard a piercing screech from inside the house. A moment later, a screen door slammed at the rear of the cottage, followed by receding maniacal laughter.

"I think he's gone," I said and started to rise. Lester grabbed my shoulder and pulled me down.

"Might be a trick."

Right. Sniffen or Duke or whatever he called himself could be circling the house, waiting to ambush us if we left the cover of the pockmarked pickup. We listened for a minute until I heard footsteps clomping along the boat dock. I peeked over the hood and saw him, one hand on a line securing a small runabout, the other grasping the shotgun. The outboard fired up, and the growl of the engine began receding across the water.

Lester reattached his prosthesis and stood up. "Okay," he said. "Let's take a look."

He led the way to the house, and I followed closely behind him. As a human shield, he left something to be desired as he's built close to the ground and I'm vertically gifted. Still, I'll take whatever cover I can get. That may sound cowardly, but if you've never been in someone's gunsights, believe me, it sucks like nothing else.

Lester was in his customary outfit: Hawaiian shirt, a flat straw boater on his bald head, Bermuda shorts with a white belt, black knee-high nylon socks, and black wingtips—the Full Cleveland. His white mask matched his belt. I was in my usual workday attire—ball cap, cargo shorts, a Green Lantern face mask, and my obscure rock band tee-shirt *du jour*, today's selection celebrating the Midget Handjob album entitled *Midnight Snack Break at the Poodle Factory*.

We were now at the front door of the cottage, which shielded us from the water in case its trigger-happy resident began shooting from his boat. I could hear a faint siren in the distance. No doubt, a neighbor had summoned the sheriff.

"We're here, why, exactly?" It's the kind of question you would have expected a rational person—or even a journalist—to have asked before looking down the wrong end of a blunderbuss. But you get used to the unexpected when you make your living writing about news of the weird.

When Lester didn't respond, I posed another question:

"How come every time somebody points a gun at me you seem to be around?"

"I could say the same thing," he replied, then gently cracked open the front door and peered in.

Fair point. Lester and I had been through a few scrapes together, including, most recently, a Key West gunfight aboard the *Miss Demeanor*, my converted fishing trawler that serves as both home and floating office.

Lester turned back to me. "You remember the movie *A Christmas Story?*"

"Of course. That kid, Ralphie, his mom warned him he'd shoot his eye out with a BB gun."

"Remember his old man's obsession."

"Don't tell me."

"Yep, we're here to retrieve that." He nodded to a leg lamp sitting on a small table by the side window.

"*The* leg lamp? The actual one from the movie?" That had to be worth a fortune. It was about four feet tall in the shape of a woman's calf and thigh enmeshed in a sexy net stocking with a gold, fringed shade perched on top.

"No," Lester said. "They used three different lamps during the filming, and they managed to break all of them. This a plastic knockoff."

"For this, we should risk getting shot?"

"No risk, no reward."

Lester was an operator for Third Eye Investigators. His old Army buddies who founded the agency employed him as a skip tracer and a "recovery specialist," meaning it was his job to find missing people and retrieve valuable stolen property. Ordinarily, he "recovered" missing money or *objets d'art*, not knockoff movie trinkets.

Lester calmly pushed the front door the rest of the way open, and we stepped inside. No drawn pistols, no hand signals, me just trailing behind him. On TV, when the cops bust in, they go room to room and clear the place. This wasn't TV, and we weren't cops.

"Relax," Lester said without turning around. He lifted the lamp off the table, and I noticed it wasn't just unplugged, but the plug, itself, had been snipped from the electrical cord.

"Kinda useless, isn't it?" I asked. The siren I'd heard moments before was now noticeably louder, even inside the cottage.

Lester began unscrewing the finial, then lifted the fringed yellow lampshade off the harp.

"Look closely," he said. He unscrewed the light bulb then, holding the lamp by its knee, turned it upside down, the mesh stocking on the shapely calf stretching as he did so. He held out the palm of his hand to catch whatever was about to pour from the socket.

"Ta-da!" he sang.

Aaaand…nothing happened.

"This is your big reveal?"

Lester began shaking the lamp, then held it up over his head and peered into the downturned socket. "Sonofagun. It's not here."

"What's not here?" I asked, beginning to wonder if my friend, the shamus, was having a senior moment.

"It's what we came here for. A computer memory card, you know, one of those small SD cards. It should have been hidden in here."

I wondered what was on the card that would be so valuable it was worth getting shot at. And if Lester would ever tell me. He might invite me along for the adventure, but he was notoriously closed-mouth about his clients.

With my phone in hand, I turned to him.

"Lester, why don't you take your leg off again. We'll set the lamp-shade on top, and I'll take your picture. Make a great *Strange Files* photo.

He ignored that and turned toward the door. "Come on. We need to vamoose."

"Uh, the lamp?"

He glanced back.

"My job was to recover the card," he said. "My client doesn't care about the lamp."

"So, you're just going to leave it?"

"Why? You want it?"

I hadn't actually written "leg lamp" on my Christmas wish list. But, I thought, why not, and snatched the lamp and shade and followed Lester out the front door.

"Mona will freak out," Lester said as we beelined to his car, parked around the block.

Mona's one of my shipmates, a mannequin I rescued from a going-out-of-business sale. She stands guard in her pirate regalia aboard the *Miss Demeanor*.

"You mean the leg being plastic and all like Mona is?"

"Exactly," Lester said. "I mean, how would Fred feel if you came home with a stuffed dog lamp?"

Fred's another of my shipmates, an eight-pound black and white Papillon, a gift from my Uncle Leo's current—and fourth—wife.

Then there's Spock, the final member of my crew. He's a cardboard cutout of James T. Kirk's sidekick. I am deeply suspicious that he and Mona may have a thing, although I've never caught them *in flagrante delicto*.

"Mona's never complained about anything," I said. "Not even when that deputy shot her. Besides, I think this will look terrific on my desk."

"What about Gwenn?"

"She'd look terrific on my desk too."

That got me an eye roll.

Gwenn's my girlfriend. She's only recently acquiesced to my living with a large-busted rescue mannequin. Would a leg lamp be too much? Would she suspect a plastic fetish?

Lester clicked open his car's locks. I briskly lowered the leg lamp into the back seat, then piled in. As we pulled out of the neighbor-hood, a green and white sheriff's cruiser swept by, lights flashing, siren wailing.

"Besides, Gwenn's in Europe," I said. "I'll post a picture on Instagram, get her used to it so by the time she returns the lamp will be old news."

"Oh, Padawan, learn you must about women." He'd been doing Yoda a lot lately. And not badly for a guy with a heavy Cajun accent.

Lester insisted on driving both of us back to his office in Naples even though my boat was docked only a few blocks away. I decided to go along for the ride. His client was waiting for us, and I was curious who was behind all the drama.

While he drove, I called up my most recent *Strange Files* column on my phone and updated it with the bounty Kitty Karlucci had posted.

THE STRANGE FILES

UPDATE: Author Kitty Karlucci Posts Bounty on Mister Manners After He Glues Grocery Cart to Roof of her Lexus

By Alexander Strange

Tropic Press

NAPLES—New York Times bestselling mystery writer Kitty Karlucci ordinarily does not do her own grocery shopping.

"I have people for that," she told me.

But her "people" are quarantined, having tested positive for COVID-19, so the wealthy "Queen of Murder and Mayhem" has driven her Lexus LS 600h L, a luxury sedan valued at $220,000, to the Publix on Tamiami Trail for the past two weeks to pick up provisions.

"I do my own cooking as everybody knows," she said. A graduate of the Culinary Institute of America, when she isn't writing episodes of her Penelope Peach mystery series, Karlucci hosts a popular weekly cooking show on the Dining Network entitled Vicious Vittles.

On her visit to the supermarket this week, Karlucci was horrified when she returned to the parking lot to discover an upside-down grocery cart on the roof of her Lexus.

"I tried to yank it off, but it wouldn't budge," she said.

It was immovable because it was Super Glued in place.

Who would do such a thing, and why? Police said a note pinned under her windshield wiper provided the answer:

"You failed to use the cart corral on your previous visit. Your discourtesy has been avenged."

It was signed "M.M."

This is the notorious calling card of a Florida vigilante that social media have been calling Mister Manners, a self-anointed punisher of those who talk too loud on their cell phones, fail to use their turn signals, neglect to use their doggie bags, and now, apparently, ignore the cart corrals in grocery store parking lots.

A spokesman for Lexus of Naples declined to say what the repair would cost, but several local body shops said it would total thousands of dollars.

Karlucci refused most news media requests for comment, but she spoke briefly to me.

"When you write this up, I want you to include a message to the son of a bitch who did this," she said. "I will find you, and I will get even."

(And today, Karlucci announced she is posting a $50,000 reward for information leading to the capture and conviction of Mister Manners.)

A passerby video-recorded part of her conversation with Naples police and posted it on Instagram. In the video, Karlucci, wearing yellow yoga pants and pink running shoes, with her hair in a ponytail, can be heard yelling about her car's damage.

"You guys need to find the f**ker who did this and string him up by his balls."

This is at least the eleventh Mister Manners escapade reported since the first of the year. In previous attacks, he has also targeted movie theater talkers, litterers, lousy tippers, red-light runners, and rude blabbermouths using their speakerphones in public.

To date, there are no reports he has silenced any telemarketers, a serious gap in his campaign, if you ask me.

Mister Manners: If you are reading this, please contact me. The world wants to know your story.

STRANGE FACT: What we call "manners" began with the French in the royal courts of the 1600s and 1700s. That would have been before the last French King, Louis XVI, met the guillotine. How rude!

Keep up with weirdness at *www.TheStrangeFiles.com*. Contact Alexander Strange at *Alex@TheStrangeFiles.com*.

CHAPTER 2

Naples, Florida

LESTER AND I HAD JUST crossed the Jolley Bridge, which connects Goodland and Marco Island to the mainland, when my phone rang. I answered without looking. I get some telemarketers that way, but also tips from readers of my column, *The Strange Files*, and I've learned the minor annoyance of crank calls is worth it. I have a stock of snappy one-liners to get rid of pests. The menu includes:

- Gotta go. My weasel needs deworming.
- Ooops, the mothership's on the other line.
- Say, you know anything about anal fungus?

But this was Kitty Karlucci calling back. She jumped right into the conversation as if it hadn't been interrupted by terrorizing and life-threatening gunfire. And if she had any lingering concerns about my wellbeing, she did an admirable job of masking her anxiety.

"Like I was saying, I've got a proposal for you. I need some help getting on the girl train."

"The what?"

"I'm talking about the book market. It's gone nuts. Every other title coming out of New York has *girls* in it. Not sure where it started, maybe *The Girl with the Dragon Tattoo*, and they just keep puking them out: *Gone Girl. The Girl on the Train. Girl in Translation. Girl*

Interrupted. Island of Lost Girls. City of Girls." She went on like that for a while. Finally, she concluded: "Goodreads has over seventeen hundred books with girl in the title and counting."

She took a breath, my cue to reply. "So, this use of the word *girls*, it offends you, is that it? You want me to write a column about it because it's sexist or something?"

"I don't give a rat's ass about that," she blurted. "Stay focused. I need a collaborator. There's money to be made in girls."

There was an obvious comeback to that, but in a rare exercise of maturity I ignored it and instead asked, "What? You're not rich enough already?"

"You can't be too rich or too obnoxious about it. And I don't have time to write these girl books myself."

"And you're calling me? I'm not an author. I'm a lowly ink-stained wretch."

She ignored that. "Have you read any of my books?"

There was a surly, annoyed tone to her gravelly voice, but maybe she was one of those people who perpetually came off grouchy. I'd read a couple of her novels. They were amusing if unmemorable, so I didn't have to lie.

"Sure," I said. "Hasn't everyone?"

"No. But I'm working on it. Thing is, people buy the brand. They see *Peach* in the title and snap it up. I want to get into the *girl* market too. Slap a title with *girl* on it and it's an instant bestseller. The moron public doesn't care whether it's any good or not. Neither do the publishers, like they'd know. It's become a phenomenon. Have you read the latest girl book? That's what everybody's talking about."

"And I'm supposed to help you penetrate the girl market how?"

"Cute. Penetrate. You're glib. That's what I need."

She paused for a moment, and I thought I heard ice tinkling in a glass.

I glanced at Lester to see him gaping at me. "Is that…"

I nodded and motioned for him to keep his eye on the road.

"Look, you're a short-form writer," Kitty continued. "Your columns, what are they, like seven-fifty, a thousand words, max?"

"If that."

"Well, that's me too. Short attention span. That's our world these days. Since you've read my books, you know all the chapters are quickies, like your columns. My books are nothing more than a collection of tightly written essays—each chapter has a beginning, a middle, and a cliffhanger ending. The trick is the plot. I outline every chapter in detail, make sure the storyline is coherent, then crank 'em out. Just like Patterson."

"But I've never…"

"Yeah, I know, you've never written a novel. And how could you write a book from a woman's point of view? Forget all that. A mutual acquaintance of ours turned me on to you. It's why I took your call last year when you wrote that snarky piece about my dearly departed ex-husband. You're funny. Glib, like I said. That's my style, too."

"And who do I have to thank for this?" I asked.

"Omar Franken. You remember him?"

"The Phoenix inventor."

"That's right. Met him at a book signing in Arizona. Said when you were a reporter out West, you totally trashed one of his creations, Stealth Car Wax. Supposed to cloak cars from police radar. You debunked it and had lots of fun at his expense doing it."

"And he recommended me to you?"

"Not so much, but he gets chatty when he's drinking, especially after sex."

"So, you're seeing him?"

"I've been scouting him. He's made my shortlist of future ex-husbands. But enough about him, here's my pitch: I'll hand you a detailed outline of the story. You write the chapters like they were your columns, hitting the plot points as you go. Maybe two short chapters a week. In six months, you'll be done. You can do it in your spare time. Turn it in and collect a check."

"Tell me about that check."

She did. It was more than I make a year writing my *Strange Files* columns. And that, naturally, captured my attention.

But I had lots of questions. Would I actually be able to write a novel? It seemed a daunting task. The payday sounded generous, but did I need the money? My life was pretty much the way I wanted it already: I had a boat to live on, a gorgeous and brilliant girlfriend who tolerated my laid-back lifestyle, and I made enough money to keep me in rum and my dog in Alpo. Taking on what amounted to a second job would run headlong into my long-held minimalist philosophy regarding work.

And Karlucci, she had a rep. Three deceased husbands; all accidental deaths. She called herself the Queen of Murder and Mayhem. Her detractors called her the Black Widow. Was she even safe to be around? And she described Omar Franken as a potential future *ex-*husband. Funny line. Except all her ex-husbands were now taking up residence in the afterlife.

Those concerns and more flashed through my mind as we talked, but I had to admit the paycheck was intriguing. I was about to tell her I needed to chew on it when she said:

"Think about it. We'll talk again in a few days." Then she hung up.

Lester was back to staring at me instead of paying attention to the road. "That was her, wasn't it?"

"Yes. Now look where you're going."

"I wasn't eavesdropping, but…"

"Of course, you were."

"She wants you to ghostwrite for her?"

"So she says."

He reached over. "Can I touch you?"

"Stop it."

CHAPTER 3

Naples, Florida

WHILE LESTER DROVE, I refocused my thoughts on Mister Manners. I'd written multiple columns recounting his skulking about Florida, punishing breaches of social etiquette, and how his antics had captured the attention of police.

But that's all they were capturing. Mister Manners, himself, was elusive. The cops didn't know his identity. He moved among us like a phantom.

His recent victims included the attention-seeking driver of a pickup truck in Panama City who played loud, profanity-laced music with his windows open outside an elementary school. For his sins, the driver found the windows of his vehicle inoperable after they'd been Super Glued shut.

A Clearwater tourist who Mister Manners had observed frightening sea birds along the Gulf shore returned to his cabana at the Sunset Beach Club to confront a hissing Burmese python curled on his bed.

The story of Kitty Karlucci discovering a shopping cart glued to the roof of her car stirred a media frenzy. Until recently, the Mister Manners story had been largely a local phenomenon. Another crazy Florida Man. Now it had gone international. I was getting calls from reporters in London (*Evening Standard*), New York (*The Post*), and, oddly, Azerbaijan (*Azer News*). The Associated Press, HuffPost, and *The New York Times* had all done their own versions of the story, as had the major news networks.

All this extra competition made it more challenging for me to score the first—and I hoped, exclusive—interview with the vigilante.

Tropic Press, where I work, is an online news service, and we have a small staff and no central office—we are, as we like to say, a "distributed" newsroom, meaning we work from various locations around the country.

I'm stationed in Gunshine State where I report on news-of-the-weird, an offbeat job by definition and hardly the sort of coverage likely to win a Pulitzer. But the idea is to ensure that our daily file of stories includes something our readers will find amusing, a brief respite from the endless doomscroll of dreadful news—especially during a pandemic.

The stories range from the simply funny (a flock of crows stealing groceries from Costco shoppers) to bizarre (a Naples teacher hit in the head by fish falling from the sky) to cringeworthy (woman attempts suicide by gator). But never dull.

There has never been a bigger story on the weird news beat than Mister Manners and his escapades. I had a long list of questions for him. And I was determined to be the first reporter to ask them. There aren't many journalists specializing in what I do. In fact, I may be the only one who does it full-time. So, this was not, under any circumstances, a story I wanted to read under someone else's byline.

Every time he struck, Mister Manners left a note explaining why he was offended by his victims' behavior. According to various police reports, the messages always ended with:

"Your discourtesy has been avenged."

Followed by the signature: "M.M."

After his first attack, someone speculated M.M. stood for Mister Manners, which got shared across social media and from there to radio, TV, and newspapers. Headline writers adopted the moniker, and, so far, none had been the object of his vengeance, so maybe he was okay with that.

I wasn't okay with not knowing more about him, and I'd been reaching out to Mister Manners through my columns, asking him to contact me. I wanted him to open up, talk about what drove this obsession of his. Ask him what M.M. really stood for.

People were calling him a modern-day Robin Hood, and he'd attracted a growing social media following. Who is Mister Manners? his fans asked. Where will he strike next? About time somebody did something about all those rude people! That sort of chatter.

If you weren't one of his victims, you might have secretly admired him. Who among us hasn't wanted to wreak vengeance on morons who fail to signal their turns, who brush against us without face masks during a pandemic, who yell on their cell phones—that sort of misbehavior?

I wanted to ask him how he selected his targets, where he got all those crazy ideas for his revenge, and if he owned stock in the Super Glue company.

To date, Mister Manners had ignored my entreaties.

Or maybe he just never saw them. Maybe he didn't read *The Strange Files*. Following the misadventures of Florida Man and his ilk isn't everyone's cup of Earl Grey. Perhaps all the social media attention went right over his sociopathic head. Maybe he was just too busy punishing evildoers to care about what other people thought of him.

After all, did Batman clip headlines? Did the Green Lantern give a hoot what anyone thought about his magic jewelry? Did Superman even know capes were no longer in fashion? Maybe to be a superhero was to obey only that inner voice that drove you, disregarding anything that would distract you from your single-minded purpose in life.

Maybe being a superhero meant you were crazy.

Was that it? Was Mister Manners simply another—if exotic— Florida loon? Yet another question to be answered.

Lester pulled into a parking spot on Fifth Avenue in front of The Third Eye's office in ritzy downtown Naples, wedging his Tahoe between a Porsche and a Bentley. But before he could turn off the engine, his police scanner began chittering about an act of vandalism in rural Everglades City southeast of Naples—not far from where we had just driven.

"Hold on, Lester," I said. "Listen to this."

After a few minutes of back and forth between a dispatcher and a sheriff's deputy, it became clear they were responding to a bizarre event, some sort of prank. Then we heard the words "Mister Manners."

"Lester, we gotta turn around," I said.

"Can't," he replied. "Client's inside. Come on in and meet her, then I'll ask Naomi to give you a ride back to Goodland. Trust me, you won't regret it."

I was already regretting the entire day, but what choice did I have? So, I grumped a bit and trailed him into his office.

The Third Eye's Naples branch wasn't large, but it was well-appointed. Naomi Jackson, a former bailiff and a reliable source of mine, was sitting at an oak desk in the front room. She'd recently signed on with The Third Eye, taking early retirement from the county after a particularly nasty tussle with a prisoner. That altercation had left a scar on her jaw below her left ear that still showed pink against her ebony skin. It left the prisoner in traction for six weeks.

She looked up from a copy of *True Detective* she was reading and thumbed in the direction of Lester's small office. We walked in.

Sitting in a comfortable leather chair next to Lester's desk was a thirtyish woman with a full head of curly black hair that glistened under the room's overhead lights. Her ringless and well-manicured hands were typing on a laptop computer balanced on her lap.

"Ms. Bhatia," Lester said as we entered. "Meet Alexander Strange. Alexander, this is Renelda Bhatia."

The woman closed her laptop and curled out of the chair. She was about five-ten, slender, with cappuccino skin. She wore faded jeans, white sneakers, and a cobalt off-shoulder blouse that matched her face mask. Nice fashion coordination there. I could see little of her face other than her coffee-brown irises and dark eyebrows, one raised slightly higher than the other as she cocked her head—a sign of curiosity, amusement, or irritation? I couldn't tell which.

But the whites of her eyes were streaked in red. Allergies? Hungover?

"Call me Rennie," she said.

CHAPTER 4

Everglades City, Earlier That Day

MILTON THROCKMORTON'S HEAD was throbbing as he staggered from his bedroom toward the kitchen, where he kept a large and frequently used plastic bottle of Advil. It was that kind of morning after.

Bare-assed naked, he paused as he stepped past his front door. Something was off, but it didn't compute. He wasn't thinking too clearly yet and wouldn't be until he downed some painkillers and a pot of coffee.

He really had to cut back on the Tito's.

After a moment of staring dully at the entryway, it finally clicked—the problem was the door's narrow window. A foot wide and four feet tall, ordinarily Throckmorton would be viewing his front porch through that pane of glass, the street beyond, the widow Hillsdale's broken-down lime green Impala parked under her stilt house across the street.

But no light penetrated the window. It was dark as a hitman's soul.

How could that be? He'd glanced at the electric clock on his nightstand before wrenching himself out of the sack, and the bright red digital readout showed it was 7:28. And that had to be A.M. since he recalled, somewhat foggily, that he'd retired around midnight following a vigorous bout of self-pleasuring while watching *The Adventures of Priscilla, Queen of the Desert.*

No, something was definitely out of kilter. Sunlight was blazing through the sliding glass doors at the opposite end of the small living room where, he irritably noted, unsightly weeds still sprouted through the cracks between the pool deck pavers despite bitching out Hector, his housekeeper, the day before. And was that a fucking frog by the pool? Jesus!

Throckmorton returned his gaze to the front entrance of his home, the darkened window, and wondered what the fuck?

He approached the door.

It is unclear whether Florida actually had—or if it did, whether it ever enforced—meaningful building codes before Hurricane Andrew, but that disaster changed everything.

Among the code improvements was a requirement that the exterior doors to homes open outward instead of inward, which is the customary direction doors swing, a welcoming gesture sweeping guests into the home.

But other parts of the country aren't regularly visited by tropical cyclones. And inward swinging doors are more easily blown open by strong winds. And when you lose your door, the next thing to go is your roof, especially if it isn't particularly well tied down, and then you with the roof unless you've tied yourself down firmly, as well.

But an outward-swinging door creates a formidable portal. It takes a daunting amount of force to push a door through its frame, so much so that it's just as likely the house will be flattened before an outward swinging door bursts open during a storm.

This building-code innovation followed the devastation leveled by Hurricane Andrew's 174 mph winds that slammed Miami killing 44 people and splintering more than 100,000 homes, many shoddily constructed. But the Throckmorton house in Everglades City, south-east of Naples, was pre-Andrew. A perfectly fine dwelling, certainly, much classier than all the unsightly houses elevated on stilts that surrounded it, but constructed before the more stringent building codes were enacted.

⊚

As THROCKMORTON APPROACHED his old-fashioned inward-swinging front door, he felt a small stab of anxiety. Or maybe it was just a twitch from the monster hangover gripping his intestines, the result of an overindulgence of martinis the night before.

Ah, yes, the night before. Throckmorton involuntarily glanced down and noticed the orange crumbs clinging to his public hairs.

Probably needed to cut back on the Cheetos, too.

Throckmorton had recently returned to Everglades City upon the death of his father, Hugo, who had been a lifelong resident and veteran of the "square grouper" drug-running era during which many of the townspeople were busily engaged in marijuana smuggling—square grouper referring to the countless bales of Columbian loco weed thrown overboard or dropped from airplanes and hauled ashore as part of a vast and sophisticated cannabis distribution network in the late 20th century.

In 1979, the federal government reported that nearly ninety percent of all the marijuana seizures in the United States took place in South Florida, with Everglades City being one of the major import centers because of its proximity to the Ten Thousand Islands where pirates once roamed, and treasure is still rumored to be buried.

As a young C.P.A. straight out of Wharton, Throckmorton was introduced to his old man's fellow smugglers, and over the years he built a growing accounting practice by establishing offshore bank accounts and reinvesting cash into multilayered limited liability corporations—an activity sometimes indelicately referred to as money laundering.

And when the Feds finally raided Everglades City en masse, Milton Throckmorton was all too eager to provide the financials the *Federales* sought in exchange for his freedom—fuck everybody else. And from there, he moved on to new clients in need of his specialized skills, finding a home with a certain New York criminal organization whose leader, a few weeks previously, had been gunned down outside his Park Slope condo. This unanticipated event made Milton's decision to linger in the land of sun, sand, and shysters not only easier but prudent.

Not that he wasn't held in high regard by the Family, but he knew a lot, including where the bodies were buried—literally. And there were activities of his own he would not want discovered. Things had to settle down in New York, new organizational charts drawn, agreements reached, and appropriate heads rolled before it would be advisable for him to resume his duties.

He was very fond of his own head and wouldn't want it to be among those rolled.

"Take some time off, Milty," he was told. "Get a tan. We'll call when everything's settled."

That call had yet to come.

Milton Throckmorton wasn't comfortable in Everglades City. Not just because it was in the middle of nowhere and flood-prone (hence all the stilt houses), but because of him a lot of people ended up in prison, including his own father. But that was unavoidable. Every man for himself, after all.

Throckmorton hadn't shared all his books with the Feds, though. He had money stashed offshore. And when the old man was finally sprung from the hoosegow, he used some of this hidden cash to underwrite his father's new start-up, a computer security business, a craft he'd learned in the federal government's excellent prison education system. He even talked his father's old public defender, now a trial lawyer, into partnering with Hugo since, as a felon, it would have been impossible for the old man to get the clearances he needed to do security work.

A lifelong smoker, Hugo finally lost his battle to non-small-cell lung cancer, and now Milton Throckmorton busied himself settling the estate. Hugo's house was the home he'd grown up in, but he was antsy to put it on the market and get back to Manhattan.

Florida was so goddamned weird. How could it be sunny by the pool and dark out the front door?

Throckmorton flipped the deadbolt latch and grasped the door handle. Just before he turned the doorknob, he scrunched his nose. What was that smell?

Then he swung the door inward.

IT HAD RAINED overnight on the fetid mound of horse manure piled against the front of the house, not enough to wash it away, but just enough to compact it into a cohesive, steaming heap molded tightly into the door frame.

The accountant stared dumbstruck at the malodorous wall of shit, and for the briefest of moments wondered what sort of animal would be capable of such a monumental feat? A burning sensation ripped through his stomach as if he'd swallowed broken glass. That was no mere hangover. It was his fucking ulcer flaring up again!

Then the quivering pile of equine excrement collapsed through the doorway burying Throckmorton under its moist, reeking mass.

CHAPTER 5

Aboard the* Miss Demeanor *the next day

IT WAS EARLY AFTERNOON in Portugal when Gwenn popped up on FaceTime. I was still drinking my first cup of coffee. She was finishing lunch at an outdoor café overlooking the harbor in Cascais, a popular tourist destination on the outskirts of Lisbon. Not as bustling today as in the past, however, with vacationers homebound because of the pandemic.

Gwenn had caught one of the few flights from the States to Europe that hadn't been curtailed. She was there on behalf of a wealthy Florida client with complicated inheritance issues involving property in Portugal and unresolved legal claims against the Portuguese government dating back to World War II.

I didn't know all the details—it sounded entangled and convoluted, just the sort of project Gwenn would relish. She's an excellent attorney but an even better researcher, and she loves unraveling knotty legal cases.

"Show me where you are," I said, and she rotated her phone around, picking up images of the patio where she was dining—O'Neill's Irish Pub—a broad plaza, and the marina in the distance where sunlight was dancing off small waves and reflecting on the hulls of sailboats.

"Gorgeous," I said when she finished the visual tour and re-aimed the camera at herself. "Cascais is pretty, too."

That earned me a big smile. "Why, thank you, sir." Her red hair was up in a ponytail today, which, with a splash of freckles on her cheeks, amplified her girl-next-door good looks.

"You're at an Irish pub?"

"Lots of ex-pats here, and a big British influence," she said. "Matter of fact, my server today was an American named Meg. She's an actress, stranded here because of COVID. So, what's happening back in the land of the free? Are we maintaining our social distancing?"

"It's a challenge on board, but I've masked Mona and Spock. Mona's mask is particularly fetching. Has a skull and crossbones. Spock hasn't said anything—what's new?—but I can tell he doesn't like it. Especially since I had to staple the straps to the back of his head.

"Ouch!"

"This is when it pays to be an introvert," I said. "Social distancing works just fine for me. About the only person I've seen is Lester. But I do wish you were here."

"It's only been two weeks."

"Really? Seems like a fortnight."

"Aren't you sweet. And how is Lester?"

"He's a little out of sorts right now. He's missing Silver."

"She just needs some time to herself."

"Yeah, Lester says she still can't get her head around the fact her brother was wrapped up with criminals. And because Lester—not to mention you and me—were involved in bringing it to light, she's, well, I don't know. She's not blaming anybody, but I agree, she just needs some time to detox."

Lester, Gwenn, and I—with a supporting cast of FBI agents, sheriff's deputies, city cops, private eyes, and others—had recently solved a pair of brutal murders in Key West in which Silver McFadden's brother played a central role, both as an unwitting member of a criminal conspiracy and a victim. Silver owns a horse ranch in Ocala, and she and Lester had become attached. And now sort of not.

"Tell Lester to be patient," Gwenn said. "Silver's been through a lot. I saw how he doted on her, how kind he was. She'd be an idiot to lose him."

"She's a flat earther and moon landing denier."

"True that. But she's not stupid. Just, I don't know, drawn to alternative facts."

"Yeah, right? We're drowning in alternative facts. Remember when the President said the pandemic was under control? Bob Woodward's got him on tape admitting he just made that up. Now he's saying Black Lives Matter protesters were throwing bags and bags of canned tuna at police."

"Tuna fish?"

"Right? If you're going to make shit up, why not throwing hand grenades, or Molotov cocktails, or fetuses?"

"But really, did they throw cans of tuna at the cops? Because I know a few cops I'd love to bean with a can of StarKist."

"Hold on, I've got the quote right here. Wait for it…wait for it… Okay, here we go, and I quote the President of these United States:

"'They really rip it, right? And that hits you. Bumble Bee brand tuna, and you can throw that, because you put a curve on it, you can do whatever you want.'"

"Do whatever you want? Isn't that what he was caught on tape saying about women?"

"Seems to be a favorite line of his."

"Well, don't get too worked up. This, too, shall pass. One day he'll be gone. It will be like a miracle."

A pelican alighted on the stern of the trawler, which set Fred off. He charged out the hatchway and began yapping at it. The bird turned its prehistoric eyes in his direction, opened its beak in what—I swear—was a yawn, then resumed scanning the marina, ignoring the agitated canine beneath him.

I told Gwenn about the shootout in Everglades City and Lester's new client.

"So, this woman, she calls herself Rennie?"

"Yeah. Like the actor, Michael Rennie."

"Wait. Who's Michael Rennie?"

"Seriously? *The Day the Earth Stood Still?*"

"It did?"

"You're pulling my leg."

"I'm happy to pull on any of your appendages, but I still haven't heard of Michael Rennie, and I thought Keanu Reeves was in *The Day the Earth Stood Still*, although I never saw it."

"That was the remake. The original was made in the fifties. Most people alive today haven't seen it, but they should. It's a classic. Uncle Leo and I watched it together when I was a kid. Part of his enormous movie collection. It's black and white. Michael Rennie plays this dude from outer space named Klaatu. He's got this robot…"

"Robot?"

"Yeah. Like Threepio, only not as mouthy and with a death ray for eyes, kinda like a Cylon. The movie was way ahead of its time. Anyway, the robot—his name is Gort—he's going to destroy the planet until Patricia Neal says the code words to make him stop: '*Klaatu barada nikto.*'"

"What does that mean?"

"*Pass the mustard*, for all I know."

"Ha."

"You know, maybe it never aired in Canada," I said.

"Could be. Montreal didn't get TV until the early fifties, although my parents said lots of people watched American stations."

"You still have dual citizenship, right?"

"You know I do."

"So, if we get married, can we live in Canada and get away from all this madness?"

"You're talking politics, not the usual crazies you write about."

"Right."

"And was that a proposal?"

"It was a hypothetical."

"Well, hypothetically, yes, but I'm not licensed to practice law in Canada, and I like what I do. So, you're just going to have to be patient. The American people will figure this out. It'll get better."

"I love your optimism."

"I'm confident we'll get a vaccine for COVID, too. Although that may take longer."

I mulled that for a moment. "Say, can you even return to America right now?"

"Not sure. But that's also hypothetical because I'm just getting started, and this is a real hairball."

She spent some time telling me about her case. There was serious money involved, something about missing Nazi gold that her client and others had filed claims against the Portuguese government to recover.

"When you're finished with that Rennie person, maybe you can fly over," she suggested. "I could use someone with your skillset."

"Which of my many skills do you require?"

"Got a lot of heavy boxes that need lifting."

"Nice."

Gwenn doesn't have a jealous bone in her body. Or so she claims. But the way she referred to Lester's client as "that Rennie person" wasn't lost on me. Maybe when I mentioned Rennie to her, I could have picked an alternative descriptor than "statuesque."

"How, exactly, does Lester's case involve you?" Gwenn asked.

"It involves me," I said, "because Rennie may help me find Mister Manners."

"How so?"

"Well, you remember Lester said his client didn't care about the leg lamp, per se, just the memory card hidden in the socket."

"Yes. So, what's on the card that's so important?"

"She didn't say, but she was uber bummed when Lester came up empty handed. He's guessing maybe it might be a backup file of financial records—stuff she might not want her mom's ex-husband to discover. Maybe her mom held out on him during the divorce or something. But that's just speculation."

"Okay."

"This is a bit of a sidebar, but the shotgun-toting lunatic who had the lamp, he believes he's Hunter S. Thompson's alter ego reincarnated...."

"Say what?"

"Yeah, he's nuts. It's why Rennie's mother divorced him. He's technically Rennie's ex-stepfather if there is such a thing. Anyway, Rennie's mom has Alzheimer's, and Rennie moved to Naples to help her with her business and is now getting her settled into an assisted living facility. She was at her mom's condo when this guy showed up demanding the lamp, claiming it's the only thing he didn't get in the divorce that he wanted—she kept it for spite, he said—and just to get rid of him, Rennie gave it away."

"Without knowing about the secret memory card."

"Exactly. So, Rennie discovers a passing reference to it in her mother's journal, calls this guy—his real name's Horace Sniffen, I kid you not—and says she's changed her mind. And he tells her she'll have to pry it out of his cold dead hands, or some such, so she calls The Third Eye."

"So, this Sniffen character's not Rennie Bhatia's real father. Her real dad was named Bhatia?"

"Apparently."

"And her mother, the one hiding financial records in leg lamps, what's her story?"

"Lawyer turned small business owner. Not sure when she remarried, but she kept Bhatia as her last name. I mean, who could blame her. Sniffen? She's kinda well-known, evidently. Margaret Bhatia. She was a public defender—just like another lawyer I know—and she represented a bunch of guys in a famous drug bust down in Everglades City years ago."

There was a pause, then Gwenn practically shouted: "Oh, I know who you're talking about. Yeah. I heard about her when I was at the Public Defenders. When you said Bhatia, it stirred a faint memory. Now I get it. Wow, small world."

"It gets smaller. One of the defendants, a guy named Hugo Throckmorton, his son is Mister Manners' latest victim. Maybe."

"Maybe?"

"It's complicated."

"So, how does this help you find Mister Manners?"

"Oh, sorry, I buried the lede. Rennie has a friend who knows him, she says."

"Nice. She give you a name?"

"No, but Rennie referred to a "her," so that narrows it down."

"Every journey…"

"Right! Anyway, when she and Lester first met, apparently my name came up somehow, and she mentioned the Mister Manners connection to him and that her friend was somehow aware I was trying to reach him, and Lester asked—on my behalf—if she would try to convince her friend to give me a call. In fact, when the phone rang, I thought it might be her."

"Sorry to disappoint."

"Oh, please…"

"So, you said the latest Mister Manners story got complicated?"

"Pun intended, it's turned into a real shit show."

THE STRANGE FILES

Did Mister Manners Miss His Mark?

By Alexander Strange

Tropic Press

EVERGLADES CITY—It appears that Mister Manners may have misfired. If it was Mister Manners' handiwork at all.

This latest installment in the continuing saga of Florida's self-appointed etiquette vigilante began Tuesday morning when an accountant named Milton Throckmorton—in town to settle his father's estate—was buried under a pile of horse manure when he opened his front door.

A YouTube video of a naked Throckmorton struggling to extricate himself from the pile of horse dung has gone viral on social media. In that video, Throckmorton, covered in feces, is seen yelling at the videographer while pulling clots of manure off his unclothed body. At one point, he charges out of his house toward the camera, then slips on the gooey excrement and face-plants on his manure-covered front porch.

The video, set to the lyrics of Sheek Louch's On That Shit, has been viewed more than 500,000 times.

A neighbor who lives across the street from the Throckmorton house, Lucy Hillsdale, told sheriff's deputies and reporters she believes the pile of horse manure that Throckmorton discovered on his front porch—and which collapsed upon him when he opened his door—was all her fault.

"I borrowed Hugo's car to take Buffy, my poodle, to the vet. But I forgot my doggie bags. I'm getting that way. Forgetful. And I guess Mister Manners must've followed me home, and when I parked Hugo's car back in their driveway, he figured that's where I lived."

Hugo is Milton Throckmorton's deceased father.

"The entire time I let Buffy do her business, I felt guilty and nervous, afraid someone was watching me. But I had no way to pick up the doo-doo unless I did it with my bare hands."

While the Sheriff's Office has included Hillsdale's statement in its incident report, it has not named anyone by the pseudonym Mister Manners as a suspect. That hasn't stopped local news stations and social media from declaring this as Mister Manners' most recent attack.

The sheriff also has not shared the telltale note Mister Manners invariably leaves behind. His modus operandi has been to leave a computer printout citing his victim's offense and declaring that the trespass has been avenged. He always signs the note "M.M."

When I asked to see the note left behind in this most recent attack, I was told that "any evidence would be part of the investigative file and will not be released." This is a consistent pattern among police agencies around the state who have universally withheld the actual notes from the public eye.

When I asked if there was, indeed, a note left behind that would indicate this was a Mister Manners attack, I was told by Detective Linda Henderson, "No comment."

While social media has popularized the "M.M." signature as Mister Manners, police apparently have no idea who the social avenger is or if, indeed, he calls himself by that sobriquet.

Adding to the confusion, the Associated Press reported that Mister Manners struck the same day in Jacksonville. In that case, the turn-signal lights were shattered on a late model sedan to which, according to police, he attached a note that read:

"You failed to use your turn signal. Your discourtesy has been avenged." It was signed "M.M."

How could Mister Manners be at two places at once?

When I called the Jacksonville Sheriff's Office, they declined to comment and, once again, refused to release a copy of the actual note.

Follow-up calls to the Collier County Sheriff's Office were met with similar no comments.

Milton Throckmorton also declined to be interviewed. However, his father was the notorious drug dealer Hugo Throckmorton who served 15 years in federal prison for his involvement in a massive marijuana smuggling network. He was arrested as part of a sweeping drug sting that ended in the arrests of more than two dozen Everglades City residents.

Dubbed Operation Everglades, some 200 federal agents and local police swept into this southwest Florida village at dawn on July 7, 1983, arresting 28 people and seizing half the town's fishing boats, which law enforcement officials said were used to haul bails of marijuana ashore after they were dropped by boats and airplanes along the Ten Thousand Islands.

This corner of Florida has long been a smuggler's paradise, home to Caribbean pirates, Prohibition rum runners, human traffickers, and the like. Marijuana was just the latest contraband to make its way to the mainland through the countless mangrove islets and sandbars where criminals have found refuge over the centuries.

Less is known about Milton Throckmorton, Hugo's son. He does not appear to have any social media accounts. He is licensed to practice accounting in the State of New York, and those records show he is 63 years old and a graduate of the Wharton School of the University of Pennsylvania.

Police sources expressed puzzlement regarding the source of the horse manure. "It would have come from a big stable. There was a lot," I was told. The largest nearby stable—indeed the biggest equestrian facility in Collier County—is the new Chitango Therapeutic Riding Center located on the grounds of the former Museum of Holy Creation off Oil Well Road.

"Whoever did this was motivated," I was told. "He went to a lot of trouble."

But was it Mister Manners?

Not unless he could have been in two places at once.

STRANGE FACT: Speaking of horse manure, before Charles and Diana's royal wedding, the carriage horses were fed dyes so their manure would match the wedding's pastel color scheme.

Keep up with weirdness at *www.TheStrangeFiles.com.* Contact Alexander Strange at *Alex@TheStrangeFiles.com.*

CHAPTER 6

Port Royal, Naples

Kitty Karlucci dropped her desktop telephone into its cradle and leaned back in her custom-built ergonomic chair, the one that allowed her to write in relative comfort for six hours a day, every day, as she churned out her contracted two manuscripts a year for the Penelope Peach cozy mystery series.

Peachy Keen, her latest book, had successfully played Queen of the Mountain against all comers, including Grisham, Child, and Barker, only recently dropping to Number Two, succumbing to the latest potboiler from that too-cute Meg Gardiner. But book Number 19—working title *Feeling Peachy*—would vault her back into first place, she was confident. The sex scenes alone would take care of that. There was more than a little *double entendre* in the title's use of the word "feeling."

Kitty had been talking on the phone to the son of an old friend who had recently succumbed to lung cancer. That friend, Hugo Throckmorton, had for years provided her with countless tips regarding the dark corners of the criminal mind. He'd also been a reliable "first reader," helping guard against embarrassing mistakes in her manuscripts.

And Hugo had been reliable in other ways too. Kitty would miss her occasional sleepovers in Everglades City, a reward she gave herself for finished first drafts. There was something exhilarating and kinky about having sex with an elderly criminal. It made her feel alive, free, nasty. She would miss dear old Hugo. And who the hell would she contact now when her computer was on the fritz?

Her call to Hugo's wretched son was prompted by a story in the *Naples Daily News*, an account of that fucking miscreant Mister Manners' latest act of domestic terrorism. The victim, Milton Throckmorton, was a sniveling little shit weasel who, if anyone deserved to be shat upon, he was the shit-ee. His gutless betrayal of his own father and countless others was execrable. And she knew through Hugo that he was asshole-deep in the mob.

But the enemy of my enemy is my friend, so she dialed Milton Throckmorton to strike up an alliance. The conversation went like this:

KARLUCCI: Milt, it's Kitty.

THROCKMORTON: Don't fucking call me Milt. Milt is fish cum. You know I don't like that.

KARLUCCI: But it suits you, darling.

THROCKMORTON: Gimme one reason I shouldn't hang up. Just because you and the old man were whatever you were, let's not pretend you give two shits about me.

KARLUCCI: I don't. But we may have an opportunity to work together for our mutual benefit.

THROCKMORTON: In your dreams. I got no interest in proofing that pablum you write. The old man might have got off to it, but I'm not my old man.

KARLUCCI: Of course you're not, dear. Your father was straight. And hard as a pistol barrel, I might add.

THROCKMORTON: Yeah, I suspected as much. Is there anyone with a hanging pair in Naples you haven't fucked?

KARLUCCI: More than I can say, but not for the lack of trying. Now, about our mutual adversary, Mister Manners...

Kitty swiveled her chair and gazed out the picture window of her study toward her verdant and perfectly manicured lawn and, beyond, the white sandy shoreline. Book publishing had been good to her. A seven thousand square foot mansion in Port Royal along Naples' Billionaire Coast validated that. Well, her dearly departed third husband and his tech company may have contributed, of course.

She glanced down at her desktop calendar. The anniversary of Number Three's demise was coming up soon. Had it only been a year? It seemed like ages. But what a way to go—knocked senseless by the swinging boom of his fifty-foot yacht off the *Cinque Terre* coast. At least that was her story. Art imitating life, she'd used that scene in *Peachy Keen*. Or would it be life imitating art? For a writer, does art begin with the publication or the conception of the plot?

She returned her gaze out the window and peered toward the horizon, across the vast blue emptiness of the Gulf of Mexico. Hadn't someone proposed renaming it the Gulf of America? Whatever happened to that? Such a splendid idea!

The call to Milton Throckmorton, she reflected, turned out better than she hoped. In the span of twenty minutes, they'd cooked up a preliminary scheme to lure Mister Manners into a trap, a sting that would end the insolent motherfucker.

Mister Manners had made a mistake. He had targeted the wrong victim. Of course, it wouldn't have happened if Milt hadn't loaned his father's car to the neighbor lady across the street to take her dog to the vet. Why was that idiot mingling with lowlifes in stilt houses anyway?

Milt's neighbor had been beside herself, caterwauling to the police that it was all her fault, she forgot her doggie bags, that none of this would have happened if her car hadn't broken down, yadda, yadda, yadda. Mister Manners must have tailed her back to Milton's house, the woman said, and he'd incorrectly assumed that's where she lived. He was punishing her for not picking up the poop.

But Kitty was delighted it happened. That scumbag deserved it, and it provided a wedge into a chink in Mister Manners' armor. Who better than she, the Queen of Murder and Mayhem, to plot that evil fucker's demise? After all, plotting murders was what she did best.

And how handy that the miscreant's latest victim had mob connections. Kitty knew all about that, of course. Hugo was a talker, and he loved to blabber about his son, with whom he had a complicated love/hate relationship. That's what happens when your kid rats you out to the cops. But that same kid also set up his father in the computer business when he got released. So, as a token of his conflicted gratitude, Hugo promptly began hacking Milton's online transactions. The apple hadn't fallen far from the tree, according to Hugo, who over the years had been supplementing his income with discrete withdrawals from his son's offshore accounts, money Milton had been siphoning from his dangerous New York clients.

All of which led Kitty to believe Milton Throckmorton may not have been the brightest bulb in the accounting world's chandelier.

Kitty's perception of Milt's dim-wittedness was reinforced by his decision to entrust Hugo with an encryption key that unlocked other documents he had stashed online, records that, if disclosed to either the Feds or the mob, would have explosive consequences. Hugo never told Kitty where he had hidden the code, but she often had wondered what secrets it unlocked.

And even though he was a dumbass, Milt's underworld connections were now proving useful. Combined with her cunning, Mister Manners' days as a living human being on Planet Earth were now counting down. Or should she say Planet Kitty? It was her world, after all. Everyone else was just a guest. It was so good to be a sociopath. And know it.

She glanced again at the phone and toyed with the idea of calling that smart-ass journalist Alexander Strange. She'd given him some time to think over her ghostwriting proposition, and she was eager to get the ball rolling. There was money to be made with *girls*.

But rushing him would be imprudent. Husband Number Two had

been an accomplished angler, and he'd told her that one of the keys was to let the fish nibble a bit before jerking the line. Strange would take the bait, she was confident. She could hear how his tone of voice modulated when she flashed dollar signs at him over the phone. What she had offered him was a fraction of what her publisher's advance would be. A small fortune to him, a minimal investment for her.

What an odd coincidence they should meet in the Publix parking lot the day after that phone call. She had shunned the other reporters but sidled up to him, buttering him up a bit more. He was a good-looking kid. Tall. Big shoulders. Kind of reminded her of that actor, what's his name in *Star Wars*. But not her type. She preferred older men, men with money, men with one foot in the grave. Gullible men. Alexander Strange had a look in his eyes. Like he was always laughing at the world around him. Mischievous. Piratical. Gullible wouldn't be her first word to describe him.

No, she needed to be patient. Give it another day. Maybe two. Don't rush it. Maybe raise the ante. Just a little. She'd reel him in eventually. It was a good deal. A genuine opportunity for both of them. And she wanted to find a ghostwriter here in Naples where she could keep an eye on the book's progress. And she already had a few ideas for the story outline she would give him.

That decided, Karlucci sighed contentedly and swiveled back to her laptop computer. She had a few more hours of writing ahead of her, and she was, indeed, feeling peachy.

CHAPTER 7

Goodland

"I HEAR YOU'RE LOOKING for Mister Manners."

The voice on the phone was female with a slight southern drawl—charming, not Nashville nasal and twangy.

"You must be Rennie Bhatia's friend," I said. "You got a name?"

"A name? Why, no. Should I get one?"

Female, southern drawl, and a smart aleck. I liked her already. But I didn't respond to that. Let her make the next move. Force her to concede something to keep the conversation going. I desperately wanted to talk to her, but I didn't want it to show. Gamesmanship. It's part of the job, learning how to get people to open up. So, I waited.

It didn't take long.

"Okay, yes, I have a name, but not over the phone, alright?"

Paranoid. And, who knows? Maybe justified.

"So, you want to meet?" I asked.

There was a pause on the line, then she said: "I'm feeling a little idle right now."

"Right now?"

"Yes. Right now."

"Gotcha. I'll be the guy in the *Toad the Wet Sprocket* tee-shirt."

"I'll be the only other person here." She hung up.

The word "idle" was the clue. It could only refer to Stan's Idle Hour, the raucous, outdoor eatery and drinkery in Goodland where, it just so happened, my boat, the *Miss Demeanor*, was docked.

But maybe not "just so happened." Too much of a coincidence. Whoever this mystery woman was, she knew where to find me. Not that you need a Q-level security clearance to track me down, but it had been a while since I'd docked in Buzzards Bay South, as the locals call it. Nowadays, I call Naples City Dock my home port. But with Gwenn out of town—out of the country, actually—I cruised over to Goodland to weather the COVID-19 outbreak. Fewer people. Except on weekends, when during tourist season Stan's gravitational pull draws into its orbit hundreds of bikers, music lovers, and other free spirits.

But it was September, and the bar would be closed for another month. It was 94 degrees outside with overcast skies and 80 percent humidity. My Weather Channel app said it felt like 104.

I came to Florida from Arizona where it was routine for the thermometer to hit triple digits. But they aren't lying when they say it's a dry heat. Blast furnace dry. But you hardly ever sweat. Perspiration evaporates the moment it hits your pores. Dehydration can be a serious issue, actually, if you spend too much time outdoors. When I lived there, I always carried a gallon jug of water in the trunk—it tasted awful, but it could keep you alive if you got a flat in the desert. In Florida, water's not an issue. Or I should say lack of water is not an issue. Here, I kept an umbrella in the car. And in my satchel.

Southwest Florida has two seasons: The Season, short for the six months of the year when the snowbirds flock back to the Sunshine State to escape the snow, sleet, and taxes up north. And Rainy Season, a subset of which is Hurricane Season. We were in the full throat of Rainy Season now. Stifling heat, humidity, and afternoon thunderstorms were the norm. Hurricanes can come calling anytime, but recently they seemed to prefer August and September visitations. But no two years are ever the same, so who knows, especially with the climate heating up.

What everyone did know, though, was that if the Big One ever hit Marco Island—Goodland being an appendage of the larger Marco, the biggest of the Ten Thousand Islands—we would all be underwater. Except for those of us with the foresight to live aboard a boat. Assuming it didn't sink, or get busted to pieces, or washed up on the mainland.

My plan come the Big One was to hightail it up the West Coast into Tampa Bay and weather the storm there. Good enough for the fabled pirate Jose Gaspar, good enough for me.

While roomy and an outstanding live-aboard, the *Miss Demeanor* is not the speediest of watercraft, so I'd need a sizeable head start to pull that off. Not that I'm neurotic or anything, but I've been known to check my weather app several times a day. That's not obsessive, is it?

Hurricanes are a definite downside to summers here, but the upside, from my perspective, was how depopulated this corner of the Gunshine State became. No traffic jams. No long lines at the checkout counters. Two-for-one deals at restaurants for the remaining customers here year-round.

Most of the snowbirds headed back north early this year, better to endure the pandemic lockdown there than risk finding themselves stranded in sweltering Florida during the insufferable summer. They fled to places like New York, where we watched in fascinated horror on television as new coronavirus infections soared and people banged pots and pans every afternoon from their windows to support the doctors and nurses risking their lives for the plague-stricken. That was then. Now Florida was the new epicenter of the pandemic.

Nobody was banging pots and pans here. We were still debating whether it was unconstitutional and a violation of our precious liberties to require people to wear masks. Can't let the cure be worse than the disease, we were told by our President and his good buddy Florida's governor, who had opened the beaches, amusement parks, and professional wrestling matches—all "essential" to the state's economy. Restaurants, bars, hotels? No problem. Party down.

And now Florida was paying the price for this greedy short-sightedness. The rate of new infections and deaths had skyrocketed. Parents were nervous about sending their kids back into the classrooms. State government was bickering with the counties and cities, which had enacted their own mask ordinances in defiance of the governor. Tourism, the state's economic lifeblood, was in the toilet. In short, it was a complete and utter clown fiesta with countless lives at risk.

And a part of me—not a small part, either—was feeling guilty about spending my time writing about weirdos like Mister Manners when the biggest story of the new century was playing out right in front of me.

My boss, Edwina Mahoney—the publisher of Tropic Press—was underwhelmed when I suggested I devote all my time and attention to the pandemic.

"And do what that hundreds of other reporters aren't already doing?" she'd asked.

Which was a perfectly reasonable question. But it was such a huge story it dwarfed everything else in the news.

"If you tumble to anything interesting, we'll talk," she said. "Until then, keep tracking down the weirdos. And keep this in mind: People are going stir-crazy, locked up, unable to see friends and family. They turn on the TV and it's a real-life horror show. What you write about, sure, it's not going to change the course of history, but it's a bright spot, a little relief from the unrelenting gloom. That's not nothing. So, go find this Mister Manners. This is your story. Own it."

As pep talks go, it could have been worse. And while I might feel the gravitas of journalistic duty tugging on me, I would be lying if I didn't admit I really wanted to meet Mister Manners. He might be crazed, but I, like many people, wasn't immune to the appeal of his antics.

So, I filled Fred's water bowl, told Spock he had the con, and I clambered over the gunwale to the dock for a rendezvous with a nameless woman who I hoped would help me score that interview.

CHAPTER 8

Stan's Idle Hour

SHE WAS SITTING at a pink and blue picnic table sheltered beneath the tin awning that stretched over the outdoor bar by the dock. And, as she said, she was the only other human being around. She appeared to be in her mid-20s. She wore a scarlet Boston Red Sox tee-shirt with a matching hat and a long, frizzy brown ponytail poked out of the back of the ballcap. Cutoff jeans and flip-flops completed her ensemble. Her cutoffs were a pale, stone-washed blue, the same shade as her surgical mask, which hid most of her face. Her white-framed wraparound sunglasses covered the rest.

I stopped about eight feet away and waved. She waved back.

"Green Lantern?" she asked, nodding toward my face mask.

"My favorite superhero."

"Hmmm."

"Let me guess. You hated the movie."

She shook her head, and a small chuckle escaped her mask. "The movie was fine. But I'm kind of a Captain Marvel fan, myself."

"Me, too. Be interesting to see who won if Carol Danvers and Hal Jordan threw down."

She nodded.

I leaned up against one of the purple telephone poles holding the adjoining thatched tiki roof aloft. "So, you're a friend of Rennie's, and you know Mister Manners, and you say you do have a name?"

"Maryanne."

"And do you have a last name?"

"I do. It begins with the letter M."

"M.M. Don't tell me. You're Miz Manners."

She shook her head and slowly—a bit theatrically, I thought—removed her wraparounds. Her eyes were hazel and pretty and set off with mascara.

"No." She crossed her legs and scratched her left knee. Naturally, my eyes were drawn in that direction, and keen observer that I am, I couldn't help but notice her excellent muscle tone. Her toes were pedicured and pink and matched her fingernails. Her hands were adorned with multiple rings, some plain metal bands, one with a large stone that might have been a turquoise, and something that looked like woven hemp.

"Me and my brother Matthew both have the initials M.M. Those were my mother's initials. She thought it was cute."

Was.

"Matthew. Is that who we're here to talk about?"

She shook her head again.

"No, Matty's not in Florida. He's a lawyer in Washington.

"Well, Maryanne…"

"You can call me Boston. Everybody does."

"Boston. Alright. South Boston? That explain that bit of a drawl you have?" A lame attempt at a joke that either went over her head, or she was too cool to acknowledge it.

"I'm a real mimic," she replied. "My roommate's from Alabama."

She seemed comfortable with small talk, so I rolled with it. I've learned never to rush these things. Better to establish rapport before getting down to tougher questions.

"So, what's with Boston," I asked. "You originally from there? You a big Sox fan or something?

She shook her head. "I'm a big fan of *Survivor*. You know, the TV show. I've been training for the past year, so when I get picked, I'll be ready."

"What's that got to do with Beantown?"

"Boston Rob? The most famous player of all the Survivors? That's my schtick. I'm going to be Boston Two. As in number two. Figured that's how I'll get Jeff Probst's attention on the videos I send him."

I nodded, just to be polite. Her odds of getting struck by a meteor were better, but we all have our dreams.

"Getting back to matters at hand, earlier you used the past-tense in referring to your mother. Your parents are deceased? If so, I'm very sorry."

I was wondering where this conversation was going. She was easy to gab with. But she wasn't Mister Manners. Her brother wasn't Mister Manners. Who was left?

She stood up and ran her hands down the sides of her face. "My Mom was killed when I was in high school. It devastated all of us, my dad especially. After Mom passed, Pops was never the same. Distant. Then very distant. As in gone."

"So, it's your father?"

She nodded, then dropped back down onto the picnic table's bench seat. "Mom was in an accident. Outside Orlando. She didn't make it. I won't bore you with the details, although you might want to get Pops to talk about it. It explains a lot."

She paused for a moment then added, "He's lost it. Obviously."

"But you say he didn't do the horse manure bit down in Everglades City."

"No. I know that wasn't him because Matty called and said he'd talked to Pops. He moves around a lot. But he said it might have been a copycat. There's some of that going on now."

"Where's he now?"

She shook her head. I wasn't sure if that meant she didn't know or wouldn't say. I decided not to press it.

"Matty thinks he's getting worse. He talks to him more than I do.

He and dad were always tight. He says Pops has been going on obsessively about how messed up the country is. Matty thinks he might do something crazy."

"You need to get him some help," I said.

"Yes, we know. He needs to get back into therapy. But, like I said, he wanders. We never know where he is any given day."

"And you don't want to turn him in."

Her eyes bulged. "We can't do that! Would you do that to *your* father?"

Since I don't know who my father is, I really couldn't answer that question truthfully, but I got her point.

I walked over to the deserted bar, hoisted myself onto it, and sat facing her. I pulled my iPhone out of the back pocket of my cargo shorts as if I were trying to avoid sitting on it, then pretended to look at a message. What I was doing, really, was trying to surreptitiously capture a photo of her, but just as I pushed the button she glanced down and all I got was her ballcap.

"So, why are you here?" I asked.

"Matty broached the idea of getting dad counseling, but he brushed Matty off. Rambled on about his life, that it's basically over, and he wants to do something dramatic before he dies."

"Like what?"

"We're not sure. I'm afraid he'll try something crazy like shoot the President or something."

"Easier said than done."

"It's been done before."

"True enough."

"And Pops is pretty good at it."

"Shooting people?"

She nodded. "He's a sniper."

I thought about that for a moment then asked, "Was he there, overseas, when your mother died?"

She nodded again. "I think that's part of the pathology. He was on temporary assignment in Syria, working with the Kurds when the White House pulled the plug on them. Just abandoned them. Everything he'd done there, it was all for nothing. He should have been home, protecting his family. That's how he felt."

"Oh, man."

She scanned me for a moment, gauging my reaction. Although projecting empathy is a good interview technique, I didn't have to fake it. I genuinely felt for her. And I guess it showed. She nodded ever so slightly, then continued:

"Whatever he's planning, he told Matty he wants to talk to a reporter beforehand to make sure his side of the story gets told."

I nodded, waiting for it.

"Pops asked Matty to help set up an interview, to use his own judgment which reporter to call. And Matty asked me to help."

"Is this where Rennie comes in?" I asked.

"Yes. We've been friends forever. She's older—in fact, she was my babysitter when I was little. She knows my father, and I've confided in her, told her Pops wanted to meet a reporter. That was about the time she met with that Third Eye detective. One thing led to another, and here we are. The detective, by the way, he said you weren't like most reporters, that you tend to get very involved with the people you write about, that the two of you have worked together."

"He said that, did he?"

"Yes. And he said The Third Eye tried to hire you, but you turned them down."

I nodded just to keep her rolling. I'd have a chat later with Lester about his big mouth.

"Rennie mentioned all that to me," Boston continued. "I talked to Matty, and we figured maybe a reporter with connections to a big private investigation firm might be an ideal combination given how weird all this is."

"Weird *is* my business," I said.

"Yeah, I read your columns sometimes. You can be pretty funny. But can you be serious? Can you help us?"

"Help how?"

"Help us with our father, of course. Keep him from doing something stupid."

"Mary...er, Boston, that's not how I operate. I'm a journalist. My job is to write stories. I don't—and don't know how to—stage interventions. Maybe you need Lester—Lester Rivers, the detective Rennie worked with."

She nodded. Vigorously this time.

"That's exactly what I told Matty, that we need to get a private eye on this. Drag dad into treatment. But he's adamant. Matty says he's insisting on talking to a reporter."

"I do want to interview your father. But it would be for publication, for a story. About talking him off the ledge, I'm not sure I could be successful at that even if I thought it was appropriate to try. Despite what Lester may have told your friend Rennie, reporters actually try to keep their distance, to be objective, uninvolved with events. I'm going to have to think about that."

She slipped her sunglasses back on, rose from the picnic table, and walked over to me, ignoring all social distancing customs. She dug into the back pocket of her cutoffs, pulled out a slip of paper, and placed it on the bar.

"Here's a number. You can reach him there. My guess, the phone's a burner, so don't think about it too long."

I glanced at the note, just a number with a Miami area code. No name. No other information. When I looked up, she was turning away.

"So, Boston, you never told me your father's name. I don't know your last name either, for that matter."

She kept walking. "Call him," she said over her shoulder. "You want his name, you can get it from him."

As she stepped past a purple trash can, she paused, pulled a cell phone from her back pocket, and dropped it into the container.

Maryanne, a.k.a. Boston, the mystery woman with no last name, wasn't the only person using a burner, evidently.

She crossed the street to where a lone vehicle was parked in the dirt lot across from Stan's, and I could hear the door lock click open as she pressed the remote. It was an older Chevy sedan, silver, parked facing the bar. There was no license plate on the front, which was normal since Florida does not issue front plates.

I was still holding my iPhone. I switched to the 2X lens, and as she pulled out onto Goodland Drive, I snapped a photo of the rear of her car and its license plate, which I noticed was from out of state. I immediately texted it to Lester with a note asking him to track down the vehicle's owner.

Boston seemed pretty sharp. And secretive. A burner, just like in the movies. It wouldn't surprise me if the car weren't hers. Maybe she borrowed it from a friend. Hell, she might have boosted it.

What I did know is that if anyone could track down a mysterious woman with no last name, it was Lester Rivers. That's what he did for a living.

No doubt about it.

But, as it turned out, it wasn't quite that easy.

CHAPTER 9

***Goodland, Aboard the* Miss Demeanor**

"This young woman with the M. and M. initials, she seem credible to you?"

It was my publisher at Tropic Press, Edwina Mahoney. We were video calling over FaceTime, me aboard the *Miss Demeanor*, she out of her mother's home in Hialeah. Her mom was one of the early coronavirus victims, and it had driven Ed crazy not being able to visit her at Jackson Memorial while she was on a ventilator. Her mom beat the odds and was now convalescing at home, and Edwina had flown from Phoenix to be with her. We were an online operation, so she could work from wherever she wanted.

And while I certainly understood why Ed would rush to the Sunshine State in an emergency like this, it was not without a few misgivings on my part. I rather liked having my boss on the other side of the continent. Ed was a terrific reporter in her day and is an outstanding businesswoman. And I liked her. But as a boss, she can be the slightest bit meddlesome.

The innocent have nothing to fear, and I had nothing to hide, but Edwina living just down the street, give or take a hundred miles, might tempt her to provide what she no doubt would consider constructive oversight—and that I would feel was backseat driving. So, shortly after she arrived, I figured we should put our cards on the table, talk to one another like two grownups.

ME: Ed, I'm so relieved your mom's alright. When you going home?

EDWINA: Actually, I kind of like it here.

ME: Oh, you won't. Traffic's terrible. People are rude. Hurricanes are a nightmare. Dengue fever. The streets flood every full moon. Pythons. Crocodiles. You'll hate it. Miami's the worst.

EDWINA: I'm touched by your concern. So, what are you doing today?

ME: Meaning what?

EDWINA: Meaning, what are you doing today?

ME: This isn't going to work, Ed, you hovering over me like this.

EDWINA: What fucking hovering? You called me.

ME: I can't handle you constantly looking over my shoulder. Makes me claustrophobic.

EDWINA: You sound feverish.

ME: What's that? I can't hear you. Must have a bad connection. I'll call later.

I didn't, and this was our first conversation since. I told her straightaway about having a bead on Mister Manners.

Good reporter that she was, Ed questioned Boston's credibility.

"I had Lester track down her license plate," I said. "Which, as it turns out, is an Alabama tag. Alabama, by the way, doesn't require plates on the front of their cars, just like Florida, in case you were wondering."

"I wasn't."

"Anyway, Boston said her roommate was from Alabama, so it's probably her roommate's car."

"Do you know anything else about who or where she is?"

"Lester's working on getting info on her roommate, but it turns out the plates are expired, and the Alabama Department of Motor Vehicles was a little turdish about releasing the information. But he finally got an ID—her roommate's a guy named Terrell Robinson, aged 25. His driver's license is still active in Alabama, but he no longer lives at the address listed with the DMV"

"Does Lester think any of that is suspicious?"

"Not necessarily. Florida's overrun with people who belong in other places—like Phoenix, for instance. And it's not uncommon for newcomers to lollygag about registering their cars down here. My old Sebring had Arizona plates when I totaled it or I still might not have a Florida registration."

"I'll have to remember that when I fly back and get my car."

That sounded ominous.

"Oh, so you think you might hang around a bit longer?"

"Actually, I'm moving here. We've registered Tropic Press as a Florida LLC."

My heart sank, but I couldn't let it show. "Well, that's why you get paid the big bucks, to make these important corporate relocation decisions. But I hope that doesn't mean you'll want me to move to Miami."

"Alexander, I don't give a flying fuck where you live. Last time I checked, you were docked in Naples. Now it's that swamp town, Goodland. Next week, you'll probably be in the Keys again. Besides corporate headquarters is my mother's condo and as much as I enjoy your company and your witty repartee, there ain't room in this town for the both of us."

That was a relief.

"Well, maybe we can visit from time to time." I thought that would be the polite thing to say. "I might have an open date on my calendar in, hmmm, let's see, November 35th, that work for you?"

"Bring it up again when the pandemic is over. In the meantime, you said something about an ethical quandary?"

I walked her through Boston No Last Name's suggestion that I help her convince Mister Manners to get psychological help.

"Why the fuck would you do that?" Edwina said. "This is a

fabulous story. I certainly don't want him to stop what he's doing. It's fantastic. Readership of your column is up sixteen percent."

Not that Edwina was cold-blooded or anything.

"All of which warms the cockles of my heart," I said. "Whatever a cockle is. But what about him maybe trying to shoot the President?"

"Do you know that for sure?"

"No."

"Are you going to ask him?"

"I imagine it could come up."

"Well, if he says yes, then we do have some decisions to make," Edwina said.

"Like…"

"Like how many photographers do we hire for the event."

"Ed…"

"Yeah, alright. We'll cross that bridge if we come to it. Whether that's in his plans or not, this story still has thorns on it. I suppose if I were teaching an ethics class in J-School, I might lecture you on keeping your distance. That it's not your job to get him into therapy. But we might also have legal issues: Let's say you interview him and learn his identity. You going to protect him, withhold his name from your story? He's a criminal. Minor league, sure, but still wanted. Even that hack author, what's-her-name Karlucci, has a bounty on his head. You protect his identity, it won't take long before cops come banging on your door demanding his ID. Then what? You say no, prosecutor drags you before a judge, and you go to jail for contempt?"

"You're forgetting Florida's Shield Law. I'm allowed to protect my sources."

"Is he a source? He's not a whistleblower. Well, except he may blow the whistle on himself. That's not protecting a source. That's hiding an outlaw. The Shield Law says evidence of a crime and eyewitness accounts of crimes are not privileged. You can't get more of an eyewitness account than from the perp himself."

"Nobody says 'perp' anymore, Ed."

She ignored that and let me digest her concerns for a moment.

"Before I interview him, I'll let him know I won't be able to shield his identity," I said. "If he wants to call it off, then he can. Or he can talk and not reveal his name and take his chances. But his whole point is to tell his side of the story, so he may not object."

"Which means he won't want to talk to you too soon before this grand finale of his, will he?" Edwina said. "He won't want anyone interfering, so it will be a last-minute thing, don't you imagine?"

"Possibly. Assuming his daughter's right about that."

Edwina appeared to be sitting at a kitchen table in her mom's condo. The corner of a stove was in the background. I could hear her drumming the tabletop with her long fingernails, a thrumming sound, probably right next to the mobile phone she was calling from. My guess is they were scarlet, her favorite color, matching her lipstick, which went vividly with her smooth, flawless chocolate skin. She raised her hand to rub her eye. Yep, scarlet.

She cocked her head and said, "So, you're interviewing him and he tells you, 'Oh, by the way, in thirty minutes a bomb's going off.' Then what are you gonna do? Call the cops? What makes you think he'd let you?"

"I can't see that happening," I said. "It would be stupid. Even if he has something like that planned—and we have no reason whatsoever to believe he does—why share it in advance and risk screwing it up? No, what he wants is to let the world know why he's done what he's done. Not what he plans to do next."

"You sure about that?"

"No."

That got a chuckle out of her. "So, you gonna call this maniac?"

"Already have. Got a recording telling me to leave a message, and I haven't heard back yet."

I could hear her fingernails thrumming some more. "And you're not concerned about your safety?"

"Nice of you to ask. But look, he hasn't injured—let alone killed—anyone yet, so I don't see why he would start with me."

She paused for a moment then said: "Don't do anything stupid."

"Come on, boss, it's me."

"Like I said."

I thought she was going to hang up, but she threw me a curveball.

"Last time we talked, you sounded antsy. You get that way from time to time, and I understand. Writing about news of the weird is funny, but it's like having dinner in a candy store. You need some meat."

"You taking me off the leash, letting me cover the pandemic?"

"Not exactly, but the pandemic will certainly be part of it."

Uh oh.

I felt a growing sense of foreboding. What did it feel like as the guillotine descended, or the trap door sprung, or the firing squad squeezed their triggers? Probably felt like this. Dammit, I just knew Edwina being in Florida was bad juju, that she'd find some way to mess with my mojo.

"It's like this, Alexander," she said. "We're nearing the biggest election in our lifetimes, and you're our reporter in the single most important swing state. The candidates know Florida's a crucial win. It's getting crazy down here. You think Mister Manners is nuts. Politics is crazier. Who knows what that madman in the White House will try to pull? Martial law? Invade China? Name Putin his running mate…"

"Kinda showing your biases aren't you, Ed?"

"Yeah, well, that's why I never covered politics. But you? Best I can tell, you don't have a political bone in your body. Do you even vote?"

"I can neither confirm nor deny…"

"That's what I thought. Look, this is right up your alley. It's Florida. It's weird. And you're an equal-opportunity hater when it comes to politicians. What could be better?"

"Uh, you saying you want me to put *The Strange Files* on hold?"

"Oh, fuck no. I want you to do both."

Of course.

God, Space Aliens and Demons Make Their Debut in Presidential Race

By Alexander Strange

Tropic Press

They say politics makes strange bedfellows. And it's hard to imagine, with only a few weeks until the election, that it could get weirder than this.

But there's another cliché to consider: In politics, a day is an eternity and a week is even longer.

This week's political news of the weird features space alien DNA, accusations that God would be harmed if the election does not go the President's way, assertions that women are prone to cancer because of demon sex, and, a continuing favorite of this political season, a renewed push for the use of a malaria drug to combat the coronavirus even though it has proven worthless.

We begin with a video retweeted by President Donald Trump about a Houston doctor and minister who touts hydroxychloroquine, a malaria medication, as a COVID killer. The President called it "spectacular." The doctor/minister also claimed face masks are unnecessary as the malaria drug is a "cure" for the virus, which is so far from the truth that Facebook and Twitter removed the speech from their sites.

Undeterred, she declared that Jesus Christ would destroy Facebook's servers if the video were not restored.

"Hello Facebook put back my profile page and videos up or your computers with (sic) start crashing till you do," she tweeted. "You are not bigger that (sic) God. I promise you. If my page is not back up face book (sic) will be down in Jesus name."

So far, Jesus has not intervened, but that hasn't slowed her down. Among her other claims:

- Women who get fibroid tumors and cysts are the victims of demonic spirits who deposit their sperm during "astral" dream sex. This condition affects "many women."

- A witch working for the "Illuminati" uses abortion, gay marriage, books, movies, Pokemon, and, naturally, Harry Potter to destroy the world.

- Speaking of gays, they practice "homosexual terrorism," and "very soon people are going to be seeking to marry children," she said in a sermon.

- Doctors are using DNA from space aliens to treat people. No word on where the aliens are kept.

- Researchers are working on a vaccine to prevent people from becoming religious.

And speaking of religion, the President said on the campaign trail that his opponent is "against God, he's against guns, he's against energy." He went further during a radio interview and said, "He's against the Bible. Essentially against religion. But against the Bible."

His opponent, former Vice President Joe Biden, who is on a first-name basis with the Pope and carries rosary beads in his pocket, called the President's comments "shameful."

STRANGE FACT: In 1484, Pope Innocent VIII issued a papal bull, which codified the existence of witches, declaring, "many persons of both sexes, heedless of their own salvation...give themselves over to devils male and female." Could this help explain the divorce rate?

Keep up with weirdness at *www.TheStrangeFiles.com*. Contact Alexander Strange at *Alex@TheStrangeFiles.com*.

CHAPTER 10

Everglades City

"GOT AN UPDATE for you. Things are more complicated than we originally thought."

Milton Throckmorton dreaded making this call, and he had mixed emotions about leaving a voicemail message. Years of dealing with his criminal clientele in New York had taught him to be circumspect about what he said over the phone. He couldn't believe he'd allowed that idiot author to prattle on the way she did when they talked the other day. What if his phone were tapped?

"Call me back on my cell," he told Kitty Karlucci's answering machine. "I'd advise you to use your cell as well."

He paused for a moment, then changed his mind. "On second thought, since you got us into this fucking mess, we need to meet in person. Squeeze your bony ass into that fucked up Lexus of yours and come down and see me. I'll meet you at the Reel and Rifle Club. Call when you get here."

After he hung up, he scanned Alexander Strange's column again. It had been reprinted in the *Naples Daily News* that morning, and he'd wished he'd seen it earlier when it had been posted online. Why hadn't the fucking cops told him it might not be Mister Manners?

That pervert couldn't possibly have been here and in Jacksonville on the same day. Something was seriously sideways.

And why did that prick Strange have to mention the YouTube video? His face was so covered in slime he was unrecognizable, and YouTube never mentioned his name. Now, thanks to his column, they were inextricably linked. What a bastard!

Throckmorton continued to smell the horseshit even though the cleaning service had scrubbed and sterilized the house. He didn't have any clothes to burn since he'd been naked, but even after half a dozen showers and several dips in the pool, the stench still filled his nostrils. Or his brain. Whatever. He could still smell it and it made him ill.

But in a few days he'd be out of this crazy state, and this would all be a receding, if hideous, memory. He never should have agreed to that stupid cunt Karlucci's harebrained scheme. Trap Mister Manners? Right! Such idiocy. Worse, he never should have made that call to New York asking for help, to send one of their goons down here. God, what a mistake! He needed to unwind all this and get the hell out of here.

He was resting in the sunny living room on his father's old brown pleather couch, idly gazing toward his front door, when he was hit with a sudden realization. Somebody who hated him knew where he lived. Forget about Mister Manners. He'd been sent a message. Like that horse's head in *The Godfather*. Throckmorton felt himself breathing more rapidly as if the oxygen in the room suddenly had been sucked into outer space.

Who in the world would do that?

Well, that could be a long list. When he'd called New York, he learned things were still unsettled, and the families hadn't sorted out everything after the hit in Park Slope. Maybe returning to the city wasn't such a hot idea after all. Maybe it was time to finally disappear. He'd planned for this eventuality. He'd stashed money offshore—lots of money.

And he'd been smart about how he did that. No paper trail. All his records were in the cloud. All the data, including bank account numbers and passwords, on encrypted documents. And those weren't the only encrypted documents he'd stored.

He'd naively believed that once he gave the FBI the books he'd kept for the "square grouper" drug smugglers back in the day, that he'd be off the hook. Wasn't it enough he sent his own father to jail? But that's not how the Feds worked. Once they had their claws in you, they never let go. They'd been on his ass ever since. It had been a stressful kabuki dance, giving the FBI just enough to stay in their good graces, and not so much that his employers detected his betrayal. It was enough to give a man an ulcer. And it had.

But if there was one thing he'd learned in his dealings with his New York clients, it was that hesitation could be fatal. If your gut says run, just beat feet out the door and don't look back. Maybe he should already be in the wind. Maybe he should grab his bags and disappear.

Like today.

Throckmorton considered that for a few minutes, weighing the pros and cons. Nothing was keeping him here. His father's lingering financials were wrapped up. The old man's partner in his computer security company, Margaret Bhatia, had turned the operation over to her daughter, Rennie, and she had agreed to buy out Hugo's share in their existing contracts. Those contracts had been lucrative—very lucrative—but it was time to walk away from that deal.

His real estate agent had listed the house for four hundred thousand. In Naples, it would sell for much more, but this was Everglades City. Location. Location. Location. Fortunately, it was unencumbered. He'd done that for his father, paid off the mortgage. Did his old man thank him? Fat chance. Like it was his fault the old fart was frog marched off to Club Fed at Eglin. It's not like he was locked up in Leavenworth or anything.

Leaving town would also solve another problem, he reflected—it would allow him to avoid any further confrontations with Margaret

Bhatia's loco ex-husband. He'd dropped by unannounced demanding one hundred large in exchange for a memory card he claimed Hugo entrusted to him. Milton Throckmorton knew exactly what was on the card since he had given it to his old man for safe keeping. If that nut job had come by sooner, it would have saved him the trouble of tearing up the house looking for it.

So the old man had given this psycho "the one thing" he'd asked his father to do for him—keep this safe and keep this secret. That card could be worth a lot more than one hundred large. It could be worth Throckmorton's life if it got into the wrong hands. Assuming Sniffen really had it.

But Throckmorton knew something that would never occur to that whack job Horace Sniffen or Raoul or whatever he was calling himself these days. It was the 21st century. Memory card data could easily be changed. A couple of minutes on the computer and that card Sniffen had would be worthless.

Which is why he'd told Sniffen to fuck off. He'd told him a few other things, too. Like take a bath and get a haircut and check into a drug rehab center. Then he threw him out of the house—physically pushed him out the door, which left him breathless. Probably needed to get the old ticker checked once he was done with this madness.

So, pack up and get out of Swampsville. But to where? Run away or return to Manhattan? After a few minutes of fraught contemplation, he made a critical decision.

He decided he needed a drink.

A little restorative would help calm his nerves, allow him to think things through anxiety-free. While it's true that hesitation could be fatal, so could panic. Sit down. Take a deep breath. Have a cocktail. And maybe a little snack. Tito's and Cheetos. Think about the situation for a minute before doing something he might regret.

After all, if somebody wanted him dead, wouldn't he already be on the wrong side of the daisies? Still, there was major fuckery afoot. But who was behind it? And why? Wouldn't it make more sense to figure that out before fleeing with his hair on fire? Before spending the rest of his life looking over his shoulder in constant fear?

Time for that drink.

He padded into the kitchen, pulled a tall highball glass from the cabinet, then pressed it into the refrigerator's ice dispenser. There were a couple of ounces left in the bottle of vodka on the countertop. He unscrewed the top, poured the remains into the glass, and swirled the clear liquid, letting the ice cubes chill it thoroughly. Then he chugged the entire drink in one continuous gulp.

It burned through him like lava, and he luxuriated in the welcome sensation of heat and spreading relaxation. Vodka! What an amazing invention. It was just what he needed to shake off his jitters—liquid courage.

But the burning sensation in his belly didn't stop. In fact, it was intensifying as if it were eating his insides. Goddamned ulcer. It was flaring up again. And no wonder with all the stress he was under.

Milk. He needed some milk. That always settled his stomach. He yanked open the refrigerator's right-hand door, extracted a carton, and poured a splash over the ice in his glass.

He downed it and waited a moment for the burning to subside.

It didn't.

Screw it. If milk doesn't kill it, I'll numb it with more alcohol, he thought. He kept a spare bottle of vodka in the freezer compartment for drinking martinis straight up, undiluted. He swung the freezer door open and...

What the fuck!

The highball glass slipped from his fingers and shattered on the kitchen's hard white tile floor. Throckmorton barely noticed. His vision tunneled, transfixed on the freezer compartment. He felt his entire body begin to tremble, his heart was racing, but he couldn't take his eyes off what was staring at him from inside the freezer.

On the shelf where his Tito's ordinarily rested was something else entirely.

Not a bottle.

A pair of frozen eyes. Eyes attached to a hideous creature.

Then they blinked.

CHAPTER 11

***Goodland, Aboard the* Miss Demeanor**

"You know, sitting out here on the poop deck, it kind of reminds me of home," Lester said, taking a sip of his French Boodle.

Even though it's my own invention, I can't stand the drink myself—equal parts Grey Goose vodka (made in France) and Boodles Gin (Travis McGee's fave). I concocted it because it was punny. Delicious, it is not. But taste is in the mouth of the beholder. Or something.

I surveyed our surroundings: Stan's Idle Hour across Buzzards Bay South, the Little Bar's back porch, a handful of pleasure craft and fishing boats bobbing in the small marina.

"Lester, none of this looks like New Orleans."

"Not the look, the feel. All those dark clouds swollen with rain, just like back home. The humidity must be a thousand percent. And that smell, it reminds me of Bourbon Street."

It smelled of grouper guts from a passing fishing boat, but I got his drift.

As if on cue, it began drizzling, and we scrambled for the shelter of the *Miss Demeanor's* cabin.

As Lester refreshed his martini, I clicked on the TV. A tropical wave east of the Windward Islands was looking ominous, and I wanted the latest update. Say what you will about local television newscasts and their "if it bleeds, it leads" shallowness, they absolutely kill with their weather reports. I checked my Mickey Mouse watch. I had another five minutes before the early news came on, so I pressed the TV's mute button.

"You covering politics now?" Lester asked. "I noticed your latest contribution to American literature was all about witches and space aliens."

"Yeah, Edwina wants me to file a weekly update on weird political news. On top of my already grueling workload."

Lester choked on that, and French Boodle began dripping out his nose.

"You all right?" I asked, slightly alarmed. The last thing I needed was for him to choke to death. How would I ever explain it to his girlfriend, Silver? If they were even still an item.

He waved me off. "Grueling workload!" He took a couple of breaths and wiped his nose on the sleeve of his Hawaiian shirt. "You tell your boss about Mister Manners?" he asked.

I ran down my conversation with Edwina, her concerns about withholding Mister Manners' identity, and her reservations about intervening on behalf of his kids because, cynical publisher that she was, Edwina—and our readers—loved following his exploits.

"She's not keen on doing anything that would slow Mister Manners down," I said.

"I'm with her," Lester said. "You worry too much. If he wants to keep his identity secret, he don't need to be talking to a reporter. That's not your problem. The issue you got, the one that always seems to tie you in knots, is stepping out of your detached, unbiased, oh so sterile and purified role as a reporter and getting your hands dirty with real people and their real problems."

"Is that a dig?"

"No. You just gotta decide what rules you wanna play by, develop your own code, so to speak. I like what journalists do. We need journalists. They're the front line of democracy. More so than us tired old soldiers, really. But who says every reporter has to sing from the same hymnal? You think Hunter S. Thomson would give two shits about something like this ethical concern of yours? You ever read *Fear and Loathing on the Campaign Trail*? Pure genius."

"Half of it was made up."

"So, he wasn't worried so much about facts. But what he did was capture just how twisted politics has become. He got the weird, nasty, insane *essence* of it."

He took a sip of his martini, smacked his lips, and set the glass down. "Let me tell you a story. I was on patrol outside Kabul when we came under small arms fire. One of my men took a bullet in the leg, and I ran over to drag him to cover. Next thing I know, another guy's helping me, and we pull him to safety. You know who that was? The guy who helped me? He wasn't one of mine. He was a reporter embedded with us, name of Jolidon.

"You think he even thought for one second about what to do? About what some professor back at college might think? He did what any decent human being would do: He came to the aid of a soldier in need."

"I'd like to think…"

"You don't need to think. You've already been there. You ran through a hail of bullets to help that cop, Jim Henderson, Linda's granddad. You know what I'm talking about. If you hadn't acted, he would have bled to death. Being a journalist doesn't mean you stop being human. And there's more than one kind of journalist. Witness Hunter S. Thompson."

"And if I discover Mister Manners is planning something terrible?"

"Fucking stop him."

"Spoken like a soldier."

"Damned straight and proud of it."

The news was coming on, and I turned up the volume:

- On the same day that more than ten thousand Floridians tested positive for the coronavirus, the Collier County Commission refused to approve an ordinance requiring people wear masks in public, with some officials calling it un-American.
- The owner of a local convenience store chain named August "Aggie" LaFrance, who had called the pandemic and Black Lives Matter protests "hoaxes," told the lone county commissioner supporting the mask ordinance that he should "go back to Cuba where you belong." The commissioner was born in Lakeland, Florida.
- And this just in, the Collier County Sheriff's Office reports that the recent victim of a Mister Manners attack, Milton Throckmorton of Everglades City, has been found dead in his father's home, the apparent victim of a heart attack.

"Jesus H. Palomino, Lester, you seeing this?"

The news anchor switched to a live feed outside Throckmorton's house.

"We're here in Everglades City, the most recent site of an attack by Florida's famous vigilante, Mister Manners," the young woman holding an umbrella aloft said into the camera. The chyron at the bottom of the screen identified her as Angela Rodriguez. "Just moments ago, paramedics removed the body of a man from the house. Neighbors said it was Milton Throckmorton who had been staying here to settle his father's estate."

The screen shifted to video images of a gurney being rolled by paramedics into an ambulance, gawking neighbors in the background. Then the reporter, doing a talk-back to the anchor, introduced a youngish man with black hair who she identified as Hector Morales, Throckmorton's housekeeper.

"Mr. Morales, what can you tell us about the situation here?" the reporter asked.

"It is very upsetting. I came by this afternoon as always, and I find

Señor Throckmorton on the kitchen floor. I check his pulse, but he ain't got one. So, I call the police right away."

"Angie, this is Kellie," the anchor interrupted. "Is he saying that when he found Mr. Throckmorton, he was already dead?"

The reporter may have been young, but she knew how to handle an airhead. "Yes, Kellie, I think that's what he meant when he said there was no pulse."

Kellie was undaunted.

"Were there any signs of foul play?" she asked.

Angie repeated the question to Hector Morales, who hesitated for a moment before answering. Angie, anticipating that he might not have understood the question, rephrased it. "What we're asking," she said, "is did it look like somebody murdered him?"

Morales shook his head. "I know what foul play is. No. He was just lying on the floor. But…"

Angie prompted him: "But?"

The man named Hector ran his hands over his face and tugged on his mask. Nervous. "Well, uh, the toad's missing."

The camera shuddered. "His toes were missing?" Angie asked, an anguished tone in her voice.

"No, toad." Then Morales rolled his eyes, turned, and scurried away before any of that could be cleared up.

The screen switched back to the anchor desk where Kellie was shaking her head, a grim expression on her face. "We'll have more on this story as it develops," she said.

Then she broke into a smile. "But on a lighter note, an alligator was found in a swimming pool at a five-year-old's birthday party…"

I switched the TV off.

"Lester, the game's afoot. I gotta go. You with me?"

He gazed at his just-poured drink, then back at me, a plaintive look on his face.

"Fine." I rummaged through the galley and found a plastic sippy cup.

He turned the green and white container in his hands, noticing the picture of Marvin the Martian on the side. He looked up at me, a puzzled expression on his face. Like there was something wrong with having a sippy cup in one's Marvin the Martian collection.

"What am I, five years old?"

I gave him palms up and shrugged shoulders, the universal body language that translated: "It's all I got for roadies, bro."

"Huh," he said. Then he ninjaed off the lid, poured in his French Boodle, and sealed it back up. "Don't dat beat all." He took a sip from the spout. "Works!"

It was raining outside, and a distant clap of thunder rumbled through the marina. Fred began whining. Like most dogs, he's terrified of loud noises. I picked him up, wrapped him in a galley towel so he'd stay dry, and rested him in the crook of my left arm like a football, which was easy enough as Fred's a little fellow.

"Let's go, buddy, you can come with us. I won't leave you here alone with all this lightning and thunder. It will be an adventure."

"Gerruff!"

"That's the spirit."

Lester was already at the cabin hatchway peeking out. "It's tapering off a little. If we go now, we might make it to the car without getting drenched."

With Fred in one hand and a key in the other, I locked the cabin door behind me and we slipped over the gunwale. My car was twenty yards away. We sprinted over and piled in before the heavens opened up again.

I buckled Fred into his little car seat and gave him one of his chew toys. That earned me another "gerruff," and he settled into gnawing his rubber bone.

I was driving a gray Ford Explorer with eighty-five thousand miles on the odometer. The SUV gave us a little extra road clearance, which we might need traversing Goodland Drive as the road is prone to flooding.

Not that long ago, I stood in that street, up to my knees in flood-water, when Sheriff's Deputy Linda Henderson shot a would-be Russian assassin to death and ran his partner into the swamp where a Burmese python strangled him.

She had since been promoted to the Investigations Department as a detective in the Special Crimes Bureau. I had a hunch she might be on the scene in Everglades City as she'd caught the earlier horse manure incident.

TV had once again referred to that attack as the handiwork of Mister Manners even though that now seemed improbable since the vigilante had also struck the same day in Jacksonville where police said he'd left his signature calling card.

Linda Henderson was a sort of friend. Her grandfather, who Lester mentioned, had been shot while he and I were unraveling the mystery of how an inmate in the Collier County jail had been murdered. It led to the discovery of a sex-and-blackmail ring run out of the Museum of Holy Creation by none other than the celebrated televangelist Lee Roy Chitango.

But even though we had that connection, she played things by the book, and I had been unsuccessful in my few attempts to wheedle confidential information out of her. Still, she steered me away from rabbit holes. For instance, when I'd asked her straight up if she'd found a note from Mister Manners in Everglades City, I got the formal, "No comment." But when I suggested to her, well, okay then, I'm going to assume it was him, she gave me a look, the squinty-eyed cop stare that said, "Don't be stupid."

But now that Throckmorton had died, I'd pester her again. This had all the earmarks of a developing cluster-fuck, the kind of case that gets mired down and cops hate because it makes them look flat-footed. Which is the perfect time for a valiant, crusading weird-news reporter to offer his services in untangling the mystery.

And which more often than not is met with sarcastic rejection, but you never know. You can't eat the wild goose until you chase it.

CHAPTER 12

Everglades City

HECTOR MORALES COULDN'T get away fast enough from the cute television reporter and her cameraman. He knew he'd already said too much, and he certainly did not need to have his face shown on the news, even if half of it was covered with a mask. What was he thinking?

Bad enough he had to talk to that sheriff's detective. Next thing you know, I'll be in a cage heading back to Mexico, he thought.

His mother had always told him, "Hector, you and your big mouth are going to get in trouble someday." This might be that day.

And why had he mentioned the toad?

¡Pendejo!

He had worked part-time for Milton Throckmorton's father, tending to the pool and doing housework. Señor Hugo also had trusted him to do his grocery shopping and to run other errands. He had given Hector a key to the house, and Hector took pride in being seen as a trustworthy employee.

Señor Hugo was a nice man, and Hector missed him.

He would not miss his son. He was demanding and disrespectful. Always complaining about his work. The bookshelves were too dusty. There was a spot on the dishes. Weeds were growing between the pool pavers. And do something about the goddamned frog.

The ignorant *imbecil* didn't even know the difference between an ordinary frog and a bufo toad.

But Hector knew. Señor Hugo's little Chiwawa, Pequeno, had been killed by a bufo. Pequeno had pounced on one loitering by the pool and bit it. Also known as a cane toad, the one that killed Pequeno wasn't that big, no larger than a softball. But like all members of its species, the bufo toad excreted a dangerous toxin when threatened. Pequeno got a mouthful, and the vet couldn't save him.

Ever since, one of Hector's duties had been to patrol the yard and eliminate any bufos he came across. Señor Hugo insisted that it be done humanely, which Hector found charming. If a toad had killed his dog, he'd be out there with a ball-peen hammer hunting them down. But Señor Hugo was not like that. He might have been an ex-con and a drug smuggler, but he had a big heart. He instructed Hector to capture the toads—using protective gloves, of course—then put them in the freezer to painlessly euthanize them.

Ordinarily, that procedure required Hector to place the toads in one-gallon Ziploc bags, but the latest bufo he'd discovered was enormous, with a body the size of a soccer ball, too big for a bag. So, he just placed it, wriggling and squeaking, on a rack in the freezer and slammed the door shut. He figured he'd remove it the next day after it went to sleep and drifted off to toad heaven.

He also knew a few other things about frogs and toads because he'd looked them up on Google. All toads are frogs, but not all frogs are toads. Most toads secreted toxic goo when frightened. It was a brilliant defense mechanism. When it came to toad toxin, though, bufos were the worst. But a few frogs were toxic, too. There was one in South America so dangerous one drop could kill a man.

So, when Hector discovered the *imbecil* sprawled on the kitchen floor, the first thing he did was *not* feel for his pulse as he told the police.

The first thing he did was approach the freezer door, which was wide open with water dripping down onto the kitchen floor littered with shards of broken glass. There was a gaping, empty space on the freezer shelf where he had deposited Señor Bufo.

Or was it Señorita Bufo? The females were supposed to be bigger, and this one was huge, the size of a cat.

Frantic, he'd rummaged through the house looking for the toad but couldn't find him, her, or it. The doors and windows were shut, so it had to be somewhere inside. What if the cops found it? What would they think? Would they accuse Hector of scaring his boss to death? Or poisoning him?

Could that have happened? How long did it take a toad to freeze to death? That was one big bufo. Maybe a long time. Maybe it jumped out and licked the *imbecil* on the face. Or maybe—oh, no!—maybe its poison, could it have dripped into the ice maker? That shattered glass on the floor. Did the *imbecil* drink bufotoxin? Was that even a thing?

Hector finally gave up trying to find the bufo's hiding place and mopped up the water and broken glass on the kitchen floor with paper towels. Then he called 911. Now Hector realized he should have looked longer for the toad, and he scolded himself as he fled the television crew. The police will find the toad eventually, then they'll be coming for me, he worried.

Hector pulled out his cell phone and checked the time. He could just make it to the Reel and Rifle Club, where he had the evening shift bartending. Between that job, the gig at the riding stables, and working for Señor Hugo, he'd done well for himself. Until now. But with Señor Hugo's death, the damned virus killing the bar business, and now the *imbecil*, things were going to *mierda*.

Hector had wanted to teach the *imbecil* a lesson. Get even for all his insulting behavior. Dumping the horse manure on the front porch had been a hilarious prank. But he wasn't laughing now. Maybe now he was a murderer. Or at least an accomplice to murder.

Can you imagine the scene in the courtroom?

And who was your partner in crime, Señor Morales?

Uh, a frog, Your Honor.

They wouldn't deport him to Mexico. They'd lock him up in Chattahoochee in a straight jacket.

It was time to get out of Everglades City. Finish his shift tonight at the club, cash out, then maybe take the bus down to Miami, blend in, get lost in the crowd of masked faces. Sure, it was the hotspot in the coronavirus pandemic, but could it be worse than this?

CHAPTER 13

Everglades City

A PRESS SCRUM awaited us outside Milton Throckmorton's house.

Three of the local network stations blocked the streets with their mobile vans, satellite antennae erect. I spotted two reporters double-teaming the event for the *Naples Daily News*, an unprecedented show of force given all the newsroom layoffs. Several photographers were jockeying for position, one I recognized, the others not, but it was hard to tell as everyone was masked.

I weaved my way toward the front of the pack leaving Lester behind to care for Fred. The TV camera crews grumbled and growled as they always do when anyone barges in on their territory. TV being a visual medium, I understood they needed clear lines of sight. But just because I understood it didn't mean I had to put up with it. One cameraman dressed even scruffier than me—which takes some doing—turned and started to give me some lip. Then he looked up, realized how I towered over him, and decided it wouldn't kill him to make a little room, take a couple of steps to ensure we maintained our distance from one another, the new pandemic etiquette.

I spotted the public information officer for the Sheriff's Office, a former *Daily News* reporter named Kristine who seemed to be organizing things. I nodded at her, she nodded back, and continued handing out what appeared to be fact sheets. I snatched one.

I glanced at the handout and didn't notice anything remarkable other than a few more background details on Milton Throckmorton: Name, age, home and business addresses in Manhattan. Self-employed. Pretty skimpy.

Kristine waved to the gaggle of reporters, photographers, and TV types to get our attention. She said a detective would brief us, but that it would be a few minutes if we would be patient. As if we had a choice.

WHILE WE WAITED, I reflected on the conversation I had with Lester on the way to Everglades City. I'd shared with him the internal debate I was having about whether to accept Kitty Karlucci's ghostwriting offer. I'd semi-concluded the only reason to do it was for the money. But was that good enough?

"You were just bellyaching about your supposed workload," Lester pointed out. "You're gonna wreck your lifestyle you keep adding stuff like this to your plate."

"Did I mention what she's offering?" I asked. When he shook his head, I told him. That earned a low whistle.

"You could keep yourself in tee-shirts for a while with that," he said.

Today's tee-shirt was red with the words "Ben Dover & the Screamers" emblazoned in black ink on the front. Yes, it's a real band, although I will confess I'd never heard any of their tunes. I found the shirt at a second-hand shop.

"You talk to your boss about this?" Lester asked. "Or Gwenn?"

"Not yet."

"You gonna?"

"Probably should, huh?"

He chuckled. "You may not be as stupid as you look."

Be that as it may, I was deeply reluctant to mention it to Edwina Mahoney. I could just imagine the ration of shit I would have to endure. You got so much free time on your hands? she would likely ask. Maybe I'm paying you too much. That sort of harassment.

Gwenn, on the other hand, would think it was terrific. Workaholic that she was, Gwenn was forever coming up with ideas on how I might more productively spend my time. Working with a famous author on a novel? That would definitely rev her engines.

But would it rev mine?

It was ludicrous that I hadn't already picked up the phone and called Kitty back. When opportunity knocks, you open the door. Or you might spend the rest of your life kicking yourself in the ass.

But something was holding me back. I really did need to run this past Gwenn. I trusted her judgment, and as a bonus, she was a lawyer. An attorney's perspective on this could be helpful. I decided to call her first chance I got.

A PLAINCLOTHES DETECTIVE—OXFORD shirt, open neck, khakis, and a Glock—took a hand-held mic from Kristine and began talking over the portable public address speaker.

"I'm Senior Detective Mark Mayweather—and yes, my initials are M.M., so let's get that out of the way. I am not Mister Manners."

That got a chuckle from the reporters.

He wasn't smiling when he said it and didn't reciprocate the laughter.

"I know there's a great deal of interest about the event here today and the earlier incident that the media has attributed to the vigilante Mister Manners. Let me be clear about a couple of things: One, the Collier County Sheriff's Office has not determined who is responsible for that earlier incident, and we have not named any persons of interest and do not have any suspects at this time. Two, because of that earlier incident, we are cautious about drawing too many conclusions about Mr. Throckmorton's death. We will not have any further information to share with you about that until an autopsy has been conducted by the Collier County Medical Examiner's Office." A collective groan rose from the crowd.

I raised my hand, and he nodded to me. "Are you with the Special Crimes Bureau?" I asked.

"I am."

"So, does that mean you are treating this as a possible homicide?"

He shook his head. "Like I said, we are reserving judgment on cause of death until we have the autopsy."

Several other reporters began shouting questions, but he still had his eye on me, waiting for any follow-up questions, which public officials with media training know to do.

So, I obliged: "I thought Detective Linda Henderson was assigned to this investigation."

That got a fleeting frown, but he quickly recovered. "Detective Henderson was on call when Mr. Throckmorton suffered that earlier attack on his residence. Now that we have a death on our hands, we're elevating the investigation."

There was a lot of shouting at that point, and he waved his hands for quiet.

"Okay, I get it. Why is this being elevated, right? Well, that's a bit of a technical matter. Any unusual death, where there can be the possibility of foul play, is automatically handled in an elevated manner..."

More shouting and more hand waving to hush the scrum.

"This is routine, people. Don't read too much into this."

Too much. He didn't say: Don't read *anything* into this.

There was more jabber, but mostly noise, very little signal. I wanted to be fair-minded about it: After all, even if there were no evidence of foul play, nobody likes coincidences, so they'd be stupid not to treat this as a potential homicide, which, despite the detective's denials, was precisely what they were doing.

But I found myself itchy about Linda Henderson getting bumped from the case. Sure, she was young and a junior detective in the bureau, but it just didn't feel routine. Something was up. I could feel it. My Weird-Shit-O-Meter was agitated.

And it had the foul taste of betrayal. This was obviously a high-profile case. To rip it away from her seemed unfair. And, of course, even if there was a lot of tension in our relationship, not unprecedented between reporters and cops, I respected Linda. She was smart, tough, and as I learned back in Goodland that day, a hell of a shot.

I don't like it when young people working on building their careers have opportunities snatched away. The senior editors at the *Washington Post* tried to steal the Watergate story from Woodward and Bernstein, too. The two greatest detectives in the history of American journalism nearly got screwed by their own colleagues. It was a scene made famous in *All the President's Men* when the paper's editor, Ben Bradlee, let them keep the story. That's how careers—and in their case, legends—are born.

This was hardly Watergate, but pulling Linda Henderson left a bad taste in my mouth.

But there's a sure-fire cure for that, and Lester already had a head start.

I needed a drink.

CHAPTER 14

Everglades City

THE REEL AND RIFLE CLUB was founded as a kind of parody of Everglades City's elegant and well-known watering hole, the Rod and Gun Club, which overlooks the Barron River and has hosted the rich and famous including five presidents, John Wayne, Burt Reynolds, Sean Connery, and Danny Glover.

The list of glitterati at the Reel and Rifle Club is much smaller and less luminescent but did include southwest Florida's most famous author, Kitty Karlucci, who Lester and I spotted sitting by herself at a table in the small barroom sipping what appeared to be a martini.

Lester beelined to her table, social distancing be damned.

"Ms. Karlucci," he announced himself, "what a thrill to see you here. I'm a huge fan."

Karlucci glanced up from her drink and offered a fleeting, if unenthusiastic, smile. She was wearing what appeared to be the same outfit she wore when she discovered her Lexus vandalized in the Publix parking lot: yellow yoga pants, pink running shoes, with her hair in a ponytail. That ponytail today was poking out the back of a blue ballcap, the front of which was embroidered with a picture of a chunk of cheese with the words "Make America Grate Again."

Lester was undeterred by her chilly reception.

"The thing I admire most is your attention to detail," he said. "I'm a detective, myself, and your description of the investigative process is flawless."

That seemed to draw a more favorable response. Karlucci cocked her head and said, "Is that so?"

Lester removed his boater, the flat-brimmed straw hat he always wore—very popular at political conventions—and pulled a business card out of the hat's lining. "Lester Rivers at your service," he said, setting the card on her table.

I was feeling a little embarrassed for him. I'd never seen him gush over anyone like this. This was a hard-bitten combat veteran and private eye who was nobody's fool, but he was acting like a teenager in heat. And Karlucci seemed to be warming to his attentions.

"Oh," she said. "The Third Eye. You *are* a real detective, aren't you."

I had drifted a little closer, still a safe six feet away, Fred by my side on a leash, and she glanced in my direction. Her brow furrowed for a moment, then her eyes grew wider in recognition.

"I owe you a phone call," she said. "You had a chance to think things over?"

I nodded. "We should talk some more."

"Tomorrow. I'll call you tomorrow."

She gestured to a nearby table. "Why don't you boys and your adorable puppy grab a seat and take off your masks." Hers was already off, resting on the table next to her martini, which was either half empty or half full depending upon your point of view.

The nearest table was at least six feet away, so I settled into a chair, removed my mask, and said to her, "So, Kitty, getting any takers on your bounty?"

She nodded. "Hundreds. No way to sort through them all, so I just forward them to the Sheriff's Office, a lot of good that will do me."

The initial surprise at discovering her, of all places, in Everglades

City had worn off, and it belatedly dawned on me that this was too unlikely a coincidence.

"Of all the gin joints in all the towns in all the world, what brings you here?"

"Meeting an associate."

Lester and I glanced at one another, no doubt sharing the same thought. What were the odds?

I started to ask her something when we were interrupted by the bartender, a lean guy of medium height wearing a black mask who, oddly, looked familiar even with most of his face covered. He asked for our orders. We both said beer. And I couldn't escape the feeling he seemed familiar. But before I could pursue it further, Karlucci spoke up.

"What are *you two* doing here?" she asked, a tone of curiosity and suspicion in her voice. Apparently, it had now dawned on everyone this was weird.

"You don't know?" I replied.

She gave me laser eyes. Kitty Karlucci did not like being toyed with.

Lester jumped in. "Milton Throckmorton. Name familiar? Allegedly the latest Mister Manners victim? You two had that in common, didn't you?"

"*Had?*" Karlucci's eyes were getting huge.

"He's dead," I said.

Karlucci gasped. "Dead?"

"Apparent heart attack," Lester said.

She whirled around in her chair. "Hector!" she shouted.

The bartender rounded the corner of the bar and scurried to her table. "Yes, Ms. Kitty?"

"Did you know about this?" She didn't bother with further explanation. It was a small room, and Hector was bound to have overheard our conversation. He stood at rigid attention, staring straight ahead at the wall behind our tables, not making eye contact.

"Hector?" Karlucci demanded.

"I just come from his house," he said. "I found him. He was in the kitchen. On the floor. By the, uh, by the fridge."

I finally recalled why he seemed familiar. "You were just on TV," I said.

He nodded, briefly glancing my way then returning his gaze to the wall.

Karlucci cut in. "Goddammit, Hector, why didn't you say something?"

The guy looked like his head would explode. A tear leaked down his left cheek. He squeezed his eyes shut, then opened them and looked down at the author.

"*Lo siento mucho,*" he said. "I...I..." He looked up, shook his head, then finally pulled a chair from our table and sat down halfway between Karlucci and us.

"I'm afraid," he finally said, his head drooping.

"Hector," I said. "You worked for Throckmorton, right?"

He nodded. "I worked for Señor Hugo, his father."

Lester snapped his fingers. "Hugo Throckmorton. Now I get it." He turned to Karlucci. "I knew that name sounded familiar when I read about the manure attack at his house. He was one of your readers, right? Hugo Throckmorton? You credit him in your books."

She ignored him.

"You should have told me," Karlucci scolded Hector. "You should have said something the minute I arrived. That's why I'm here." She glanced briefly at Lester and me. "We were supposed to meet."

"About Mister Manners?" I asked, following a hunch.

She gave me the evil eye again, then her expression softened. She nodded, then took a big sip of her martini. The glass was now definitely half empty.

"And you," I said to Hector, "what was it you told the TV puke? Something about a toad?"

CHAPTER 15

Goodland

UNCLE LEO WAS incredulous. "So, you all end up at this joint in the middle of nowhere, and the bartender confesses to killing this Throckmorton fellow? Sounds like the cheesy ending to one of Kitty what's-her-name's insipid mysteries."

"Not quite."

"You said he spilled his guts."

"Yeah. Lester badged him, and he kind of fell apart and just started sobbing and jabbering. Went on and on. Poor guy's scared to death he may really have killed Throckmorton."

"He put a poisonous toad in his refrigerator. What the fuck did he think would happen?"

"Well, we don't know that was the cause of death."

Uncle Leo grumbled something I couldn't quite make out over the phone, then I heard the rattling of ice in a glass. I checked my Mickey Mouse watch. It would be 6 p.m. in Arizona, well into the cocktail hours for Leo.

"So, the cops know about this Hector character?" he asked.

"They talked to him about discovering the body, but he told us he didn't say anything about the toad. I'm thinking the cops might like knowing that little detail."

"I'll bet."

"I think I may share all this with Linda Henderson, maybe use it as leverage to get a little more out of the Sheriff's Office about Mister Manners."

"And who is she?"

"Oh, sorry. Linda's been the lead detective on the Throckmorton horse manure attack but got yanked from the case now that he's dead. Which, I gotta tell you, I find not only annoying because she's a semi-friend, but my Spidey sense tells me something odd is going on with all this."

I filled Leo in on the press conference outside Throckmorton's house, how Linda Henderson had been replaced, ostensibly because the case had been "elevated" now that there was a death that could be suspicious.

"I seem to recall her," Leo said. "Wasn't she a deputy, a rookie? Shot a couple of Russians to death?"

"She shot one and chased the other into a mangrove swamp. He ended up getting strangled by a python."

"Oh, yeah. How could I forget? Pythons."

"She recently got promoted to detective in the Special Crimes Bureau."

"And they pulled her? What for? They need a few extra hands to tear-gas peaceful protestors somewhere?"

Leo wasn't a big law enforcement fan despite being a cog in the Phoenix criminal justice system. Uncle Leo to me, Maricopa County Superior Court Judge Leonardo D. Strano, to you. He was a liberal trial lawyer long before his appointment to the bench, and he harbored deep suspicions about the authoritarian impulses of government and the police.

"Gwenn says this too shall pass," I said, trying to steer the conversation away from politics. "She believes the American people will straighten this out."

"Spoken like a true Canadian."

There was a pause on the line, Leo probably taking a sip of whatever his cocktail of choice was this evening, then he said:

"Hey, you think she could get us into Canada?"

"Funny, I just asked her if we got married could we move there."

"You didn't propose, did you?"

"No. And she doesn't want to move back to Montreal, anyway."

Leo's tone of voice when he asked the question—had I proposed?—felt off.

I was a child when my mother, Alice Strano, died. Leo, Mom's older brother, took me in, got me through public school, off to college, and even helped me get my first job as a reporter for the *Phoenix Daily Sun*.

Mom drowned during a flash flood that inundated an Austin cave where she was staging a sit-in to save the habitat of an endangered spider. At least, she is presumed to have drowned. Her body was never recovered. Nor the spider's, for that matter.

I never knew my biological father, so for all intents and purposes, Leo was the father I never had—in fact, legally, he was my father since he adopted me. He also helped me change my last name to the English translation of Strano—Strange.

And he was my best friend.

But he had a checkered matrimonial history. His current wife, Sarah, was his fifth. With his first four wives, I recalled a certain souring in his attitude regarding the holy union of matrimony preceding each of those divorces. And I was picking up that same vibe right now.

"Things okay there on the home front, Your Tortness?" I asked.

"Meaning what?"

"When you asked if I'd proposed, you sounded a little freaked out."

"Nah. Gwenn's a nice girl. She's smart. And she's got a steady job—no small matter considering what you do for a living and the state of the news business."

He hadn't actually answered my question, so I pushed it.

"And how's Sarah?"

I heard ice tinkling again. "Sarah's fine. We're fine. You worry too much."

He clicked off the call. Abrupt. Anyone else, it would be insulting. But that's Leo. When he's said all he wants to say he hangs up.

Still, the conversation was troublesome. Sarah was much younger than Leo and, without question, the nicest, most decent, and, certainly, the most attractive of his many wives. She adored him. I didn't want to borrow trouble, but the conversation left me a little unsettled.

CHAPTER 16

Goodland

IT WAS LATE, AND I was sitting in the lounge of the *Miss Demeanor* playing fetch with Fred, our nightly ritual before he curled up for the evening. Fetch with Fred is a little different than with most dogs. I threw a chew toy across the cabin. He charged after it, then he ran away to hide it somewhere in the bowels of the boat. Shortly thereafter, he'd come back for another. Toss, hide, repeat. I was continually stepping on and tripping over Fred's toys all over the trawler.

What do you call a dog who won't retrieve? An unretriever? A misfetcher?

He was scampering back from my stateroom, ready for another round, when the phone rang. "Twenty-four hours a day, seven days a week, this is Alexander Strange," I announced when I took the call.

"You called me first. Whaddya want?" it was Linda Henderson.

I'd left her a message after my conversation with Leo but didn't expect to hear back so soon.

"I was out in Everglades earlier," I said. "At the presser for Throckmorton. Met the new suit on the case. I asked him where you were, and he said, and I quote, that the case has been elevated, whatever that means. And I kinda got concerned about it, to tell you the truth."

The line was quiet for a moment. I thought maybe I heard traffic noise in the background.

"Concerned." A statement, not a question.

"Okay," I said. "Maybe this is just misplaced loyalty on my part, but I got some history with the Hendersons, and I don't like seeing you tooled around. And that's what this feels like. Unless you want to tell me otherwise."

The line was quiet. I heard the muffled sound of a horn. Definitely in a car, windows up.

"Not hearing any response," I said, "I gather I'm not off base being annoyed on your behalf."

"Who am I talking to?" she finally asked. "Is this Alexander Strange the reporter, or Alexander Strange, the guy who saved my grandfather's life and my acquaintance?"

"You just can't say it, can you?"

"What?"

"That we're actually friends."

"I'm a cop. I don't have friends. I have the job."

"Is that a line from *Dragnet*?"

"You haven't answered my question."

"This is Alex, your friend. I'm not taking notes. I'm not recording you—and I wouldn't without telling you, by the way. I'm concerned. But, open kimono, this is starting to feel like a dumpster fire. A guy gets attacked by Mister Manners and next thing you know they're carting his body to the morgue? Seems kinda sketchy to me."

"Does, doesn't it."

I took that as an opening. "Look, I called for more than to express my sympathies. I got something that may help you."

The line was quiet for a beat or two, then she finally responded: "I'm gonna owe you, aren't I?"

"No strings attached, Linda," I said, even though, yes, absolutely, I did want her to see red in her ledger. "I know something that happened in that house, with or to Throckmorton, that may help the investigation."

"Hold on. Should you be sharing this over the phone?"

"Why not?"

"I don't trust phones. I think maybe we should talk in person."

"Well, I suppose it can wait until tomorrow…"

"No. Tonight."

"Tonight?"

"This, whatever it is you're going to tell me, it's important, right? You're not fucking with me?"

"You're gonna to think it's pretty important."

"And it involves Throckmorton's house?"

"Yes. And something that may still be in the house that you definitely will want to know about."

"Still in the house, huh? Okay then. We need to meet tonight. Kill two birds with one stone."

"Meaning?"

"You'll find out."

"Alright. Where you want to meet?"

"Everglades City."

"Are you shitting me? I just got back from there a little while ago. And I was just about to pour myself a cocktail. And it's late. And dark."

"Yes, that's the point. It's dark. I've got something I gotta do. And I need it dark. I'm going to let you tag along, but you need to keep your mouth shut about this. Agreed?"

Agree? Without knowing what the heck she had in mind? How stupid would that be?

"Sure," I said.

"Wear dark clothes. And meet me in the parking lot of the Rod and Gun Club. Say thirty minutes."

"Thirty minutes?"

"Drive fast."

CHAPTER 17

Everglades City

LIKE ME, LINDA Henderson was wearing all black.

I pulled up beside her car—a cobalt blue Honda Civic, not her Police Interceptor—and slipped into the front seat beside her.

"I gather whatever we're up to, it's off the books."

She nodded and pulled out of the Rod and Gun Club parking lot.

There was a scent in the air I couldn't quite make out. Not cologne. Sort of like bananas soaked in alcohol. Or something. "What's that smell?" I asked.

She glanced at me and sniffed through her mask. "What you're talking about."

"It's not perfume," I said.

"I don't wear perfume."

Of course not.

I sniffed obnoxiously loud just to get a rise out of her.

No reaction.

"Seriously, you can't smell that?" I asked.

She turned, cocked her head, then said, "Oh. Gun oil. I just cleaned my Glock."

Naturally.

"And you can stop flirting. Your lawyer girlfriend wouldn't like it."

She was right about some of that. Gwenn hated Linda Henderson. Before Linda was promoted to detective, she filed a couple of complaints with the Bar Association against Gwenn, accusing her of fabricating abuse allegations against her handling of two of Gwenn's clients. This was back when Gwenn was an assistant public defender.

The complaints went nowhere because Gwenn was able to substantiate that her clients—both petty criminals who Linda had arrested—verified the claims that Linda had roughed them up. And the Sherriff's Office, after a brief inquiry, concluded that Linda's arrests did not violate policy.

But bad blood lingered between them.

The last place any sentient male should place himself is between two warring women, but I couldn't help myself. I liked Linda. I mean, nothing was charming about her whatsoever, she was all business and had a dour disposition. But she was a pro. And I admired people who were good at their jobs.

But flirting? That part, no. No way.

"Linda, I promise you I was not flirting with you. The only time I ever even touched you, you threatened to cut my balls off. And I was saving you from stepping on a python. Trust me, I'd just as soon flirt with a panther."

"It would be safer."

She parked the Civic about a block from Throckmorton's house and killed the headlights.

"You going to tell me what we're up to?" I asked. "This about that dickhead who stole your investigation?"

Linda's hand had been on the door handle, but she withdrew it, settled back into the driver's seat, and turned toward me.

"Don't misread the situation," she said. "Mayweather's not a bad guy. He didn't take the case away from me."

"At the press conference, he said the case had been, his words, elevated."

She nodded. "That's right. And here's partial payback for whatever it is you plan to tell me, but you did not hear this from me."

"Okay."

"The case has been elevated, alright—right out of our hands. We're no longer the lead. The Feds are. But the sheriff doesn't want to advertise that."

That was a surprise. So, I asked the obvious questions:

"Why's the sheriff shy about it, and what are the feds up to?"

She shot me with her finger. "Great questions. The sheriff's annoyed, for one. And I think the Feds have told him to keep it on the down-low for reasons I don't know. As for why the Feds are so interested, your guess is as good as mine, but it's curious, isn't it?"

"You're saying the Feds are keeping you in the dark?"

"Like a mushroom."

"So why are we here?"

"I'm allergic to fungus."

CHAPTER 18

Everglades City

SEÑORITA BUFO WAS warmer now. She'd been so cold that she barely had been able to move. Now she was hungry and thirsty. And lost.

She was also alone, which made her edgy. Although, being a toad, she wouldn't know how to express that emotion in a sound a mere human could comprehend.

She might have been pleased to know that some humans, like Hector Morales, had made an effort to understand her. He'd read up. He knew frogs were surprisingly intelligent creatures capable of running mazes just like rats, that they expressed their wide range of feelings in song, and that toads became stressed when lonely.

And Señorita Bufo was very lonely at the moment. And frightened, which was an unusual sensation because she didn't have many natural enemies being toxic and all. Not a lot of friends, either, for that matter, and for the same reason.

Señorita Bufo was startled by an unusual sound, unnatural, nothing like near the river. It was grating, scratchy. And she vaguely recalled hearing it before, when she had been carried inside and put in the cold box. She wouldn't know it was a sliding glass door opening and closing, but she associated it with danger.

And despite her desire to get back to the river, she decided to remain hidden. She stopped singing and became motionless, buried beneath a pile of soft material, not like leaves but smooth, with a funky smell.

If she had been human and were it not so dark, she would have recognized the tiny orange flakes on the pile of rumpled clothes in the closet as Cheetos.

CHAPTER 19

Everglades City

LINDA HENDERSON SWEPT a small penlight around the darkened kitchen until it fell on the refrigerator, then she lowered the beam toward the white tile floor.

She crouched to her knees, then sprawled prone and rested the penlight on the tile, which caused its beam to flare into a wide arc.

I stood over her for a moment, wondering what this mysterious ritual was about, then dropped beside her.

"You see what I see?" she whispered.

I examined the floor in front of me carefully, wanting to pass the test. If I was going to play Watson to her Holmes, I didn't want to make a fool of myself.

"No question about it," I said, "this is an immaculate floor."

She rolled to her side and glanced at me. Her black mask matched her black long sleeve tee-shirt, which, even in the dim light, I noticed clung to her nicely. Her eyebrows rose in—was that approval?

"Very good," she said softly.

Then she scuttled backward like a crab away from the fridge. I followed her, feeling like I was five years old playing army. "Look now," she said.

"Hmmm," I said thoughtfully. "Floor's not as clean here."

She nodded. "Very good. What does that tell us?"

I thought about that for a moment. "That Throckmorton's house-keeper sucks?"

She groaned, and I knew I'd flunked the test. Some Watson I was. She leaned to her side again and rolled her hand over several times, the universal signal to keep trying.

"So, somebody mopped down the area in front of the fridge, right?"

That earned a nod.

"Which is where Throckmorton's body was found. Would the lab techs have done that?"

She shook her head.

"Did somebody mop up the blood?"

"Don't know."

She was hedging. "But there *was* some blood, right?"

She pointed to her nose. "Mayweather said it looked like he fell and hit his nose. There was a trickle on his face."

I considered that, then said: "You knew exactly where to look, didn't you? You came straight to this spot in the kitchen. The crew that was here earlier, somebody spotted this and tipped you off. Was it Mayweather?"

She cocked an eyebrow, which I took for a yes.

"And we're here because he doesn't like being sidelined any more than you."

Another cocked eyebrow. "He wanted me to take a look at this. See if I had the same reaction he did. Wants me to think about who could have done this and why. And, for that matter, if it's important."

"Mayweather wanted you to take a look, so he left the sliding door unlocked. Why didn't he just give you a key?"

She beetled her eyebrows. I was starting to get good at eyebrow reading. "Ah. The Feds have the key."

"And they told us to leave the scene intact, no digging around, to wait for their people."

What Linda didn't know is that I already knew the answer to who could have, and most likely did, clean up the kitchen floor. Hector Morales hadn't said anything about mopping up by the refrigerator but that's who it had to be. And why would he do that? He told Lester, Kitty, and me that he was afraid that if the police discovered he put the toad in the freezer he'd end up in jail. I could imagine him arriving here, Throckmorton collapsed on the kitchen floor, the freezer door open and melting ice leaking all over the place. He must have cleaned it up, figuring it would help cover his ass.

I rose to my feet, and Linda joined me.

"Check out the trash can," I said.

"This about what you plan to tell me?"

I nodded.

She swung the small flashlight around until she found the cabinet under the sink. She opened it, and there, where you often find them, was a small kitchen wastebasket. I didn't have to tell her what we were looking for.

She aimed the light into the little trashcan revealing a wad of damp paper towels. The towels on top were not discolored, so whatever they had mopped up had been clear. Like melted ice.

Linda pulled the wastebasket out and gently removed some of the paper towels and set them on the floor. And when she did, we heard the unmistakable tinkle of broken glass.

Linda was wearing latex gloves, and she began pulling the shattered pieces out of the pile and pushing them together until it was apparent we were seeing the remains of a highball glass. There was a milky film on the inside curve of the pieces.

"Your forensic people would have found this right away," I said.

"If they had been allowed. Feds are bringing up a special team from Miami in the morning. It's a stupid waste of time."

"So, we're going to need to put this all back."

She nodded.

I signaled Linda to hand me the penlight, and I shone it more closely on the broken highball glass, specifically the milky film on the inside curve of one of the pieces. "I have a hunch what this might be," I said.

"You talking about that film?"

"Can you get a little swab of it and secure it. Safely. And don't touch it whatever you do."

She looked at me curiously.

"What are you thinking?"

"Poison."

Linda reached into a fanny pack she was wearing—some kind of detective field kit—and extracted a Q-tip. She wiped the inside of the glass, then slipped the swab into a plastic bottle and sealed it.

"Have your guys test it for bufotoxin," I said.

"Bufo what?"

"Toxin. As in the poison from a cane toad."

She put her hands on her hips and gave me the dead-eye cop stare. "Okay, you need to spill it. What do you know?"

I didn't want to waste time inside the house telling her the whole story. The longer we lingered, the greater the odds we might be discovered. "I'll fill you in when we get back to your car."

Linda reached back into the trashcan and pulled out another wad of damp paper towels. This time no broken glass, but we noticed a diluted pink stain on one of the towels.

"Oh, boy," I said. "Whoever wiped this up really fucked up the scene, didn't they?"

She nodded and began returning the paper towels and bits of broken glass into the can. "Yeah. And we don't want to make it worse. Mayweather will definitely want to know about this."

When she had returned the trashcan under the sink, I held my index finger up to my mask and stood very still. The house was silent. The AC had been turned off, so the usual woosh of blowing air was absent from the background. No sound penetrated the interior of the house from the outdoors.

"What are we listening for?" she finally whispered.

"Toad song."

CHAPTER 20

Everglades City

SEÑORITA BUFO WAS very still. The house around her was quiet, too. Earlier, there had been shuffling sounds. Distant. Away from where she was hiding. But not now. She wriggled, feeling slightly less anxious.

Then she heard it—a rustling noise on the carpet. Of course, she didn't recognize it as a rug, but, rather, a rough grassy place with an odd, unpleasant smell. But the sound of the anole's tiny feet moving through the fibers was a familiar sound. It was the sound of dinner.

She peered out from the pile of dirty laundry and saw the tiny lizard. A Cuban brown anole—pronounced *uh-knoll-ee* by Floridians, although she wouldn't know that. It was about four inches long and oblivious to her presence.

The little lizard, like Señorita Bufo, wouldn't last long inside the hot, dry house. They both would dehydrate and die. The anole was not moving fast, struggling to make its way through the carpet's fibers. Lethargic. Maybe already on its last legs.

Señorita Bufo's lightning-fast and very sticky tongue spat out and snared the little lizard and just as rapidly reeled him into her broad mouth. She swallowed it whole.

This cheered up Señorita Bufo. She was so happy she sang a little song.

CHAPTER 21

Everglades City

"What was that?" Linda Henderson whispered.

It was a rapid series of throaty staccato clucks that anyone who's spent time outdoors on a South Florida evening would find familiar.

"That's who we're looking for. You got any more gloves?"

She pulled another pair of latex gloves from her kit, and I slipped them on. Tight fit. By now, our eyes were fully adjusted to the dim illumination of her penlight, and I nodded her in the direction of the sound.

"It's coming from that end of the house."

Linda gently pushed open the first door we came to off a short hallway. It swung wide. A bathroom. We froze and listened. The sound we'd heard moments before hadn't repeated itself.

She shone the penlight around the bathroom, behind the toilet, into the tub. Nothing. We slipped inside. It was a tight fit, and I brushed against her hip. I swear it was inadvertent. Fortunately, she decided not to shoot me.

There was a small door to our left—a linen closet—and I opened it. She lit up every shelf, but all we saw were a few towels and washcloths and rolls and rolls and rolls of toilet paper. Throckmorton had been one of the hoarders.

I glanced at Linda and whispered, "What a douchebag. No wonder somebody iced him."

Something twitched behind her mask. Could that have been a smile?

We re-entered the hallway and stood motionless for a few moments hoping for more toad song, but the house remained still.

The next door on our left was open. Linda aimed the penlight at the ceiling, and it dimly reflected across the room. It was the master suite. The bed was neatly made, and a blue silk bathrobe was casually flung atop the creamy white comforter. We peered around and noticed the mirrored sliding door to one of the twin closets was half open. Unlike the room's general orderliness, there was a mountainous pile of clothes bunched on the closet floor.

Linda directed her light to the heap, and a pair of button-sized reflections bounced back.

The toad was pretty well hidden inside the pile of clothes, but after a moment we could make out a snout and broad mouth attached to those glowing eyes.

"Detective Henderson," I said. "I believe we've found an eyewitness to the crime."

CHAPTER 22

Goodland, Aboard the Miss Demeanor

"So, how'd you get that froggy out of there?"

Lester and I were eating donuts and drinking coffee on the *Miss Demeanor's* poop deck. I was filling him in on the previous night's adventure.

"Very carefully. That toxic gunk covered her. Fortunately, Linda had some of those latex crime scene gloves."

"A she-froggy?"

"That's just a guess. Females are bigger, and this little lady's huge, Lester. With her legs extended she's as big as Fred. Never seen anything like it. And her skin, it's not all that toad-like either. It has the warts you expect on a toad, but she isn't completely covered in them. And she's greenish like a tree frog, not brown. But she's way too fat to be climbing trees."

"A mutant froggy," he said.

I took a bite of my donut—chocolate-covered cake. Eating chocolate for breakfast seemed very civilized to me. I'd read somewhere that Europeans do it all the time. I'd have to ask Gwenn about that.

"We found a large plastic trash bag, and I wrestled her into it," I said after chasing the bite of donut with a swig of coffee. "And that wasn't easy, let me tell you. She was one unhappy toad, all squirmy and slimy."

"Where she at now?" Lester asked.

I nodded toward the cabin. "Mona's watching over her."

Lester choked on his coffee, spilling some down the front of his Hawaiian shirt. "Here? You brought the froggy here?"

Lester bounded out of his chair and bolted into the cabin. There, on the lounge's coffee table, sat a medium-sized wire dog crate that I sometimes use for Fred. I'd put a bowl of water in the crate, which appeared untouched. The toad sat motionless as if in shock.

"Uh, froggy looks unhappy," Lester said.

"Linda's going to find a place to take her today," I said. "A vet or wildlife rescue place. Maybe a biologist or something. We need to hang onto her so we can compare the toxin on her skin with the milky stuff we found on the broken glass at Throckmorton's place."

Lester leaned over to take a closer look, and I waved him back.

"Careful, buddy, she'd kinda cute, but she's deadly."

"Huh." He inspected the toad for a few more seconds then asked, "What do you feed her?"

I hadn't thought of that.

"Tourists?"

"Better look it up," Lester said, "or you could have a dead froggy on your hands."

Turns out the answer was grubs, spiders, insects, worms, snails, and small reptiles. That was for ordinary-sized toads. Ours probably ate small mammals, too. I'd locked Fred down in my stateroom for safety's sake. Now I was doubly glad I did.

The *Pirates of the Caribbean* theme song filled the cabin. It was my new cell phone ring tone. Linda Henderson was on the line.

"Where you docking that scow of yours these days?" she asked.

"This excellent example of American watercraft is currently gracing the marina next to Stan's Idle Hour."

"She back up on bricks and oilcans in that vacant lot like the last time I was there?"

"Nope. She's afloat. In fact, she's been down to Key West and back since then."

"Okay. I'll be by shortly. Found somebody to take the toad off your hands. A vet I know. And she's got contacts at the University of Florida in their biology department. They got people there who specialize in this sort of thing if you can believe that."

"And they can analyze the toxin for us?"

"That's the plan, Sam."

She was unusually chipper, which was not at all like the Linda Henderson I knew. Maybe she already arrested somebody this morning and it cheered her up.

"I got donuts and coffee when you get here," I offered.

"Lights and sirens then."

CHAPTER 23

Port Royal

KITTY KARLUCCI COULDN'T believe her eyes when she walked into her study. She'd just returned from the grocery store securing ingredients for the next episode of her TV show, *Vicious Vittles*, and there, sitting in her custom-made ergonomic chair behind her expansive mahogany desk, was a huge man with a gleaming bald head, wearing a black mask and holding a smoldering cigar in his gloved hand.

She screamed at him.

"Who the fuck are you and why are you in my chair and why are you smoking in my house?"

He slowly set the cigar down and pulled out a gun.

"Look what I found," he said calmly. He had a slight New York accent. Brooklyn? The Bronx? He wagged the pistol for a moment then tossed it at her.

Karlucci surprised herself by catching it one-handed. She examined the compact semi-automatic, a Glock 19, the one she kept in her top drawer. It had been years since she'd even touched it. She glanced back at the interloper, his filthy stogie no doubt smudging the desk's surface, and thought, what the hell?

She pointed the pistol at him and pulled the trigger.

Click.

"You didn't think it would be loaded, did you?" He raised his massive fist and let a trickle of copper-jacketed nine-millimeter bullets rain down. They splashed onto the polished mahogany in a clatter, like hail on a barn roof.

"Fucker!" Karlucci yelled and hurled the empty pistol at his head.

The man didn't move. It flew past him, missing his head by mere inches, but he never flinched. Cool customer.

"We need to have a little talk," he said, gesturing to a guest chair across the desk.

"You're in my seat!" Karlucci said, no longer screaming but still agitated and, if she were honest with herself, more than a little frightened.

The man nodded. "And in your house. Sit."

She sat.

He wanted something from her, obviously. It was his play. She crossed her legs, composed herself, folded her hands in her lap, and waited for his move.

"Nice," he said. "You recover quickly. Let me get to it. You were an acquaintance of Milton Throckmorton. And the two of you cooked up a plan to lure this Florida character, Mister Manners, into a trap. Milton called his, uh, associates in New York. They called me. I do business with them from time to time."

Karlucci shook her head. "Deal's off. Milton's dead. I've already decided to cancel the bounty I put on Mister Manners."

The man picked the cigar off the desk as if to inhale, then seemed to remember he was masked, and set it back down, flicking ash onto her laptop computer. She cringed inwardly but tried not to show it. This was all an act designed to intimidate her. She couldn't let him see her sweat.

"This isn't about that anymore," he said. "My employers wanted me to ask Throckmorton some questions. They are displeased he no longer can provide the answers they are seeking."

"You don't talk like your ordinary hoodlum," Karlucci said, asserting herself.

His eyes hardened. "What? Not ghetto enough for you?"

"Don't pull the race card on me, buster. My second husband was black. I study how people talk. Your diction is precise, measured. You must be college-educated. Why are you doing this?"

His eyes relaxed. "Thugs come in all shapes, sizes, and colors. We're a varied lot. Plus, the money's good and I get to interact with such interesting people." His eyes tightened again. "If ever so briefly."

He rested the heel of his left boot on the surface of the desk, not quite in Karlucci's face, but she understood the body language was unquestionably designed to emphasize his dominance. She'd used the technique herself from time to time.

Karlucci recrossed her legs, leaned back in the chair, and made an effort to smile, show a little confidence. She unclasped her hands. Relaxed and open body language.

"So, Milty had some problems with the mob?" she said. "That why you're here? There's a surprise. That little ratfucker put his own father in the slam. Why would any criminal organization trust him? Your employers, they need to have their heads examined."

He gave her a slight nod. "The organization has undergone some…hmmm…restructuring. Certain inconsistencies have surfaced. So when Throckmorton called, my employer felt this would be an opportune time to straighten things out. The timing of his death is inconvenient."

Not his death, just the timing.

"Reading between the lines, what you're saying is dear old Milty was ripping off the mob." She already knew he'd been skimming— Hugo had confided that. She waved her hand in dismissal. "Be that as it may, it has nothing to do with me."

"Except," he said.

"Except what?"

"Except you were one of the last people to talk to him. And you were working together on this Mister Manners caper. You knew his father. Very well, from what we've heard. So, you may be in a position to assist us."

Kitty Karlucci took that in, and her immediate reaction was to push back, say something snarky like, "Why the hell should I do that?" But there was an obvious reason why: It might be extremely unpleasant not to. So, instead, she asked, "How?"

"I have to start somewhere to find the answers for my employers, which means it might be useful to find out who killed Milton Throckmorton. So tell me, little lady, did you have anything to do with that?"

"Me? Fuck no. What are you talking about?"

The man studied her for a moment. "Then who?"

"How the fuck should I know? Do I look like a killer?"

The man studied her for a moment more. "You just pulled the trigger on me. So, yes, I'd say so."

Karlucci rolled her eyes. She couldn't help herself. "Yeah, well, no shit. I come home and you—look at you—sitting in my chair, throw a gun at me, it was instinct is all."

"And three dead husbands?"

"They were old. People die. We all kick the bucket eventually."

He nodded. "Sure."

Then he sat there waiting. Her move.

"Look," she said. "I was surprised as hell that Milton died. We don't even know what killed him yet. There's been no report from the medical examiner that I know of. He was in terrible shape. Could be natural causes."

She was rambling and knew it. And she was annoyed that he had made her lose her composure.

"We were supposed to meet. We were going to call the whole thing off, this plan we cooked up…"

She paused for a moment realizing an opportunity, then continued. "It was his idea, Milt's, not mine, actually…"

The man chuckled. "Not what I heard."

"Well, it was. His father was a friend of mine. You apparently already know that. Milt was so upset about the prank Mister Manners played on him, that horseshit thing, I felt sorry for him. But then we found out it probably wasn't Mister Manners after all."

"What makes you say that?"

"Because Mister Manners pulled one of his stunts in Jacksonville the same day. He couldn't be in two places at once."

The man frowned, then leaned forward.

"That pile of manure didn't get there by itself. Somebody had it in for Throckmorton. I want to know who and why."

Kitty Karlucci started to interrupt, but the man held up his hand. He took a deep breath and continued:

"You're a smart woman. Let me explain. When Throckmorton died, he took his secrets with him. Murdered, heart attack, doesn't matter to me. What matters is I get some answers for my employers. I have to start somewhere. If he *was* murdered, it might be useful to know who did it and why and what they know. Not for revenge. For answers. *Capisci?*"

Oh, for fuck's sake. *Capisci!* Give me a break, Karlucci thought, but nodded, figuring it was better to keep him happy.

"Good," he said. "Now you're going to help me, let's say, do a little networking, give me some names, a place to start."

She nodded. "I can do that."

His smile widened. "Excellent. Like I said, a smart woman. But before we get started on that, I'm going to need one more thing from you. This is going to take longer than planned. I need to cover my expenses. Let's agree I'm entitled to an advance on that bounty. Twenty large. How's that sound?"

"I should do this, why?"

The man pulled an enormous stainless steel revolver from his waistband and set it on the desk in front of him. It landed with a heavy thud, its barrel pointed straight at her. "This one's loaded."

She blinked several times and found herself in the unusual position of being literally without words. But only for a moment.

"I'll write you a check," she said.

He shook his head and snatched the revolver from the desktop and pointed it at her for a menacing moment. Then swung it over his head in a violent backhand motion smashing it against the Paul Arsenault watercolor of the Naples Pier above her credenza.

Karlucci gasped as the gun's long barrel bounced off the frame, and the frame rebounded, swinging open on hidden hinges revealing the door to a concealed safe embedded in the wall behind it.

He dragged his boot from the desk and stood, glancing briefly at the safe. "I'll thank you for the combination," he said. "And then you're going to tell me everything you can think of that will help me track down this Mister Manners character, starting with why he showed up at Throckmorton's house..."

"But he didn't..."

"But somebody did, right? If not Mister Manners, who? And who would know Milton was staying in his old man's house? Think. I need to connect some dots. Who knew Milton Throckmorton, who were his friends or his father's friends or business associates?"

As anxious and angry as she was, a small part of Kitty Karlucci had to acknowledge that this mob enforcer from up north had a point. There might even be a win-win in all this. Give him the twenty thousand, better than dropping the full fifty she'd been offering, and maybe this tough guy could actually rid the world of Mister Manners and figure out why Milton was killed—assuming the sorry sack of flatulence hadn't just dropped dead of a coronary. It would be good to know. Always better to know than not to know. And maybe she could work all this into her next book.

Art imitating life and all that.

"There's a woman," she said. "She and Hugo—Milton's father—ran a computer security business together. But she's *non compos mentis.*"

The thug gave her a cocked eyebrow.

"*Non compos mentis.* That's Latin for…"

"I know what it means," he said. "I'm just surprised you do."

Fucker.

CHAPTER 24

Goodland

"HOW'S OUR EYEWITNESS?" Linda Henderson asked as she slipped over the gunwale a few minutes after Lester departed.

"She seems stressed," I said.

I led her into the lounge, and she walked over to the crate. "Yeah. She's so still. Well, I'll get her to the vet. We wouldn't want anything to happen to her. You got gloves? I used all mine last night."

I'd carefully disposed of the latex gloves I'd worn during our B & E job at Throckmorton's house, but I had a pair of work gloves down in the engine room, and I fetched them and set them atop the crate.

"You mentioned something about donuts?"

"Yes," I said. "And coffee. How you take it?"

"Black."

She settled in, removed her mask, and took a sip. Then she raised the coffee cup to me appreciatively—I'd given her a Wonder Woman mug. I was sipping my third cup of the morning out of Batman.

The *Miss Demeanor's* lounge is surprisingly spacious, and we managed to keep six feet apart. I'd left the hatchway open, and a muggy breeze was blowing through the cabin. Safe enough. I hoped.

"Couple of things," she said. "First off, thank you." She nodded to the cage. "This is huge. I filled in Mayweather this morning. He flipped out."

"He pissed you brought me along?"

"I might not have mentioned that."

"Ah."

She took a big gulp of coffee, then said, "I'm gonna share this with you but you didn't hear it from me, okay?"

"Agreed."

This was the second time Linda had offered information on the condition that I protect her as the source. Interestingly, she didn't say I couldn't use it, just not to name her. I fleetingly wondered if she knew the difference. She was still new in this job and might be unused to dealing with the press, but she kept talking and I let her.

"Mayweather met the FBI's forensic team out at the house this morning. He said they were very thorough. In fact, they're still there. They found the wet paper towels and broken glass in the kitchen trashcan right away and bagged it."

"They notice anything out of the ordinary in the bedroom, like a missing gigantic toad?"

Linda bit her lip and thought for a moment before responding. "No. We're keeping that to ourselves for the moment."

I gave her a curious look.

"It's like this: Mayweather asked me to look around, get my own impression of the scene, so we could compare notes. Just because the Feds are claiming they have jurisdiction, this is still our county and our case. At least that's how we see it."

"Okay, but about the frog..."

"So Mayweather couldn't very well tell them that we broke in and removed evidence, could he? We didn't anticipate this. If you and I had seen something besides a toad—say a syringe, or a threatening note, or whatever—we wouldn't have removed it."

"You thinking we should have left the toad there?"

"Too late to look back."

"I understand."

But not really. Linda Henderson was operating well outside of how I had her pegged. Where had the play-it-by-the-book cop I knew disappeared to? We were breaking into houses, and she was withholding evidence from the FBI. Who was this woman?

It turns out she was a mind reader.

"I see the expression on your face."

I shrugged. "This all seems out of character, is all. Not that I'm objecting."

"Nothing about this case is ordinary."

I nodded in agreement, just to keep the conversation rolling. "Did Mayweather get anything out of the Feds? Like why they're taking an interest in this?"

She stared at the ceiling of the cabin for a few moments, thinking about how—or whether—to answer. Then she said, "Not from the Feds, but the sheriff. Mayweather talked to him last night. Over drinks. The sheriff likes to drink, and when he does he talks, sometimes more than he should. In a nutshell—and you really, under all circumstances, must keep this to yourself, you can't use it, alright?"

So, she did understand the difference. Good. I offered her my standard reply: "I won't use anything you're about to tell me unless I get it from another source."

That seemed to satisfy her. "It seems Milton Throckmorton was leading a double life," she said.

"He was closeted?"

"Likely. But that's not what I'm talking about. Apparently, he worked for one of the New York families. He was their accountant."

"Holy shit. So when you say double life are you suggesting…"

"Let's just say the Feds are unhappy that he died and want to know what happened to him. They are tearing his house apart looking for any documents or files he might have there. Mayweather thinks they'll be getting warrants for other searches, too."

I thought about that for a few seconds while she took another bite of her donut. She'd passed on the chocolate-covered and selected a plain glazed. Guess she didn't care what they ate in Europe.

"I'm surprised the Feds told the sheriff about this," I finally said.

She nodded. "Sheriff's got a friend, a buddy in the bureau. Very high up. They met at Quantico. It's actually illegal to discuss this stuff. I'm surprised, too."

She polished off the glazed.

"But I figured you should know," she said.

"I'm glad to know, but why…"

"Because we're talking about the mob, Strange. We poke around this thing, who knows who we might irritate."

We.

"They thinking maybe this was a hit?" I asked.

"No way of knowing, but the possibility's obvious."

"Just to be clear, so I don't go running around wrong-headed, the gist of this is that Throckmorton was feeding the Feds information about the mob? That kind of double life?"

"Be my guess, but it would just be a guess. I didn't get anything like that from Mayweather, so I don't think the sheriff got anything like that from his buddy in the bureau. All we know for sure is that he was mob-connected, and the FBI is curious."

"Which means the FBI either had something going with him or had a close eye on him, right?"

She shrugged. "Feds seem unusually interested, so maybe that. Maybe something else. Although I agree, it seems reasonable."

She took another sip of her coffee and set the mug down. "There's one more thing, the thing I really wanted to share with you."

"I'm all ears."

"Like I said, you can't print this. If you did, it could blow our whole investigation into Mister Manners."

She had my full attention.

"Last night, when you told me about Hector Morales, the conversation you had with him, how he put the toad in the freezer, all that? I wanna let you know, I appreciate and respect that you took me into your confidence. Obviously, what he did could turn this investigation around. This bad girl might have killed him."

She gazed at the bufo for a moment and shook her head. "Why do I just kinda like this frog?' she mused.

I nodded. "Yeah, in an ugly, fat, green way she's sorta cute. If deadly."

"Anyway, Mayweather talked to Morales at the scene. But he got nothing from him about a poison toad in the freezer. I'm impressed you got that out of him."

"What can I say?"

What I could have said was that between Lester's badge and Kitty Karlucci's ass-chewing, Hector Morales was a shattered wreck, and I just happened to be there when he spilled his guts. But why spoil a good story with tedious facts, right?

"We missed that, then we got shoved off the case. I like having this information, and I like that the Feds don't."

"You're welcome."

"Grandpa said I could trust you. I see what he meant now. So, there's something else I want to share with you. You've been writing about Mister Manners. And, officially, I got nothing to say about that. But I've noticed you've been reaching out to him in your columns, asking him to contact you."

She let it end there, waiting for an acknowledgment. I decided to hedge my bets and not mention that I'd already called him, left a message, talked to his daughter, all that.

"I have and I want to. It would be a great interview."

She nodded.

"Well, buyer beware."

"What's that mean?"

"It means, there are imposters out there."

"Copycats," I said. "I understand the numbers are growing."

She nodded, sipped her coffee, then said: "Have you ever wondered why everyone calls him Mister Manners?"

I shrugged. "I figured somebody tossed it out there on social media and it stuck."

"Right. But it didn't show up out of nowhere. A reporter at a newspaper in the Panhandle, the *Northwest Florida Daily News*, you heard of it?

"Sure."

"This reporter, she's got some pretty good sources in law enforcement up there, and somebody leaked something that we've been working very hard to keep under wraps."

I was back to nodding, encouraging her to continue.

"You know the notes Mister Manners leaves behind? How he always says the same thing at the end. 'Your discourtesy has been avenged.' That?"

"Of course."

She shook her head.

"That's not what the notes really say. They actually say, 'Your *bad manners* have been avenged.' That's where the *manners* in Mister Manners originated. It's what the Panhandle cops were privately calling him, and this reporter picked up on it."

"Okay. And you guys are hiding the real language, why?"

"It's one way we know the real Mister Manners from the copycats."

"Ah, ha!"

She cocked her head, waiting for me to finish the thought.

"And you think this is how I'll be able to tell the real deal from a fraud if I arrange an interview."

She shot me with her finger.

I gave her my best Elvis: "Thank you. Thank you very much."

She smiled—a pretty smile. "You're welcome."

I considered all this for a few more moments then asked, "Kitty Karlucci and her car, was that the real Mister Manners?"

She nodded.

"What about at Throckmorton's? Was there a note?"

"Yeah, there was. We just didn't acknowledge it."

"Because it wasn't the real Mister Manners," I ventured.

"Right. We've been playing down the copycat attacks. We don't want to encourage this. At Throckmorton's, it wasn't even that. The writing was garbled. Clearly not written by anyone who speaks English as their primary language. My guess would be Spanish."

"A native Spanish speaker with access to enormous amounts of horseshit?"

She nodded. "Which is why, after I drop off the toad, I'm heading out to the Chitango stables."

"See if they're missing any manure?"

She shrugged. "It had to come from somewhere, and that's the biggest stable of horses around here."

"Makes sense."

"Then I'm circling back to Everglades City to have a conversation with Hector Morales."

"Feds might not like that."

"Feds can bite me."

Linda finished her coffee, and I donned the gloves resting atop the crate and carried it out to her Interceptor.

Hector Morales was about to have a very bad day. Or so I imagined. Little did we know, at that very moment he was on a bus motoring southeast on the Tamiami Trail, destination Little Havana where he planned to disappear.

I'd left Fred napping aboard the trawler, and as I watched Linda pull away I replayed in my mind the exact words she used when she'd told me about the FBI's interest in the Throckmorton case. I'd promised not to name her as a source regarding the FBI's involvement, but nothing was restricting me from using that information if I could confirm it independently.

There were several ways I could go about that, but the quickest and most direct solution would be to simply get in my car and drive over to Everglades City to see for myself. Occam's razor. Sometimes the best answer is the simplest one.

From the corner of my eye I spied motion in the parking lot across from Stan's Idle Hour. A beat-up old camper van was pulling out onto Goodland Drive. I remember thinking: Looks like the snowbirds are returning.

I would later learn that was no snowbird.

CHAPTER 25

Goodland

ALEXANDER STRANGE WAS a tall son of a bitch, the man known as
Mister Manners thought as he peered through the Schmidt and Bender
PM2 scope that he'd detached from his Remington 700 sniper rifle.
He was built, too. The kid worked out.

His daughter had told him all that, but it was good to confirm with
his own eyes. He had a fondness for big men. They were easier targets.

Mister Manners was sitting in a hard-driven Coachmen Orion
camper van—his home on wheels—parked across the street from
Stan's Idle Hour in the otherwise empty unpaved lot that, during tourist season, was packed on the weekends with visitors, bikers, and other
revelers. In the heat and humidity of hurricane season, not so much.

He'd gotten Strange's voice message but wanted to check him out
first. He was not encouraged to see a sheriff's cruiser parked nearby,
nor the familiar way Strange seemed to interact with the plainclothes
cop who had just driven off.

Was it all that unusual for reporters and cops to know one another?
Maybe not. But what was in that crate they loaded into the rear of
her Interceptor?

He hadn't survived all those tours in the sandbox by failing to
listen when his instincts were sending warning signals.

He set the scope on the passenger seat and cranked the camper's engine.

Let's find out what's in that crate, he decided. Alexander Strange, he could come back and check out anytime he wanted. That old trawler wasn't going anywhere. Certainly not at any speed.

He pulled onto Goodland Drive, keeping his distance from the cruiser. This was the only road out of the village, and it dead-ended at San Marco Road. From there, a right turn would lead over the Stan Gober bridge to the mainland, a left to the City of Marco Island.

He'd keep far enough back to avoid attracting attention but close enough to see which way she turned. Then, once in traffic, he'd tighten it up, but only just enough not to lose her if she exited the highway.

A camper van was not the most inconspicuous of vehicles, certainly not ideal for tailing anyone. But it was Florida, and they weren't exactly a rarity down here. Still, he'd have to be careful.

And he knew how to do that. People might think he was crazy, but he wasn't careless.

He knew how to be sneaky. He was a sniper, after all.

THE STRANGE FILES

Local Grocer and Mask Protester Plans Massive Flotilla for Trump

By Alexander Strange

Tropic Press

NAPLES—Declaring "we're going to take our country back," a local political gadfly is organizing what may be Florida's largest flotilla in support of President Trump's re-election combined with a massive anti-masking protest.

"Two thousand boats. We're going to fill Naples Bay, blockade Marco Island. You'll be able to walk across the water, just like Jesus, boat to boat from one side of the bay to the other without getting your feet wet," August "Aggie" LaFrance announced at a press conference staged outside one of his convenience stores in Golden Gate Estates.

Asked if he had a permit to clog the waterway as he envisions, he replied, "We don't need no stinking permits. No masks, neither."

When I asked LaFrance specifically from whom he is trying to reclaim the country, he said:

"White people made this country great, but the immigrants, and drug dealers, and rapists, and socialists are taking over. We're taking our great nation back, restoring America, just like it was when it was founded."

Does that mean you propose to reintroduce slavery, take away women's right to vote, turn back the clock on gay marriage, the forty-hour workweek, child labor laws, Social Security, all that?

"F**k off," he replied.

He went on further to declare that rules requiring the wearing of masks during the pandemic were not only unlawful but "part of the deep state conspiracy to rob us of our freedom and turn us into socialist zombies."

It would be easy to dismiss all this as the fever dream of a deranged local crackpot, except Donald Trump is encouraging these "Trumptillas."

"We are doing great," he said of the support he is getting from Florida mariners. "You see the boaters out. There are thousands and thousands of boats every weekend, and we appreciate it, but nobody has seen anything like it ever. And we have that in many other states with boaters and bikers and everybody."

LaFrance declared: "We're going to set a world record, get in the Guinness book with our flotilla. This is more than a single event. It's the start of a navy, and we're ready to go to war. Naples Bay today, the Potomac tomorrow."

But while the watery publicity stunts may buoy Trump's hopes for re-election, law enforcement officials are concerned about radical right-wing groups, such as the Proud Boys, infiltrating these events.

One official, who spoke on the condition of anonymity, told me: "Don't underestimate the level of emotion and plain old-fashioned hatred of these groups. They're not rational. They live in an alternative reality, feeding on nonsense. Some of them really believe Washington is overrun with cannibals who eat children. They believe the craziness they see on social media. These are dangerous people."

STRANGE FACT: In 2016, a 28-year-old armed man stormed into a Washington, D.C. pizza joint believing he could "rescue" children imprisoned in the basement where they were to be eaten after they were sexually molested. He believed online conspiracy theories suggesting Bill and Hillary Clinton were using the restaurant as their headquarters for a pedophile ring. But there was no basement. There were no captive children. There was no Pizzagate coverup. But to this day, the rumors persist, such is the viability of hate-filled nonsense on social media and the consequences it can bring.

CHAPTER 26

Goodland

I FINISHED POSTING the Trumptilla column after I returned from
Everglades City. I had written this piece to replace one of my
"evergreen" columns, articles I stash for use when news is slow, or
I'm feeling lazy, or poisonous toads start killing off local mobsters
distracting me from my usual nine-to-five.

I was devoting more time now following political news, thanks
to Edwina. If anything, politics was so weird it made Florida Man
capers seem semi-sane in comparison. Thankfully, I'd been able to
talk Edwina out of her original idea: Whenever either of the presidential candidates was campaigning in Florida, I would be there,
she'd ordered.

"Ed, that won't work," I told her. "For multiple reasons. First off,
Florida's big. It's nine hours' drive-time from here to Pensacola, for
example. And there are no non-stops if you want to fly. You gotta go to
Atlanta or Charlotte first. Even if it's someplace closer, it's still hours of
highway time. Plus, Florida's a political war zone. There will be a can-
didate or a surrogate here every day. Plus, I don't have credentials from
the campaigns, so I'm not going to be in the reporting pool. That's
already established. I can get the feeds from the pool reporters, but it's
pointless for one reporter to run around all over the state like that."

Surprisingly, she bought my argument. Which, in hindsight, I realized was just a negotiating ploy on her part, maneuvering me into accepting a less onerous solution, which is how we settled on me writing an additional weekly column summing up campaign weirdness, of which there was sure to be plenty.

How I was going to juggle that with my Mister Manners story and digging into Milton Throckmorton's death, as well as my regular columnizing, I didn't know. Let alone start writing a novel for Kitty Karlucci. There was a serious threat that my heretofore considerable leisure time could be in jeopardy.

Linda Henderson had called to report she'd dropped off froggy at a vet on Marco Island. She was heading out to eastern Collier County to check on any missing horse manure and promised more info when it became available.

Fred had been napping, but he came bounding up the stairs from my stateroom and started jumping up and down, his dance signaling it was time to take him for a walk or I could kiss all that house training goodbye.

I scooped him up, walked out to the *Miss Demeanor's* stern, and legged over the gunwale onto the dock. I clipped on his leash, and we set out for a stroll about Goodland.

I like Goodland. It's rustic and real. Snooty is not a word you would ever use to describe this place, unlike neighboring Marco Island or Naples. In Naples you play golf at the country club, here you go fishing. Duck Leg Confit and Coq Au Vin grace Naples menus; grab yourself a burger and some grouper balls here. You could go hunting with Horace Sniffen's alley sweeper all over Goodland and never find a Bentley to perforate; you trip over them on the mainland. Etcetera, etcetera.

Fred and I meandered around the little marina, past the Crabby Lady Restaurant, the Little Bar, and over toward the tiny post office. He found a bush that required irrigation then hunkered down for some more serious action. Fortunately, I had a plastic doggie bag in my pocket, so I needn't worry about Mister Manners taking revenge on me. I responsibly deposited Fred's droppings in a trash can outside the post office.

We wandered some more and found ourselves by the entrance to the Drop Anchor mobile home park on Papaya Street. Back when the *Miss Demeanor* was drydocked in Goodland, a woman who lived there, Mrs. Overstreet, was Fred's regular dog sitter. I figured it would be neighborly to stop by and say hello.

We strolled to her single-wide, and I knocked on her door. It took a few moments for her to emerge, and I used the time to check out her neighborhood. It was a tidy and well-kept group of trailer homes, clean with freshly manicured landscapes. Several had Trump bumper stickers in their windows. Didn't see any for Biden. No surprise there. Collier County is overwhelmingly Republican. Eventually, Mrs. Overstreet stepped out.

"Oh, my goodness, look who it is!" she screeched as she swung her front door open. She bolted down the concrete steps and snatched Fred's leash from my hand.

"Freddie. I missed you so much," she cooed as she picked him up and nuzzled him. Fred, ever polite, gave her a lick just so Mrs. Overstreet would know she was appreciated. Fred's a natural-born diplomat.

"Did you bring Freddie for a visit?" she asked, her face filled with anticipation.

"Well, actually, we were out for a walk and..."

"Good, good, good. You go for your walk. Freddie's going to stay with me for a while. You go get your exercise."

With that, she turned and ushered Fred into her place, never looking back.

"Uh, bye, Fred."

But by then, he was gone.

I was wearing my running shoes, and it occurred to me that Mrs. Overstreet had a good suggestion. It had been a couple of days since my last run, my exercise routine having defaulted to twelve-ounce curls. Time for some sweat. I could knock out about five miles, add on some pushups, then take a nice cool shower, maybe a nap. Rest is every bit as vital as exercise, after all.

A run would give me a chance to think about the zaniness unfolding around me: A gigantic poisonous toad. A dead mob accountant. A famous novelist—who wanted to hire me—posting bounties on an insane vigilante. And a cop who had always kept her distance suddenly taking me into her confidence.

I needed to push aside the distractions and focus on my two most important missions—scoring the interview with Mister Manners and dodging Edwina lest she conjure more ways to interfere with my lifestyle.

After all, it wasn't my job to figure out how Milton Throckmorton croaked. The medical examiner and the Feds had that assignment. It could turn into a story. But it required nothing from me at the moment. Linda Henderson might want to go off the reservation and unpeel whatever motives the Feds had to investigate Throckmorton's death. And I could tag along for grins and giggles if I felt like it. But the primary mission had to be Mister Manners. Right?

Why did I think that was too easy? Probably because it was. Then my cell phone rang. It was Lester.

"Got us an opportunity for personal growth," he said.

"Most excellent."

"Kitty Karlucci just called. She's a pretty tough cookie, but she sounded a little shaken up."

"About what?"

"She had an uninvited guest earlier today, a guy she described as a hitman for the mob."

"The mob, as in guys with vowels at the end of their names and a fondness for cannolis?"

"Yeah, that mob. Turns out, our buddy Throckmorton was a bag man for one of the New York families. That's what she says, anyway. They're concerned about his untimely demise. This leg breaker, they sent him down to help Kitty and Throckmorton with a scheme to trap Mister Manners, something they were cooking up. That's why she was going to meet him at the Reel and Rifle Club."

"Funny how that didn't come up when we talked to her."

"Yeah, she said that with him dying and all, it escaped her attention."

"You think much escapes her attention, Lester?"

"No, but this enforcer may have loosened her tongue. As she tells it, the Family back in New York, it isn't pleased that Milton's gone home to Jesus. They're a suspicious lot. They're wondering if someone knocked him off. And why. At least that's her story."

This was a little awkward. I'd just learned about Throckmorton's underworld connection from Linda Henderson, but I had promised to keep that confidential. I didn't like not sharing that with Lester, but I had no choice. I'd given my word. Then again, it seemed dearly departed Milt's illicit activities were no longer a tightly wrapped secret.

"Uh, this is getting real, isn't it," I temporized.

"Afraid so, Padawan."

"What's Karlucci want from you?"

"She wants to talk about hiring The Third Eye to guard her place. You wanna come along?"

"Well, not that it wouldn't be fun, but what's any of this go to do with me? You mentioned the mob. Like I don't have enough to worry about already?"

"This thug, he was asking questions about Hugo Throckmorton, Milton's old man, the drug smuggler, and he seems very interested when she told him Hugo was in the computer security business and his business partner was Rennie Bhatia's mother."

"She told him that?"

"Yeah. He leveled a gun in her face."

"Persuasive interviewing technique. Wonder what else she knows."

"Right? I hear the words computer security business and mafia, and we have to remember Milton Throckmorton had a habit of turning state's evidence, and now a leg breaker from Up East has taken an interest, and I'm wondering what all was on that SD card in the leg lamp that Rennie was so eager to get back."

"Huh."

Lester hadn't answered my question—what any of that had to do with me—but now my curiosity was aroused, so it didn't much matter.

"I'm heading over to Kitty's place in a bit. I'll text you the address. Catch up with me there, say in about an hour and a half. Got some things I need to clear up here in the office first."

"I can do that. But, Lester, why doesn't she just call the police?'

"Ixnay on the opscay."

"How come?"

"Won't know until I talk to her. And when you meet me, throw that leg lamp in your car."

"Well, it's not mine, so sure, but you're thinking what?"

"If nothing else, it's evidence. You don't need it in your possession, might come back to haunt you."

"Haunt?"

"Hell, I don't know. Just a hunch. Bring it."

And I would have, too. Except, when I got back to my boat, an imposing man with a very large gun had other ideas.

CHAPTER 27

Goodland

"Uh, I don't believe we've met."

He was tall, nearly my height, and clearly spent more time than me at the gym. Probably juiced up on 'roids for breakfast and bench-pressed Volkswagens. His skin was nearly as dark as his black mask and his scalp gleamed. Had to shave it daily. Leather gloves encased his huge hands, which allowed him to effortlessly grip the cannon he was aiming at me.

"I dislike thieves," he said.

"But you've no qualms about breaking into my boat." I made a slight shuffle in the direction of the galley where my speargun rested on the counter.

He cocked the revolver, and I froze. The pistol was stainless steel and enormous. Probably a .44 Magnum. Maybe after shooting me, he'd go elephant hunting with it.

What an idiot. There are no elephants here.

Random, nonsensical thoughts like that were bouncing about in my skull. Not that I was frightened or anything, just suffering from adrenalin poisoning.

"That lamp," he said, waving his pistol in the direction of the leg lamp on my little desk. "It doesn't belong to you."

"Finders keepers," I said. "Found it in an abandoned house down the street."

He shook his head.

"On your knees," he ordered.

Okay, I was scared. I won't lie about it. Any sane person would be. But I was also more than a little peeved. This fuckwad had broken into my boat—my home—and now was waving his .44 Magnum in my face like Clint Eastwood in *Dirty Harry*. What next? Would he start bragging it was "the world's most powerful handgun"?

And did he think brandishing that cannon meant he could push me around? Well, of course he did. And he was right. To a limit. But if he was going to "blow my head clean off" it sure as hell wouldn't be while I was on my knees.

Fuck him.

"Knees," he repeated.

"You're not my type," I said, keeping my voice steady, adopting a tone of cool dismissal as if assassins waved firearms at me all the time.

He grunted, then raised the barrel to my face. I braced for oblivion.

IN THE HISTORY OF humankind, there have been no reliable journalistic reports datelined AFTERLIFE. Nor, for that matter, HEAVEN or HELL. So, nobody really knows what the moment of death is like. We've all read imaginings in books and visualizations on the big screen, but it's just speculation. All of it.

Is it instant lights out? Or while the brain discharges its final sputtering synapses does your life pass before your eyes? And does that hurt?

I've always voted for immediate oblivion, figuring the afterlife was identical to the pre-life—in other words, nothingness. And painless.

But my date with The Big Sleep was postponed. The thug didn't pull the trigger.

Somebody else did.

I DIDN'T HEAR the shot. But the shattering portside window startled me, and I whirled in that direction as broken glass showered the cabin. The next sounds I heard were the heavy thump of the gunslinger's body collapsing and the clatter of his huge revolver smacking the teak deck. Even though it had been cocked, the gun didn't go off.

I lurched from the window and stared at his inert hulk, limbs akimbo. A rivulet of blood was oozing from above his right ear. His bloodshot eyes bulged open, not in surprise but a blank stare into nothingness.

I was hyperventilating and dropped to the deck. I took several deep breaths to steady myself, then leaned over and retrieved the fallen pistol, which had skittered several feet from his outstretched hand.

I don't own a gun, but I'm not unfamiliar with them. I'm an American, after all. I gently lowered the hammer, pushed the release button, then opened the cylinder and checked for bullets. There were six of them. I clapped the cylinder shut and looked for a safety lever or button. I didn't see one.

The big man on the floor was still leaking blood. Is that normal when you're shot in the head? Doesn't your heart stop when the brain dies? I looked more closely. His eyes were now shut. I couldn't tell if he was breathing. And I wasn't about to crawl over to him and check his pulse.

I gripped the pistol tightly in my right hand, and with my left I fished out my cell phone and punched in 911. I relayed a brief description of the situation to the dispatcher then hung up, ignoring her urging me to stay on the line.

While I waited for the cavalry to arrive, I listened intently to the sounds outside the boat. No footsteps on the dock nor the deck of the *Miss Demeanor*. No click of a gun cocking. After a minute, I could hear the faint screaming of sirens in the distance. Maybe the shooter had skedaddled.

Why would someone want to kill this guy, still spilling blood on my teak deck? Then an unsettling thought occurred to me. What made me think the shooter was aiming at him? Maybe the gunman saw a target through the window and assumed it was me.

Terrific.

I never heard the gunshot, so the shooter may have used a suppressor or fired from long range—which would be a neat trick in flat Florida. For a long-distance shot, he would have had to fire from elevation, and we have a desperate shortage of mountains in the Sunshine State. And Goodland has no skyscrapers.

So, a suppressor. Or maybe a suppressor on a gun firing a subsonic load so there wouldn't be the sharp crack as the bullet broke the sound barrier. I knew a little about ballistics, and I recalled that subsonic loads usually are accompanied by big bullets. The .45-caliber semi-automatic pistol, for instance, uses a subsonic load, but the bullet is huge and makes up for its comparatively slower speed with enormous mass. Mack trucks are subsonic, too, but you don't want to get hit by one.

The fucktard bleeding on my deck was still unconscious. Or dead. I didn't know which. The sirens were growing louder. I figured it was safe to check out the cabin. A large caliber bullet, would it have passed through his head? And if so, might it have lodged somewhere in the boat?

I found it immediately. It had blown a clean circular passageway through the thigh of the leg lamp and buried itself into the bulkhead.

The leg lamp. Lester had told me to bring it. And the guy bleeding on my deck was interested in it, too. Did this douchebag think something was still hidden in it? And where would he have gotten that idea?

I looked more intently at the downed gunman. I still couldn't detect any breathing, but if the bullet penetrated his head wouldn't there be a bigger mess, a Sam Peckinpah bloodbath? Maybe it just grazed him, knocked him out cold. But for how long?

Blue flashing lights began playing on the bulkhead through the shattered porthole. The cops would be clambering aboard any minute. I cracked open the revolver's cylinder, ejected the bullets, and then set the pistol on the deck. The last thing I needed was for the police to storm the boat to encounter me holding a loaded heater. It wouldn't be a good look, and it wouldn't be for long.

I started to toss the bullets on the deck, then thought better of it. What if Fred got hold of one? Wouldn't be good for him. Lead and all. Or what if he bit the primer? Would it go off? I mean, we've all heard the expression "biting the bullet." I briefly wondered if that ever happened. And even as that fleeting thought took temporary residence in my mind, I knew I was still jittery with adrenalin and not thinking entirely straight. I shoved the bullets into the pocket of my cargo shorts.

Oddly, the lamp hadn't been blown to pieces by the round passing through it. The leg's plastic was pretty thin, and I suppose it hadn't offered much resistance. It did leave an unsightly run in the net stocking, however.

What was so special about this lamp? It no longer served as a hiding place for the mysterious SD memory card. What other possible value could it have?

I glanced back at the bleeder on the deck. Still out. Then turned back to the lamp, picked it up, and examined it. There were no hidden notes pressed between the sexy net stocking and the plastic leg. The lampshade was amber and translucent. It had a liner, but anything secreted there would be visible. Where else? I flipped it over and checked out the base of the lamp. It was circular, wooden, black, but on the bottom there was an indentation covered with felt where the electrical wire fed through.

Could something be hidden in there?

Sheriff's deputies were exiting their Interceptors across the marina. I set the lamp down and walked out onto the deck, hands raised, and waited patiently as they approached. They took their time, unsure of what they were walking into.

There were two of them, one I happened to know. His name was Garcia. The other deputy I hadn't seen before. They approached hands on their holsters, about ten feet apart from one another—good tactical training there.

"Hey, Garcia," I said.

"Somebody been shooting up your scow again?" he asked.

This was an inside joke between us because the first guy to shoot a hole in one of my windows was Garcia when he was startled by my mannequin, Mona. He blew a hole through her chest and out the front window. But that was ancient history. The county paid for the window's replacement, although Mona still wore a Band-Aid.

"Who's inside?" he asked.

"Never seen him before. He broke into my boat. Somebody shot him through the portside porthole."

Garcia's head swiveled from left to right.

"Port. That's left to you landlubbers."

"What's his status?" Garcia asked as he climbed over the gunwale.

"He's been shot in the head. But there's not as much blood as I would have thought. Maybe it creased his skull. But he's out cold."

The other deputy began mumbling into his shoulder mic, probably calling for backup. I could hear another siren now, most likely an ambulance.

"And you say he was armed?"

"Great big revolver. He was about to shoot me when that shot through the window took him down."

"Jesus."

"Gun's on the deck. I unloaded it."

He nodded.

"Okay. Stay here." Garcia took the lead and entered the cabin, gun drawn, the other deputy behind him, his piece also out.

They stepped inside, and after a moment I followed, ignoring his order to stay put.

"Where is he?" Garcia asked.

There was a small puddle of blood on the floor, but the man had vanished.

His empty pistol was also missing.

So was the leg lamp.

CHAPTER 28

Goodland

WHILE THE TWO DEPUTIES cleared the boat, ensuring the massive hitman wasn't hiding in the head or the engine room or the microwave, I stepped outside onto the dock and placed a quick call to Lester.

"I'll have to give a statement," I said. "They're going to ask me what he wanted. When I tell them the leg lamp, that will open up another line of questions, like where I got it? And did it belong to me? And what's so special about it? And I don't feel like telling them, 'Oh, you mean the memory card that was supposed to be hidden there and is now missing?'"

"Answer all their questions truthfully," Lester said calmly. "But don't volunteer anything they don't ask."

"I figured I should check in with you first given the, uh, unusual way we acquired it. Didn't want to complicate your life."

"I appreciate that. And the truthful answer is neither you nor I know what was on that card. And that's between me and my client, and if they have questions about that they can contact me."

"And if they ask me who your client was?"

"Tell them to contact me."

This was standard Lester: Never lie to the cops, but don't give up anything you don't have to, especially when what's going on is still a mystery. Don't impede the police investigation. Don't complicate your own.

"Lester, there are two big questions here. The first is who's the shooter and who was he shooting at? But we got another issue.

"Which is?"

"Which is, how did this thug know to come here? How would he know I had the leg lamp?"

There was a pause on the line.

"Let me call you back." And he hung up.

TWO HOURS LATER, deputies were still scouring the marina looking for whatever—a cartridge from the bullet that nicked the gunslinger, maybe? Tire tracks? Witnesses? The crime scene techs, an all-female crew, scraped his blood from the deck, sprayed Luminol to trace blood splatter, and made a mess with their black fingerprint powder.

With time to kill while waiting for the cops to finish up, I briefly wondered what I should call this guy. Thugzilla came to mind. He certainly was big enough to be a "zilla." But despite brandishing that six-shooter of his, he didn't act at all thuggish. In fact, he behaved like a pro. A professional bad guy, sure, but not street scum. I could call him Dirty Harry, but who would get it? Just because Uncle Leo made me watch all those old Clint Eastwood flicks didn't mean anyone else would connect the dots with a fifty-year-old movie.

He was a hired gun. Working for somebody. An enforcer, juiced on steroids.

I also spent some time considering how he managed to sneak off the boat while I was right outside waiting for the cops—especially carrying a bulky lamp in the shape of a woman's calf and thigh. He must have slipped out of the cabin at the bow while I was standing on the stern. Then he could have dropped over the gunwale into the water while out of sight from the approaching deputies, shielded from view by the cabin.

Stealthy bastard.

I suggested to the deputies he might have re-emerged somewhere else in the little marina. But there were no traces of wet footsteps elsewhere dockside or other signs of where a man might have come ashore.

Could he still be hiding aboard one of the other boats? Deputies fanned out around the harbor to look, but they didn't find him. A swimmer in good shape, with healthy lungs, could have swum underwater out of the cove, maybe surfacing only once or twice for air. Maybe he made it all the way around to the Crabby Lady or someplace else where he could have emerged out of sight.

On the one hand, I kind of kicked myself for not staying with him inside the cabin. On the other hand, if he had jumped me inside the boat, it might have gotten messy. Me being the mess.

Mrs. Overstreet called. She'd heard the sirens. "Don't tell me, young man. You've gotten yourself into trouble again, haven't you?"

"Mrs. Overstreet, I swear it's not my fault. This guy, he just showed up to rob me."

"Oh, my goodness. Are you alright?"

"Yes, ma'am. I'm fine.

"But is there a burglar here, somewhere?" she asked, her voice strained.

"Uh, no, Mrs. Overstreet. I'm sure you're safe. He got what he came for."

"What was that, dear?"

"A leg lamp."

"A what? Did you say leg of lamb?"

"No ma'am, a lamp, in the shape of a woman's leg."

"Why on earth would you have ... oh, never mind. I'll keep Freddie until you get this straightened out." She hung up.

The deputies searching the area were thorough, but nobody saw or heard anything unusual around the marina. The questions they asked me were easy to anticipate: Did I know this guy? What did he say? Had I ever seen him before? Why was he on board my boat?

I followed Lester's advice and answered their questions truthfully.

Who might want to shoot him? Or me?

No clue.

I had one sneaking suspicion that I kept to myself. Whoever fired on my boat would have been a very able marksman, not just to put one through the window, likely at some distance, but to hit his target, through glass, even if not fatally.

Assuming, of course, that the intruder was the intended victim, which is what I wanted to believe. If the shooter used a scope, I wondered, would he have been able to distinguish between us through the window?

It would have been dark inside the boat, and we would have been shadowy. The intruder was directly in the bullet's path, so most likely he was the intended target. I was not visible from my position in the lounge—I didn't even get sprayed with the shattering glass as the bullet blew through the window. On the other hand, the shooter could have assumed it was me when he saw a man in the window, not knowing there was someone else aboard.

No matter, he was an excellent shot, and who did I know with skills like that?

Linda Henderson was a sharpshooter, of course, and Lester was the best one-legged marksman the army ever produced. But it obviously wasn't them.

Which left the only other person I was aware of with the requisite skill: A retired sniper who everyone was calling Mister Manners.

Detective Mayweather eventually showed up and grilled me, asking many of the same questions I'd already fielded from the deputies.

"I don't like coincidences," he finally said, flipping his notebook closed.

"What coincidences?" I asked, playing dumb.

"That we should meet again so soon after the Throckmorton press conference."

Then he really wouldn't like knowing I'd helped Linda break into Throckmorton's house. But I kept my mouth shut.

He glanced around the *Miss Demeanor's* lounge, his eyebrows raised. "You have some unusual shipmates," he said, nodding at Mona and Spock.

"Best crew ever."

And then I remembered the bullets. I reached into my cargo shorts and fished them out. "You might want these," I said.

I opened my fist so he could see what I was holding, and his eyes bulged. "That from his gun?" he asked.

"Yep."

"Jesus." He signaled one of the crime scene techs. She wagged a small paper bag at me, and I dropped the bullets in.

"Forty-four magnums," she said. "You handle them much?"

I nodded. "Unloaded the revolver, put them in my pocket, and now handed them to you, so I guess so."

"Jesus."

"What? You'd rather I left him a loaded gun?"

Mayweather said, "So he grabbed his gun and the leg lamp and somehow snuck off the boat unnoticed carrying, what, a lamp you said was four feet high?"

"Looks that way."

"So why'd he steal it?"

"The leg lamp?"

"No, second base. Of course, the leg lamp."

Before I could figure out how to answer that truthfully and still avoid mentioning the memory card fiasco, there was a rap on the cabin hatchway. Outside, one of the two divers the Sheriff's Office had summoned stood in the stern of the trawler, dripping wet. Dangling from his left hand was a sopping replica of a holiday movie prop, water draining out of the bullet hole in its leg.

Mayweather walked out onto the deck, and he took it from the diver's hands. "This is it, right? Just to confirm?"

"May I?" As if a closer inspection was needed. As if there would be another *Christmas Story* leg lamp lying on the bottom of Buzzards Bay South.

I turned it bottoms up and, as I feared, the felt on the underside of the lamp's base had been torn off, revealing a small indention that could have held something, but it looked like a tight fit for an SD card.

"Yep, this is the one," I said, as if there were any doubt. "See the cut cord? Unmistakable."

"Okay, then," Mayweather said. "Why'd he bother to rip it off only to dump it in the harbor?"

"Weird, huh?"

CHAPTER 29

Goodland, earlier

MISTER MANNERS HAD returned to the parking lot across from Stan's Idle Hour and was waiting for Alexander Strange to show up.

Earlier, he had tailed the plainclothes sheriff's detective to, of all things, a veterinarian's office on Marco Island. He'd been too far away to see what kind of animal she had inside the cage and debated with himself whether to concoct some story, try to flim-flam his way inside the clinic to find out. But to what purpose? Just to satisfy idle curiosity? He was spinning his wheels. He was either going to sit down and talk to the reporter or not.

By then it was noon, so he drove around looking for a decent place to eat with uncrowded outdoor seating. He finally settled on Doreen's Cup of Joe where he ordered a Corn Flake Chicken Sandwich, only because he'd never heard of such a thing. It came on ciabatta bread, which he liked. And the service was good. And he hadn't run into any rudeness in the restaurant. All of which pleased him.

Until he walked back to his camper, where several middle-aged couples were huddled around his vehicle, maskless, gabbing away at one another, spewing God knows how many virus particulates into the surrounding atmosphere.

"Move away from my camper, please," he ordered them.

Startled, rather than disbursing they froze in place.

"And wear your goddamned masks," he said. "We're in the middle of a pandemic."

One of the bolder members of the gaggle pushed back: "We don't need masks. Who do you think you are?"

Oh, man. If that moron only knew. How would he avenge this? Maybe ram a dozen surgical masks up his tailpipe? That would be entertaining. But they'd seen him and his camper van, so, no, he couldn't make it easy for the cops to get a physical description of him or his vehicle. They had no idea how close they'd come to being a headline.

Mister Manners drove back to Goodland with a sense of frustration that he'd let those idiots go unscathed but with a clearer picture of how his final act of vengeance—his grand finale—might play out.

He parked his camper van and glanced across the clutter of colorful picnic tables and the empty bandstand to the marina beyond where he made out Strange's aging and, he had to say, not-so-shipshape trawler. The reporter's Explorer was still parked across the street where it had been before, so maybe he was aboard.

Mister Manners tried to detect movement aboard, but saw none. He'd been cleaning his guns the night before, and his black-market VSS Vintorez—a Russian sniper rifle used by Spetsnaz units—was still lying on a towel on the floor. It was renowned for its built-in suppressor and quiet operation. Of all the firearms he owned, this was his favorite for several reasons, not the least of which because it was challenging to find one in the West.

It had an excellent scope. He picked the weapon up and peered into the trawler through one of the portholes but saw nobody stirring.

Then he spied a woman standing very still. Utterly motionless. She was wearing a black mask emblazoned with a skull and crossbones. He focused in on her and realized she was dressed in full pirate regalia, holding a sword. And still she hadn't moved.

What was up with her?

He trained the scope's crosshairs on her head. She had beautiful brown eyes. Her skin was flawless. Too flawless, he suddenly realized.

Jesus Christ! It's a fucking mannequin. What kind of pervert was this guy?

Then he spotted motion out of the corner of his left eye, turned, and saw a large man wearing gloves and a black mask boarding the trawler. He carried a stainless steel revolver in his left hand, either a .357 or a .44 Magnum, he guessed. In his right hand, he held a metal object. Looked like a shim. He plunged it into the space between the hatchway and frame, jiggled it for a moment, and the door sprung open. He slipped inside.

Mister Manners retreated from his cracked doorway into his camper and opened the metal box where he stored his ammunition and loaded the Russian sniper rifle. He wasn't sure what was going on, but this had bad news written all over it. He reopened the door a crack, positioned himself on the floor of the camper, prone, and waited.

He was so intent keeping his scope on the intruder—and his gun—that he spotted Alexander Strange boarding the *Miss Demeanor* too late to warn him. He retrained his scope on the intruder holding the pistol.

And when the intruder raised his gun and pointed it at Strange, Mister Manners didn't hesitate. Not even for a nanosecond.

Strange would have been pleased to know he'd guessed correctly. The gun fired a subsonic round, which helped keep the noise down. No gun, not even a BB gun, is completely silent. But the sound of a single shot from a heavily suppressed weapon such as this is nearly indistinguishable from myriad other noises, and, even if someone heard it, the odds of associating the muffled snap with gunfire were remote.

The sound was further diminished by Mister Manners shooting from inside his camper through his cracked-open door. He took the shot, set the gun down, closed the door, and pulled out of the parking lot. He drove the camper van to the Goodland Baptist Church several blocks away, parked, then strolled back, just in time to see the first flashing blue lights arriving.

He meandered over to the Little Bar, saw two deputies approaching the trawler, and then Alexander Strange emerged from the cabin, hands raised over his head, waiting for the cops to board.

Then he noticed movement on the bow of the boat. What the fuck? It was the gunman he'd had in his sights.

Had he missed? Had the glass deflected the shot that much?

Goddammit.

He shaded his eyes and stared intently as the man quietly slipped over the side of the boat into the little bay. Even at this distance, the streak of blood on the side of his head was easily visible.

The shot must have grazed him. That was embarrassing. Definitely need more time back at the range. And what the hell was he carrying? It looked like a lamp in the shape of a woman's leg.

Jesus. Only in Florida.

Mister Manners walked over to Papaya Street, keeping an eye on the water. The swimmer's bloody head bobbed up near the bay's inlet, near the Paradise Found bar. Good lungs, staying down that long. Especially after getting his bell rung. Impressive.

Would the swimmer turn left or right? Right would take him to the tie-ups by the Crabby Lady. He wasn't sure what all was over past Paradise Found, but he recalled it looked industrial when he had driven in. He stayed on Papaya and walked to the water's edge waiting for the swimmer to resurface.

But, no, he must have gone left.

Dammit.

Now he found himself on the opposite side of the cove from where the swimmer would have to emerge. By the time he circled back, past Stan's Idle Hour over to the other side, the guy would probably be gone.

Nothing for it, though. Might as well try.

Mister Manners began retracing his steps, but he didn't get far before his progress was interrupted outside the Little Bar by a sheriff's deputy.

There were several white and green cruisers and an ambulance at the marina now. And he could see other deputies fanning out, no doubt looking for a shell casing or other evidence of where the shot had been fired through the porthole.

The deputy approached him. He was young, late twenties, early thirties, Hispanic, fit. Nametag said GARCIA.

"Hey," the deputy said. "You seen or heard anything out of the ordinary around here in the last few minutes?"

Mister Manners shook his head. "Just out for a walk. Only thing unusual is you guys. What's up?"

The deputy ignored the question. "You hear a gunshot by any chance?" he asked.

"Gunshot? No, man. Somebody get shot?"

The deputy shook his head and moved on.

Mister Manners continued his trek along Harbor Place until he circled to the opposite side of the cove. The little street was set back from the water and dead-ended in a sandy pathway that he followed as it meandered to the rear of the handful of buildings at the water's edge. Past them, it was all mangroves. The swimmer could have emerged anywhere.

If he had, there was no sign. He was gone.

Also gone was the opportunity to talk to the reporter. Not today. Too many cops hanging around. He could return in a day or two when things settled down.

Be good to know what that gunman wanted, though, before he came back. Why did he swipe that lamp? Was that worth shooting Strange for? None of this made any sense.

He knew better. He really did. But that's the thing with his compulsions. Even as he was acting on them, punishing the ill-mannered, he knew it was stupid, risky.

But his curiosity was aroused. What the hell was going on around here?

His instincts screamed he should just blow this whole idea off. Fuck a bunch of talking to a reporter. Especially one that seemed to draw trouble like a magnet. Yeah, just forget it.

But he knew he wouldn't.

CHAPTER 30

Goodland

WHILE THE COPS and crime scene techs were crawling over my boat and scouring the neighborhood for witnesses, I received two phone calls—the first from Linda Henderson, the second from Lester Rivers.

"Guess who we know who spreads horseshit for a living," Linda asked.

"Rudy Giuliani."

"Besides him."

She was playing Holmes to my Watson again. The correct answer would have to be a mutual acquaintance or the question made no sense, which was helpful: It eliminated almost everyone I could think of.

"I surrender. Who?"

"Hector Morales."

"He works for Throckmorton *and* at the Reel and Rifle Club *and* the stables? When does he sleep?"

"Immigrants. They're so industrious."

"Hold on. The stables? Are you saying he's the guy who unloaded all that horseshit on Throckmorton's front porch?"

"He's now officially our prime suspect. And there's something else he is."

"And that is...?"

"AWOL."

"You mean you can't find him?" I asked, stating the obvious and giving her a priceless opportunity for a sarcastic rejoinder. Some people don't know how to play the straight man in a comedic duo, but I always thought Bud Abbott was funnier than Lou Costello in those old-time radio shows Uncle Leo used to make me listen to. And I've learned that mirroring back to sources often prompts them to show off, prove how smart they are, many times revealing more than they originally intended. I wasn't pulling that on Linda, though. It's simply become ingrained in my conversational *modus operandi*.

But she didn't seize on the opportunity, which was a bit of a letdown. I mean, who passes on a chance to be a smartass?

"Yes, that's right," she said. "I can't find him. Driven all over Everglades City. Tracked down his crib, and he's vanished. His landlord has no idea. He doesn't answer his cell phone. And I'm annoyed we let him slip away."

And I was more than a little annoyed that I'd been with Hector Morales when he confessed that he stuffed the bufo toad in Throckmorton's freezer but never let on he was a Mister Manners copycat. A potentially great column had slipped right through my fingers while I sat there unawares.

"Well, this all just sucks," I grumbled.

"Oh? What's with you?"

"Oh, let's see. I took Fred for a walk. Chatted with a neighbor lady, Mrs. Overstreet. Strolled around Goodland a bit. Then a robber pulled an enormous gun on me. But that worked out okay when he got shot in the head. But then he swam away with my leg lamp."

I paused my monologue, letting it dangle, then I filled in the details. She listened without interruption, and when I was done, she said:

"And Mayweather's there?"

"Yeah. For some reason he thinks it's unusual that an armed robber would go to all the trouble of breaking into a boat, stealing a movie trinket, then drown it. And he finds it weird we should meet again so soon."

"Did he…"

"No. He didn't say anything about our break-in at Throckmorton's, nor did he ask about dangerous toxic toads."

"And what's so special about the lamp?"

"That's a different story. Still fuzzy on some details. Like most of them."

"Don't go anywhere," she said. "I'm coming over."

I wasn't about to go anywhere, not while the cops were still swarming over my boat. But I did take that break in the action to call my insurance agent.

"So, looks like I have a broken window, Shannon," I told her.

"Oh, too bad. Windshield?"

"No. Porthole. On the side. Portside, actually. But it's a big porthole, probably two feet in diameter."

"Sounds more like a round window. What happened."

"Mmmm. Something hit it. Not exactly sure what caliber."

"Vandals?"

"Or Visigoths. Hard to know."

She didn't miss a beat. "We'll call it vandalism."

"So, what's my deductible?"

"Well, Alex, you'll recall when we wrote your policy, you insisted on the least expensive rate, which means you have high deductibles. In your case, it's a thousand dollars for vandalism."

"What if we call it something else?"

"Still a thousand."

Then Lester called.

"I need you to meet me here in Naples," he said without preamble.

"Where you at?" I replied, unabashedly dangling the participle.

"NCH. Standing in the parking lot right now, outside the Emergency Room."

Naples Community Hospital is the big downtown medical center, a sprawling facility overworked of late with coronavirus patients.

"What's at NCH?" I asked.

"Rennie Bhatia. She's in the ER. I went to her place right after I talked to you. You asked an important question—who would know you had the leg lamp? She was the only person I could think of. When I got there, the medics were hauling her out. A friend—maybe that daughter of Mister Manners—found her unconscious and, from the looks of it, a little roughed up.

"Jesus. So that's how the sonofabitch found me. He beat it out of her. But how did he know anything about Rennie in the first place?"

"Had to be Kitty Karlucci. Remember, she said the thug who showed up at her place asked about Hugo Throckmorton's computer business. She told him Rennie's mom was Hugo Throckmorton's business partner and that Rennie was running the store for her now."

"And he would care about that, why?"

Lester said, "Great question and the only answer that comes to mind is the missing memory card."

"So, this dickwad beats the shit out of Rennie to find the leg lamp even though there's no memory card in it?"

"The thought occurs to me that Rennie might not have been forthright with him about that detail."

"Forthright."

"I'm a professional investigator for The Third Eye. We all took college."

"Have you spoken with her?"

"No. I need to bamboozle my way into the hospital. They got the place locked down to visitors because of the pandemic."

"Where's that miracle Trump promised us?"

"Don't blame Trump. Not his fault people refuse to drink Clorox."

I took a few moments to process all that, then said, "You know,

Lester, that asshole was unconscious in my boat. And I had his loaded pistol in my hand. Should have held him at gunpoint."

"Alexander, he's a professional killer, according to Karlucci. Not the kind of guy you want to tangle with, especially in close quarters. You're a big guy, and I know you can handle yourself, but it could have turned out a lot worse."

"Still feels like a lost opportunity."

"Okay."

I took a few moments to catch him up on what had happened since we talked last, and I finally told him, "Divers found the lamp, by the way."

"Divers?"

"Yeah, that douchebag tore the felt off the bottom of the lamp's base. There was a small indent underneath."

"Looking for something."

"Or finding something."

"It occurs to me," Lester said, "Ms. Bhatia may not have been entirely forthright with us, either."

"It does. And it occurs to me that all of this is something the cops should know about, don't you think?"

He hesitated a moment, then said: "Yes. But. Let me see if I can get in to see Rennie. And I need to have a chat with Karlucci. Maybe some of this will make more sense then."

"That would be a nice change of pace. But there's a complication."

"Now what?"

"Linda Henderson."

There was a pause on the line while he thought that over. "She took you along when she broke into Throckmorton's and grabbed the froggy. She's trusting you and you don't like not being straight with her."

"Yeah."

"I understand. She's a comrade in arms. You feel a sense of loyalty and obligation to her. That's admirable." Another pause. I didn't say anything, letting him complete his thought. "But she's also a cop."

"Who's operating off the books."

"And you think I should trust her like you do."

"That's up to you. You got your own deal. You're a private eye. There's a reason people hire you. They want things kept private. You don't want to mention Karlucci to Linda. I get it. Then again, since this thug threatened Karlucci right before he messed up Rennie, Kitty must have given him Rennie's name. Which makes all that evidence, doesn't it?"

"You're not wrong. But you only know that because I shared that with you."

"Which is confidential."

"Correct."

"Well, you see where I'm coming from."

"I do."

"Any advice?"

"Suck it up for now. Let me talk to Karlucci, then we'll regroup."

CHAPTER 31

Goodland

THE CRIME SCENE techs packed up and left, following Mayweather and the deputies out of the marina. I duct-taped a black plastic garbage bag over my ruined porthole—enough to keep out the rain if not interlopers—and was locking up the cabin when Linda Henderson materialized on the dock beside the trawler.

"You just get here?" I asked. "You missed your pals."

She shook her head. "Parked down the street. Didn't want Mayweather seeing us together. It'd raise too many questions."

"Speaking of questions, any news from the vet?"

"Yeah, as a matter of fact. First off, she's never seen such a gigantic bufo toad. Said she has to be some kind of record, a real biological marvel, maybe even some sort of crossbreed because her coloration is unusual."

"She? So froggy's a chick, like we guessed. How'd she figure that out?"

"Probably used science. Anyway, she's not a frog expert, but she jumped on a Zoom call with a biologist at the University of Florida, and she said the guy about shit himself when he saw the size of that toad. He had her poke it—gently but firmly, she said—to stimulate toxin release, and it was enormous."

"Enough to kill a man?"

"Not sure. But, maybe, yeah."

"Any word yet on Throckmorton's cause of death?"

"Waiting on the toxicology report. We asked the M.E. to check first for bufotoxin—that raised a few eyebrows—but I'm hoping we'll at least get that result soonish. We asked them to prioritize it."

"So, Linda, it comes back he was greased by frog poison, you gonna let the Feds know?'

"That's Mayweather's call. But all the more reason to find Hector Morales, just in case."

"You think he might have bugged out?"

She shrugged. "He has a twenty-year-old Dodge truck registered in his name. I found it parked behind the duplex he's been renting. Guess what was in the bed of the truck."

"Horse manure."

She shot me with her finger.

"If he's on the lam, he didn't take his truck, which would have made it easier to track him down," she said. "If he wants to get lost, maybe he hopped a bus or hitched. He's got a green card and a driver's license, so we've broadcast his mugshot to Trailways, Greyhound, FHP. Even TSA while we were at it. Of course, he could have gone to ground and holed up right here. We'll see."

"And you and Mayweather are keeping all this on the down-low for now."

She nodded. "Look, Alex, nothing about this is normal, okay? There's something sketchy with the Feds poking their noses in the way they have, being so secretive about why they're here. Them insisting on using their own evidence techs, for instance. That was odd. It delayed matters. Them bigfooting around doesn't just complicate things but—and don't take this the wrong way—I don't trust them."

"How would I take that the wrong way?"

"If you assumed it was just the usual local cops hating on the Feds thing. My gut tells me there's more to this."

She was looking at my window repair job. "I gather they never found the shooter."

"Nobody saw anything. No shell casings lying around. But whoever shot out my window probably saved my life."

"And the asshole who broke into your boat, he wanted the lamp?"

"Or something hidden in the lamp."

"Huh. What didn't you tell Mayweather?"

"The same thing I'm not going to tell you."

The blood rushed to her face and her eyes turned to slits. "And why the fuck not?"

What I couldn't share, of course, was anything I knew about Lester's business—his employment by Rennie Bhatia to recover the memory card that was supposed to be hidden inside the leg lamp, and how Kitty Karlucci was now engaging him after a gunman threatened her—undoubtedly the same guy who just absconded with the self-same lamp after pointing a revolver in my face.

"If I tell you, can you promise me that you won't share this with Mayweather?"

Her shoulders stiffened. "Depends."

"Exactly." So by not telling you, I keep you out of hot water. I'm giving you deniability."

"Give me a fucking break."

"That's exactly what I'm doing."

"You think so, do you?" Defiant.

"Linda, we're on the same side. You gotta trust me on this."

"Or I could arrest you."

"Or you could arrest me, but what would that get you?"

She chewed on that a little bit, then said, "You're a pain in the ass, you know that?"

"I get that a lot. Look, I'm heading downtown. Maybe we should restart this conversation there."

She frowned at that, either not liking my changing the subject or wondering what the hell else was going on. "What's downtown?"

"The hospital. I'm meeting Lester Rivers there."

"Is he injured?"

"No, but a mutual acquaintance is. She's in the ER."

She frowned again and cocked her head, clearly not liking any of this. "Does this have anything to do with Throckmorton?"

She was connecting dots, and I had to admire her instincts, but I shook my head. "I don't know. I really don't. It potentially has something to do with what happened here today, and that's what I need to find out."

"You and Rivers are working on something, aren't you?"

I nodded.

"This involves a client of his; that's why you're so closed-mouth all of a sudden."

"I'd rather not discuss that." Which really meant "yes" without my explicitly saying so.

She placed her hands on her hips and lowered her head in thought. But just for a moment. "You know what? You may be the most annoying person I've ever met."

"It's my superpower."

"Yeah, well, if you have information bearing on my case, I'm putting you on notice right now that you need to cough it up, buster."

"Well, don't you pretty much have it wrapped? You got your suspect, right? Hector Morales? If he's the guy who dumped that horse manure on Throckmorton's front porch, that clearly shows his hostility. And he had a key to the house. And he put the bufo toad in the freezer, right where Throckmorton dropped dead. What's left besides catching the guy?"

Linda had been studying her cell phone while I was talking. She looked up, a scowl on her face, and said, "There's a complication."

"The fact that Morales is missing?"

She shook her head.

"What, then?"

"I'd love to tell you, but, well, you know how it is."

"How what is?"

"You have your secrets. I have mine."

CHAPTER 32

En route to Naples

LINDA WAS PILOTING a green and white sheriff's cruiser, and I expected her to fire up her lights and sirens to clear the way downtown. Instead, she drove the speed limit, which meant that traffic balled up around us, nobody wanting to draw the attention of the fuzz.

Despite the storied tension between reporters and cops, most of them I've had dealings with seemed okay. Differing personalities, of course, like everyone else. But not utterly humorless and sadistic. I hadn't run into too many cops I thought would get their rocks off kneeling on somebody's neck. But, obviously, they're out there.

Linda had always struck me as among the more hidebound cops I'd encountered when it came to doing things by the book. Then she started sneaking into houses and sharing confidential information, so it was clear I had a lot to learn about her. Still, there were some rules Linda Henderson apparently wouldn't bend—like putting the pedal to the metal when it wasn't a Code 3.

We continued to chug along at the speed limit, which nobody ever drives, but here we were setting a record for how long it would take to get from the island to downtown. I fleetingly wondered if she were doing this on purpose, just to aggravate me. But that was a non-starter on so many levels, not the least of which was that Linda Henderson didn't have a passive-aggressive bone in her body. When she was pissed at you, she got in your face and said so. As she had.

I wondered what this big secret was that she taunted me with right before we pulled out. Was it really something or was that just payback for me holding out on her? If her goal was to torment me, it was working. She'd been scanning her phone right before. Was it about Hector Morales? If so, what? Had they found him? But why would that be a "complication?" Yep, she had me going.

I flipped on the radio. I don't have a fancy, schmancy police scanner in my car like Lester, and I only listen to so-called news channels, avoiding the music stations. I have this odd thing with earworms. I know, I know, everyone gets them, but I have this annoying compulsion to play the lyrics over and over in my mind rewriting them, almost always terribly—not the most comfortable thing to admit when you scribble for a living.

That doesn't mean I don't like music, though. Think of it as a kind of allergy. You might like the taste of shellfish, but you don't welcome a trip to the Emergency Room.

After all, if I hated music, I wouldn't have such an extensive collection of obscure rock band tee-shirts, which is my usual workday attire. Today, I was sporting one of my faves: Elvis Hitler, a Detroit psychobilly band whose music I'd heard only once.

My tee-shirt collection has taught me that there are two kinds of people in the world—those who notice when I'm showcasing a particularly outrageous band—say, the Exploding Fuckdolls or Diarrhea Planet—and those who seem oblivious. I've learned it's hard to predict how people will react.

Linda Henderson, you'd think a cop—especially a detective—wouldn't miss a detail like a shirt celebrating Lyin' Bitch and the Restraining Orders. I would have expected at least a comment or a little squinty eye. But, no, she never seemed to notice. She either has an observational deficiency or she has awe-inspiring discipline. Probably the latter.

One of the right-wing gasbags on the radio was signing off, and the station was offering up a few brief snippets of local and national news.

Pollsters were saying a majority of voters thought Donald Trump's performance in the first presidential debate was disturbing, the way he continually interrupted Joe Biden and the moderator. Respondents were aghast at how he seemed to call out white supremacists to help him disrupt the election.

Closer to home, convenience store owner and political gadfly Aggie LaFrance was interviewed about his plan to hold the country's largest pro-Trump and anti-mask boat rally, the goal of which was to flood Naples Bay with more than two thousand yachts, sailboats, and motor craft sporting Make America Great Again banners. "We're going to take our country back," he said. "This is war and the first battle will be fought right here in Naples."

Police reported a single-engine plane missing from a hangar at Collier Wings Estates, a residential community built around a runway in east Naples populated by aviation enthusiasts. All the homes have hangars for garages, and the thief apparently broke into one of them in the middle of the night and flew off, destination unknown. I made a mental note to learn more about that incident. It had all the trappings of a *Strange Files* column waiting to be written.

Snake hunters had killed a record eighteen-foot, nine-inch Burmese python in the Everglades. The red tide outbreak along the coast was continuing to pile up dead fish along the beaches. And the county commission had decided to schedule a new vote on whether to enact an ordinance requiring mask-wearing in public places. At the rate they were dithering there might not be anyone left alive to wear them.

And The DJ—or whatever they call the radio host on a channel that doesn't play music—broke to a National Weather Service report. The tropical depression in the Caribbean had been upgraded to a tropical storm named Olivia and was expected to become a Category 1 hurricane over the next twenty-four hours. Olivia was leading a parade of storms stretching across the Atlantic from coastal Africa—all heading our way. The forecasting "cone of uncertainty" showed her swinging northward to graze Florida's east coast with an anticipated landfall five days out. If Olivia stayed on that track, there'd be nothing to concern ourselves about on the Gulf coast, but vigilance would be required.

My iPhone began ringing, so I switched off the radio and put it on speakerphone. "Twenty-four hours a day, seven days a week, this is Alexander Strange," I said after seeing Gwenn was on the line. "Have pencil, will travel."

"I wish you'd bring your pencil over here," she replied.

I started to say something witty in response, but she kept talking before I could get it out.

"But you can't. At least you shouldn't. We're at what they're calling COVID Level 3. It just isn't safe. Not just because of the disease but hospital availability."

That did not swell me up with happiness. "Uh, so maybe you should get out of there. Not sure it's that much safer here, but at least I could bring you chicken noodle soup."

"No, I'm pretty safe since I'm spending all my time indoors, mostly by myself, poring over a mountain of paperwork. I've got at a few more days of this before I can even see where this is going."

"I'd be lying if I told you I'm grief-stricken you aren't having the time of your life without me."

That got a laugh.

"You sound like you're in the car," she said.

"Yup. Heading into Naples, NCH specifically. You remember Rennie…"

"The Bhatia woman…"

"Yes. Somebody beat her up. She's in the ER. Lester's there now. I'm meeting him."

I deliberately did not mention that Linda Henderson was accompanying me. Not the way Gwenn despised her. She had enough on her mind without that.

"Beat her up? Does this have anything to do with this business you're working on, finding Mister Manners?"

"Short version: Somebody's still after the leg lamp, and they roughed up Rennie to find it."

"Last I heard, it was on your boat."

"Yeah. And the guy who manhandled Rennie broke in and stole the lamp."

There was a pause on the line as she digested this, for which I was grateful because I had to decide how much detail to burden her with. I didn't want her worrying about me while she was busy with her own business on the other side of the world.

"No fair!" she shouted. "I'm missing all of this."

So much for her anxiety.

"But wait!" she said. "How do you know it was the guy who beat up Rennie? That he was the one who broke into your boat?"

"I'm inferring since he wanted the lamp."

"You were there? While he was aboard?"

"Uh, yeah, I got back and there he was, ripping me off."

"What'd you do? Beat him up? Did the cops arrest him?"

"No. He got away. The bullet only grazed him."

"Bullet? You're holding back. I want the details. All of them."

So I told her everything, including that I was working with Linda Henderson. Her reaction to that surprised me.

"Good. You know I don't like her, but the bitch can shoot. Between her and Lester, maybe they can keep you from getting killed."

Traffic tightened up as we got closer to downtown. Somehow, a MINI Cooper Clubman and a Harley had wedged their way between

Linda's cruiser and me. I figured we were less than five minutes from the hospital at that point.

"Don't have much time," I told Gwenn, "but I got one more thing I need to get off my chest."

"Now what have you done?"

I filled her in on Kitty Karlucci's proposal.

"Oh, that is so cool. My boyfriend the author. You're going to say yes, aren't you?"

"Well, I thought I should run it past you…"

"Go for it."

"And I suppose I need to mention it to Edwina."

"Why? What you do on your own time is your business. Tell her when it's done. Otherwise, she'll dog you about spending time on it when you should be doing your column."

"I had that same thought."

"One more thing," she said.

"What's that?"

"This shouldn't be a handshake deal. You need an actual contract. And you should negotiate for up-front money, an advance on the work you'll be doing, just like authors get from publishers."

"Huh. Never thought of that."

"This is a business proposition. If it isn't in writing, it isn't real. Before you sign, scan it and send it to me."

"This is one of the many benefits of dating Ally McBeal."

"I'm twice the lawyer she ever was."

"Better looking, too."

"And's that's why you get my friends and family rate."

I told Gwenn I was pulling into the hospital parking lot, but she had one more question.

"How's that frog you captured? Is it okay?"

"She's at a vet's, and as far as I know she's fine. But since when did you start caring about poisonous amphibians?"

"I Googled bufo toads. They're ugly and gnarly and everybody hates them. I guess I've got a soft spot for under-loved creatures."

"Lucky for me."

"Exactly.

CHAPTER 33

Naples

Lester, Linda, and I met in the crowded hospital parking lot outside the emergency room entrance. We were standing our obligatory six feet apart, wearing masks. I'd been in close contact with each of them, but you can't be too careful. Masks aren't fun to wear, but they beat the hell out of a ventilator.

"You get in to see her?" I asked.

Lester shook his head. "No. They're hard-assed about visitors. People are dying in there, and their loved ones can't even get in to say their goodbyes."

"Jesus."

"But I did talk to her. Took a chance and called her cell, and she answered. She's still being observed in the ER, but it doesn't look like they're going to admit her. They're waiting for test results to make sure there's no concussion or anything."

"She a friend of yours?" Linda asked Lester.

"Client."

"How badly was she hurt?" There was an edge in her voice, some barely contained anger. "And did she ID him, give a good description?"

"He slapped her around, from the way she described it," Lester said. "At one point, she fell and smacked her head on something, maybe an end table. She might have been knocked out for a minute or two, says her memory's hazy. Got a cut lip, nasty bruise on the side of her head, and she's got a few stitches over her right eye."

"And the ID?" Linda asked.

"Matches Alexander's description of the thug who broke into his boat. He waved a revolver at her. She said it looked silver, which also matches the description of the gun he pointed at you, right?

I nodded.

"I need to ask you something, Mr. Rivers," Linda said.

"Major," I interrupted.

She cocked an eye at Lester. "Army?"

He nodded.

"Major Rivers, this client of yours, she's mugged by the same goon who threatened Alexander. I don't like coincidences, do you?"

Here we go, I thought. How will Lester play this? But he'd already anticipated the question.

"My client, Renelda Bhatia, hired me to recover some lost property. Which I did."

"We talking about that preposterous leg lamp?" Linda asked.

"We are."

"She say what was so damned important about that stupid lamp? Why somebody would beat her up, threaten Alexander?"

"When I talked to her on the phone earlier, I explained to her that this would be one of the questions she could anticipate being asked by the police," Lester said.

I jumped in. "Linda, will you be investigating this?"

Linda shook her head. "Templeton's the lead. You've met. He joined Special Crimes same time as me. They had a batch of retirements right as COVID-19 started getting serious. I talked to him while we were driving over. He's inside there now."

"Is Templeton also the lead on Alexander's break-in, the shooting?" Lester asked.

"Mayweather," Linda said. "Although we're probably going to have to roll all this up into one investigation. Speaking of which, what is it you and Alexander aren't telling us? I know there's something. Is someone else involved?"

Lester's eyes crinkled in a grin.

"Detective Henderson," he said. "You have excellent instincts. I have a client…"

"Who?"

"I'm sorry, but I can't divulge that right now." He cocked his head in my direction. "We should be going."

Linda put her hands on her hips and shook her head ever so slightly. Then she turned to me. "And you know who his client is, don't you?"

I shrugged.

"And you're not going to tell me."

"It's his call. His client."

"You find out something we should know about, I expect a call," Linda said, then turned and marched toward the emergency room.

As she disappeared through the ER's entrance, the automatic glass doors shut behind her. It occurred to me that those weren't the only doors that had just closed on me.

CHAPTER 34

Naples

LESTER AND I TALKED FOR a few more minutes, then agreed we would caravan to Kitty Karlucci's place in Port Royal. I had just cranked my Explorer's engine, ready to follow him, when from the corner of my eye I spotted Linda Henderson running right back out of the emergency room door.

What on earth would cause her to rabbit like that after just showing up at the hospital? Something was up, but was it about this dumpster fire or something else? Her cruiser was parked two rows over, so I slowly backed out of my slot and waited to see what she would do.

My phone rang. It was Lester. "I lose you already?"

"Game's afoot. Linda just ran out of the hospital and she's pulling out now. You go ahead. Call me crazy, but I'm going to tail her."

"You're crazy."

I punched off the call and peeled out behind Linda's green and white. She'd fired up her lights as she turned out of the parking lot. At Ninth Street—Tamiami Trail—she turned left, and as she accelerated away her sirens screamed to life.

Tamiami Trail is the main north-south artery through Naples, eventually veering to the southeast and continuing through the Everglades, where it ultimately dead-ends in downtown Miami. We were heading in the opposite direction, north through the city's crowded commercial corridor filled with restaurants, banks, furniture stores, and other businesses, a route with frequent cross-streets and traffic lights.

While fire departments and ambulances in Collier County employ ingenious devices known as EVPs—short for Emergency Vehicle Preemption Systems—that let them change red lights to green, sheriff's cruisers do not. So, tailing Linda through intersections could have involved red-light running, which in addition to being dangerous and illegal could also earn me the ire of Mister Manners. Fortunately, she hit a green at the first signal then turned right over to Goodlette-Frank Road, another north-south byway. Three blocks later, she pulled into the parking lot of the Collier County Memory Care Center. Two other sheriff's cruisers were already there.

The lot was only half full (or half empty, take your pick), and Linda wheeled her cruiser into a spot to the left of the entrance. A few seconds behind her, I pulled around to the right and killed the engine.

It was pure instinct to follow her here, and like the proverbial dog who catches the firetruck, the next question is always: Now what?

Linda solved that quandary for me. She bypassed the entrance and marched directly to my car and rapped on the window.

I rolled it down. "Holy cow, what a coincidence," I said. "I thought you were at the hospital."

"What the fuck do you think you're doing?" She had her hands on her hips and was barely suppressing a snarl.

"Uh, Linda, your mask?"

"Cut the crap, Strange."

She wouldn't bother to confront me if an emergency inside demanded immediate attention, so I assumed we weren't dealing with a hostage situation or anything requiring the SWAT team. Then again, there were no ambulances, which you frequently see at retirement homes and elder-care facilities, so this wasn't a medical emergency, either. Something odd was going on.

Who did we know who might be living in a place like this? Someone important enough to draw Linda from NCH with lights and sirens. I didn't have to be the sharpest pencil in the drawer to grok the answer.

"It's Rennie's mom, isn't it?" I said. "She said her mother has Alzheimer's. Did that fucker who manhandled Rennie show up here?"

"Get out of here or I'll arrest you."

"For what?"

"For being a pain in the ass."

With that, she turned on her heel and stormed into the facility.

Yep. I'd say our days of playing nice together were over. Now what? Leave or risk a pair of steel bracelets? I pondered that question briefly, knowing the answer, really, just stalling, when my cell phone buzzed. It was Lester.

"Where are you?" he asked.

"Outside a place called Collier County Memory Care. You wouldn't happen to know if this is where Rennie took her mom, would you?

"It is. Rennie just called me. They're discharging her right now, and I'm heading back to NCH to give her a lift. We'll meet you there. Stay put."

"What the hell is going on?"

I heard Lester take a deep breath.

"Her mom's disappeared."

"She wander off? That happens sometimes with dementia patients."

"Don't think that's it."

"Why's that?"

"Rennie got a call from the nursing home. A man came to visit her mother. Fits the description of the character aboard your boat. A nurse went to check on Rennie's mom, and she was gone. The visitor's missing, too."

"It's that gunslinger. He must not have found what he wanted in the leg lamp."

"That would be my assumption."

"And he's grabbed Rennie's mom, why?

"Leverage. Force her to cough up the memory card."

"But Rennie doesn't have it."

"You know that for sure?"

"Well, that's what she said."

"Trust no one."

Lester seemed to be having second thoughts about the credibility of his client. And she wasn't on my all-time Favorite Humans list at the moment, either.

"If this asshole is still trying to find the memory card, that means it wasn't in the base of the lamp, which Rennie certainly knew," I said. "Yet she thought nothing of sending a hired killer after me."

"Right. And that's annoying. But she was scared."

"Yeah? Me too. For all we know, it was never in the lamp. Which could mean Sniffen took off empty-handed when we cornered him in Goodland."

He gave me Yoda, which he has a habit of doing at the most unlikely times:

"Much we don't know, there is."

CHAPTER 35

Collier Wings Estates in East Naples

MISTER MANNERS WAS MORE than a mere trigger-puller. He was also a pilot, a fair mechanic, and he knew his way around a soldering iron—which at that moment he was wielding, lying on his back on the floor of an airplane hangar that was attached to a house in Collier Wings Estates.

The police reported a plane stolen from the aviation-themed community, where every home came with its own garage/hangar that backed onto the landing strip serving as a spine through the center of the housing development.

How could a thief just fly off with a plane unnoticed? That was the question the cops and everyone else wanted to know.

Mister Manners didn't know either, nor care, because that's exactly what he didn't do. Instead, he had rolled the Cessna 172 from its hanger at 3445 Skyhawk Way across the runway to 2872 Aviator Street and into the empty hanger of U.S. Army Col. (Ret.) Tony Frahm, who was on an extended vacation in Alaska with his wife where they had flown themselves in their Beechcraft King Air twin-engine C90GTx.

Mister Manners met Frahm during one of his overseas tours, and they had stayed in touch. When Mister Manners had mentioned that he might be spending some time in Florida, the colonel asked if he would mind checking on their property from time to time while they were away. He was more than happy to do so. Indeed, it served as an inspiration for what he imagined would be his final grand gesture before retiring his role as the Sunshine State's most celebrated vigilante.

Mister Manners did not see himself as a criminal, even though his behavior was illegal. But he knew hubris was the enemy of all outlaws, the sense of invulnerability that comes from getting away with lawlessness unscathed, much like young soldiers who come away from their first firefight uninjured and enjoy a fleeting sense of invincibility. Then reality sets in. Mister Manners knew that eventually the police would catch up. You had to know when to fold 'em, as Kenny Rogers sang.

But first, there would be his final statement. A signature event that would cap his career, cement the legend. Then he would literally be in the wind, never to be seen again. At least, that was the plan.

He'd spent a career defending America from its foreign enemies, but in recent years he'd seen the development of a new threat, a rising surge of selfishness and disregard for others that seemed to have infected the culture, enabled and encouraged by lying elected officials—leaders who had sworn to defend the nation against all enemies, foreign and domestic, just as he had, but were now undercutting that foundation.

This behavior needed to be called out. Rudeness, self-dealing, deception—these were not the characteristics of the America he believed in. Already others were taking up the torch. The police were calling them copycats, but he saw the beginnings of a new cadre of involved citizens pushing back against cultural rot.

His final act of vengeance would be an inspiration.

Mister Manners looked up at the undercarriage of the Cessna as he busied himself fastening two pairs of custom-made pods—built from fiberglass from a mold he had created. Nothing fancy, and not too durable. But they would only be needed for one flight.

The trick was attaching the pods securely to the underside of the wings, then running the wires into the cockpit to release the makeshift bomb bay doors he had installed at the bottom of each of the pods. It might be jerry-rigged, but it still needed to be fastened securely and be aligned correctly for the sake of aerodynamics.

He had flown Cessnas before, but those were larger aircraft with hardpoints built into the wings to attach armament. On this plane, he had to create his own attach-points using solder and Super Glue.

Filling the pods would be a bitch, he realized. Each pontoon-shaped container would hold approximately a hundred bomblets, and they wouldn't be loaded until after the pods were attached to the underside of the wings. He would have to think about how to stuff the ordnance in there with the bomb bay doors opened. Maybe some kind of net to hold them in place. He needed to figure that out.

If only the pods could be made detachable. Then he could load the armament, then fasten the pods. He should have thought of that earlier, but now it was too late. But he'd sort it out. He had to. The day of the planned attack was rapidly approaching.

CHAPTER 36

Naples

I PULLED MY EXPLORER around to the side of the memory care center, figuring maybe it would buy me enough time to avoid arrest until Lester arrived with Rennie Bhatia. If I continued to loiter out front, Linda might just cuff me for spite, and there was no need to make it easy on her to do something she'd regret.

See, this wasn't just me being cautious, I was also looking out for her best interest, right? Call me Mister Considerate.

I could still see the entrance from my new vantage point, but I didn't imagine Lester would show up all that soon knowing how hospitals dawdle when releasing patients.

I called Mrs. Overstreet and told her I might be late returning to the island. She seemed in a better mood than the last time we talked and told me she'd keep Fred overnight. Mrs. Overstreet is the best dog sitter ever.

With a bit of time to kill, I Googled Rennie's mother, Margaret Bhatia, just to see what might be floating around in the Twittersphere about her. Quite a bit, as it turned out. During her time as an assistant public defender, she'd handled some high-profile cases, Hugo Throckmorton among her more infamous clients. And I also read a complimentary write-up about her computer security business, which

I had assumed was a mom-and-pop operation, maybe working with local businesses to help protect them against hackers—that sort of thing.

But I underestimated her. The company did that. But more. A lot more, as it turned out. The *South Florida Business Journal* story noted that Tech Proof Security Consultants had landed a lucrative contract with the U.S. Department of Homeland Security, specifically to provide computer security services to the Drug Enforcement Administration's thirteen offices in Florida.

Now that was interesting. The DEA was employing a company to secure their computers run by a woman whose partner was an ex-con who served time for drug smuggling. How could that happen?

I read the story more closely and noticed there was no mention of Hugo Throckmorton. That was curious.

I picked up my iPhone and punched the number for Lester's office. As I hoped, Naomi Jackson picked up. Naomi and I had a complicated history. She'd been the bailiff for a judge who committed suicide after I confronted him about his involvement in a sex trafficking ring. His suicide had devastated her, but she was tough, sharp, and, according to Lester, a hell of a detective.

"Naomi, got a question."

"There's a surprise."

"I could use help with something, and I can't do it from here. I'm waiting for Lester to show up…"

"You at that Alzheimer's place?"

"Yes. I take it Lester's checked in."

"He's good about that."

"Okay, I just texted you a link to a story about a computer business here in town. Is there any way you can look up its articles of incorporation or other official documentation about the business that would show who the principals are?"

"Can I? Of course. I'm a licensed private investigator. Am I looking for anyone in particular?"

"A man, recently deceased, by the name of Hugo Throckmorton."

The line went quiet for a moment, then she said, "Okay, I'm on it. I think I know where this is going. You and Lester have got a tiger by the tail, don't you?"

"Could be."

"We billing this to Tropic Press?"

"Sure, put it on my tab."

"You don't have a tab."

"Well, there's that."

I rang off and double-checked the parking lot to make sure Lester hadn't pulled in while I'd been distracted on the phone. He hadn't. It dawned on me that I'd been sitting here with the motor still running, the AC keeping the car nice and cool, but that seemed environmentally irresponsible, so I lowered the window and turned off the engine. I idly wondered if leaving the car running might be an offense that Mister Manners would punish. Then I ruminated a bit about all his acts of vengeance, and it occurred to me that maybe him being on the prowl was having a salubrious if subtle effect on my behavior. Was I more conscious of bad habits that I needed to clean up? Wasn't that a good thing? Was that why Mister Manners was doing all this, to be a societal change agent of sorts, a one-man army trying to teach us to behave ourselves?

Or was I glorifying a lunatic?

It would be nice if he returned my call so I could ask him that question. Also be good to know if he was the shooter who took out the asshole aboard my boat. Somebody was either out to kill me or protect me. I'd prefer to think maybe it was Mister Manners looking out for me, but that could be a flight of fancy.

And even if it were true, what the hell was he doing snooping around Goodland? Was he spying on me? If so, what for?

The past few days had turned into a raging dumpster fire, not the least of which—setting aside life-threatening gunplay—was Kitty

Karlucci's ghostwriting offer, which she had yet to revisit with me. Then again, crazed hitmen wagging enormous pistols in your face could interrupt anyone's carefully considered agenda.

A car pulled into the parking lot, and I sat up in my seat anticipating it was Lester and Rennie, but, no, just a middle-aged woman in a Cadillac, probably there to visit a relative. I slouched back down and picked up my phone. I had a text from Naomi asking me to call her.

"It's like this," she said. "The company is registered by the Florida Secretary of State's office as a limited liability corporation. Margaret Bhatia is listed as the registered agent and manager. No mention in the state records of Hugo Throckmorton. I'm no expert, but if this was a formal partnership, there should be a record of that, I'd think."

"Huh."

"Also checked Collier County business permits and the Florida Department of Business and Professional Regulation. Same story. LLC. Margaret Bhatia, manager."

"Sounds like they wanted to keep old Hugo's involvement on the down low, doesn't it?"

Naomi said, "Could be. Also could be a simple explanation that I don't see. I'm no expert on business law. I'll make a couple of calls over to the courthouse, ask if there's something I'm missing. But unless you hear from me, I'm thinking, yeah, he was a very silent partner." She rang off.

I glanced up again. Still no Lester. I checked the time on my phone. I'd been sitting in the parking lot for half an hour. Not that long. Just seemed glacial.

With phone in hand, I checked my weather app. Olivia had just been designated a Category 1 hurricane but still following a path that would scrape Florida's east coast. However, the "cone of uncertainty" was drifting westward a bit. But I figured the *Miss Demeanor* was safe enough in Goodland, no need to evacuate. As long as the storm didn't grow any stronger.

I switched to my news apps. *The Miami Herald* was fretting about the Dolphins' quarterback situation. The Orlando paper was reporting on Disney's reopening plans. The *Naples Daily News* noted that more than two hundred people had signed up to speak at the next meeting of the Collier County Commission to protest the rehearing of a proposed mask ordinance, Aggie LaFrance claiming mask-wearing was "unconstitutional and a violation of our sacred rights." As if people had the right to infect one another.

I looked up from my phone. Still no Lester.

A text from Edwina showed up in my notifications.

"You see the latest Mister Manners story out of Key West?"

I scrolled through my newsfeeds until I found it. The *Key West Citizen* was reporting a house tee-peed with dozens of rolls of toilet paper with a note thumbtacked to the front door claiming it was the work of Mister Manners. An enterprising reporter had taken a picture of the note and published it along with the article. It read: "You are guilty of hoarding toilet paper during the pandemic. Your discourtesy has been avenged." It was signed "M.M."

And I now knew, thanks to Linda Henderson, this was not the genuine calling card of the real Mister Manners. His notes actually read: "...your bad *manners* have been avenged."

I knew the *Citizen* reporter who wrote the story. Her name was Hermina Hermelinda Obregon. Her initials—H.H.O.—matched the chemical composition of water, which is why everyone called her Agua. I shot her a text:

"Push the cops on that tee-pee story. It's a copycat."

She texted back immediately:

"You know this how?"

"Can't say but trust me it will be a better story."

Then I texted Edwina back:

"Copycat attack. Happening a lot and deserves own story. On my list. Talk later."

I looked up and another car was pulling in. It was Lester's Tahoe. He and Rennie went straight inside. I stayed in my car and waited.

My phone dinged again. It was Edwina:

"You owe me a column."

"Shit!" I had completely forgotten. I quickly scrolled through my files of pre-written columns that I kept backed up on my phone. Many stories I pursue about the antics of weirdos are datelined from Florida (you fish where the fish hang out). But every now and then I cover news from further afield, including this one from overseas that was too, um, tasty to ignore.

THE STRANGE FILES

Woman Alarmed by Mysterious Krakow Lizard

By Alexander Strange

Tropic Press

This is a test.

There are two images accompanying this article. One is a photograph of an iguana, a kind of lizard. The other is not. Can you tell the difference?

If so, your powers of observation are keener than some. Specifically, better than a woman in Poland who called the authorities when she saw an unusual object in a lilac tree outside her home.

The object had been there for a few days, and the longer she looked at it, the more she became alarmed it might be an iguana.

Why someone would panic when they spied a lizard in a tree is another question entirely, although they are considered invasive species in some locales. Not sure about Krakow.

Anyway, when wildlife officers arrived, ready to do battle with this mystery animal clinging to the limbs of the woman's tree, they found something they concluded definitely was not a lizard.

It was a croissant.

Now, The Strange Files does not hold people up to ridicule.

Unless it's funny. But, really, do you see any similarity? One is a bakery product. The other a reptile.

In all fairness, both are edible. Some people call iguanas the "chicken of the trees." Sources tell The Strange Files that iguanas taste remarkably like poultry, then again chicken itself is almost flavorless, which is why so many things taste like chicken.

But we cannot imagine it tasting anything like a croissant or a Danish, or a donut, or other breakfast treat. After all, it's scaly, not crusty. But who knows? Maybe roll that critter in dough and deep fry it? Let us know if you give it a try.

But, for sure, they don't look anything alike. Can we all agree on that?

The Krakow Animal Welfare Society reported that officers were able to capture the tree-borne creature "bread-handed." They speculate that someone threw the croissant out a window in a half-baked effort to feed the birds. And they assured the woman she did the right thing by calling.

We can only imagine the phone conversation if this had happened in the States, say here in Florida where I live and which is becoming increasingly overrun with iguanas:

911 Operator: What's the emergency?

Concerned Citizen: I'm looking out my window and I think I see a lizard.

911 Operator: I'd be surprised if you didn't. What's the issue?

Concerned Citizen: Well, it's been there for three days.

911 Operator: Probably dead. Let us know if it really tastes like chicken.

STRANGE FACT: You shouldn't feed bread—or croissants—to birds, according to the never-wrong internet. Bread has low nutritional value and moldy bread can kill our avian friends.

Keep up with weirdness at *www.TheStrangeFiles.com*. Contact Alexander Strange at *Alex@TheStrangeFiles.com*.

CHAPTER 37

Goodland, the next day

"So, THIS RENNIE PERSON, she admits the memory card wasn't in the leg lamp after all?"

It was Gwenn on the phone from her apartment in Cascais, Portugal. I was walking Fred home from Mrs. Overstreet's place at the Drop Anchor mobile home park. Mrs. Overstreet had to work today—she's a part-time server at the Little Bar—so Fred would be my wingman as I headed out shortly to meet Lester.

"Rennie now claims her mother removed it from the lamp and hid it somewhere in her condo. Decided the lamp wasn't safe enough. Or some such. It's still a little confusing."

"And she just now found out about this?"

"Apparently. Her story is she visited her mom at the memory care place, and her mom made a joke about the quote-unquote stupid leg lamp. One thing led to another, and her mother told Rennie she couldn't remember exactly where she hid it."

"How convenient. Rennie could say anything she wanted and attribute it to her mother, and how could you prove otherwise? She's throwing her demented momma under the bus."

"Or maybe her mom really doesn't remember."

"No matter, she knew damned well it wasn't in the leg lamp when she sent that killer your way."

"Yeah. I find that a little, hmm, shall we say, nettlesome."

Gwenn laughed. "I'll bet you do."

"My guess is she needed to buy some time, throw that juiced-up enforcer off the scent long enough to find the card and hide it someplace else."

"Like where?"

"I'm getting all this second hand, you understand, but here's the play-by-play:

"I was in the parking lot and Lester showed up and escorted Rennie into the Alzheimer's place. I stayed put. If I'd tried to bluff my way in with them, I would have gotten thrown out anyway."

"Well, in all fairness," Gwenn said, "you didn't have any legitimate business being there."

"Right. Not that I'd let that get in the way, but yeah. So, I cooled my jets some more, and in about half an hour they all came out, Lester, Rennie, Linda Henderson, a deputy, and another detective who arrived shortly after Linda, name of Templeton. You remember him? He stood guard over us in Goodland after those Russians attacked my boat."

"I do. Rugged looking guy. Handsome."

"Hair lip. Stutters. Anyway, Linda took Rennie with her, and they peeled off and Lester filled me in. Apparently, the enforcer was there earlier. Signed himself in as a Mr. Stephen Hawking, claimed to be Margaret Bhatia's life coach or some such, gave them ID, obviously phony. Sometime later, they realized the old lady's missing."

"How'd he get out without anyone noticing?"

"The doors have alarms. They need them to defend against patients wandering off on their own. Somehow, he disarmed one and snuck out the back."

"Good grief."

"Later last night, Lester got an update from Templeton, who—and I didn't know this—he's kept up with."

"Lester's Rolodex is impressive."

"Right. He's excellent at developing contacts."

"And?"

"And short version: Linda drove Rennie home, and when they got there they found the old lady passed out on the couch in the living room—but otherwise unharmed—and the condo ransacked."

"Holy shit. And let me guess. The memory card's gone."

"This is where it gets a little sketchy. And bear in mind this is Lester's version of Templeton's version of Linda's version…"

"Carry on, soldier."

"So Linda immediately called for backup, medics arrive, check out the old lady and conclude she's fine, just intoxicated. She tells everyone a nice young man took her for a ride, and they had drinks and a delightful time, and then she woke up."

"And the memory card?"

"And Linda calls in the Crime Scene crew and they dust for prints and all that and, naturally, she asks Rennie if anything—like say a highly sought after computer memory card—is missing.

Gwenn jumped in: "Let me guess. She asks her mother, "Hey, Mom, where'd you hide that memory card?"'

"Good guess."

"And Mom looks befuddled and says, what card?"

"You're clairvoyant."

"So did they even look for it?" Gwenn asked.

"Rennie told the cops she'd already turned the place upside down looking for it."

"And did she say she didn't find it?"

"No. Her exact words, according to Lester, were, 'It isn't here.'"

"Which is not the same thing."

"And when Linda pressed her on that, Rennie suddenly started feeling woozy—she did take a blow to the head—and said she had to lie down, let's talk later, and, so, things are still murky."

"Murky. Or devious. But wouldn't it be good news if that awful hitman actually found the card?"

"How so?"

"That man, what'd you call him, a juicer? Because he uses steroids?"

"I thought about calling him Thugzilla."

"Whatever, if he found what he was looking for, you don't have to look over your shoulder anymore."

"That *would* be good news."

"Well, I'm the bearer of even more. Good news, that is."

"You've wrapped up your client's case and you're coming home?"

"No and yes. Still have loads more work to do, but I have the outlines of a plan. There's a local lawyer assisting me who will carry the ball for a couple of months until I can return."

"Fan-fucking-tastic."

"Got a flight out in two weeks, which will give me time to get things at this end cleaned up."

"How'd you pull that off? I thought all air travel was suspended."

"It's a special charter. Bunch of Americans here working at NATO. Found out about it from a guy at the embassy who's been helping me. But there's a catch."

"Oh, no."

"Oh, yes. We'll be barracked at Joint Base Andrews for fourteen days of coronavirus quarantine before I can return to Florida."

"Can they make you?"

"Part of the deal."

"What if I drive up and rescue you?"

"My hero."

CHAPTER 38

Naples

Kitty Karlucci was annoyed at Lester for standing her up the day before. He had a good excuse, of course, and it bore directly on why she wanted protection. Still, she was being churlish and told Lester her calendar was full and she couldn't possibly see him until early afternoon. As if the delay would ruin his day.

Lester and I agreed to meet beforehand downtown and talk things over at a socially distanced lunch. Dozens of restaurants line Fifth Avenue South, most with outdoor seating. I picked a new place, Café 6809, where a friend of mine had just started working. Lester ordered a blue-cheese burger with a Budweiser chaser. I selected the chicken Caesar and a Diet Coke.

"Real men don't drink Diet Coke, you know," he said.

"Trump drinks Diet Coke."

"Like I said."

"Will it turn me into a raging narcissist, too?"

"Don't think you can blame the Coca-Cola company for that."

A pink-haired server strolled over to say hello. "That you, Alex? Hard to tell with the mask. But who else in this town would be wearing the Green Lantern?"

"Hey, Gabby. You remember Lester Rivers?"

"Sure do. How could I forget that hat?"

Lester, per usual, was wearing his straw boater. He tipped it toward her and said, "So nice seeing you again. Alex told me you're the lead singer in a band now. What was the name?"

"The Swamp Vixens."

"Fabulous." He extended his elbow, and they bumped.

Gabby had been tending bar at Stan's Idle Hour the day I met Lester, the day a faceless body floated up to the docks setting off an adventure that saw us tied up in a barn at the Rev. Lee Roy Chitango's Museum of Holy Creation, now the site of the Chitango Therapeutic Riding Center where Hector Morales scored his manure.

"You know Mrs. Overstreet, Lester," I said. "Gabby's her niece."

He nodded. "Small world."

Gabby bent down and patted Fred on his little head. He was gnawing on a snack I'd set down next to his water bowl. "Fred's such a good little guy," Gabby said.

"Your aunt loves him."

"She does. She's pretty fond of you, too. She told me once she thinks of you as the son she never had."

I felt my face growing hot.

"You're blushing. That's adorable."

With that, she scampered off, and it was impossible not to notice how her waitress gig was working wonders at toning her calves. It was also impossible not to notice the clutch of maskless men at a four-top across the restaurant and the loudmouth leading their raucous conversation. He was stocky, bald, and sporting a deep walnut tan that screamed "future melanoma patient."

Lester turned to match my gaze. "That's Aggie LaFrance, is it not?"

"How can you tell?"

"I keep hearing the words *hoax* and *take our country back*."

"Ever wonder who we need to take the country back from?" I asked.

"It's whom. And last time I read any history, didn't we steal it in the first place, from the Indians?"

"Indigenous Americans."

"I stand corrected."

LaFrance looked up from his conversation and noticed us staring at him, which, to be fair, is impolite, but nothing a sane, well-balanced person would go to war over. But this was Aggie LaFrance.

We could hear him grumble something to his pals, then he rose from his chair and strutted over to our table. He was wearing jeans, work boots, and an untucked long-sleeved blue denim shirt that strained to contain his prodigious midsection. I could see a bulge on his right hip. Knowing Lester, he wouldn't have missed that, either.

"You got a problem?" he asked, hovering over the table.

"Lester leaned back in his chair, removed his boater, looked up, and smiled. "You mean besides you breathing on us?"

"I could see you talking about me."

Lester glanced at me, a look of astonishment on his face. "Do you know this person?"

I shrugged. "He's probably homeless. If you've got any change give it to him and he'll go away."

"If I give you a dollar," Lester said to LaFrance, "would you wash my windshield for me?"

LaFrance hunched his shoulders. "Think you're smart, huh." He raised his shirttail to expose his pistol. But in so doing he flashed his hairy, distended belly, a sight so appallingly grotesque that my eyes suddenly hurt—probably my optic nerves strangling my retinas in self-defense.

Lester just shook his head. "Glock 17. Be careful you don't shoot yourself in the leg. That trigger can be tricky for amateurs."

Gabby, showing uncommon personal courage, stepped over. "Everything okay here, guys?" she asked.

"Everything's fine," I replied. "Needledick the Bugfucker here was just showing us his pee-pee, weren't you Needledick."

I rose from my chair, towering over him, although with his porcine midsection he might have outweighed me. "Get away from us. And wear a mask when you're in public. Nobody wants your germs."

He still had his right hand on his shirttail by his Glock, and he hovered for a moment glaring at me. This is where things could have become exciting. Florida's infamous "stand your ground" law gives wide leeway for people to use deadly force when they feel threatened. Fortunately, one of LaFrance's buddies scurried over and grabbed him by the bicep. "Come on, boss, don't let these snowflakes get your goat."

LaFrance snarled at us for a moment longer, no doubt expecting us to quiver, then pivoted and stomped off with his little posse.

"Making friends wherever you go, huh, Alex?" Gabby said. She had a slight warble in her voice.

"It's a gift."

"Weren't you worried he might shoot you?"

"Lucky for me a heavily armed licensed private investigator was by my side, right, Lester?" He always carried a .38 Special holstered on his hip, hidden by his Hawaiian shirts.

"What? You thought I might club him with my leg?"

"You *are* carrying, right?"

He shook his head. "Locked in the car. Didn't figure I'd have to shoot my meal."

"Terrific."

"You know, Padawan," he said after Gabby drifted off, "we live in crazy times and we're surrounded by unstable people. Maybe you should think about getting a weapon."

"How many journalists you know carry guns?" I asked.

"Outside a combat zone, none. But it's not like you spend your days in courtrooms or city halls. Let's face it, you manage to get yourself into unusual—and sometimes hazardous—situations more than your ordinary stateside reporter. Partly it's the nature of your work. When you spend your time around weirdos, no telling what can happen."

"Lester, the last time I shot anything it was with my speargun, and I almost decapitated Brett Barfield." Barfield was a Third Eye op who was with us in Key West when we faced down a maniac on Duval Street. I was aiming for the maniac, not Brett. I shook my head. "I'd probably just shoot my eye out."

"Maybe taekwondo, then? There's an excellent dojang in Naples. I've resumed my training there, myself. You should join me."

"I didn't know you were into martial arts."

Lester nodded. "Everyone in the military gets unarmed combat instruction, of course. But I've trained off and on over the years in taekwondo. Earned my first black belt before my little accident in the sandbox." He tapped his prosthetic leg. "Just getting back into it."

"So you could teach me?"

"Better if you attend class. There's much to learn, but if you apply yourself, you could test in three years."

"For a black belt?"

"Yes. First rank."

"How many ranks are there?"

"Nine."

"Okay, Lester, what happens if a first rank black belt, say me in three years, gets into a fight with a higher rank?"

"You get your ass kicked. But here's the thing. By the time you test for your belt, you will have had your ass kicked more times than you can remember. And you learn two important lessons from that."

"Like pain?"

"Yes. You learn that you can handle it. Fear is the biggest enemy in any physical confrontation. Once you know you can take a punch, you no longer fear it. That's a great advantage in any fight."

"What's the other important lesson?"

"You learn that your most powerful muscles are in your legs."

"So you can kick?"

"No, so you can run away."

CHAPTER 39

Port Royal, Naples

PORT ROYAL IS THE ritziest address in a ritzy city, occupying the southern tip of a peninsula bordered by the Gulf of Mexico on the west and the Gordon River on the east. Canals comb through it like watery fingers ensuring that the multimillion-dollar homes and mansions all have access to the ocean.

Some of the Gulf-side estates rival those of Palm Beach, Key Biscayne, and other fabulous Florida hangouts for the rich and richer. Kitty Karlucci's wasn't the biggest manse on the beach side of Port Royal, but it was impressive nonetheless with a sprawling lawn the size of a football field sloping down to a two-story gray stucco heap resting near the water's edge. The double wrought-iron gates guarding the red-bricked drive were wide open, and we drove through.

"Fabulous security you got here," I said to Lester. We had decided to carpool from downtown. I'd left my Explorer on a side street off Fifth Avenue, and I hoped that douchebag LaFrance wouldn't find it and slash my tires.

"Naomi's here," Lester said. "She's running a quick security assessment. I texted her before we left the restaurant and told her to open up."

Lester parked on the circle in front of the entrance, and we climbed a short set of stairs to a pair of massive double doors set in an imposing archway. They appeared to be solid oak, giving the entrance the sturdy feel of a medieval castle. All that was missing was the portcullis.

Before we could knock, the doors groaned open, and Naomi greeted us.

"Gentlemen. So glad to see reinforcements."

"Going well?" Lester asked.

"Just emailed you my preliminary report. Technically, the house has all the bells and whistles. Alarm system. Exterior lights and infrared cameras. Impact glass. Swept it for bugs. It's clean."

"Then how'd that asshat break in?" I asked.

"Did I mention the door locks? They only keep out bad guys if you remember to use them."

Lester said, "This is a user-interface issue, then."

"Yes, and this user is a real piece of work. Good luck." With that, she waved us inside, bent down and patted Fred on the head, then stepped out onto the landing.

"You're leaving?" I asked.

"It's a safety issue. If I'm around her another minute, I think I'll kill her myself."

As we stepped across the threshold, Naomi reached back and grabbed Lester's sleeve. "Hang on a sec. Got that info you wanted."

She opened the portfolio she was carrying, extracted a slip of paper, and read from it.

"The car you asked about was registered in Alabama to one Terrell Robinson, age 25, and the plates were expired. This we already knew. Robinson has since applied for and received his Florida driver's license, and we now have his Florida address in Estero. However, yesterday, I drove there and it's his mother's house, which, apparently, he uses as a mail drop but does not live there."

"You talk to his mom?" Lester asked.

"I did. I told her I got her address from the Department of Motor

Vehicles. She may have inferred I worked there. I asked where I could find her son, and she said that he just rented an apartment in Bonita Springs, but she didn't have his new address yet. She did volunteer that he dropped by most afternoons to pick up his mail. I told her that it was urgent that he get in touch, gave her my number, and left."

"Now what happens?" I asked.

"I'm driving back over there now and staking it out. When Terrell shows up, I'll follow him to his new digs. I assume you want me to stay on this until we track him down, right boss?"

"Yes," Lester said. "This takes priority."

"I'm all over it," she said and trotted down the steps.

"I should have tailed her when she met me in Goodland," I mumbled to myself. I could have at least tried to follow "Boston" home and, if I had, none of this legwork on Naomi's part would have been necessary.

"Shoulda, woulda, coulda." Lester chuckled.

The polished marble entryway led to an atrium, a circular expanse into which you could drop half a tennis court. On the right-hand side was a horseshoe-shaped bar, well-stocked with liquor and wine. To the left, a winding wooden staircase rose to a balcony encircling the yawning space where a voice drifted down from the second floor.

"I'm up here."

Kitty Karlucci was seated behind a broad mahogany desk, one shoeless foot resting on the desktop, the other curled under her butt as she lounged back in what appeared to be a custom-engineered chair. Her PowerBook rested in her lap.

"Nice," I said, looking out her window to the Gulf of Mexico beyond. "Can't imagine how you get any work done with this view."

"It's like anything else, houses, beaches, husbands—they all get tiresome after a while. Pull up some chairs, you two. And I see you brought your puppy. How sweet."

"He's my therapy dog."

"Well, if it *therapees* on my rug, you can buy me a new one."

Lester plopped down in a dark green leather occasional chair across from her desk. There was a small, round table with two accent chairs by the window. I grabbed one of them and dragged it over beside Lester. I looped the end of Fred's leash under one of the legs. He circled his tail twice then collapsed onto the carpet.

"Your associate seemed very thorough," she said to Lester. "But she bitched me out for not locking my doors."

Lester nodded. "She does that."

"Well, she's not wrong. They don't do a fucking bit of good if you don't use them. I'm used to my housekeeper locking up around here, but she's been hospitalized with COVID, terrible thing."

"That's too bad," I offered.

"No shit. I've got no help whatsoever now. Have to do my own grocery shopping. Place hasn't been cleaned in two weeks. I'm overwrought."

Lester and I glanced at one another. Was she being ironic? He shrugged and turned back to her. "I spoke briefly with Naomi when we arrived. I'll read her report completely, but from what she said, your security infrastructure seems sound enough."

"Right. But I want guards. Guards with guns. When can you get them here?"

"The Third Eye, as I explained over the phone, has a security division, and I can have people stationed here within twenty-four hours. I will make myself available in the interim if you like. I should caution you that this is not inexpensive…"

She waved that off with a dismissive sweep of her hand.

"…but you should also know we have reason to believe that the intruder who broke in here could possibly have already found what he was looking for. Although that is far from conclusive."

Kitty beetled her brows. "Oh yeah? What's that about?"

Lester gave her a thorough rundown of the past twenty-four hours ending with discovering Margaret Bhatia in Rennie's condo, which appeared to have been thoroughly searched. "My understanding is that Ms. Bhatia told police the memory card is no longer at her place."

"He found it?"

"That's one possibility."

She had listened restlessly, squirming, her eyes growing big from time to time, occasionally gnawing her knuckles as Lester described the beating, the kidnapping, the missing memory card, and the shooting aboard my boat.

"That's the same gun he pulled on me," she said. "Big fucking pistol. But who the hell fired that shot, the one that grazed his skull?"

I shook my head. "No idea. Cops prowled the marina. No witnesses. No shell casings. Nobody heard a gunshot."

"You got a theory?"

I shrugged. "Assuming the shooter was aiming for this hitman and not me, which is what I want to believe, he would have been a hell of a marksman. I have no reason to believe this other than a lack of other possibilities, but my first thought is Mister Manners."

"Mister fucking Manners!" she screeched.

"He's a former sniper. I know that much about him. I've been reaching out to him. I'm trying to interview him. Maybe he came by to check me out and intervened."

"That seems pretty far-fetched."

"Everything about this is far-fetched, wouldn't you say?"

"There's one more thing," Lester interjected.

"Of course, there is."

"This thug, he attacked Rennie Bhatia right after harassing you, if I understand the timeline correctly. She gave up Alexander, said he had the leg lamp where the memory card was supposed to be hidden, which is how that hitman ended up on his boat. This chain of events traces its roots back to you. The police are aware that I have a client who may have information that would be useful to their investigation, but I have not yet given them your name."

"Where's this going?"

"There's been a shooting, an abduction, assault and battery, and you could provide information to the police that would be helpful to their investigation. You are a material witness."

"What if I don't want to?"

"You should consult your attorney, but you gave this gunman Rennie Bhatia's name, did you not? You told me he was looking for information about Milton Throckmorton, and you pointed him to her because of the business relationship between his father, Hugo, and Ms. Bhatia's mother. Correct?"

"I told you all about that, yeah."

"Well, that could be considered aiding and abetting."

"He was holding a fucking gun on me."

"Yet you didn't call the police when you could have. After a man threatened you with a gun. You called a private investigation firm about security, not to report a crime. The police might find that... uh...curious."

"I don't like cops. And for good reason."

When she didn't expand on this, I said, "And that reason..."

"They call me the Black Widow, right?" she said. She ran her hands through her hair and shook her head as if to rid herself of a chill. "Woman writes murder mysteries and has a succession of real-life husbands buying the farm. Guess what? The police have not always been my best friends. They don't like coincidences, all those dead hubbies. They're a cynical lot. I've learned I have less heartburn when I don't have anything to do with them."

"Of course," Lester said. "And I'm not saying the cops would charge you. But my advice: You'll be better off making a call to the police to get ahead of this rather than letting them piece it together on their own, which they will. And then they will begin to question the assistance you may have provided—even under duress—to this mob enforcer."

Kitty drummed her fingernails on the desktop for a few moments while she digested that. It reminded me of how my boss, Edwina Mahoney, had done the same thing during our recent phone call. Then she pinched her nose, rubbed her eyes, and snapped the lid on her laptop computer closed. Finally, she curled out of her fancy chair and walked over to the window, turning her back to us as she stared out at the Gulf.

"I blame Muriel for all this."

"And who is Muriel?" Lester asked.

"My housekeeper. If she hadn't gotten sick, I wouldn't have gone to that goddamned grocery store, and that fucking Mister Manners wouldn't have vandalized my car, which got this whole shitstorm stirred up."

"So what are you going to do?" Lester nudged.

"It's obvious, isn't it?"

When neither Lester nor I offered to guess, she made it clear:

"I'm firing that bitch and getting a new housekeeper."

"Jesus!" I blurted. "That's a little cold-blooded, isn't it?"

Her back was still turned to us, and I glanced at Lester. He was rolling his eyes. I now understood why Naomi bolted. And I was supposed to work with this sociopath?

She turned around, shaking her head. "Don't blow a gasket, I'm just venting. I won't fire her. It would be terrible PR. Go ahead, give me the number of the sheriff's detective I need to call. Let's get this over with."

CHAPTER 40

Port Royal

FORTY-FIVE MINUTES LATER, a gaggle of detectives was knocking on Kitty Karlucci's front door.

"Be a dear and one of you get that for me, would you?" she said.

"I'm on it," I said.

We were still hanging out in Karlucci's spacious, book-lined study. Did I mention the books? I should have. An entire wall of shelves stuffed with hardback and paperback novels. An impressive collection suggesting a lifetime of reading and scholarship. Until you looked closer. They were all her own titles. Every single one. Multiple copies of each of her Penelope Peach novels. You've heard of ego walls? This was an ego library. Someday soon, a novel I've written for her might grace those shelves. But my name will not appear on the cover, I found out.

While we waited for the cops to arrive, Karlucci handed me a contract to read. I didn't even have to ask, as Gwenn had told me I should. Karlucci had anticipated it.

"You got a lawyer?" she asked.

"Do I ever."

"Have him..."

"Her."

"Have her look it over, make sure you are entirely comfortable. This is a business deal, after all. It needs to be in writing."

"My lawyer advised me that I should ask for this. Looks like there was no need."

"Two of my three late husbands were attorneys," Karlucci said. "One thing I've learned is to always get any deal in writing and always make sure you like the terms. Contracts. Prenups. And wills. Especially wills."

"That's very thoughtful of you."

"And that's the first naïve thing I've heard you say. This isn't for your benefit, it's for mine. When you turn in the manuscript, you will get the balance of your advance. But I will get complete rights to your work product. And there's a deadline, as you will see. My editor is a stickler about deadlines, so I must be as well. Your final check will depend upon timely delivery."

"When will you have an outline for me?" I asked.

"Two weeks from the day you return a signed contract."

"Precise."

"You bet your sweet ass. Make no mistake. Like I said, this is a business."

I LUMBERED DOWN the curving staircase from Karlucci's second-floor office and swung open the front door. Linda was flanked by three other detectives, including Mayweather and Templeton from the Collier Sheriff's Office and a guy named Martinez from the Naples PD. Anything happening in Port Royal would be on the City of Naples' turf, so it appeared the two agencies were working cooperatively.

"Greetings," I said. "Kitty Karlucci asked me to show you up to her study."

"You're what, her butler now?" Linda asked, getting her snark on.

"This place is massive. I wouldn't want you wandering aimlessly in a strange house."

Lester was still reclining in the occasional chair by Karlucci's desk when the detectives strolled in. He held Fred in his lap. Fred loves company, and Lester gripped him to prevent the little guy from running around, pawing everyone's leg.

Mayweather and Martinez marched over to Karlucci and extended their hands. At first, I thought they intended to shake—a definite violation of protocol in a pandemic—but then I saw the business cards they were holding. Kitty took the cards, and Mayweather introduced his colleagues. He gave Lester a brief nod then looked around for a place to sit.

"Shall we talk here?" he asked.

"Sure. Pull up a seat. She gestured to the remaining chair by the window, and Lester, sensing this was his cue to exit stage right, set Fred down and rose to his feet.

"I supposed we should be going," he said to Karlucci, but she wagged her finger at him. "Don't be in a hurry. I want to talk some more about security. Why don't you and Alexander stick around. I might want witnesses to this interrogation."

Martinez jumped in. "We're not here to interrogate you, ma'am. We're just looking for information that will help us find the man who threatened you."

"Ma'am!" Karlucci blurted. "God, I can't remember the last time anyone called me that. It's Kitty. Y'all want a cocktail or anything? There's drinks over there in the corner."

Y'all? I snuck a glance at Lester, and he was rolling his eyes again. Suddenly Kitty Karlucci was getting her Southern belle on. Maybe that's how she charmed all those husbands of hers. The persona switcharoo was a bit disorienting, but I had to admit she was good at it. Both Mayweather and Martinez appeared to be smiling behind their masks. Templeton seemed expressionless. Linda Henderson had lingered by the window, and I glanced her way. She noticed me look-ing at her, and she squeezed her eyes shut for a moment as if she were in agony.

I was happy to stick around while Karlucci spilled her story. I was curious whether the version she gave the cops would match what she'd told Lester. And I was a little surprised that after she ran down all the events of the previous day, not only did she share the identical spiel she gave Lester, but she also added a few details, including the twenty thousand dollars the hitman had relieved her of.

"You say he held you at gunpoint and made you open the safe?" Martinez asked, repeating what she had just told them.

"There an echo in here?" she said, a touch of annoyance in her voice, then caught herself and dropped back into character. "My apol-ogies, detective, I know you're just doing your job." She laughed. "Yes. He had a gun. A very large gun. I think it's called a revolver."

Linda couldn't take any more of the Southern charm. "You write detective novels, do you not?" she asked.

"Why, yes."

"And you don't know the difference between a semiautomatic and a revolver. What do they use in your books, bows and arrows?"

Karlucci's face empurpled, and she stared daggers at Linda. Linda just smirked. "Well, was it a revolver or not?"

"Yes, it was. And it was big. And while there are guns in my books from time to time, my character, Penelope Peach, is terrified of them, and so to stay in character, I avoid knowing much about weapons at all."

"Peach?" Linda asked. "She from Georgia?"

"Why yes she is, darlin'. Atlanta. I may have a copy of one of my books lying around if you'd like one."

Linda rolled her eyes and resumed leaning against the wall by the window.

Templeton asked Karlucci if the gunman had touched anything

in the house, and she nodded and, on impulse, did something very stupid. She reached into her center desk drawer and pulled out a pistol.

"He rifled my desk and tossed this at me, daring me to shoot him, but he took all the bullets out."

"You *own* a gun?" Linda asked, exasperated.

Karlucci instantly realized her mistake but recovered quickly. "Yes, but I've never used it. And it won't do you any good, anyway."

"Why's that," Mayweather asked.

"He was wearing gloves."

Mayweather turned to me. "Refresh my memory. Was the shooter on your boat wearing gloves?"

I nodded. "Yes, that's consistent. I distinctly remember looking at his hands because they were holding that huge gun."

Then I thought of something. "You guys get any prints off those bullets I gave you?"

Mayweather ignored that.

The questioning continued for a while before the cops finally closed their notebooks.

Karlucci had struck me as a cool customer, but she had lost a little of her edge and seemed slightly frayed by the cops' questions. It was clear she was either lying about something or withholding a critical piece of the puzzle.

I wondered what.

CHAPTER 41

Port Royal, Naples

KITTY KARLUCCI SHOWED Alexander Strange and Lester Rivers out the front door and bolted it behind them. Then she walked straight to the atrium bar, pulled out a fresh bottle of McCallum's, and poured herself a half glass, straight up, and swallowed it in one long, continuous gulp.

"Jesus, Mary, and Joseph," she muttered to herself.

Could she have fucked that up any worse? Pulling out that gun? What the hell was she thinking? And trying to charm a quartet of cops with her phony Southern charm, like this was a Penelope Peach book signing or something? All she had to do was play it straight. Just the facts, ma'am. But no, she had to embellish, had to show off.

And flat-out lie.

She saw the looks Alexander Strange had given her. That kid knew something was up. So did that female detective, so young and smug and full of herself. She saw right through her *faux* naivete about firearms. Called her out, and she barely recovered. She could only imagine what the cops said about her after they left.

Well, the last thing she needed was to have a bunch of CSI nerds tromping around, pulling prints, sticking their noses where they didn't belong. Wouldn't you think saying the gunman wore gloves would put that to rest? But no. They insisted on sending a crew. You never know, they argued. And what was she supposed to do then? Tell them to get a warrant? That was the last fucking thing she needed.

Not that there were any actual bodies buried here.

Husband Number One had been cremated after choking to death at their dinner table despite what she told police were her valiant efforts to perform the Heimlich maneuver. But Herman had weighed in at over 300 pounds, well more than twice her body weight. Not her fault she couldn't save him. She'd scolded him for eating too fast. Told him to chew more thoroughly. So what if he died eating one of her home-cooked meals? Could just as easily have happened at a restaurant, right?

Husband Number Two had fallen off a balcony during a vacation to Mexico. Their relationship had been a little rocky. She knew the lecherous pettifogger was untrustworthy when she married him. But he was also something else: very rich. But his indiscretions were getting out of hand. A little second honeymoon would reinvigorate their marriage, she told him. They celebrated with margaritas she mixed herself on the twelfth floor of their resort hotel. Who knew he had such a lousy sense of balance? His two ex-wives and three children screamed bloody murder when the will was read. Tough shit. She'd earned every penny. Millions and millions of pennies.

Husband Number Three. Well, he should have learned how to swim if he was going to go galivanting around the coast of Italy in a sailboat. He'd been the most fun of them all. And by far the wealthiest. He was so rich, she hadn't even bothered altering the will, not like the first two, and was delighted to split the estate with his brother, whom Marty had envied his entire life. He always had to prove himself better than his big brother. Had to have the bigger house, the faster car, the more expensive boat. Well, he had the most lavish funeral, and he beat his sibling to the grave—if a watery one—so he finally won at something.

Gluttony. Lust. Envy. Three of the seven deadly sins and all her exes met their maker because of them. They had only themselves to blame. Mostly. Thank God she had the foresight to ensure their last wills and testaments—and accidental death policies—reflected their undying devotion to her.

So, no, there were no bodies buried here. But there was paperwork. And ghosts.

Kitty poured herself another generous slug of scotch and wandered out to the patio overlooking the Gulf. The sun was inching lower toward the horizon and a cooling breeze was moving onshore, unfortunately carrying with it the lingering scent of dead fish, the consequence of the recent red tide outbreak. That aside, it would be another beautiful, if somewhat malodorous, evening in paradise. She plopped down in an Adirondack chair, kicked off her shoes, and set the bottle of McCallum's by her side on the marble deck.

She was unremorseful about her choices, how she had schemed her way into relationships that paid off so handsomely. Eat or be eaten. It was the law of the jungle. Let the CSI twerps waste their time dusting for prints. After that gun-toting fuckhead left, she'd spent the entire afternoon wiping down every possible surface he might have touched, a chore that goddamned Muriel should have been here to do.

The last thing she needed was for the cops to get a positive ID on him—or, God forbid, catch him. He might rat her out, the entire Mister Manners plot, how she had arranged through that dickhead Milton Throckmorton to have a hitman sent down here in the first place. How they would lure the vigilante into a trap and cap his ass. They might start asking embarrassing questions, like how did she know Milton had mob connections? And what did she know about killing people?

What the hell had she been thinking?

Seven deadly sins. One of them was wrath. And she had let her anger get the better of her. So was pride. She'd allowed her hubris to lull her into behaving carelessly, as if she were invulnerable, beyond the reach of the law. Such foolishness.

But life was a continuous improvement project, was it not? She would learn from this. Maybe even figure out how to use this experience. Perhaps she could work it into the outline she needed to write for Alexander Strange.

Alexander Strange. Damn, but he had broad shoulders. He'd make an excellent playmate. Not husband material, of course—too young, too poor, and not nearly stupid enough. She daydreamed a bit about playing cougar to his cub. The scotch was definitely kicking in, her mind was wandering, and she was enjoying it. Some of her most creative ideas came from sessions like this: scotch and sunsets, a perfect combination for letting the imagination run wild. What was that saying? Oh, yes: Write drunk, edit sober.

Towering cumulus clouds were piling up at the edge of the world, and the sun was slipping behind them, tinting the sky orange. No green flash tonight. She'd only seen it once, that brilliant flash of emerald as the tip of the sun sinks beneath the waves. Most people never see it, try though they might. Or they lie about it.

Gazing at the cloud buildup, she recalled that the National Hurricane Center had revised its predictions for the newly formed Hurricane Olivia's path. The storm was bending westward. Instead of sliding past Florida's east coast, grazing Miami, it now seemed possible it might run smack into the Everglades, maybe even rumble its way up into the Gulf of Mexico. If so, no telling what it might do as the warm soup of the Gulf fueled its fury.

Oh well, she thought. This mansion is impregnable. I couldn't possibly be safer—as long as I remember to lock the doors. She'd finally concluded that she didn't want armed guards running around. The fewer people here, the better. And Lester Rivers, she didn't need him hanging around, either. He wasn't the lackey she thought he might be, not like the gumshoes in her stories. He seemed to have a calculating nature. No, she didn't need him sniffing around. Although she had been flattered by the attention he'd shown her when they first met.

She raised her glass and saw that it was empty. One more, then. She leaned to her side to snatch the bottle of scotch from the deck, but her hand only found air. She looked down. The McCallum's was missing.

What the fuck? She wasn't that drunk, was she?

She twisted around to check the other side of her chair, and that's when she saw him—standing there with a self-satisfied smirk on his face, wagging the bottle at her.

"Looking for something?"

CHAPTER 42

Naples

LESTER AND I HAD JUST pulled out of Kitty Karlucci's Port Royal estate when my cell phone began vibrating. I looked at the screen and, somewhat to my surprise, it was Linda Henderson's caller ID.

"We need to talk," she said.

"And by *we* you mean…"

"All of us. We're over at the bandshell in Cambier Park. We only saw a Tahoe at Karlucci's. You and Lester carpooling?"

"Ten-four."

"Good. We want him here, too. What's your ETA?"

"We're inbound, five minutes out."

I punched off the call and turned to Lester. "They want a confab."

He chuckled. "You surprised?"

"I'm surprised Linda's talking to me at all. She was pretty pissed off yesterday."

Lester nodded. "She didn't like us holding out on her. She made that pretty clear."

"I've thought about that, Lester, and the more I do, the more I keep coming back to one very annoying conclusion: Linda's happy to pal around when it's all on her terms, when she's in control. But the moment I push back—even just a little bit—she reverts to type, all Sergeant Joe Friday."

"Yeah, but I understand where's she's coming from," he said. "They're trying to track down a bad guy. A bad guy who abducted, assaulted, and robbed three women—and who might very well have ended you. Anything—or anyone—getting in their way doesn't flip their pancakes."

"But you persuading Kitty to talk to them, that had to help lower their blood pressure."

"Maybe that's why they're willing to talk now. And speaking of which, Ms. Kitty didn't exactly blow up anyone's skirts with her performance. She seemed off her game."

"Yeah, there's something she's not telling us. Starting with why that gunslinger came to see her in the first place. She was pretty vague about that."

"You don't buy her story? That he was running down all of Milton Throckmorton's acquaintances?'

"And this guy breaks into her house just because he wants to talk to her? Flashes a gun? Steals money from her? No, there's more to that story. You think Mayweather bought that?"

"No."

"They think something's squirrely too."

"I assume that's why they want to compare notes."

"Speaking of which, now that Kitty's fired you, aren't you off the hook, free to share what you know?" I asked.

"Well, for the record, she didn't fire me. She just changed her mind about requiring our services."

"Right. And you still have Rennie as a client. That still ties your hands a bit."

"It would if that statement were correct."

"What's not correct?"

"The part about her being a client. She called me earlier today and said she no longer needs my assistance."

"She say why?"

"It was a very brief conversation. She said she's changed the locks and thinks she's safe enough now."

"Does that scan?"

"Not really."

"I don't trust her, Lester."

"You have every reason not to trust her. She sent that hitman to your boat knowing full well the leg lamp no longer contained the memory card. But our kidnapper outflanked her, grabbing her mom."

"Yeah, but then he let her go."

"What does that tell us?"

"At first blush, I would have guessed it meant he found what he was looking for," I said.

"But, according to what I was told, Rennie didn't confirm that. She was vague. Said it wasn't there, not that it was taken."

"Okay, Lester, but if so, why'd that juiced-up badass give up her mom? Why not keep her as a bargaining chip?"

Lester shook his head. "That's inconsistent, I agree."

"Something else about this nags at me," I said. "Why didn't he search Rennie's place when he was there in the first place?"

"She's a convincing liar, I suppose. He believed her when she said you had it. Bought herself some time."

"To do what?"

"This is just a wild ass guess," Lester said, "but what if her mother had a moment of lucidity and told Rennie where she hid it? Rennie might have needed time to retrieve it. Or something."

"Or something."

Lester shook his head. "Be nice to know what's so special about that card, don't you think?"

"Has to be something valuable."

"Or damaging."

"To who?"

"Whom."

"Whatever."

"I am curious about one thing, Padawan."

"Lay it on me."

"If you think Ms. Kitty's shady, why'd you agree to do business with her, to ghostwrite that book?"

"I haven't said yes. Not yet. I want Gwenn to look over the contract, and I want to think about it a bit more. And whether I take the deal or not, I want to keep that connection open with her until we get this clusterfuck figured out."

"You're stringing her along?"

"No. It could be an excellent opportunity. But first things first, and there are too many balls up in the air. We've got Sniffen shooting up the joint so he doesn't have to give up the leg lamp, which we now understand to have been worthless. We got a mob bagman dead after a copycat Mister Manners attack…"

"Copycat?"

"Yeah, apparently he's spawned a following. We still don't know Throckmorton's cause of death. Could be frog poison. Or something else entirely. And now a New York crime family is showing a hell of a lot of interest in whatever might be on that memory card—endangering the lives of a demented old lady, her daughter, a famous novelist, and lest we forget, the world's most famous weird news reporter."

"I didn't know you were world famous."

"If I say it, it has to be true, right?"

"Anyway, I take your point. We have a lot of players to sort out."

"Right. And I just touched on some of them. I have a hunch that with this many people involved, something will have to break sooner rather than later.

"Why sooner?"

"I've invented a new crime stoppers theory. I call it The Strange Rule."

Lester looked over at me, a perplexed expression on his face. He stared so long I had to signal him to turn around and keep his eyes on the road. "What's The Strange Rule?" he finally asked.

"The time it takes to solve a mystery is inversely proportional to the number of people involved."

"In plainspeak," Lester said, "the more witnesses, the easier to solve the crime?"

"I like my way better. Sounds more scientific. Anyway, we have a big cast of characters, some of whom—I got that right, didn't I, whom?'

He nodded.

"Some of whom may know everything, some who know bits and pieces, but with this many actors on the stage, this hairball ought to start untangling."

"Hairballs untangle?"

"No, I guess not. Maybe gets coughed up?"

"Keep working on it."

"Anyway, the question about ghostwriting for Kitty turns on whether she has any culpability in all this." I paused for a second, then started over. "What I mean, really, is the deal's off if she's in the hoosegow. Be bad for my brand to be affiliated with a criminal."

"You have a brand?"

"I'm the inventor of The Strange Rule. Of course I have a brand."

CHAPTER 43

Naples

CAMBIER PARK IS A LOVELY tree-covered oasis in downtown Naples adjacent to the city's art center. It features a bandshell used for church services, concerts, and clandestine meetings between cops, private eyes, and weird news reporters.

It was dusk by the time we arrived, and the tennis players at the adjacent Allen Tennis Center had retired their racquets for the evening, leaving the park blissfully free from the thunks and pops and cursing of the games next door.

Lester parked his Tahoe on Eighth Street. I leashed Fred, and the three of us walked through the park toward the bandshell where the sheriff's detectives were engaged in animated conversation. Martinez, the Naples PD detective, wasn't invited to the party, evidently.

Fred paused by one of the live oaks and contributed some moisture to the park's ecosystem, then we continued on. Mayweather looked over and spotted us approaching.

"Thanks for coming," he said. "Thought we'd compare notes."

"Always happy to assist our friends in law enforcement," I said.

Linda grunted. "Right."

This was getting old. "Can you please give it a rest?" I said. "Lester shared confidential information with me, and I agreed to protect it.

That's what reporters do. I even protect sources in law enforcement, from time to time."

"Fine."

She said *fine*, but what she meant was *bite me*, but I'd made my point. After all, she was one of those sources in law enforcement whose identity I protected.

"You two have any thoughts about all this?" Templeton asked, drawing us back on task.

"This a two-way or one-way street?" I was still a little peevish.

"Talk to us and we'll see," Linda said.

I turned to Lester. He ran his hands over his bald pate, a contemplative gesture as if he were giving it some serious thought. But knowing Lester, he would already have foreseen this: the cops always wanted to take, not give.

"What would you like to know?" he replied, returning the ball to their court.

Most interviews begin with open-ended questions, softening people up, building rapport, then slowly peeling the onion, layer by layer, getting to the heart of the matter. I knew that. Lester knew that. The cops knew that. And we all knew we all knew. Lester was forcing them to cut to the chase.

"What didn't Kitty Karlucci tell us, for starters," Mayweather said.

Lester chuckled. "The same things she didn't tell us, I'm afraid. Starting with why this gunman broke into *her* house, of all people."

"You don't buy her story?" Templeton asked. "That this tough guy was looking for information on Milton Throckmorton?"

"Oh, I imagine that's true," Lester said. "I don't think she lied about that. It's what she didn't say."

"I told you," Linda said to Mayweather. "We need to press her on that."

"Before you do that," I said, "what's the latest on the missing memory card?"

Mayweather looked to Linda and Templeton, maybe checking their temperature about answering my question, maybe seeing who would be the first one to tell me to go pound sand. Templeton was poker-faced. Linda was chewing her lip.

"Look, guys, we want to get to the bottom of this as badly as you do," I said. "The last few days have been a total shit show. Maybe we can help." Fred seconded the motion with a low "gerruff." Not sure what prompted that. Maybe he spotted a lizard.

Mayweather glanced at Fred then said, "Strictly off the record. Your word this goes no further. Both of you."

Lester nodded.

"Off the record," I agreed.

"Okay, but first tell me about you and Rennie Bhatia," Mayweather said to Lester. "She hired you to find that missing lamp, is that correct?'

"Yes, she hired The Third Eye to recover the leg lamp she had given to her mother's ex-husband, Horace Sniffen. You know the background about all that?"

"Think so," Mayweather said. "She told us he pestered her, said he wanted it back, should have gotten it in the divorce, and to get rid of him she gave him the lamp. Only later she figured out maybe something was hidden inside it when she went through her mother's paperwork."

"Right," Lester said. "An SD memory card. I took the assignment, found the lamp for her…"

"She told us it was both of you," Linda said.

"Yes, Alexander accompanied me, but for another reason."

"What was that?" Templeton asked.

I knew Lester would be reluctant to tell them the real reason—that he wanted to introduce Rennie to me because she might have a friend who knew Mister Manners. So I jumped in to let him off the hook.

"He wanted me to meet her. She had information on another story I'm working on."

"What story?" Linda asked.

"Maybe we can circle back to that later," I suggested.

Linda was giving me a curious look, no doubt wondering what else I hadn't told her. And, of course, what I hadn't shared was how Rennie had put me in touch with Mister Manners' daughter. Linda was already annoyed with me for not giving up Lester's client. When she learned that I had also held out on her about Mister Manners, she'd have a conniption.

Mayweather told Lester, "Keep going."

"Right. Well, we recovered the lam…"

"Where was it?" Linda again.

"In his living room."

"You broke in?"

"No, actually, he left the door open for us."

Which was clever and not entirely untrue. Horace Sniffen hadn't bothered to lock his door when he ran out the back and motored away in his skiff. And he hadn't bothered taking the lamp with him, either—the lamp he went to so much trouble to reacquire from Rennie Bhatia. Which had led us to believe he must have grabbed the memory card hidden in the socket and skedaddled. Why else leave the lamp?

That was before. Now we'd learned the memory card wasn't there after all, that Sniffen had gone on a wild goose chase. That didn't explain why he felt the need to empty his shotgun at us. But maybe he was just having one of those mornings. Might not pay to overthink the motivations of a guy who believed he was reincarnated as a fictional character from a gonzo journalist's fever dream.

Lester was still filling the cops in on our encounter with Horace Sniffen. "You recall a report of shots being fired in Goodland a few days ago?"

Templeton nodded. "Guy's pickup truck was shot to hell with double-ought."

"Horace Sniffen was using the truck for target practice. He ran off when Alexander and I arrived."

Linda said, "That was you guys? He was fucking shooting at you? Neighbors reported seeing two men hunkered down behind that truck."

"A misunderstanding," Lester said. "After all, Sniffen did leave the lamp for us."

"Yes," Mayweather said, "but there was no hidden memory card. You can confirm that?"

Lester nodded. "That's correct."

"Which brings us back to the original question," I said. "What's the latest on the memory card? Has it been found?"

Mayweather shook his head. "Let me ask you," he said. "Do either of you have any information about what's on that card, why so many people are interested in finding it?"

"What? Didn't Rennie tell you? Not even after her condo was trashed?"

"Mayweather gave me the evil eye. "How do you know about that?"

"I know something else, as well. You just referred to multiple parties interested in the card."

Mayweather shook his head. "Slip of the tongue."

Now it was my turn to shake my head. "No, it wasn't, and we all know it."

EARLIER, LINDA HAD confided that the FBI was bigfooting all over the sheriff's case, information she shared on the condition that I not name her as the source. I had promised to protect her, but that didn't mean I couldn't independently confirm the FBI's involvement.

After she had taken off to deliver the toad to the vet on Marco Island, I'd driven to Everglades City to verify that the Feds were at Throckmorton's house, as she had said. The black SUVs with white

U.S. Government plates parked curbside were dead giveaways. I pulled up to the house, then walked to the front door and knocked. A man in his forties with salt-and-pepper hair, a coal-black mustache, and a badge on his belt answered the door.

"You order a pizza?" I asked through my mask.

I could have passed for a delivery guy. I had my usual uniform on—cargo shorts, ballcap, and an obscure band tee-shirt, this one celebrating the musical prowess of Commander Cody and His Lost Planet Airmen. But he didn't buy it.

"Who are you?" he demanded.

I handed him my Tropic Press business card.

"Why's the FBI interested in Milton Throckmorton?" I asked.

He closed the door in my face. But it was all the confirmation I needed.

"I WAS THERE," I told Mayweather. "I spoke to one of the FBI agents at Throckmorton's. It wasn't a slip of the tongue. How about being the stand-up guy everyone says you are and level with us. What's going on with the Feebs? And what did Rennie's mother tell you?"

"We can't discuss that."

"Then what was the point of insisting on off-the-record ground rules if you weren't going to share anything off the record?" My decibel level might have been up a few clicks.

Mayweather shook his head. "We wanted to compare notes with you about Kitty Karlucci. Not open our whole case file to you."

"Can you at least tell us if the M.E. has released Throckmorton's cause of death?"

"Thanks for stopping by," Mayweather replied, ignoring my question. "We have to go now."

He nodded to Templeton and Linda Henderson, and the three of them marched off. I stared at them as they neared Eighth Street and their three cars parked at the curb, side-by-side. Templeton and Mayweather were the first to pull out. Linda hesitated a moment before opening her car door. She looked at me across the park for a moment or two, thinking who knows what. Then she slipped behind the wheel and she, too, drove away.

I turned to Lester. "Everybody's hiding something."

"Speaking of which, that question you asked Mayweather about the FBI. You just stumble across them?"

I shook my head. "Had a tip, went over to confirm it. The FBI's running the Throckmorton investigation."

Lester rubbed his chin as he thought about that. "I'll bet Mayweather loves that."

"Not so much."

He continued: "We know Throckmorton was mob-connected. At least that's what Ms. Kitty told me."

And it's what I also learned from Linda, and that was strictly off the record, so I just nodded.

"And both the mob and the Feds are looking for this memory card. The mob has a jump on it thanks to your new employer, Ms. Karlucci," Lester said.

"You think that's a lousy idea, don't you? Me writing that book for her."

"As you said, you haven't signed the contract yet. And it could be that it's just bad luck she got caught up in this."

"And this thug, he could be in the wind by now."

"Yes, if he got what he wanted."

"Which is why we need to know what Rennie and her mom know about all this. Rennie, who out of the blue fired you. You, the guy who was Johnny on the spot when she was discharged from the hospital, and now she's not talking to you."

"Yes."

"They're afraid, like you said before, aren't they?"

"Yes. And the more I think about it, the more I wonder if I was wrong."

"About the juicer?"

He looked at me curiously.

"That's what I've been calling him. Steroids. You know."

Lester nodded. "Where I was going with this, I'm wondering now if he really did get what he was looking for."

"You're having doubts, why?"

"Because of Rennie's evasiveness with the police when she was asked flat out about it. But also because of something you said and that I dismissed without thinking about more carefully."

"Why he trashed Rennie's place when he could have searched it before kidnapping the old lady?"

"Yes."

"And going all the way back to Horace Sniffen, try this out for size: He knew there was a memory card hidden in the lamp, which is why he wanted it. But when he got it, it was gone. He must know what was on it. But what's it to him?"

"Money," Lester said. "It's always about either sex or power or money. Has to be money."

"Valuable to him?"

"Or someone who might be happy to pay for it."

"Like the mob."

"Or somebody."

"Good thing we're narrowing this down."

We started walking towards his car. "So now what?" I asked.

"Well, I no longer have any clients, so, technically, I don't have a rooster in this fight."

I nodded. "And my real interest is finding and interviewing Mister Manners. All the rest of this has been a distraction."

"Not our problem, anymore," he said.

"We can totally walk away."

"Right."

"So, you can just drop me off at my car, and we'll call it a night."

"Sure thing."

"That's not quitting," I said. "Nobody bats a thousand. Strikeouts are inevitable. You said it, you're out of clients, and I have other priorities. No sin in walking away."

"Can't win 'em all."

"Gotta know when to fold 'em."

"Keep talking," Lester said. "Maybe we'll convince ourselves."

"Yeah, right."

CHAPTER 44

Port Royal

THE SMUG EXPRESSION on the gangster's face evaporated when he heard the doorbell chimes. He flipped the bottle of McCallum's over the low patio railing into the yard below—fucking threw a nearly full bottle of McCallum's away with the top off, the asshole—then pulled out his enormous revolver.

"Goddammit, that liquor's expensive," Kitty Karlucci growled. "What the hell's wrong with you?"

She was furious and frightened. Angry with herself for declining Lester Rivers' offer to spend the night and watch over her place. Such arrogance! When would she learn? And why the hell was this fuckstick back with that big gun of his? Even though she owned one, she really, truly was terrified of firearms, just like her character Penelope Peach.

"Don't answer the door," he said. His voice sounded a little hoarse. Then he coughed. Oh, fucking great, she thought, the bastard's caught the virus. And I don't have my mask.

And then it hit her. He wasn't wearing a mask, either. Which was alarming for more reasons than the pandemic. Now she could identify his face. This was not good, not good at all.

She glanced at the empty scotch glass in her hand. It was one of those moments—either do it or die—no time deliberate. She reared back and hurled it at his head.

Just like when she'd thrown her pistol at him, the gunman didn't flinch. He was way too cool for that. Too in control. Too macho.

But forgetful.

The glass hit him square in the face, next to a line of stitches where a bullet had creased his skull. The glass shattered and fell the patio floor. Kitty Karlucci did not throw like a girl. He should have remembered that.

As he staggered backward, she bolted for the patio railing and hurtled over. She stumbled when she hit the grass, rolled to her feet, and charged through the sprawling lawn toward the beach. She ran as hard as she could, legs pounding, never looking back.

She heard herself screaming, and she could feel tears streaming down her cheeks. Would she hear the shot? Would it hurt?

Just run.

Run!

At the water's edge, she veered right—north—and kept running. There was no point seeking help from her neighbors. Most of the mansions along the Gulf were empty and would be until after hurricane season. She knew that. But would he? Maybe she could head toward one and lose him in the deepening shadows.

She was barefoot and the beach was littered with seashells, and as her right heel landed on the broken edge of a conch, she cried out in agony and stumbled. She looked back over her shoulder, terrified that she would see that fucking monster on her tail.

But he was gone. Was he hiding, waiting to ambush her again when she returned? And who was that at her door ringing her bell? Had she not closed the gate? Goddammit, no wonder she kept getting broken into.

She turned her gaze back to the beach, and to her surprise, a man was approaching. She did a doubletake. Had that fucking gunslinger outflanked her? But no, this was a white guy. Scrawny, long, bleach-blond hair, sunglasses even though the sun had set, and no mask. No wonder the fucking coronavirus was spreading like wildfire with all these morons running around breathing on one another. Although, she reflected, she wasn't wearing a mask either.

Walking now, her right heel on fire from the seashell she'd landed on, she edged closer to the water's edge to put some distance between her and the beach bum. Dead fish littered the shoreline, and she looked down to make sure she didn't add to her injury by stepping on some sharp—and bacteria-infused—bones.

Then it clicked. The beach bum. She'd seen him before. Couldn't quite place where and when, but that face was familiar.

And that familiar face had detoured from his path on a vector straight for her. Before she could scream, before she could run, he grabbed her with his right hand.

His left hand held an ice pick.

CHAPTER 45

Corkscrew Swamp

MISTER MANNERS FELT edgy as he waited for his daughter to meet him at their pre-arranged rendezvous point.

She had insisted on a face-to-face meeting, and he worried it would be unpleasant. She would try to talk him out of it. She would beg him to get psychiatric help. As gently as possible, he would dismiss her pleas, and she would be upset, and he would feel guilty, once again letting his family down.

This wasn't the first time. But maybe it would be the last.

He was sitting in his camper, parked on the edge of a dirt road near Corkscrew Swamp Sanctuary, out in the boonies halfway between Naples and Immokalee. A short time earlier, a sounder of wild pigs had drifted by, either oblivious or unconcerned by his presence. He'd spotted an owl in a nearby gumbo limbo tree. It was hooting, a forlorn sound, a call for companionship. Otherwise, it was quiet. And dark.

After a few minutes, headlights turned onto the dirt road where it branched off Rookery Lane, and in a few moments a car pulled up behind him.

He stepped out of the camper and walked back to the sedan as the car's window rolled down.

"Hello, Missy."

"Hi, Pops."

She wore a big smile, displaying those perfect teeth. Perfect after a small fortune in orthodontic work. She was a pretty girl. And smart. Took after her mother. And that made his heart ache.

Suddenly her eyes got big. "Oh, sorry." She leaned over to the passenger seat and grabbed her face mask and strapped it on. "Can't be too careful."

"Good girl."

"I like your wheels," he said, patting the hood of the Honda Civic.

"Thanks. Now that I got my new job, I don't need to borrow Terry's junker anymore."

"You like that boy, don't you." It wasn't a question, more of an acknowledgment.

"I do. He's a good friend. So, you talk to that reporter yet?"

"You know, I was about to when the damnedest thing happened." He leaned against the car, pulled a pack of coffin nails from his shirt pocket, and fired one up. As he smoked, he told her the story of how he'd discovered Alexander Strange being accosted and how he had intervened.

She was shaking her head by the time he'd finished. "Jeez, you saved his life."

"Yeah, but the bad guy got away."

"You still planning on talking to him? I have to tell you, I got kind of a good vibe from him. Not a jerk. Seemed legit."

"I think so. But there's something strange going on…"

"That's a terrible pun."

"Unintended. This reporter, he's caught up in something, and I think he's in over his head. And it has nothing to do with me. Something else he's involved with."

"One way to find out."

He nodded.

They were quiet for a moment. It was an opening for her to lecture him, all the words he'd been dreading. But she didn't.

"Thanks," he finally said.

"For what?"

"For not…" He found he couldn't talk; his throat had tightened up.

She reached out through the window and patted his hand. "Pops, I'll love you three thousand no matter what. Just don't get hurt. If there's anything I can do to help—well, short of ending up in jail—let me know."

He smiled behind his camouflaged mask. "Well, since you asked, I have a list of ordnance I need." He pulled a sheet of paper out of his back pocket and handed it to her.

"Ordnance?"

"You can read it later."

"Oh, almost forgot, I need you to do me a favor, too," she said.

"Anything."

"Take this." She handed him an envelope. He could feel a small, flat object inside. Rectangular in shape. "My friend Rennie asked me to find a place to keep this safe."

"What is it?"

"No idea. But she seemed worried. Which worries me. I figured, well, if you don't mind…"

"Got your six."

CHAPTER 46

Goodland and Naples

IT HAD BEEN A LONG night, and I slept in. This did not please Fred, who is a creature of habit and insisted on taking care of his morning business at zero dawn thirty. Every. Single. Day. No exceptions for hangovers, sleepovers, or silly humans lacking the good sense to bed down at a reasonable hour.

I ignored his whining and pawing the side of my berth as long as I dared, then leashed him, walked him, fed him, poured him a fresh bowl of water, then crawled back under the sheets for some extra shuteye.

Now my iPhone was buzzing. I glanced at it and the ID showed "Leonardo Strano." Uncle Leo, like Fred, is an insanely early riser.

Well, I only had myself to blame.

LESTER AND I WERE frustrated with the conversation in Cambier Park with the sheriff's detectives. They were all take and no give and had wasted our time. As a reporter, I was used to loitering on the outside looking in when dealing with cops and their cases. But I'd gotten a little spoiled, I suppose, hanging with Linda. Now I'd been cut off. And Lester had, essentially, been fired. Happy campers, we were not.

My first impulse had been to get a drink—or several—but that would have involved sitting at a crowded bar packed with maskless people, which, next to attending a professional wrestling match, was the dumbest thing you can do during a pandemic. Why Florida hadn't permanently closed all indoor dining and drinking—let alone wrestling—was no mystery, though. Science did not dominate governmental decision-making here in the Gunshine State. Money did.

And if Lester was right, it was money that drove Horace Sniffen to retrieve the leg lamp and the prize he assumed it contained. But what about the Feds and the mob? What was in it for them?

"I thought we agreed we were done with all this," I said as Lester drove us to Rennie's place.

"Don't look at me. This is your party. Myself, I could live the rest of my life completely content not to give this another thought. Why, I'm so over it I've almost forgotten where we're going."

"Oh, really?"

"Yes. I'm Zen. I am one with the universe."

"Well, okay then. Let's turn around."

"No fucking way."

The door to Rennie's condo had one of those peepholes at eye level, and we could see the light dim as she peered out to check who would be calling at this hour. We heard a couple of clicks, locks unlatching, then she opened the door a crack.

Fred said hello—"gerruff"—and Rennie glanced down. She bent over and patted him on his head. "How cute." Then she stood up and whispered: "Mom's asleep." I could smell the strong scent of wine on her breath. "Come on in. Let me get my mask."

We stood in the small foyer until she returned from her bedroom and signaled us to join her in the living room. She tottered over to a cream-colored leather couch, where a full glass of white wine awaited her on a coffee table. She seemed slightly unsteady—apparently not her first drink of the evening—which I found encouraging: *In vino veritas*. Maybe we'd get some straight answers out of her. Maybe that's why she let us in. Shields down. Thank you, ethanol.

She wore a small bandage over one eye and a bruise was yellowing on her upper cheek, so if I had been in a more charitable mood I might have attributed her shakiness to the lingering effects of her injuries. Maybe it was both.

"You guys want something to drink?" she offered.

This is where private eyes have it all over cops. "Please and thank you," Lester said. No nonsense about drinking while on duty.

"Alex?"

"Sure. Whatever's handy."

She returned from the kitchen with two more glasses and a half-empty bottle of a New Zealand sauvignon blanc. "Help yourselves." Then she retreated to the kitchen again and returned with a small bowl of water and set it down by Fred, who had curled up at the base of my chair. Fred's not much of a night owl. He was out. But I was impressed with her kindness.

Ordinarily, I'm not a white wine drinker, but any varietal in a storm. I poured a glass for Lester and one for myself and leaned back into a chair of matching cream-colored leather across from the coffee table. Lester wheeled over a chair from an informal dining table and sat down.

I lowered my mask and took a sip. "How are you, and how's your mom?" I figured I'd get the perfunctory part of the conversation over with.

"Mom's down for the count. She has to stay here for two weeks in quarantine before they will readmit her. They're very strict about keeping the place locked down. Got a call, and they're now restricting visitors in light of what happened with Mom. That's the bad news. The good news is she wasn't hurt. He got her drunk, and she passed out. She was fast asleep when we got here."

I was looking around her living room, and if I didn't know the place had been tossed, I never would have guessed. No broken glass.

No cushions slit open. No lingering fingerprint powder. It was immaculate. "You did a nice job putting things back together," I said.

She nodded. "Worked all day. Mom helped. Guy came and changed the locks, added that second deadbolt."

She glanced apologetically at Lester. "I figured that's enough protection."

"Speaking of your mother," Lester said, ignoring her lame effort at explaining why she fired him, "was she able to recall what happened?"

"Surprisingly, yes. She said the man told her he was a doctor and was taking her for a ride. She recalled the conversation clearly. Usually, it's her short-term memory that fails her, but for some reason this stuck."

She took a long pull of sauvignon blanc, then reached over and poured the rest of the bottle into her glass.

"We were worried your mother might have been injured," Lester said.

She nodded. "Yeah, after the way he shoved me around. But he didn't hurt her. Instead, he got her sloshed—I bought a case of this wine from Trader Joe's; well, it used to be a whole case—and he tried to cajole her into telling him where the card's hidden. That's what she said, anyway."

"It work?" I asked.

"By then I'd found it."

"So, what's on the card that's so important?" I asked. I might have come off a little curt.

Rennie instantly picked up on the tone, stared at me for a moment, her brows beetling. She knuckled her eyes and inadvertently rubbed her bandage, which made her wince.

"Look, I'm sorry. That asshole scared me to death. All I could think was finding a way to get rid of him. I should never have answered the door. So, I told him about the memory card, and I said it was in the lamp. The police told me what happened to you and..."

She shook her head and averted her eyes. She might have been genuinely embarrassed. Or it might have been an act designed to spark a sympathetic impulse on my part—*sure you sicced a hired killer on me, but don't cry, you poor thing.* Call me a cynic, but I didn't buy it.

"Come on, Rennie. It's just us chickens here. Cough it up."

"Wha…what?"

"What was on that card? What's so important about it?"

"Like I would know."

"And your mother?"

"She doesn't know."

Rennie rose from the couch and walked back into the kitchen. She opened the refrigerator door and pulled out another bottle of wine, twisted off the cap, and returned with it.

"How could your mother not know?" Lester asked. He was being gentle, soft-spoken, understanding. It dawned on me we were playing good cop/bad cop, and I hadn't even realized it was happening. I was fine with bad cop.

"Hugo Throckmorton gave it to her. Told her to keep it safe. That it had important personal information on it or something, she never knew. Didn't try to find out."

"So where is it now?" I asked. "Did that guy find it when he ran-sacked your place?"

She shook her head. "Couldn't have," she said, gulping a hearty slug of wine. "It wasn't here."

"Where is it?" Lester asked. "Have you turned it over to the police?"

She shook her head again, sending her wavy ebony hair bouncing around her face. "More wine?" She tipped the bottle in our direction, and Lester held up his hand.

She wagged the bottle at me and I said, "It's all yours." Maybe if she drank enough she'd eventually get around to telling us what she did with the damned card.

"Here's the way I figure it," she said after topping off her glass.

"Whatever's on that card must be dangerous. And I don't need that in my life right now. Neither does Mom. She just did Hugo a favor, and we don't need any more involvement in this. My opinion? Hugo always seemed shady. I mean, yeah, he was a drug smuggler in his day. But, you know, there still was always something about him. Shifty."

"So, the card?" Lester asked again. He needed to move it along before she became incoherent the way she was guzzling her wine.

"After I found it, I decided I didn't want to destroy it. And I wasn't even sure if I could copy it, and even if I could that would just double my problems. So, I gave it to a friend to keep for me."

"A friend?" Lester was incredulous. "Did you tell the police this?"

She shook her head.

"Why not?" I asked.

"I'm scared. Mom says she doesn't know what's on the card, says she never did, but what if she just doesn't remember. What if there's something on there that implicates her in something. After all, her business partner was an ex-con."

"Then what'd you tell the cops."

"I told them I didn't have it anymore."

"And they settled for that explanation?"

She shook her head again.

"Detective Henderson, she was mean. Said I had to tell her or I would be in big trouble. But that's crap. How would I be in legal trouble for not giving her that memory card? It's my property, right? What right does she or anyone else have to it?"

"But why would you want to hang on to it?" I asked. "I mean, I get it, maybe it has something about your Mom on it, but you don't know that for sure."

"It's insurance," she said.

I wasn't sure where she was going with that, and I guess she read the puzzled look on my face.

"He called me."

"Who?" Lester asked. "That thug?"

"Yes. He called and said if I didn't give him the card, the next time I wouldn't find Mom alive."

"Did you tell the police?"

"He told me that if I did, or if I gave the memory card to the police, he'd kill both of us."

"So you gave it to a friend?"

"Yes. If anything happens to either one of us, I've left instructions with my friend to hand the card over to the police. And I told him so. He can't touch me now."

Lester was shaking his head. She was naïve. All the mobster would have to do is snatch her mother again and he'd have Rennie over a barrel. And she'd admitted she knew where the card was and that she could get it back. She'd put herself in a box.

I wouldn't have thought it possible, but I now was feeling sorry for her. What a freaking mess. Once again, no good deed goes unpunished. She was here to help her mom, and now mobsters were after her scalp. Assuming everything she'd shared with us was true. If it wasn't, she was a terrific liar.

Now I wanted another glass of wine. I picked up the bottle and poured. I wagged the bottle in Lester's direction, but we waved me off. He was scowling, not liking anything about the situation.

"Let me ask you one more thing, Rennie," I said. "Lester and I have been puzzled why your stepfather..."

"Ex-stepfather..."

"Yes, Horace Sniffen. He had to know the memory card had been hidden in the leg lamp, right? That must be the real reason he wanted the lamp back because he just left it when we showed up. But the question is: How would he know about it?"

She cocked her head and thought about that for a moment. "You know, he helped Mom with her computer security company and got to know Hugo Throckmorton in the process. They became pretty good pals, Hugo and Horace."

Lester perked up. "You agree he had to have known all along?"

She shrugged. "Pretty weird he should show up when he did, right after Hugo's death, now that you mention it."

"And you haven't heard from him since? He hasn't bugged you about the card or anything?"

She shook her head.

I heard a door click open, and an older woman peered around the corner. Rennie's mother. She was medium height, with gray streaks in her dark hair, and as wide as she was tall.

I had wondered why the juicer left her here when he failed to find the memory card. He could have used her for leverage to blackmail Rennie. Now I thought I understood. If Mom had gotten drunk and passed out, he probably didn't have a choice but to leave her unless he wanted to roll her out.

"Is it a party?" she asked.

"Hi, Mom." Rennie scooted over to the far side of the couch and patted it, a signal for her mother to come and sit. She waddled over and plopped down, bouncing Rennie up from her cushion.

"Oh, wine. I love wine." Then she frowned. "But why do I think I shouldn't?"

"You were a little overserved yesterday," Rennie said.

"I was? When?"

"When that man was here. You remember. He said he was a doctor, brought you here. You talked to him about your business?"

Margaret Bhatia frowned again and shook her head. "Nooo." She looked over to Rennie and cackled. "Oh, you! You're joking me again."

Rennie glanced at me and blinked. "This is how it is."

Lester, still sounding patient and sympathetic, introduced us then said, "Do you mind if I ask a few questions?" He addressed the query to Margaret, bypassing any chance Rennie might object.

"Fire away!" Margaret said, sounding chipper. She was looking at Lester, then turned her gaze to me and, for the first time, spotted Fred asleep on the floor by my chair. She took a big breath and pointed. "Oh, how sweet. A puppy. Yours?" she asked.

"I nodded."

"How old is she?"

"His name is Fred, and he's a teenager."

Lester cleared his throat. "We've been talking about your ex-husband, Horace Sniffen. We, uh, encountered him when we got your leg lamp back."

"That stupid thing," Margaret said, now giving Lester her full attention. "You can have it."

"We understand you used it to hide something."

She laughed and slapped her knee. "That's what I told Horace, yes I did."

"What?" Rennie blurted. "Wait. Wait. I thought you got that card from Hugo."

Rennie's face was crimson and I thought she might reach over and throttle her mother. And her mom seemed to be enjoying her frustration. She chuckled again.

"It was Hugo's, alright. A little SD card. He gave it to Horace, and Horace told me to find a place to hide it. And he told me not to tell anyone where. Including him. But I couldn't resist. I told him I hid it in the socket of that stupid leg lamp of his. He about died. It was hilarious. He was ranting and raving, yelling that if anyone turned the light on it would fry the memory card. I about wet myself it was so funny. So, I pulled the plug out of the wall and cut it off with a pair of scissors and Horace nearly had a stroke. He was so upset. He really did love that lamp."

"Then later you turned around and hid the card somewhere else, right?" I asked.

She shook her head and stared at me. Like this was some sort of game and I had to guess the right answer.

I took a breath. What had I missed?

"This is a standard sized SD card we're talking about, right?"

Margaret's head bobbed up and down. I glanced at Rennie and she was rolling her eyes, impatient, like my question was pointless.

"Would that actually fit in a light socket?" I finally asked, silently kicking myself for not questioning that before now.

Margaret's laughed and began bobbing her head up and down. "Good for you. You're the first person to figure it out. Horace never did."

"Oh, for fuck's sake, Mother," Rennie groaned. "You mean all this time…"

"Language!" her mom shot back.

"So, ma'am," I asked, "could you tell us what's on the card?"

She threw her hands in the air. "Who knows? Who cares?"

She sank back into the sofa, drew a deep breath, and exhaled slowly. "I do miss him."

"Miss who, ma'am?" I asked.

"Horace."

"Horace's still alive, you know."

She shook her head. "Not the Horace I knew. He's been gone a long time. Fried his brain. Couldn't resist sampling the evidence."

"What evidence?" Lester asked, now totally confused. I shared the emotion.

"Drugs," of course. "Cocaine, LSD, Ketamine, heroin, you name it. Horace was always borderline personality-wise. But that stuff finally blew his circuits."

"You called it evidence," I said, wondering where she was taking all this.

"Yes. Evidence. Couldn't keep his hands out of the cookie jar."

She saw the puzzled expression on my face.

"Didn't you know? Horace was a DEA agent."

UNCLE LEO WAS ebullient on the phone and eager for an update on the unfolding Mister Manners story.

"It's gotten a little twisted," I said.

"Naturally. You're a magnet for weirdness. You're one of the few people I've ever known who has absolutely, positively found the calling he was destined to serve."

"Writing about crazy people?"

"It's a strange job, but it has to be done."

"Ha, ha."

I updated Leo on all the zaniness that had transpired since the last time we talked, ending with the revelation that Horace Sniffen had been an agent for the Drug Enforcement Administration.

"And he was pals with an ex-con who went up the river for drug smuggling."

"Yes, and who, according to his ex-wife, was heavily into narcotics, himself. And her company landed a big contract with the DEA's Florida operations."

Leo thought about that for a few seconds, then said, "So this mysterious memory card, you thinking it has something to do with drugs, then?"

"Be my guess. The mob's after it. The Feds want it, apparently. Rennie told us before we left that the FBI is searching her computer business today, and they want to interview her, too."

"Taken them a while to get to her, hasn't it?" Leo asked.

"Kind of feels like they're behind the mob on this, playing catch-up. But once Rennie tells them her story, that'll change, and I'm guessing they'll be on the hunt for this mob enforcer, too. And I'm sure they'll make Rennie tell them who she gave the SD card to. She might have gotten away with stalling the local cops for the moment, but I can't see the *federales* putting up with that."

"Not a chance."

"And I've got a pretty good idea who has the card now."

"Who's that?"

"Rennie's best friend is Mister Manners' daughter."

"Oh, for fuck's sake."

"Lester's pulling out the stops to track her down. Hope we can get to her before the Feds."

"Why?"

"Linda Henderson doesn't trust them. The local cops don't like the way they've stuck their nose into the sheriff's business."

"Typical."

"Yeah, but maybe there's more to it. My Weird Shit 'O Meter is pinging."

"Well, not to change the subject, but I have some news."

"Lay it on me."

"Last time we talked, you asked about Sarah and me. You sounded worried."

My heart sank. This was precisely what I was afraid of. Leo was about to crash and burn another marriage, this time with a woman I genuinely liked.

"Oh, Leo," I muttered.

He laughed. Actually chortled. "No, no, Nephew, this is good news. Are you sitting down?"

In reality, I was still lying in bed.

"Sarah's pregnant. And we just found out. It's a girl."

CHAPTER 47

Goodland

"I THINK THAT MEANS I'm going to be a step-brother."

"Nuh-uh," Gwenn said. "A cousin."

"Leo's my biological uncle, right? But since he adopted me, legally I'm his son. So she would be my step-sibling or something, wouldn't she?"

"And I'm my own grandma."

I called Gwenn immediately after hanging up with Leo. With the time difference, it was early afternoon in Portugal. I was slightly alarmed when she answered the phone as her voice sounded a little scratchy.

"I'm fine. Just got a little sinus drainage."

"Not the plague? You're sure?"

"Not to worry." Then she coughed. "Well, maybe I caught a little cold or something. But I've been very careful."

I told her about Leo's news, and she seemed as shocked as I was. "How old is Sarah anyway?" she asked.

"Forty-something, maybe forty-fiveish, not entirely sure. She looks younger than her years."

"That's remarkable. The odds of a woman getting pregnant in

her mid-forties are tiny. And with an older man even smaller. Was this planned?"

"Don't think so. But I have to tell you, I'm a little amped about this."

"Really?"

"I know it's weird and all, Leo having a kid at his age. But, you know, I've never been part of a real family before. It was just Mom and me, then she died. Leo was pretty much a stranger when he adopted me. No brothers or sisters, let alone cousins. Or a father, for that matter. No big Thanksgiving dinners and family gatherings at Christmas. None of that. Now, maybe a family."

"And maybe you'll start a family of your own, one of these days," she said.

"Yes. If only I knew a woman who had an interest in such a thing."

She coughed. Which at first I thought was for comic relief. But it didn't stop, and it sounded like she was about to lose a lung.

"Gwenn, that's *no bueno*."

"Yeah, maybe I'll go get tested."

CHAPTER 48

Marco Island

Señorita Bufo was afraid. So many strange noises. And it was cold. Not like when she was in that dark place, the box with the ice, but, still, it was uncomfortable. She preferred habitats with fresh air and moisture, darkness and warmth, not here, so shiny and chilly.

And lonely.

The bright overhead light especially displeased her. She had excellent eyesight and could see nearly three hundred and sixty degrees—useful for a creature who could not turn her head. And her night vision was superb, which made her an effective hunter in the dark but made the constant glare above her disturbing.

And although her sight was good, it was drawn to motion. It was said that a toad could starve to death surrounded by food if it weren't moving. But there had been no shortage of tasty snacks hopping about her prison. At least she had that going for her.

But once again, she was by herself. No one answered her songs. She felt exposed and vulnerable. And she was deeply unhappy.

Suddenly, she felt herself swaying, and the world outside the bars that surrounded her began to dance. If she could have observed herself from outside the cage, she would have seen a man in a blue outfit lifting the container in which she was imprisoned and walking it out the front door.

The man strode over to a plain white panel van and set the cage holding Señorita Bufo inside it.

He spoke, but his sounds made no sense. A woman standing beside him understood, however, and she told him:

"Take good care of my girl."

"I will, ma'am," the man replied. "No stops, straight to Gainesville."

What Señorita Bufo couldn't know is that the woman was anxious about what might happen to her once she arrived at the University of Florida laboratory. She was promised that all the lab techs needed was a sample of her bufotoxin, that no harm would come to her.

But the woman was concerned that once they saw this creature's size, they might be tempted to experiment on her.

Like her friend Linda Henderson, the veterinarian had grown fond of Señorita Bufo. Of course, she loved animals. That's why she became a vet. But Señorita Bufo was special. Maybe it was her imagination, but she couldn't help but feel a sense of heartbreak in her toad song.

Was that crazy?

No, Señorita Bufo would have told her, that it wasn't crazy at all.

CHAPTER 49

Bonita Springs

LESTER CALLED SHORTLY after I hung up with Gwenn. I told him I was worried that she might have contracted the coronavirus, and I was feeling frustrated I wasn't there to help her.

"Can't help you with that," he said, "but I do have something that will cheer you up. We got a lead on Mister Manners' daughter."

That did perk me up.

"Naomi tailed Terrell Robinson to an apartment complex in Bonita Springs. The office was just closing when she arrived, but she sweet-talked the girl there into confirming Robinson's apartment number—don't ask me how she did that—and that he does, indeed, have a roommate, Her name is Maryanne Mulligan."

"M. and M."

"Yep."

"Any way to check out retired army snipers named Mulligan?" I asked.

"What makes you think he's army? Lots of different sniper teams in the sandbox, not all military, either. Be easier just to go talk to her."

Which is precisely what we decided to do. An hour later, we were sitting in my Explorer at an apartment complex parking lot off

East Terry Street in Bonita Springs, a town just north of Naples in Lee County.

We'd driven around to see if we could spot "Boston's" car, the one with the Alabama tag, but it wasn't there. So we pulled out, found the nearest Dunkin' Donuts, and grabbed coffee and half a dozen glazed, and we were back staking out the joint.

"I'm getting a little nervous about Olivia," I said.

"That's not her name."

"No, the hurricane." I had the weather app open on my phone. "The cone of uncertainty has bent all the way into the Gulf now. I probably should have moved the *Miss Demeanor* up to Tampa or something."

"Or you might be safer right where you are. It's only a Cat 1."

"Hard to know."

"You ever hear the story about the man who wanted to protect his family in the runup to World War Two?"

"Does this have any bearing on what we were talking about?"

"Italian guy. Saw the war coming. Europe would be in flames. So he took out his world map and calculated the very safest spot on the planet, packed up the wife and kids, and sailed to the South Pacific. He'd found a lovely island where they would be far away from the war. Know its name?"

I shrugged.

"Iwo Jima."

"And the lesson, oh Jedi master, is be careful where you hide to avoid wars?"

"Hide with care from hurricanes, you should."

For a guy with a Cajun accent, he really did a mean Yoda.

I finished my doughnut and asked Lester, "How long you figure we'll be here?" It had been an hour, and I was going stir crazy.

"Relax. Could be days. I once was stuck on a stakeout for five straight. Five miserable days and nights in the sandbox without food or water. Couldn't pee, couldn't poop. It toughens you up.'

"You're full of shit."

"As a matter of fact, I was very full of shit before it was over."

Off to our left, we heard a vehicle door slam. I spotted a middle-aged man walking our way from an aging camper van, which seemed familiar somehow, although I couldn't put a finger on it right away.

"Looks like we have company," Lester said.

He was medium height, fit, sandy hair cut short, clean-shaven, best I could tell from the edges of his camo mask, wearing jeans, a plain white tee-shirt, and combat boots. He walked over to the SUV and rapped on the glass.

I rolled the window down. "Howdy," I said. "Why do I think your camper looks familiar?"

He nodded. "Maybe because you've seen it before."

"I'm Alexander Strange, but I have a feeling you already know that."

"What gave it away?" he asked.

"What are the odds of us sitting in the parking lot of Mister Manners' daughter and a complete stranger comes over to say hello?"

He nodded.

"She's not here," I added. "At least her car isn't."

He shook his head. "She's got a new ride since you saw her in Goodland. That's hers over there."

"Ah. And that was you, wasn't it?"

"You're welcome."

"Hell of a shot."

He shook his head. "Glass was thicker than I figured. Had no intention of just grazing him."

He stepped back a couple of paces from the door to give me room to step out, and Lester joined us. "This is Lester Rivers," I said. "He's with The Third Eye. You guys may have been in the service at the same time."

Mister Manners cocked an eye.

"INSCOM," Lester said. Which was militaryspeak for U.S. Army Intelligence and Security Command.

"You buy that in Trashcanistan?" Mister Manners asked, nodding toward Lester's prosthetic leg.

"Half-price sale at the Taliban store."

Mister Manners nodded.

"You follow us here?" I asked. "Didn't spot you."

He shook his head. "How'd you find her?"

I nodded to Lester. "Third Eye wizardry."

"And you're here why?" His voice was even, controlled, but this wasn't just Mister Manners we were talking to. This was "Boston's" father. A trained professional killer who might not be the most stable person on the planet and who would be understandably protective of one of his children.

"We believe—and I'm honestly guessing here—that Rennie Bhatia has given your daughter something for safekeeping. You checked out on the latest, how Rennie was beat up, her mom abducted, all that?"

He was quiet for a moment, then he said, "No. I'm not aware of any of that. But you're going to tell me, right?"

"The item that Rennie may have given your daughter is dangerous. Both the mob and the FBI are after it. The guy on my boat that you shot? It's what he was after. Your daughter possessing it potentially puts her at risk. We came here to talk to her. To check on her."

"That's why *I'm* here."

"Is that wise?" I asked. "Aren't you risking someone making the connection to your identity showing up at your daughter's place?"

"She's my daughter."

He turned on his heels and began marching toward the apartments. We followed him.

"I called earlier. She didn't pick up and didn't return my call," he said over his shoulder. "That's not like her. I need to make sure she's okay."

The apartment complex was a two-story structure, U-shaped, with a swimming pool centered between the two long wings. We walked through one of several entryways to the inner courtyard and approached a set of stairs leading to the apartments on the second story.

We heard a door slamming shut above us, and Mister Manners froze. From our angle, it was impossible to see who was up on the landing. Mister Manners turned and signaled us to follow him behind the stairway, out of sight, lest we be spotted.

Footsteps clomped down the stairs, two people from the sound of them, and as they neared the bottom, the voice of a very agitated woman spoke out.

"You're hurting me, goddammit."

Mister Manners tensed. I'd recognized the voice, too. I glanced at him and put my hand on his chest to hold him back. "Let me distract them," I whispered. "Then you come up from behind."

I rounded the corner, and there at the base of the stairs was the girl I remembered from Stan's Idle Hour and the tall, musclebound thug from my boat with his big fist locked firmly on her left bicep, pulling on her as they stepped off the staircase.

Just like on my boat, he was wearing a black face mask and leather gloves. The coronavirus sure made it easier for criminals to fit right in while they concealed their identity.

"Maryanne!" I greeted them. "Wow, small world, so good to see you again. What are you doing here? Is that your boyfriend you keep telling me about? Hi, my name's Alexander. What's your name? Wow, do you lift weights, or did your shirt shrink on you?"

They froze. The juicer didn't miss a beat. "What the fuck are you doing here?" he growled.

"Thwarting a kidnapping, obviously."

With his right hand, he reached behind his back, no doubt to whip out his monstrous stainless steel revolver, but before he could pull it from his waistband, a pair of highly motivated hands grabbed his forearm and jerked it up from behind into a hammerlock.

He bent over and twisted, and in the process released his grip on Maryanne. I reached over, grabbed her arm, and pulled her away just as Lester rounded the corner behind me, his .38 Special raised and aimed at the center of the kidnapper's body mass.

"Please do something stupid," he said. "I haven't killed anybody in ages." His voice was surprisingly calm and even and yet somehow all the more menacing for it—the voice of a man who meant exactly what he'd just said. The mob enforcer stared at him, and the defiant look in his eyes morphed into something else. He was facing one of his own, a professional killer, only this one had been trained by the United States government.

Mister Manners yanked his arm higher, and the thug winced. We had things totally under control. I had Maryanne. Lester had a bead on the bad guy, and Mister Manners had him pinned.

Then everything fell to shit.

CHAPTER 50

Bonita Springs

I DIDN'T HEAR HIM coming—but Maryanne's eyes bulged—and before I could react, someone slammed into my back, bouncing me into Lester, who buckled and collapsed on the sidewalk, me stumbling over him.

I heard a highly agitated male voice scream: "What the fuck are y'all doing?"

Maryanne yelled back: "No, it's okay, Terry."

Then I watched, horrified, as the mobster rotated out of Mister Manners' grip, pivoted, and elbowed him in the jaw with a ferocious spin move. Mister Manners flew backward onto the stairway, and the mobster whipped out his pistol and swung it toward Lester.

His .44 Magnum erupted, and the concrete next to Lester's head exploded, sending fragments flying. One hit me in the leg. But the real damage was done to Lester, who now was lying prone, his .38 on the ground by his outstretched hand, and blood streaming from his forehead.

Just as the mobster started to sweep his gun toward me, Mister Manners lunged from the stairs and grabbed his arm, pulling it down, and the weapon discharged again. I sprang to my feet and threw myself at him, and my right shoulder slammed into his solar plexus, knocking both men backwards and onto the sidewalk.

The mobster's pistol went flying with the impact, but he rolled over, staggered to his feet, and began running toward the courtyard entrance and the parking lot beyond.

Maryanne was screaming hysterically. Terrell Robinson was shouting maniacally. Mister Manners had hit his head when he fell and was trying to get to his feet, but staggered and sat back down again. Maryanne rushed over to him. Terrell just stood there paralyzed. And Lester was out cold and still bleeding.

I could have chased after the enforcer. And maybe I should have. I had plenty of reasons later on to second guess the decision. But I had only one thought—more of an instinct, really—and that was to help Lester.

He was face down on the concrete, and it took a little effort to roll him over. A wave of relief swept over me when I felt his neck and a strong pulse. I inspected his wound. It was a deep, elongated gash and still bleeding. No way of knowing if it was from a ricochet or flying cement. But his heart was beating, and I could feel his breath. And in a moment, his eyes fluttered and he groaned.

Terrell finally came to his senses and dialed 911. With the two blasts from the mobster's cannon echoing through the apartment complex, it probably wasn't the first call to the police. Terrell started jogging out of the courtyard, still holding his phone and yelling at the 911 dispatcher, trailing the escape route the mobster took. Not sure what he planned to do if he caught him, but at least it kept him busy doing something besides tackling unsuspecting weird news reporters.

Mister Manners, with his daughter supporting him, staggered to his feet.

"Where'd he go?"

"He's in the wind," I said. "Maybe Terrell will spot him. And speaking of being in the wind, you think maybe you should be, too? Cops are on the way."

He shook his head, and I didn't argue the point. Not my job to protect Mister Manners' secret identity, just to interview him.

Lester tried sitting up, then gave up. "Why does my head hurt?"

"You stopped a bullet. Or at least some flying cement."

He touched his forehead and inspected the blood on his fingers. "Red. No gray. That's a good sign."

Mister Manners had his arm draped over his daughter's shoulders, comforting her when Terrell returned to the courtyard.

"You see him?" Mister Manners asked.

"Car was pulling out, two men in it. That dude was in the passenger seat. Didn't get a look at the driver."

"You get plates?" I asked.

"Took a picture." He showed me the image on his phone.

"Text that to me right now." I gave him my number.

It arrived momentarily, and I sent it to Naomi with a message to call ASAP.

My phone began vibrating before I could stuff it back into my cargo shorts.

"That's a getaway car," I told Naomi. "We need to know who owns it. Lester's down. Head injury, but he's conscious, and I think he'll be okay. Can you get on that, then I'll fill you in."

"Ten-four."

"You did good, Terrell," I said. "We're tracking down the car's plates now."

"I'm sorry," he muttered in a deep drawl, his head downcast. "I misread the situation, obviously."

Mister Manners shook his head. "You acted," he said. "That's admirable." Then he turned to Lester. "How is he?"

"He's pretty hard-headed, but we need to get him checked out."

He nodded.

"Hey," I said, "We still going to talk?"

"Yes. I still want to do that."

"You got a name?"

"Why, you think I should get one?"

I guess smartassery ran in the family.

"Maryanne," I said. "How did he find you?"

It was an obvious question. We worked like hell to track her down using the sophisticated resources and shoe leather know-how of The Third Eye. How'd this guy get here ahead of us, and how did he even know to look for her?

She was shaking her head. "I don't know."

"Who knows you live here?"

She shrugged. "I haven't kept it a secret. It's on my driver's license."

So to find her, the mobster just needed to know her name.

That had been our big stumbling block. But not her kidnapper's. I realized I'd asked the wrong question, but even as the words were leaving my lips, I knew the answer.

"So how did he know your name?"

There could only be one answer, Rennie Bhatia.

CHAPTER 51

Naples

LESTER INSISTED THAT I get back to Naples to check on Rennie and her mother. He'd been trying to call her to no avail, and we were both worried.

"I don't need babysitting," he said. "I'll let the medics take a look and then deal with the police. Hit the road or you'll be tied up here for hours."

It was clear the only way the mob enforcer could have even known to look for Maryanne is if he had gotten her name from Rennie. When she didn't answer his call, I immediately punched up Linda Henderson on my iPhone.

"We may have a serious problem," I said the moment she answered.

I was expecting more petulance, but I misjudged her. "Talk to me," she said.

"You need to send someone over to Rennie's. There's a good chance that thug returned. She's not answering her phone, and she and her mother could be in trouble."

"I'm in the neighborhood, but what's this about?"

"Hold on." I let myself into my car, pulled out of the apartment complex parking lot, and aimed the Explorer south toward Naples. I punched the speaker on the phone so I could talk hands-free.

"Lester and I talked to Rennie and her mother last night. We learned that Rennie did, in fact, have the missing memory card in her possession, just not when she talked to you."

"So she didn't technically lie when she told me it wasn't there."

"That's what she says. Her story: She gave it to a friend for safe-keeping. And a few minutes ago, that friend was being abducted by our friendly neighborhood *pistolero* when Lester and I showed up to talk to her."

"Crap. What happened."

"We thwarted him."

"Thwarted."

"Yes. Spenser says that all the time."

"Spenser, who?"

"Never mind. The important thing is the only way he could have learned about her would be if he got her name from Rennie."

I heard her talking on the cruiser's radio. There was some police code I didn't catch, but I gathered from what I did hear she was calling for backup. Then her sirens began screaming.

"Where is this friend of Rennie's now?" Linda asked.

"At her apartment in Bonita Springs. Lee deputies and EMS are on the way. I'm inbound, heading for Rennie's place."

"EMS? She get hurt?"

"No, but Lester did. I think he'll be okay."

"You got an address for her?"

I gave it to her. I knew her next step would be to alert Mayweather. And he would send someone up to Bonita to liaise with the Lee deputies.

"You think our guy is at Rennie's place now?" she asked. "I'm pulling up."

"Doubtful. Last we saw, he was fleeing the apartment complex with a wheelman. Got the tags and sent them to Lee County. If I can text them without driving into a ditch, you'll have them momentarily."

"How far out are you?"

"At least fifteen minutes. You got backup?"

"On the way."

By then, I was at a stoplight at Tamiami Trail and Immokalee Road with a dozen cars and trucks in front of me. I texted Linda the photo of the getaway car while I waited. The light finally changed, but the idiot at the head of the caravan was busy daydreaming or trimming his nails or otherwise engaged in some task far more urgent than actually driving, and we remained stalled. Horns blared, and finally the line of vehicles began inching forward. But by the time I hit the intersection, the light had changed again. Where was Mister Manners when we needed him?

Well, back at his daughter's apartment, of course. Before I left, Maryanne confirmed that Rennie had given her the memory card. So I asked her straight up: "You still have it, right?"

She shook her head. "No. I could tell from the way Rennie acted that it was a hot potato, so, no, I don't personally have it."

Lester, who by then was able to sit up, sputtered: "And what the hell does that mean, exactly?"

That earned him a dirty look from Mister Manners. Guess he didn't like anyone disrespecting his daughter.

"You have to understand," I intervened. "This damned card has been passed around and around, and we have been on a wild goose chase for days trying to find it. Everyone who's had it—or believed to have had it—has been threatened or beaten because of it. The information on the card holds the key to why all this mayhem is occurring, why that thug grabbed you."

"Missy told you, she doesn't have it," Mister Manners said. "End of story."

Well, no, it was hardly the end of the story, far from it, but I didn't have time to debate it with him then and there.

Once again, it seemed, the memory card had been handed off

like a radioactive baton in a deadly relay. I wondered if the recipient understood the danger he or she might be in.

As I pulled into Rennie's condo complex, I spotted three green and whites, including Linda's Interceptor. The door to Rennie's unit was closed. I walked over and rang the doorbell, fearing the worst.

In a moment, the door swung wide. It was Rennie. "Oh, good, now the media's here, too. Come in. Join the party."

In the living room stood Linda Henderson, two uniformed deputies, and Rennie's rotund mother, sunk into the couch in the exact same spot we had left her the night before.

"I thought you might be in trouble," I told Rennie. "Maryanne Mulligan was just assaulted by that thug. I figured he must have gotten her name from you."

She shook her head and gestured to her mother. "Not from me. From big mouth over there. And it wasn't that thug."

"Who, then?"

"Her ex."

"Horace Sniffen?"

"None other."

Apparently, Sniffen had dropped by and Margaret Bhatia had welcomed him in like a long-lost lover and friend, no hard feelings, so glad to see you again, and sure I know who Rennie gave the memory card to. Ironically, Rennie had left her mother alone to visit the Alzheimer's facility to speed up her readmittance.

"How'd he know your mother would be alone?" I asked.

Rennie shrugged. "Got lucky, I guess."

"Any security cameras here?" I asked Linda.

She shook her head. "This is why they teach us at the academy to hang with reporters."

I turned to Rennie. "The reason I asked about cameras is because there might be video showing not only if Sniffen staked the place out waiting for you to leave, but also whether he was traveling alone. That mob guy who just grabbed Maryanne Mulligan had a driver. Be good to know if it was your ex-stepfather."

Even as the words left my lips, I realized something: "But I guess that doesn't make any sense, does it? Sorry. How would they know each other?"

"Oh, they're in cahoots, alright," Rennie said.

Both Linda and I turned to her and said: "What?"

Rennie's head was bobbing up and down. "This one," she gestured to her mother, "wanted to talk some more about dear old Horace last night after you left. She was feeling all nostalgic…"

"I don't like your tone, young lady," her mother snapped.

"Turns out, she remembered something. The night that thug brought her home, plied her with liquor…"

"He did no such thing…"

"…they had an unexpected visitor. Horace."

"Oh, I do remember that," her mother said.

"After tearing the place apart, they must have left together. Of course, mom was passed out by then."

"No such thing…"

I heard a toilet flush off the hallway that led to the bedrooms. In a moment, a middle-aged man with salt-and-pepper hair and a black mustache walked into the living room. He took one look at me and froze.

"I've seen you before," he said.

"Yeah. You owe me for that pizza."

It took him a moment to digest that, then he shook his head. "You're that reporter." He turned to Linda Henderson. "Get him out of here."

Linda had been standing beside the sagging couch suffering under the weight of Rennie's mother; now she walked over to me. "Got a second?" She nodded to the door, and we both stepped out on the condo's landing.

"The Feds finally caught up with you, huh?"

She shook her head. "No comment."

"Was he here when you got here?"

She nodded, then said, "Now, let me ask you something and I want a straight answer. Do you know who has the memory card right now?"

I was tempted to parrot back *no comment*, but we were past fun and games. I shook my head. "No. Maryanne Mulligan confirmed she had it. Past tense. Rennie gave it to her, but she played hot potato with it and handed it off to someone else to hide. No idea who."

"Okay. Mayweather should be there by now. And as soon as I finish up here, I'll join him. You think she'll tell us?"

"All you can do is ask."

"Right."

"You guys looking for Sniffen as well as this leg breaker?" I asked.

She nodded. "Sniffen seems to have abandoned his place in Goodland. It was a rental. He's now officially a person of interest, and we've got a BOLO out for him."

"The plates I sent you. That his car?"

"Yes. Thanks for that. And…" She paused as if trying to sort out what she wanted to say.

"And, what?"

"And that was pretty good thinking on your part, connecting Sniffen and this mobster. I hate to say it, but I'm impressed."

Her cell phone buzzed, and she took the call. I couldn't hear who spoke to her, but her replies escalated from, "Okay." "Got it." "You're shitting me." To finally, "Holy fuck!"

She clicked off, pocketed her phone, and looked me in the eyes.

"You tackled that fucker?"

I shrugged. "It was either that or stand there and let him shoot me."

She gave me a lingering look of appraisal, as if saving my own skin were a surprising instinct.

"Linda," I said. "Rennie's been acting like an idiot. She declined

Lester's offer to have someone watch over her. You guys going to get her some protection?"

She paused for a moment as if, once again, calculating her response. "I think that's being handled, yes."

Then she walked back inside and shut the door behind her.

I piled back into my Explorer and retraced my route to Bonita Springs. By the time I got there, Lester was gone. One of the Lee County uniforms lingering in the parking lot told me he'd been taken to Lee Memorial, the regional trauma center.

That was alarming. I'd hoped he'd be treated for a scratch and turned loose.

"They gurneyed him out," the deputy told me, "but I think they were just overly careful. He was bitching and moaning about it the whole way."

Everyone else was gathered up in Maryanne and Terrell's apartment, and I knew it was unlikely I'd be welcome, so I retreated to my car to wait it out. My plan was to let the cops disperse, then I would sit down with Mister Manners and his daughter and see if I could fill in the blanks, starting with where the traveling memory card was now.

I placed a call to Lester's cell phone, but he didn't pick up. Not a big surprise. He might be getting a CAT scan after a blow to the head. Or, more likely, he might be neck-deep in insurance forms before anyone would see him.

Then I called Lee Memorial's emergency room to confirm his arrival and got the usual runaround, patient privacy, the federal HIPPA Act, yadda, yadda, yadda. Again, no surprise.

It would be pointless to rush up to the hospital just to sit around for hours in the parking lot waiting for him to be discharged when I could be sitting around for hours in a parking lot right where I was.

It was overcast and gusty, and the temperature was in the high eighties. The fronds of the sabal palms overhead were dancing in the breeze, their trunks occasionally yielding to the force of the wind then springing back. In a canal behind the apartment complex, I spotted a pair of river otters playing, not a care in the world. Oh, to be an otter.

I checked my Weather Channel app to learn Hurricane Olivia was still a Category 1 cyclone, but the cone of uncertainty had continued to shift westward, and the eye of the storm was now forecast to scrape Florida's west coast arriving within forty-eight hours.

Elsewhere in the news, a two-year-old Facebook post from a Georgia congresswoman resurfaced in which she suggested space lasers owned by a Jewish financial conglomerate were responsible for setting all the California wildfires. She also had said at one time or another that 9-11 was an inside job, that the school shootings at Parkland and Sandy Hook were staged, and that Donald Trump was secretly battling a worldwide child-sex-slavery ring run by the Clintons.

Closer to home, another loon, Aggie LaFrance, held a maskless rally attended by more than five hundred supporters outside one of his convenience stores in the name of promoting herd immunity. At the rally, he announced that his plan to fill Naples Bay with the largest "Trumptilla" in history had nearly six hundred boaters signed up, with more people joining every day.

It occurred to me that Edwina may have been prescient in suggesting I start expanding my search for news of the weird to the world of politics. Florida Man's got nothing on these bozos.

Linda Henderson eventually showed up. I stayed in my car and watched her walk up to the apartment. After about half an hour, she and Mayweather emerged, followed in short order by another plainclothes officer—a Lee County detective, I presumed—and a couple of uniformed deputies. After a few minutes of chit-chat, they pulled out, and I exited my car and climbed the stairs.

I could hear a heated conversation inside the apartment as I neared the door. It sounded like Terrell was giving someone a piece of his mind. I imagined the recipient was probably Maryanne. And I further imagined Mister Manners' patience being tested.

I decided to save Terrell's life and knocked on the door. The voices went quiet and in a moment, Mister Manners swung the door open, saw it was me, then turned back to Maryanne and Terrell. "Keep packing."

He stepped outside on the landing.

"They're getting out of here?" I asked.

He nodded. "Yes. I have a place where I'm staying. They'll be safe there until we can get this sorted out."

"I assume since you haven't been deprived of your liberty…"

"No reason for them to suspect."

I nodded. "Does Terrell…"

"No."

I nodded again.

"You've got it, don't you?"

He nodded. "I told the police it's in a safe deposit box. I'm supposed to meet them at Fifth Third Bank tomorrow morning to get it."

"You got a safe deposit box?" I asked.

"No."

"So, what's your play?"

"Job One, protect my daughter. Job Two, find this cocksucker and take him down."

"You know what's on the card?"

He shook his head. "Not yet. But I will soon."

"Something you need to know," I said. "That leg breaker? Lester and I have reason to believe he's under contract with one of the New York families to find that card. And he's not the only one looking for it. So's the FBI. This is bigger than one thug running around threatening people. My advice: Turn that card over to the cops."

He studied me for a moment, then said, "I'll take that under advisement."

Then he added:

"Thank you. You and your friend Lester may have saved my daughter's life. I won't forget that."

"I think this makes us even."

He nodded. "If I should need to find you tomorrow, you going to be around that boat you live on?"

"I can be."

"I'll drop by."

"Be nice to know your name," I said.

He nodded. "I'm sure it would."

"Care to share?"

He fished out his wallet, extracted an ID card, and held it up. "Same ID I gave the police."

CHAPTER 52

Goodland

"I FIGURE I OWE YOU ONE, so I'm giving you a heads up. The Medical Examiner's issuing a statement this afternoon you'll want to know about."

It was Linda Henderson. That she was calling at all was a surprise. That she was offering a tip was stunning. I guess she decided we could be pals again.

"Autopsy results in?" I asked.

"Preliminary. He's going to rule it a possible homicide."

"Possible? That's not much of a ruling, is it?"

"It's complicated. Toxicology reports came back, and Throckmorton had trace amounts of—hold on, let me look at my notes—a chemical listed as 5-hydroxydimethyltryptamine, which, his words, 'theoretically could have a causal relationship with the onset of cardiac arrhythmia.'"

"We're talking bufotoxin?" I asked.

"That's my understanding. We got a briefing a little while ago. Although they stressed the amount was tiny."

"So, it could just be a regular old heart attack?"

"What we were told is that Throckmorton was in bad health. He had coronary artery disease, showed evidence of a previous heart attack, and—now I'm paraphrasing—an ulcer the size of Saturn."

"But the M.E.'s not calling it natural causes?"

"Well, there's a wrinkle. Sometime after Throckmorton collapsed in the kitchen—and we were told he was probably unconscious at this point or maybe even dead—somebody messed him up."

"You mean someone broke in?"

"Doors were unlocked, so not technically 'broke in,' but, yes, the M.E. thinks someone attacked Throckmorton after he was already down."

"What'd they do to him?"

"It's unclear right now whether he was still breathing at this point or not, which is why the ruling is preliminary. If his heart had already stopped, it could be a case of defiling a corpse. If he was still on this side of the Pearly Gates, it might have been the final straw.

"What might have been the final straw?"

"Remember that little bit of blood we found on the paper towels? And that the first responders thought maybe he hit his nose when he collapsed? That it was the reason for a small nosebleed?"

"I do."

"Well, when they got Throckmorton back to the morgue, and they opened him up, they discovered something else."

"You're killing me. What already?"

"There's a medical term for it. Something called a transcranial puncture. But in layman's terms, somebody shoved an ice pick through his nose into his brain."

CHAPTER 53

Goodland

I WAS BUSY ON THE PHONE for more than an hour after I hung up with Linda. The first call was with Lester. He had just awakened and still sounded groggy, but other than the stitches in his forehead itching like crazy, he said he was feeling okay.

But his memory was a little fragmented, either from the pain medication or the chunk of concrete that skulled him.

"I remember our talking in the car," he said. "But everything after that is foggy. I think that's when the meds must have kicked in. Strong stuff."

I'D PICKED LESTER up at Lee Memorial after they released him. He'd taken a nasty blow to the head, but no concussion. On the drive back to his place, I'd filled him in on my conversation with Mister Manners at Maryanne and Terrell's apartment.

"I asked him his name, and he pulled out a plastic card with an embedded computer chip that identified him as Hercules Mulligan."

Lester laughed out loud. "Oh, my God."

I thought the name amused him. Hercules certainly was unusual. But that wasn't it.

"Hercules Mulligan was, arguably, the most successful American spy during the Revolutionary War. He reported directly to Alexander Hamilton, and his intel saved George Washington's life at least twice."

"You know this how?" I'd asked.

"Army spy school. Tell me about this ID he showed you."

"Well, it was white, had U.S. Government across the top in blue letters, and an alphabet soup of an acronym that I didn't see all of because of the way he held it. His thumb covered part of the lettering."

"Unquestionably fake."

"What makes you so sure?"

"Besides the fact he's not likely to reveal his true identity? And that name? You suggested earlier that I try to track down any recently retired military snipers. Made a call to a buddy in the Pentagon. Wasn't as hard as I thought it might be. There aren't all that many Mulligans compared to some other names. No hits from any branch of service."

"So, what are you thinking?"

"He's not military. Know who makes the best phony IDs?'

"Guy named Gary when I was in high school."

Lester had smiled behind his mask. "CIA. They run their own assassination teams through their Special Operations Group. No-shit James Bond stuff. Had some dealings with them. That'd be my guess."

"Huh. And if that's so, then Maryanne…"

"Yeah, I'd have some questions about her bona fides, too."

I FILLED LESTER IN ON THE Medical Examiner's ruling that would be announced later in the day.

"Linda says they're anticipating that the news media will go apeshit and jump to the conclusion that Mister Manners is now a killer."

"Is Mayweather connecting the dots that way?" Lester asked.

"No. They're confident Hector Morales was responsible for the manure attack. And they have other evidence Morales was just trying to copycat Mister Manners' moves."

"They going to say that?"

"Yes. They're going to name Hector as a person of interest. They've already got a BOLO out on him."

"They think he's the ice picker?"

"Linda says they've no clue. Not that she asked for my opinion, but I told her I didn't believe it, that my impression of the guy is that he's scared to death the toad he stashed in the freezer might have killed Throckmorton. I don't see him doing anything violent like that, do you."

"No. But he's a handy suspect. And cops like the path of least resistance. If I were Hector, I'd be making myself real scarce."

MISTER MANNERS SAID he would drop by, so I figured I better stick around the marina. The wind had picked up overnight, and I began tightening the *Miss Demeanor's* mooring lines. The success of this exercise assumed, of course, that the dock itself would survive the storm. I noticed that several of the smaller boats had been pulled from the water. It was too late to try to outrun the storm, and where would I go, anyway, with Olivia barreling northward along the coastline? If anything, the hurricane would only get stronger the longer it churned in the Gulf, so tying up on the southern end of its path was probably as safe as it was going to get.

Gwenn FaceTimed me and suggested I evacuate to her second-story apartment in downtown Naples. I had a key, and it might be a smart move. No point going down with the ship if I didn't have to. Plus, I had the safety of my crew to worry about. Fred loved trips to Gwenn's as she always had special treats for him. This would be Spock and Mona's first visit, and it would probably do them some good to have a change of scenery.

I'd scanned the contract Kitty Karlucci had given me and emailed it to Gwenn. "It all looks pretty straightforward to me," she said. "I went online and perused similar deals. They're essentially work for hire contracts, twenty percent upfront, the balance on delivery. The money seems pretty generous given this would be the first time for you doing something like this."

But I could tell by her tone she had reservations, and when I pressed her, she conceded her only concern was Kitty Karlucci, herself. "She does have a controversial history, all those dead husbands. So far, no dead book collaborators, but still, you'd be tying your name to hers, at least in a small way. Something to think about."

The good news was she seemed to have recovered from whatever had been causing her coughing fits the last time we talked.

"It was probably some bug or pollen, I don't know. But no fever. My taste buds are working. I'm fine."

That was a relief.

Edwina also FaceTimed, inquiring about my hurricane prep, and I assured her I would be okay—like I knew anything about riding out a hurricane, having spent all but the last couple of years of my life either in central Texas or Arizona. I briefed her on the latest, including my pending interview with Mister Manners.

"When's the interview?" she asked.

"Not sure, but he confirmed it's still on. I'm hoping he'll drop by sometime today. Maybe I'll learn what's on that damned memory card that has everyone so riled up."

"Good. In the meantime, not to tell you how to do your job, but I read in the *Miami Herald* that whatshername, the Jewish space laser congresswoman, is coming to Florida to stump for Trump. What would you think about interviewing her about all her nutty conspiracy theories?"

"But they're lies."

"Yes, but they're weird."

"True that," I said. "But, Ed, here's the thing. When I write about people jumping in alligator-infested canals to commit suicide, or morons who get shot by their dogs, or even when Mister Manners glues shopping carts to the roofs of cars, it's all strange, but it's also factual."

Edwina interjected, "And when a member of Congress starts blaming space lasers for forest fires, it's also true that she says it."

"Sure. But it's horseshit. Do we want to give it more credibility by publicizing it? Doesn't that trouble you? All these lies are circulating on social media. People are getting conned. And riled up. Shouldn't we be about helping to set the record straight?"

There was a pause on the line for a moment then I heard her exhale. "Yes. Of course. So use it as an opportunity to debunk all that malarky she spouts."

Fair enough, but there was something about Edwina's tone that was off. She was one of the strongest, toughest, and smartest people I knew. Ordinarily, I could push back when I disagreed with her, and she'd give it right back to me. Now, she almost seemed to be pleading.

"What's wrong, Ed? You don't sound like yourself."

Old Ed would have responded with something like: "Spare me your psychoanalysis."

This Ed said, "Nothing you need to worry about."

Which, naturally, worried me.

"We in trouble?" I asked. "Financially?" We'd recently gotten some grants that would allow us to hire some more reporters. I assumed we were in good shape. I was hoping to hear something reassuring.

"It's not that."

Then it wasn't business. Had to be personal. My heart sank. "Umm, Ed, how's your mother?"

She shook her head, and her voice sounded weary when she replied: "She's back in the hospital."

AFTER I HUNG UP WITH EDWINA, I sat down at my small desk and wrote a brief news story about Milton Throckmorton's cause of death, and I filed it to the news service.

I'd asked Linda if she would fade any heat for sharing the Medical Examiner's preliminary results, but she said Mayweather knew and had approved it.

"He agrees we owe you one," she said. I told her I'd keep their names out of it and simply cite "sources" in county government.

And while I was grateful to have the exclusive on this story, I also knew that leaking it in advance of the press conference served the Sheriff's Office's interests. My story emphasized that Mister Manners was not involved in Throckmorton's death, and that would take some of the air out of the story.

It also was no accident they planned on making the announcement while everyone was busy battening down the hatches for an approaching hurricane. Nothing like a busy news day to help bury a story you don't particularly want too much attention focused on.

There were still too many questions they had no answers to—or that they would prefer not to discuss—like how Throckmorton might have ingested bufotoxin and who would want to take an icepick to an unconscious man who might already have been dead? The more attention people paid to all this, the more pressure they'd face to provide answers, to make arrests.

It was in their interest to buy some time.

"So why say anything at all?" I asked Linda. Not that I wanted the cops to clam up, but it was curious.

"No choice," she said. "Medical Examiner's got a bunch of open records requests for the autopsy. No way we can keep a lid on it."

I knew that to be true. One of those requests was from me.

CHAPTER 54

Goodland

I WAS TOPSIDE FASTENING a circular piece of plywood over my shattered porthole. Ever tried cutting a circle with a handsaw? I wouldn't recommend it as a hobby. But with a hurricane approaching, a plastic garbage bag wouldn't do. I needed something sturdier.

"I guess that's my fault," a voice behind me said.

I turned around, and there he was, standing on the dock. I never heard him approaching.

"Afternoon, uh, Hercules, if that's what you want me to call you," I said. As if he hadn't fooled me for one minute.

He was wearing a mask, but I could see his eyes crinkle in a smile. "Call me Herk if you like."

"Whatever you say."

"That piece of glass going to be expensive to replace?" he asked.

"Worth every penny. Saved my life." I finished applying the last strip of duct tape to the outside and would repeat the process from the inside later on.

"Welcome aboard. Cocktail hour's fast approaching. Can I get you anything?"

"Coffee?"

"Coming right up."

We retired to the *Miss Demeanor's* lounge. It was late afternoon, hot, humid, and windy. I had the dockside power connected and the AC running, but I left the hatchway open for extra ventilation. He settled into one of the lounge's two occasional chairs while I brewed a fresh pot of Café Bustelo. Earlier in the year, I had finally ditched my Keurig in a fit of guilt over all the landfill plastic it produced.

When the coffee machine finished dripping, I gave him a cup in the Batman mug. He took it black. I was Green Lantern with a dash of half-and-half. Fred was sipping water out of his Marvin the Martian dog bowl. Three guys drinking from cartoon character containers. Is this a great country, or what?

"So, you give the police the memory card?" I asked. Figured I might as well get right to it.

"Yes. And here's something for you. I think you've earned it." He tossed a thumb drive to me.

"Thank you. You looked at it?"

"It's a line of sixty-four characters, letters—both caps and lower case—numbers, and symbols."

"Sounds like a passcode."

"I looked up encryption passcodes, and you're right. It appears to be a key to decode a 256-bit AES encryption, which I'm here to tell you I have no idea what that means, but I gather it's a very secure way to protect data. Unbreakable."

"Okay," I said. "But where's the encrypted document?"

"Beats the shit out of me."

"Who'd you give the memory card to?"

"That detective, Mayweather."

"Did he ask if you looked at the contents on the card?"

"He did. And I told him the truth. I said no. Because I didn't examine the file on the memory card. I looked at the copy I made."

"Nice. Did Mayweather say anything about the actual document this is the key to?"

He shook his head.

"He fill you in on the history?"

"No. I was hoping you would."

I walked him through the entire shaggy dog story, including how we initially believed the card was hidden in the leg lamp. I told him about Hugo Throckmorton's sordid past, his drug smuggling conviction, and how his recently deceased son, Milton, was rumored to be a bagman for the mob. How the mob's enforcer appeared to be here on behalf of one of the New York families to discover what secrets Milton might have left behind, and how the FBI was also interested in finding the same info the mobster was chasing. How the Feds searched Throckmorton's house and, later, the computer business owned by Margaret Bhatia and dearly departed Hugo.

"The FBI know about the memory card?" he asked.

"I think it's likely they do now. There was an FBI agent at Rennie's place when I drove over to check on her. Hard to imagine she didn't spill her guts."

"So, if I got this straight," he said, "out there somewhere is an encrypted document this is the key to opening. It's an electronic file, which could be hidden anywhere—on a computer, or phone, another memory card, or in the cloud. Right so far?"

"I guess so."

"And it originated with Hugo Throckmorton?"

"That's what we were told."

"But this mobster and the FBI, they seem interested in Hugo's son, Milton, right?"

I saw where he was going with this, and it occurred to me that Mister Manners was more than a sharpshooter—he was a sharp thinker.

"I've thought about that, too," I said. "Seems to me that Hugo might have been doing all this on behalf of his son, the bagman with a history of betraying his clients. Hugo was a trained computer geek and would be a handy guy to know if you needed to hide something electronically."

"And the FBI's already searched Milton Throckmorton's house and his father's computer security company," he said.

"So, for all we know, they've already found the encrypted files, and they just need this key."

He nodded. "And if that's correct, then that would explain why the mob is so desperate to keep it out of the hands of the Feds. It has to contain stuff very damaging to them. Maybe financials, who knows what?"

"But let's not forget," I added, "that one of the players mixed up in this is a retired DEA agent who worked closely with Hugo and Margaret Bhatia."

Mister Manners frowned. "Where does that lead?"

"Not sure. Maybe DEA agents on the mob's payroll? Maybe nothing? But it's hard to ignore."

CHAPTER 55

Port Royal

IT WAS MISERABLE ENOUGH locked up in her own home, but now Kitty Karlucci thought she would really and truly lose her mind if she had to listen one more minute to her cellmate's vapid whining.

"Hector, for the last time, if you don't shut the fuck up, I'm going to crush your skull with one of these."

She walked over to the bottle-lined wall of her wine cellar holding the remains of her Dom Perignon collection. Champagne bottles would be the best for beating someone to death, she figured. The glass was extra thick to contain the carbonated *vino* under pressure.

Trapped in her own fucking wine cellar. How humiliating. Worse, her captors had removed all the glassware and wine openers, and there wasn't a bottle—not a single one—with a screw cap.

But she didn't need a corkscrew to open champagne, so she had been getting pleasantly soused, drinking straight from the bottles, and hiding the empties in one of the cellar's cabinets so that fucking hitman and his execrable accomplice, Horace Sniffen, wouldn't discover her secret.

"I shoulda stayed in Miami," Hector Morales moaned. "*Qué idiota.*"

"That's it, fucker, you're dead."

Kitty opened the cabinet where she'd stashed all the empties and grabbed one by the neck. No sense ruining a full bottle of Dom on this sissy.

Hector raised his hands and his voice, pleading with her. "*No, no señora.*"

"Pipe down, you jackass, and die like a man."

THE DOORBELL HAD rung just as she'd been confronted on her patio by that big leg breaker from the mob, providing her the distraction she needed to make her escape, only to be caught on the beach by Sniffen, who evidently was in cahoots with the mobster.

It had been Hector ringing the doorbell, hoping the sometime girl-friend of his former employer would offer him shelter. Instead, when the door swung open an enormous man in a black mask, bleeding from his forehead, grabbed him by the throat. And shortly thereafter, Kitty joined him in the wine cellar—a converted bathroom, remodeled, expanded, and insulated to keep the wine chilled. A perfect prison.

When he wasn't weeping about cruel fate, Hector had told her about his disastrous trip to Miami. He had hoped to hide, blend in. But he had been spotted shortly after exiting the bus station at Miami International Airport, ironically located next door to a Customs and Border Protection office. Apparently, the Collier County Sheriff's Office had circulated his photo. He had fled on foot, finally making his way to the Tamiami Trail a few blocks away, where he hitched the first ride he could find. Which is how he ended up right back in Naples.

"I'm so stupid," he had confided to Kitty Karlucci.

"You ain't wrong, but I'm in here with you." It was her first and last attempt to console him.

During the hours of their captivity, Kitty Karlucci had kept her ear glued to the wine cellar's door, catching snippets of conversation between the two men. She'd learned how they had teamed up, and that they were now on the run. But even criminals need a place to rest. So why stay in a cheap hotel or the backseat of a rental car when Naples offered mansions by the Gulf? Mansions with safes stuffed with cash. And kitchens full of food.

They had to know she would be missed if this went on too much longer, which meant they'd have to take off at some point. But would they leave witnesses behind? She wouldn't.

HECTOR WAS STILL pleading—loudly—and she was bouncing the champagne bottle in the palm of her hand. "I warned you," she said.

Suddenly, the door swung open, and Horace Sniffen's bedraggled form filled the entryway. "What's all the racket in here?" he demanded.

Kitty Karlucci turned away from Hector to see Sniffen standing there, hands on his hips, and realized this was an opportunity not to be missed. In one step, she was in Sniffen's face.

"Good night," she said, and swung the bottle.

CHAPTER 56

Goodland

THE INTERVIEW WITH Mister Manners took about an hour, including the time we spent establishing ground rules.

"I can't use the Shield Law to protect your identity," I told him straight up. "Once this is published, the cops may come knocking on my door demanding to know who you are. The law allows reporters to protect their sources, but you're a wanted man, so it doesn't cover this situation."

"I assumed as much," he said. "But what about timing?"

"That's negotiable. I can agree to delay the release date of the story. And there's something else we should discuss."

Mister Manners wagged his empty coffee cup at me, and I grabbed the pot in the galley and refilled it.

"Maryanne says you have some grand finale planned. I would love to know what that is. But I have to tell you that if you say you're planning to kill someone or do something violent, all bets are off."

"Then I shouldn't mention it."

"Again, your call. But are you really planning to harm anyone?"

He shook his head. "That's not my style."

"And there's one final thing."

"Sounds like you're trying to talk me out of this."

"Just want to be straight with you."

"So what's this final concern of yours?"

"Your family. If your identity is discovered, your kids will be in the spotlight. Sitting for this interview increases that risk, gives anyone trying to track you down more information they can use. Have you talked to them about all this?"

He nodded. "Yes. I wouldn't be here if they objected. They're on board, and they know there could be some fallout."

"Okay, then. We doing this?"

"Yes."

He had some ground rules, too. Ten questions, no more. Then he had a final statement he wanted printed verbatim. Would I agree to that? I was disappointed with the limit on the questions I could ask, but that certainly wasn't a deal-breaker. But I balked at giving him *carte blanche* for his statement. "I won't promise you that until I see what it is," I told him. "But unless there is some ethical reason why not, I will include it. But to be clear, that will be my decision." He didn't like that but finally consented.

He insisted that I couldn't video or audio record him, and he didn't want any photos taken. That was also disappointing but hardly unexpected. We would conduct the interview with pen and paper only, a blast from the past.

I pulled out the Waterman fountain pen Uncle Leo gave me for my birthday—yes, it's old-fashioned, I suppose, but I love the way the nib glides over paper, how writing with this pen is such an enjoyable tactile experience. I flipped open my reporter's notebook.

"Ten questions," I began. "Let's start with the one thing most people want to know: Why are you doing this?"

My final question to him set the record straight about his identity. I asked him: "Have you shared your real name with anyone?"

He smiled, having guessed a question about his name would be coming in one form or another. He paused for a few moments then answered.

WE HAD WRAPPED up when I heard footsteps on the dock. Since I couldn't peer out of my plywood-covered porthole, I rose and looked through my open hatchway. It was Lester clambering over the gunwale, one hand on his boater, trying to keep it from launching off his head in the wind. The National Hurricane Center was predicting the eye of Hurricane Olivia would pass about fifty miles offshore around midnight. We'd get buckets of rain and some tropical-storm-force winds, but it could have been so much worse.

Mister Manners met Lester at the hatchway, and they fist-bumped. "You feeling okay?" he asked Lester.

"Never better. Slept like a baby. Gotta get me some more of those drugs." He turned to me. "Is it cocktail hour yet?"

"For you, the bar's always open."

I stepped over to the galley to make Lester a martini. The boat was rocking a bit now, and it would get choppier through the night. Might not be a bad idea at all to button up the *Miss Demeanor* and drive over to Gwenn's. I was overdue to water her plants anyway.

Lester's idea of a martini is vodka shaken with ice in a tumbler without ever even thinking the word "vermouth." I prepared his drink and handed it to him. He planted himself across from Mister Manners in the lounge's other occasional chair, the one I had been occupying during our interview.

"Anything for you, uh, Herk?" I asked.

"I'm good. Gotta check on the kids." He rose and strode over to the hatchway. "Don't forget that date I gave you."

I nodded as he stepped out to the deck, climbed over the gunwale, and strode across the marina toward his camper van.

"What date's that?" Lester asked.

"It's the release date for the interview. Can't publish it until after then. It coincides with his grand finale."

"He say what he's gonna do?"

I shook my head. "But he told me to get a front-row seat, I might want to be hanging out on the Jolley Bridge at high noon."

"Mysterious."

"He is, indeed."

I FINISHED TAPING the plywood to my damaged porthole and double-checked the lines. The winds were now gusting up to forty miles per hour, and the *Miss Demeanor* was bouncing around a bit more.

Fred had pretty good sea legs, but like most dogs, storms frighten him, and I knew he'd be more comfortable on dry land. I looked around the boat to ensure I didn't forget anything. I had my laptop, camera, and an overnight kit. I'd packed Fred's food, water bowls, snacks, toys, and his Alpo in his own travel bag. I decided to leave Spock and Mona aboard to watch over the trawler rather than trying to cart them out to the Explorer in this wind. Neither were susceptible to drowning, but Spock, being cardboard and all, could get a little waterlogged. I noticed Mona seemed to be tottering a bit. She has a metal peg that rises from her floor stand into her left heel, and it's been wobbly forever. I gently lowered her to the deck for safekeeping so she wouldn't topple over. I set Spock atop my berth in case the deck got sloshy.

"You have the con," I told him. He said nothing in reply. Typical.

Lester had taken off a few minutes before. He rents a condo in Old Naples, south of downtown, just a few blocks from Gwenn's place. He had a pizza in the fridge, and I told him that as soon as I got Fred settled, I'd stop by for a bite.

Before I could step outside and head for the car, my cell phone rang. It was Mrs. Overstreet.

"Are you and Freddie going to spend the night in the marina?" She asked, her voice sounding a little concerned.

"You worried about Fred?" I asked.

"Not so much. But I don't like storms and I thought that, well, maybe, if you wouldn't mind, it would be nice to have some company."

I knew she wasn't talking about me. "You want Fred to spend the night with you, is that it?"

"Would that be okay?"

"Of course."

If the Weather Service had been predicting a storm surge of any consequence, the answer would have been no. I fact, I would have invited Mrs. Overstreet to camp out with me over at Gwenn's. But I knew Fred would be fine with her.

Which meant I really could just stay aboard the Miss Demeanor for the night with Fred in safe hands. I won't lie and claim that all the bouncing around doesn't bother me, but I could handle it. Fred less so. Gwenn, not at all. She was strictly a fair-weather sailor.

But I had promised Lester I'd stop by, so I threw my things in the car just in case I decided to spend the night downtown and headed out.

As it turned out, it really wouldn't have mattered. I wouldn't be getting much sleep at all.

CHAPTER 57

Port Royal, Naples

KITTY KARLUCCI WAS in good physical condition. Yoga, cooking, and runs on the beach gave her strength, agility, and a physique that belied her age. And she could swing a mean champagne bottle.

It made a satisfying thunk as it collided with the side of Horace Sniffen's head. He collapsed like a felled sapling.

Unfortunately, a very large enforcer for one of the New York crime families was standing right behind him holding a small handgun. Kitty recognized the pistol right away. It was hers. Fucker was stealing her stuff.

The mobster stepped astride Sniffen's prostrate body and pointed the gun in her face.

"That wasn't very nice," he said, his voice raspy.

She froze and the bottle dropped from her hand onto the marble floor. It did not shatter. Champagne bottles are tough.

The mobster wagged the pistol at her. "Back in your cage."

She backed up, bumping into Hector Morales, standing there like a statue, paralyzed in fright.

The gunman knelt down, never taking his eyes off Kitty, and felt for a pulse in Sniffen's neck. He shook his head and rose to his feet. "Looks like that champagne packed a wallop."

"It was self-defense," she said.

The gunman shrugged. "Saved me the trouble. Grab his arms and pull him in there with you."

"Are you kidding me?"

"Pottery Barn rules. Can't have dead bodies littering the place. Fucks up the feng shui." He turned his malevolent gaze toward Hector, who nearly wet himself. "Help her."

"*Si. Si.*" Hector bent over, grabbed Sniffen's wrists, and tugged. The body slid with surprisingly little resistance across the slick marble floor, leaving a smudged red streak in its wake.

Kitty heard a muffled sound coming from outside her line of sight, and the gunman quickly glanced in that direction. Was there someone else in the house?

"Calm down," the thug ordered and then coughed several times.

"Catch the COVID?" she taunted. "You don't sound so good."

He kicked the empty bottle of Dom through the door then shut it in Kitty's face.

"I can't believe it," Kitty mumbled.

"*Si, señora,*" Hector said, trying to mollify his fellow captive lest she recall who she originally intended to bean with that bottle.

Kitty shook her head. It wasn't forcing them to drag the corpse into their champagne-lined cell that she found incredible, although it was certainly disgusting. It was that the gunman didn't at least search the body beforehand.

She knelt to inspect the corpse, then noticed the empty champagne bottle on the floor beside him.

"Step over here, Hector," she said. "Pick that bottle up and stand guard by the door."

He hesitated a moment, then did as she ordered, grasping the bottle by the neck. Kitty smiled. Assuming they got out of here alive, somebody had to take the rap for clobbering Sniffen, and now Hector's prints were on the murder weapon. It had been self-defense, of course, but it never hurts to have a fall guy just in case she needed one.

She began running her hands through Sniffen's pockets hoping to find a cell phone but struck out. Then she patted him down more thoroughly, just like the cops did in her novels, starting with his upper body and working her way down his torso. She paused when she got to his left ankle. There was a lump. She felt her heart skip a beat.

"Our lucky day, Hector," she said.

She rolled up Sniffen's pants leg to reveal a Sig P365 in an ankle holster. She slipped the 9mm pistol out of the holster, popped the magazine, and saw that it was full. There was even a bullet in the pipe.

"Well, Hector, do we shoot out the lock right now and hope for the best? Or do we wait for an opportunity, maybe with better odds?"

It took Hector a moment to identify the hot wet sensation slipping down his thigh.

Kitty sniffed the air. "Oh, for fuck's sake."

CHAPTER 58

Collier Wings Estates

MISTER MANNERS WHEELED his camper van into the hangar and squeezed alongside the borrowed Cessna 172 that now sported four fiberglass pods under its wings, all painted DayGlo orange. A growing stack of ordnance rested underneath each pod waiting to be loaded.

He pushed the remote, and the hangar door began closing. It had been a wobbly ride, the camper getting blown all over the road by the gale-force winds. He stepped out and strode toward the door connecting the hangar to the house. He had left Missy there with specific instructions not to venture outside, to just hang out until police had captured the mobster who assaulted her.

"It'll just be a day or two," he had promised.

She didn't argue. Terrell, however, pushed back, said he didn't intend to "curl up like a fetus," that he had things to do. But he had promised to return that evening.

As Mister Manners reached for the door, he paused. Something was wrong. He did a three-sixty, scanning his surroundings, then it struck him: His daughter's car was missing.

"Goddammit," he muttered to himself. He quickly entered the house through the kitchen and walked room-to-room confirming she was gone. He then checked his cellphone to see if she had left a message. Nothing. However, he had received a text from Alexander Strange asking him to call.

First, he dialed his daughter's number. After several rings it rolled over to voicemail. "Fuck."

What now? He decided to return Strange's call. Maybe he knew something useful. "What is it?" he asked when Strange answered.

"Uh, I just had a small follow-up question I should have asked, but you sound like someone shoved a phone pole up your ass. Is everything okay?"

He thought about hanging up but then reconsidered. Strange was a reporter with his own agenda, and he knew enough about how the news media worked—at least how it was supposed to work—that reporters didn't take sides.

But Strange had been straight with him, even asking whether his family would be alright with the interview before proceeding, which was stand-up. And when Missy was threatened, Strange had thrown himself at the gunman, risking his own life. He was as close to an ally as he was going to get, and he might need help.

"Missy's gone," he said.

"She leave a note?"

He'd been so frantic he hadn't thought of that. He walked back into the kitchen, checked the counters for any stray slip of paper, but found nothing. Then he noticed the magnetic whiteboard on the refrigerator. The kitchen appliances were white, and the blank board blended in unnoticeably. But now in red marker ink was written:

"Shopping for more ordnance. Boston."

Boston. He wasn't a fan of her new nickname and thought her dream of being selected for *Survivor* was a waste of time and a ticket to disappointment. He had always called her Missy and wasn't about to change now despite her bugging him about it.

He looked at his hand clutching the cell phone and remembered he still had Alexander Strange on the line.

"Yeah, she did leave a note. Good call. Said she's out shopping."

"For crying out loud."

"My sentiments exactly."

"Wait. What kind of shopping?"

He started to reply, "ordnance," but he couldn't let on that Missy was in any way helping him with his grand finale.

"Probably the grocery store."

"So, where's the nearest one? I'm surprised they're still open."

"Okay, I see what you're saying. There's a Winn-Dixie just down the road. I'll drive over."

"Hey, let me know, okay? You've got me a little concerned now."

"Will do."

He hung up and redialed Missy's number. Still no answer. Dammit. He wasn't excited about driving in and out of the hangar during daylight hours, but he didn't have a choice. He glanced out the kitchen window. The palm trees were bending steeply in the wind, and the rain was blowing horizontally. Not ideal weather for a top-heavy vehicle like his camper.

He redialed Strange.

"Got a situation here. I can't drive my camper in this weather. I wonder…"

"What's your ten-twenty?" Police code for location.

"I'll drop a pin and send you the gate code."

"I'm en route."

CHAPTER 59

Collier Wings Estates

I HAD JUST PUNCHED in the gate code to enter Collier Wings Estates, where Mister Manners told me he was housesitting, when my cell phone buzzed.

"You almost here?" he asked.

"Pulling through the gate now and heading to your address."

"Just got a call from a detective up in Lee County. They swung by Missy's apartment, but she wasn't home."

"Of course not."

"But her car was."

"What's going on?"

"I don't know. She's not answering her phone. Only thing I can figure is she must have gone back over there to pick up something. We left in kind of a hurry."

"For good reason."

"Detective told me there was no response when he knocked on the door. He was able to peer into the living room and didn't see anything out of order. But I'd asked to be notified if anything seemed amiss. That's why he called."

I looked ahead and saw him standing in the shelter of the front porch of a large one-story house attached to an aircraft hangar. He was holding an elongated leather carrying case of some kind. I pulled to the curb out front. He pocketed his cell phone, sprinted to my Explorer, and piled inside, drenched. He set the case between his legs.

"Reach behind you," I said. "There's a towel in the backseat. Might have a little sand in it from the last time I went to the beach."

He twisted in his seat, scooped up the towel, and began wiping off his dripping face. He wasn't wearing a mask. I opened the center console and pulled out a package of KN95s and handed it to him. He nodded, slipped one out, and put it on.

I turned up the AC to maximum to circulate the air as much as possible. "Where to now?"

"Her place."

I had imagined that when I met Mister Manners I would encounter, not necessarily a lunatic, but someone burning with anger and a compulsive sense of vengeance, driven by events in his own life that had twisted his psyche and caused him to act out. I guessed he would be clever, manic, self-assured, and, most likely, an asshole, although an asshole with some redeeming qualities.

The man sitting next to me was downcast and anxious. A worried father. He might be unbalanced, but that wasn't the face he was showing now.

"What's in the bag?" I asked.

He reached down and raised the bag to his lap and unzipped it so I could glimpse inside. It was a rifle with a suppressor and telescopic sight.

"It's Russian. It's what I used to shoot that fucker aboard your boat."

"You thinking you might need it today?"

"I hope not."

I called Lester, put him on speakerphone, and filled him in on our situation.

"We're en route to Maryanne's apartment right now," I told him.

"It'll be an adventure. The rain is blinding. Let you know what we find when we get there."

"The Lee County detective, he still on site?" Lester asked.

"Yes, he's waiting for us."

Fifteen minutes later, we rolled into the apartment complex. Parked next to Maryanne's car was a plain beige sedan with Lee County plates. Through the rain, we could see two people sitting in the car. We pulled up alongside and looked in.

Sitting in the passenger seat next to the detective was Maryanne.

CHAPTER 60

Naples

"So what was her story?" Lester asked while chewing a bite of pizza.

"In the rush to evacuate her apartment, she forgot her cell phone. She realized it on the way to the grocery store or somewhere—she was kinda vague about why she'd taken off in the middle of a storm. That's why she couldn't reach her father, why she left a note for him instead of a text or something."

"Well, all's well that ends well, right? Pizza's getting cold, dig in."

He had poured us a couple of beers, and I'd dried off after the dash from my car to his doorway. I had a square piece of Crust pizza in my hand, about to devour it, when the *Pirates of the Caribbean* theme song filled the room.

I reached into the pocket of my cargo shorts and pulled out my damp iPhone. ID showed "M.M." Now what? I wondered.

"We have a situation," he said.

"Of course, we do."

"Yeah, the fun never stops. Missy just got a call. Good thing she found her cell phone. Those assholes that grabbed her? They snatched Terrell."

I put the call on speakerphone.

"I'm with Lester. You're saying Terrell has been abducted?"

"They want a straight-up trade. Terrell for the memory card."

"So just give it to them. They won't know it's a copy."

"Small problem."

"What's that?"

"I've got a version on a thumb drive like I gave you. I don't have an SD card or I'd do just that, copy it over. All the stores are closing because of the storm. No idea where to get one."

"Well, you called the right guy. Got my gear with me in the car, including my camera, which uses SD cards, and I have a handful of them in my bag. You remember what brand card, what size?"

"Aren't they all the same?"

"No, there are several different sizes, but I was thinking of capacity."

"Oh. Yeah. Hold on. I took a picture of it. Let me look at my camera roll." There was a pause while he fiddled with his smartphone. "Okay, here it is. It's a SanDisk. Sixteen gigs."

"I'll run and get my bag and take a look. I know I have SanDisk cards. Not sure about anything that small, though. I usually use 128 gig."

"There's an alternative," Lester interjected. "We could call the sheriff, get them to make the copy with the precise card."

"No cops," he said, "or they kill the kid. Missy's going out of her mind right now, terrified. I can't bring the police into this. If something went sideways, she'd never forgive me. And, besides, they don't know I kept a copy. And I don't want them to know because then they'll start asking questions, like who else has one, and that's you, and I don't imagine you want that known by the police right now either, do you?"

"I've already made copies and stored the data in the cloud," I said, "so I'm not concerned about that. Anyway, it's not important right now. I'll burn the data to a memory card for you if that's what you want. But where's all this supposed to come down?"

"Don't know. They're going to call back with instructions. I stalled, told them I hid it and had to go retrieve it."

"Do they know where you are?"

"No, I checked Missy's car for trackers. It was clean. And we weren't followed back here."

"Then how'd they find Terrell?"

"No idea."

"Well, here we are in the middle of a hurricane, but I guess we need to meet somewhere so I can give you the card. I'll make the copy for you while you drive over."

I turned to Lester and he nodded, so I gave him Lester's address.

"We'll be there in half an hour."

"We? You're bringing Maryanne?"

"Can't leave her alone. She's too upset. She's blaming herself for all of this. Thinks she should never have let Rennie Bhatia talk her into taking that stupid memory card in the first place."

"Alright. But think some more about getting the police involved. This could get ugly."

The line was quiet for a moment, then he said:

"Ugly is what I do."

CHAPTER 61

Port Royal

IT WAS APPROACHING nine o'clock at night, and the city was dark. Florida Power & Light had cut the power until the storm passed, a standard hurricane precaution so downed lines don't start fires or electrocute people.

But I could see light through the windows of Kitty Karlucci's house, and the thrum of generators from somewhere in the back of the property reverberated over the howling wind. Naturally, a home this grand would have its own backup power supply. Probably an entire electric utility.

Maryanne insisted on accompanying us, so we put her to work as our driver. She dropped Lester and Mister Manners at the entrance. We figured since they were the marksmen, I should be the delivery boy. By now, Lester would be crouched down, sheltering his pistol from the rain, hidden behind a fountain around which the driveway flowed as it approached the house. Mister Manners would be invisible, secreted in the lush shrubbery fronting the house, his Russian-made sniper rifle trained toward the heavy wooden double doors.

Maryanne pulled up to the entrance, and I stepped out of the SUV and sprinted through the deluge up to the front porch. I watched as she drove out the open gate where she was to park on the edge of Gordon Drive.

Why had the gunman selected Kitty Karlucci's mansion as the place for the exchange? Was she okay? Burning questions with no answers. The mobster had given Mister Manners the address with no explanation.

When that call came, I insisted we call the police. But Mister Manners—and, surprisingly, Lester—argued against it. Their reasoning boiled down to this: The two of them had better training—and more experience—than the local cops in dealing with a possible hostage situation. Bringing in the police might further endanger Terrell. And we had no time for that. We had to get going.

And that's what we did.

I took a deep breath and pushed the doorbell button. The entryway provided a bit of shelter from the wind and rain, but not much. I waited a few seconds then punched the doorbell again. I repeated the process several times, but the doors remained closed and I could hear no activity inside. But with the roaring wind around me, that was unsurprising.

I hadn't expected the doors to swing open and the juicer to just walk right out, of course. But this was taking even longer than I expected. I pushed the button again and continued to wait. I was now thoroughly drenched. And where I had been filled with anxiety when we first pulled up, that emotion had been replaced with irritation.

Come on, fuckhead. Let's get this party started.

Then I heard a cough off to my right in the darkness.

Finally.

"You should get that checked out," I said.

"Where're your friends?"

I ignored his question. "Is it true the .44 Magnum is the world's most powerful handgun? Oh, but you lost yours, didn't you?"

He coughed again but didn't take the bait. I had hoped to get him talking, make it easier for Lester and Mister Manners to get a bead on his location. But he was playing it smart, hiding in the shadows, avoiding the light from the window. On the other hand, he had chosen to approach from the north, which meant he was facing the southerly onslaught of wind and rain. Not so smart.

He coughed again, this time for what seemed like a full ten seconds. I thought I could see faint motion in the darkness. Not enough detail to tell if he was alone or if Terrell was with him. It would have been nice if we had night vision goggles, but you can't have everything.

"Really, dude, that sounds bad. You should probably lay off the juice. You're just feeding the virus."

He stopped hacking long enough to croak, "Inside."

I shook my head. "Not a chance."

Anticipating this response might not please him, I continued:

"Remember that head shot through the porthole of my boat? Trained sniper." I raised my voice to ensure both Lester and Mister Manners could hear me above the howling storm. "You're in his sights right now. He has night vision. And he's close enough he can hear every word."

That wasn't entirely a lie. All humans have night vision to one degree or another. It just isn't very good.

I'd been standing facing him, taking the brunt of the rain and wind on my back. Now I turned and gestured toward his left as if that's where the sniper was in hiding. "Come on out of the shadows. Let's get this done."

And he might have. Except at that moment, we were startled when gunshots exploded inside the house.

I reflexively threw myself sideways away from him, hoping against hope I was faster than a speeding bullet. As I hit the patio brick, I saw Mister Manners rise from the bushes, his sniper rifle trained in the mobster's direction. Lester burst from behind the fountain and sprinted toward us. I glanced over to where the mobster's voice had come from, but it was impenetrably dark.

And the only sounds were the fury of the wind, the crackling of the palm fronds above our heads, and a woman's voice inside the mansion screaming, "Come out, you cocksucker, I'm gonna blow your balls off!"

CHAPTER 62

Port Royal

IT WAS MIDNIGHT, AND if the forecasters were correct, the eye of the storm would be directly off the coast by now, fifty miles out.

It was howling outside, and the rain smacked the impact glass of the mansion's windows like buckshot—a sound eerily reminiscent of Horace Sniffen's shotgun blasts when they pelted the truck Lester and I had hidden behind.

The difference was Lester and I were still on the green side of the grass. Not so Horace Sniffen, a.k.a., the reincarnated Raoul Duke.

"What happened to him?" I asked Kitty.

"Champagne disagreed with him."

Which wasn't an answer. His scalp was bloody, and an empty bottle of Dom Perignon was lying next to his corpse in the wine cellar.

"So, who clobbered him?" I asked.

Kitty replied, "Let's just say he wouldn't be there right now if it weren't for Hector, right Hector?"

"*Si, Señora Kitty*. Whatever you say."

Hector had a nervous tick in his voice. Was it fear? After all, the guy went into hiding after Milton Throckmorton croaked. Maybe he was nervous about yet another possible murder rap. Or was it something else? Who would be more likely to club somebody, a fraidy cat like Hector or the Black Widow herself? I made a mental note to grill Hector about that if I could catch him alone.

Kitty told us how she found the pistol on Sniffen's body and that when she heard the doorbell ringing she realized it was her chance to make a break for it. The shots we heard were her shooting the wine cellar's lock to pieces.

Hector and Kitty escaped. But Terrell Robinson was unaccounted for, and Maryanne was miserable about that.

"Did you see or hear anyone else here?" she asked Kitty.

"I heard that asshat talking to somebody, telling him to pipe down or something, so I assume there was someone else here. But we couldn't see."

Hector had been embarrassed about his soiled pants, but once again Mister Manners impressed me with his fundamental decency.

"Go get yourself cleaned up, son," he told Hector. "You're not the first guy to brown his skivvies. Happens all the time. Nothing to be ashamed of."

Kitty told Hector where to find something to change into—maybe some of her yoga tights? They were about the same size. "And bring some towels back for everyone else," she ordered.

As she watched him climb the stairs to her bedroom, she said, "Huh."

"What?" I asked.

"I'm going to need a new housekeeper. Muriel didn't make it. Hugo always raved about him."

Her casualness about the death of an employee was chilling. Did I really want to have anything to do with this woman? But I passed on the opportunity to confront her and instead said:

"Medical Examiner's issued a preliminary ruling in Milton Throckmorton's death. They found traces of bufotoxin, but maybe not enough to implicate Hector. And they don't know if Throckmorton was already dead when he got ice picked."

That got curious looks from everyone, so I backed up and recited the Reader's Digest version, how Throckmorton may have ingested toad poison because of the bufo in his freezer, but that someone stabbed him after he collapsed on his kitchen floor. I skipped the part about how Linda Henderson and I had found the toad during our little breaking and entering adventure.

"You saying he was stabbed with an ice pick?" Kitty asked.

"That's what the autopsy shows."

"We need to look around here. When Horace grabbed me on the beach, that's what he was carrying. An ice pick. It must be here somewhere."

While the rest of them began exploring the house, I texted Linda Henderson:

"Sniffen ice picked Throck. Sniffen dead. At Karlucci's."

I waited for a reply, but nothing arrived. I checked my phone, and the message screen showed the text had transmitted. Well, I'd done my duty, nothing for it now. Nobody would be out and about until the winds died down.

While searching for the missing ice pick, we also checked the downstairs doors and windows to make sure they were locked. And we decided the wine cellar was as good a place as any to leave Horace Sniffen's mortal remains. It was the coolest room in the house, after all.

After about twenty minutes of prowling around, Kitty finally shouted from the kitchen. We ran in there to see her standing by an open dishwasher. "It's in here," she said.

Lester walked over and examined the dishwasher's contents. "Hasn't been turned on," he said. "Dishes in here are dirty. Don't touch anything." Then he shut the door.

Maryanne was leaning against a kitchen counter shaking her head. I walked over to her and said, "Hey, I know you're worried, but I'm sure Terrell's okay. It's in that thug's interest to keep him safe. It's the only bargaining chip he's got."

She nodded. "He was probably outside. We could have gotten him back. Then Annie Oakley here ruined it all." She gave Kitty a withering look.

"Next time," Kitty said, "you can be the one locked in a room with a rotting corpse waiting to be executed. We'll see how you play it."

"I wonder how far he'll get," I mused.

"However far it is, he'll be traveling in style," Kitty said. "He looted the rest of the money in my safe. Thirty grand."

I rechecked my phone. Still no reply. And I noticed I had no bars. I tried my Weather Channel app but got no service. We were cut off.

"You got a landline?" I asked Kitty.

She shook her head. "It's Comcast, and cable's down."

Not that it would have made a difference. I only had Linda's mobile number, which would be unreachable with cell service down.

Mister Manners put his arm around his daughter's shoulder. "We'll find him. That thug still wants the memory card, and Terrell's his ticket to get it, so he'll be okay."

I hoped he was right.

CHAPTER 63

Port Royal

THE NICE THING ABOUT weathering a hurricane in a mansion is that there are plenty of spare bedrooms, and we eventually crashed at various locations throughout the sprawling house. Although the odds seemed remote that the mob enforcer would make an encore appearance in the middle of a raging storm, we agreed to take shifts standing sentry duty in the atrium with its access to the entirety of the dwelling.

I took the first two hours, and Lester gave me his .38 Special. "Don't shoot your eye out," he cautioned, then trundled off to grab a few hours of shut-eye. Mister Manners, who had identified himself to Kitty as Hercules Mulligan, relieved me around 2 a.m., and I fell asleep the moment my head hit the pillow despite the sound and the fury outside.

We were awakened by a pounding on the front door shortly after dawn. By the time I sleepwalked downstairs, Lester already had the door open, and Linda Henderson and a uniformed Naples patrolman were standing in the entryway.

"You got my text," I said.

"Yes. Everyone alright here?"

"It's been busy. And we have one casualty. He's in cold storage."

The rain had stopped and the wind had dropped considerably as the hurricane trundled north through the Gulf.

"How bad is it out there?" I asked Linda.

"Nothing like Irma. Power's coming back up, downed lines here and there and lots of debris, but not so bad. Good thing it stayed offshore. Let's see this casualty you mentioned."

Kitty Karlucci had already been up for an hour. Like Uncle Leo, she's an impossibly early riser. But the benefit of that for all of us was that she had brewed coffee and set out pastries to help us fend off starvation.

The Naples uniform called in to the city's Criminal Investigations Division and told us a detective, a CSI, and the medical examiner would be arriving as soon as they could get themselves organized. I assumed the detective would be Martinez, the guy who'd been here before.

While we drank our coffee and ate our Danish in the kitchen, Kitty directed Linda and the officer to the wine cellar and told them her story of how the mobster had broken in and how she escaped to the beach only to be captured by Horace Sniffen, who was in cahoots with the mobster. How she had been imprisoned in the wine cellar and how Sniffen threatened her.

"How's he end up here?" the patrolman asked.

"Hector," Kitty replied.

"Hector Morales?" Linda interrupted. "He's here?"

"Asleep upstairs in one of the guest rooms."

She briefly huddled with the Naples uniform, told him he was sought in connection with a suspicious death down in Goodland, and they broke away from Kitty and climbed the stairs to the second level.

Well, Hector, sucks to be you this morning. Nothing like waking up to cops and handcuffs. But I still had my doubts he was the one who clubbed Horace Sniffen, not that the lunatic didn't deserve it.

The sounds of doors opening and closing and cops stomping

around drifted down into the atrium, and finally Linda Henderson leaned over the balcony and announced, "Are you sure he was up here? There's no sign of him."

Kitty pointed to the other wing on the opposite side of the atrium. "There are a couple of more rooms over there, down the hall from my office. Check there."

In less than a minute, Linda and the uniform were tromping down the stairs.

"You take that side, I'll look over here," she said, and they resumed their search through the dining room, lower floor bathrooms, storage closets, and other potential hiding places.

A few minutes later, the patrolman called to Linda. "Found something out here."

"Sounds like they're in the garage," Kitty said.

Curious, we all followed Linda to the four-car garage where the uniformed officer was pointing to a door that opened to the side yard.

"This was unlocked," he said to Kitty. "Didn't you say you guys checked all the doors last night?"

"We did," she replied. "That was locked, as was the door from the garage to the house."

"How about that?" Linda asked, nodding to the entryway door from the garage to a mudroom leading into the kitchen.

The patrolman shook his head. "It was unlocked. I just turned the knob to enter the garage."

"If he got out that way, I never saw him," I said.

Lester and Mister Manners concurred.

"Well, he's not here, and somebody had to unlock those doors," Linda said.

She gave me a hard look. "You got a theory?'

"I'm working on it."

CHAPTER 64

Port Royal

DETECTIVE MARTINEZ SHOWED up at Kitty Karlucci's with a CSI and two additional uniforms, followed shortly thereafter by Detective Mayweather. Kitty showed the detectives and techs to the corpse in the wine cellar while the uniforms prowled the grounds to see if they could spot anything suspicious.

That sounded like a fool's errand to me. Surely anything useful—tracks, prints, whatever—would have been washed away in the storm. But what did I know? Better to look than not to look, I suppose, even if the odds were marginal.

While Kitty was retelling her story to Martinez and Mayweather, I slipped over to the stairway.

I was harboring doubts about Hector killing Horace Sniffen. On the one hand, what did it matter? Sniffen was an asshole, and I wasn't even slightly unhappy he no longer would be haunting the living with his demented presence. Kitty? Hector? Somebody deserved a gold star for bashing his brains in.

But Hector was on the run, a person of interest in Milton Throckmorton's demise. And wasn't it just too convenient that the guy Kitty credited with killing Sniffen was now in the wind where he couldn't be questioned about her account of events?

How could he have gotten past any of us standing watch downstairs? Unless there was a dumbwaiter or a secret stairway hidden in a wall somewhere, he couldn't have avoided descending the staircase, and either Lester, Mister Manners, or I were right there.

The more I thought about that, I realized the only person who could have unlocked those doors was Kitty, herself, when she was putzing about in the kitchen this morning while most of us were still asleep. I'd asked Mister Manners if he'd seen her come downstairs from her bedroom, and of course he had.

I'd confided to him my suspicions and asked him: "Any chance she could have stepped away for a few seconds and unlocked those doors?"

He shrugged. "Maybe. I wasn't paying any attention to her. She wasn't a threat. But why would she do it?"

That was the question. My hypothesis was elementary: If, for whatever reason, Kitty didn't want to admit killing Sniffen, then it would be easy enough to pin it on Hector. But the guy would never hold up under any kind of interrogation. So how hard would it be to shuffle Hector out into the storm, tell him to run like hell and never look back?

But Hector couldn't have gotten past us standing guard in the atrium. The only other way out of the house would have to have been from upstairs.

And maybe he did sneak out on his own. But if Kitty helped him—or forced him—she might want to make it look like he got out somewhere else. The unlocked downstairs doors could be a red herring.

Was that too convoluted? Maybe not for a mystery writer for whom planting false trails was *de rigueur* in her stories.

While Kitty was busy giving her statement to the detectives downstairs, I strolled up to her master suite on the second floor. The double doors were closed but not locked. The room was enormous, at least a thousand square feet, with a canopied bed in bleached wood with matching dressers. At the western end of the room, two sliding glass doors opened to a balcony. I wandered over. The carpet by the doors looked damp. I bent down and felt it, and it was drenched, as if the door had either leaked or been opened during the storm.

Out on the balcony, heavy wrought-iron furniture had been shoved around by the wind and bunched up against the north side of the railing. And that railing opened to a stairway that curved down to a sprawling marble patio below.

Kitty could easily have spirited Hector out of the house this way, then unlocked the downstairs doors to make it look like he fled on his own.

That was at least one possibility.

But stairs lead up as well as down. Was this how the enforcer had broken into her house in the first place, came up this stairway, maybe jimmied the lock like he did on my boat?

I pulled out my cell phone and dialed Mister Manners. "Did you check the doors leading from Kitty's bedroom to the balcony last night?"

"No. She said it was locked tight up there."

I spotted a box of tissues on one of her matching dressers and pulled one out and wrapped it around the fingers of my right hand. Then I grabbed the sliding glass door's handle and tugged. It slid silently and effortlessly open.

I stepped outside and examined the exterior of the door. Not sure what I was looking for, maybe scratches where someone had pried it open. That's the sort of thing they do in movies, anyway. But the paint was unmarked.

I stepped back into the bedroom, slid the door shut, and pushed up the little button to lock it. As an afterthought, I grabbed the handle again to test the lock, and to my surprise the door slid open again. I examined the locking mechanism on the edge of the slider, and when I pushed the lock up and down nothing happened. It had been jammed or broken or otherwise rendered unfunctional.

I pulled out my cell phone again and called Linda Henderson. "Where are you?" I asked.

"Hold on." In a few seconds she got back on the line. "I was sitting in with Martinez and Mayweather. What's up."

"I'm upstairs in Kitty's bedroom. If you can do it without attracting attention, sneak on up here. I want to show you something."

A few minutes later, Linda arrived. "What the hell are you doing?" she asked in a hushed voice. But she wasn't scowling.

"Know a cop who taught me how to break into houses," I said. "Watch this."

I showed her the broken lock on the sliding glass door. "She might have snuck Hector out through here," I said. "That way he couldn't contradict her story that he was the one who killed Sniffen. It also could be how that thug broke in, although Kitty already admitted she's lackadaisical about locking her doors."

Linda shook her head. "Martinez didn't buy her story either. He pushed her on it, and she finally admitted she was the one who hit Sniffen with the wine bottle."

That surprised me. "So, why'd she lie before?"

"Says she didn't. And, technically, she may be right. When we asked how Sniffen ended up dead in the wine cellar, she said it was Hector. Because Hector dragged him in there after she clobbered him. What she's saying now is that Sniffen was threatening them, and she hit him in self-defense and he fell outside the cellar. Then that hit man ordered Hector to drag the body back in there with them."

I shook my head. "She was trying to weasel out of it, hanging it on semantics, hoping Hector wouldn't be around to contradict her story. Wonder what changed her mind?"

We were standing side by side in the bedroom, gazing through the sliding doors toward the Gulf. The sky was still overcast and we could see a band of showers out over the water. But the gale-force winds had subsided and scattered patches of blue sky were now visible in the south.

She pointed down toward the southwestern corner of the house almost directly below us. I slid the door open and stepped out onto the balcony and peered over. The two Naples uniforms were having a conversation with a man seated on the ground, his back leaning against a royal palm. He was wearing a soaked tee-shirt and yoga pants.

Hector Morales hadn't gotten very far.

"One of the cops stuck his head in before I came up here and told Martinez they'd found Hector. That's when she changed her story."

"Quick thinking," I said.

She shrugged. "Or we just finally got around to asking the right questions."

Suddenly we heard a woman's voice yelling from across the lawn. "Hector, Hector, are you alright?"

Kitty Karlucci strode across the patio and knelt next to Morales. She threw her arms around his neck and hugged him. We could see her whispering something in his ear, then aloud she said, "Come inside. I need to get you out of those wet clothes."

She helped him to his feet and escorted him into the house with her arm around his shoulders.

"Now that's a side to her that I haven't seen before," I said.

Linda shook her head. "Give that woman an Oscar."

DEALING WITH THE corpse in the wine cellar occupied the cops' immediate attention, but they eventually got around to grilling us about how we all ended up in Kitty Karlucci's mansion in the middle of a hurricane. Pajama Party? Seance? What the heck was going on?

We had anticipated the question, of course, and expected the police to go ballistic when we confessed we were here to meet a kidnapper. In fact, I was a little surprised it took them as long as it did to get around to it. But, in all fairness, the aftermath of a hurricane, a dead body, a missing criminal suspect—there was a lot to process.

Lester had pulled Mister Manners, Maryanne, and me aside earlier and advised us that we should not lie to the police, that they might be pissed, but that what we did wasn't technically illegal.

"Florida doesn't recognize misprision of a felony," he said, which generated a lot of blank stares. "Means it's not a crime to fail to report a crime," he clarified.

But we had done more than simply fail to call the cops, we'd actively negotiated with a kidnapper. Legal terminology like "aiding and abetting" and "obstruction" and "accessory after the fact" came to mind, and I said so.

"Look, it was an emergency," Lester argued. "We were in the middle of a hurricane. We were given twenty minutes to get here or else. There wasn't time. And you contacted Linda Henderson as soon as you could. I think we're covered."

And that was our story, and we stuck to it, and the tongue lashings we got from both detectives Mayweather and Martinez were endurable. They saved the bulk of their wrath for the answer to the question: What did the kidnapper demand in exchange?

And the answer was, of course, the memory card.

To which Mayweather said, "Yeah, but you gave it to me, right?"

"That's right," the man posing as Hercules Mulligan said.

"So what were you thinking?"

"We were thinking," I said, following Lester's earlier rationalization, "that we had no time and no options, and it was better to get here and see if we could do some good than sit on our hands."

This generated a lot of grumbling about "amateurs" and such, which, really, was the best possible outcome. At no point were we forced to lie about having made copies of the memory card, which probably would have resulted in a nuclear meltdown.

In the end, none of us was shoved into the back of a cruiser with cuffs on. But both the Sheriff's Office and Naples PD issued more BOLOs, sent uniforms to both Maryanne and Terrell's apartment and Terrell's mother's house. And Mayweather and Martinez extracted promises from all of us that we would call them immediately if contacted again.

Interestingly, Linda Henderson didn't join the ass chewing. And at one point, I caught her eyeing me, and she closed her eyes and shook her head ever so slightly, the universal sign that she didn't believe a word of it.

CHAPTER 65

Port Royal

KITTY KARLUCCI CLIMBED the stairs to her room, stripped off her clothes, and crawled into bed. She glanced at her sliding glass doors where a locksmith had extorted her out of four hundred dollars to repair the latch. Lester Rivers had insisted upon that, or he said he wouldn't leave the premises.

And she needed some alone time.

It had taken hours for the police to clear out, carting Hector away in handcuffs. Thank God she'd had a chance to whisper to him before the cops started their grilling. Her message had been simple: "It was self-defense. Stick to that. I'll get you a lawyer."

It *was* self-defense. At least as far as she was concerned. But it never hurts to make sure you keep your stories straight. As for a lawyer, well, that depended on what Hector was accused of. If anything. She'd talked about that, briefly, with Mayweather. He seemed far more personable than that smug bitch Henderson. With Milt no longer among the living, they might not even bother charging Hector in the horse manure prank. At least, she got that impression. Frog poison? That was another matter altogether. Depended on whether it actually killed the sonofabitch or whether it was Sniffen's ice pick that did the job.

The CSIs had bagged the ice pick as well as the champagne bottle.

And they'd made a mess of things, as they always seemed to do, with that nasty fingerprint powder and luminol spray. She desperately needed a new housekeeper. Maybe she should post bail for Hector and put him to work.

Mayweather had played good cop to Martinez's bad cop during their interview. They insisted on calling it that—an interview, not an interrogation. She knew the difference. In an interrogation, cops push a theory, try to get a suspect to admit guilt, or get caught in a contradiction. This was just fact-finding, they claimed.

She kept with her story that the hitman from the mob had shown up out of the blue. But the fact that they wanted to revisit that question was troubling. They obviously had their doubts. Well, Milt was dead, so who was left to say otherwise? Even if that mobster got caught and tried to say he was in Florida to help hunt down Mister Manners, she would just deny it. After all, Milt made that call to New York, not her.

But they were smart, and they had another line of inquiry she knew to answer honestly: How did the mobster and Horace Sniffen know one another? Did she know anything about that?

She had told them earlier that when the hitman originally broke into her mansion, he was looking for names, connections to people who knew Milton Throckmorton. Margaret Bhatia, his father's business partner, topped the list, as did her daughter, Rennie, who had taken over the business with the old lady losing her marbles. But she'd also dropped Horace Sniffen's name because he and Hugo had gotten to know one another through the computer business.

And while she was held captive in her wine cellar, she'd overheard the mobster and Sniffen talking.

"They were both looking for the memory card," she told the detectives. "I couldn't hear everything they were saying, but somehow they hooked up. I know the hitman was looking for him. But so were you, right?"

Mayweather nodded.

"I got the impression they both may have shown up at the same time at Rennie Bhatia's condo, that maybe Sniffen had been skulking around the place and ran into the hitman, maybe after he ransacked it? Would that be consistent with what you guys know?"

Cops were used to people trying to turn conversations away from their own questions, and didn't take the bait. She hadn't expected otherwise. But their reactions told her that maybe what she told them was helpful. Or confirmed something they already knew or suspected. And she wanted the police to see her as an ally and not a person of interest. She wanted their interest in her at zero or lower if possible. She did, after all, have secrets. And the sooner the cops got out of her hair, the better.

She fluffed her pillow, then pulled a sleeping mask from her bed-side table drawer. A little nap, then back to work. She had more murder and mayhem to plot.

But she was restless, and she tossed and turned, couldn't quite get comfortable, and at one point pulled off her mask and stared at the ceiling.

She really didn't like sleeping alone. Maybe it was time to move ahead with plans for husband No. 4. She closed her eyes and began running through her list of candidates.

And that put her to sleep.

CHAPTER 66

Goodland, three days later

LINDA HENDERSON TOOK a sip of coffee. We were sitting in the *Miss Demeanor*'s lounge, and she had arrived bearing a gift.

"And exactly what am I supposed to do with her?" I asked.

"Possession's nine-tenths of the law. Your cage. Your frog."

"She's not being held as a material witness or evidence or anything?"

"The M.E.'s updated the official cause of death. Going to announce it this afternoon. He's now saying that Throckmorton was likely still alive when he was ice picked. Blood on the ice pick we found at Karlucci's matches Throckmorton's. So we'll be officially closing the case with Sniffen as the perpetrator. The M.E.'s concluded the trace amounts of bufotoxin found in Milton Throckmorton were not, in his words, 'determinative.' Therefore, this big girl is free to go."

"And Hector?"

"We got no beef with him on Throckmorton's death now, and there's nobody left to press charges on the horse manure stunt, so we've cut him loose. Last I heard, Karlucci's hired him as her new housekeeper."

"And Horace Sniffen's death?"

"State attorney's office has the file, but I don't think anything will come of it. Hector backs Karlucci's story that Sniffen was threatening them. Her lawyer will cite the Stand Your Ground statute. And, hell, she was being held prisoner in her own home. Seems a clear-cut case of self-defense to me."

But for the past three days, there had been no word about Terrell Robinson. No kidnap demands from the mob enforcer. Nothing. I had written the interview with Mister Manners, and it was ready to go once his grand finale took place. I'd spoken to him every day by phone. Maryanne was still distraught, and he was worried she might become clinically depressed.

I had shared the code on the memory card with Lester, and Third Eye data gurus confirmed that any document so encrypted would likely be unbreakable.

"Your techs still analyzing the memory card?" I asked Linda.

"No comment."

"You turn it over to the Feds yet?"

"No comment."

"Any luck finding the encrypted document?"

Her face empurpled. "How do you know about that?"

"No comment."

CHAPTER 67

Goodland

THE NEXT DAY, MY PHONE rang just as I finished my morning walk with Fred. ID readout on my screen said "Unknown Caller," which ordinarily means it's a telemarketer, but I answered anyway.

"You know who this is?" the voice on the phone said.

It was Mister Manners.

"This a new phone?" I asked. I had his old number stored in my contacts list.

"It's a burner. Now listen up. Missy just got a call from Terrell…"

"He okay?"

"That asshole's still got him, but Terrell told Missy he's unharmed. Then she gave me the phone and—what are you calling him, the juicer?—he came on the line. Wants the same deal, a swap, the card for Terrell."

"Where the fuck's he been?"

"I asked him the same thing. He didn't say, but he sounded like his throat was raw, and he coughed a few times during the conversation, so my guess is he caught the crud."

"So when's the swap supposed to happen?" I asked.

"Tomorrow. Noon. On the Jolley Bridge."

"Wait. That's where you told me to be. To witness your grand finale."

"Yeah. he picked the day, so I picked the time and place since I knew you'd be there."

I would be there because Mister Manners had said it would give me a front-row seat to his final act of vengeance. He didn't say what that would be, but it was also the day of Aggie LaFrance's huge Trumptilla boat parade, the route of which would take his navy of mask protestors under the bridge that connects Marco Island to the mainland.

"I'll be there, but I should volunteer to do this, why?"

"Because I've got nobody else I can turn to."

Like that was supposed to be persuasive? Was I to feel guilt-ridden for the rest of my life if I declined?

"I seem to recall a reaming from the cops last time we did this. Weren't we warned in no uncertain terms to never, ever do this again? Didn't we have to pinky swear?"

"Does that mean you won't?"

"No. Just venting. Where do you want to meet?"

"It's all you, Kemosabe."

"What?"

"I've already got big plans for that day."

"And you've already told him I'd be there with the memory card, didn't you?"

"It's a dirty job…"

"Very funny, but I'm not going solo. I'm contacting Linda Henderson. And I'm asking Lester, too."

"And Missy."

"Whaddaya mean, Missy?"

"You think she's going to sit on the sidelines for something like this? She's my daughter. It ain't in her genetic makeup."

He seemed right about that.

"One more thing, Kemosabe. Linda Henderson. Maybe that could be at the last minute, so there aren't dozens of flatfoots milling around and wrecking our chances of pulling this off?"

He rang off.

I thought about that for a minute or two, then dialed Linda.

"You working tomorrow?" I asked.

"Why?"

"Any chance you could be on Marco, say noonish?"

"Again, why?"

"Be ready and come alone. I'll call."

CHAPTER 68

Collier Wings Estates

LOADING THE ORDNANCE into three of the four pods mounted under the Cessna's wings was a bitch and a half, and it took the better part of two hours to secure the payloads. The fourth pod was easier. It held the message.

Fortunately, the aircraft had been fully fueled when Mister Manners borrowed it from the hangar across the landing strip. He had stenciled new N-Numbers on the side of the plane, just making them up so it would be harder to track the Cessna's real owner. That and the DayGlo orange pods should render the aircraft unrecognizable from the original.

He hated the idea of leaving Missy behind to deal with Terrell without him. He knew he was abandoning her in the middle of a personal crisis. That's what obsessions do, they override your judgment, compel behavior you know is insane even while you're in the midst of doing it. But over the years, he'd learned to read people, especially who he could trust to watch his six. He felt confident Alexander Strange could pull it off. He had to.

He was doing the final check on the aircraft when Missy strolled into the hangar.

"So this is it, the grand finale," she said.

He nodded. "Ordnance is loaded. Just about set."

"You sure about this?" As was so often the case lately, he could hear the strain in her voice, her concern.

"My final act, Missy. Then I'll be done. You'll never have to worry about me again."

"That's a promise, right?"

"My word."

She nodded. "You talk to Alexander?"

"Yes. Just got off the phone. He's on board."

"He know I'm going to be there?"

"He wasn't happy, but it's not like there's anything he can do about it. But, Missy, you've got to promise me something too."

"Like what?"

"Like you won't get hurt."

"Anybody gets hurt, I'll be the one doing the hurting."

CHAPTER 69

Goodland

I HUNG UP WITH MISTER MANNERS, called Linda, then made sure Fred's water and food bowls were full.

"Going out for a little bit, Fred. You're in charge. I'll expect a full report when I return, especially about Mona and Spock. Make sure they behave themselves. But if they don't, I want pictures."

I'd harbored suspicions that Spock might be nearing Pon Farr, the Vulcan mating season. Although Gwenn assures me that cardboard cutouts of Star Trek characters can't actually get it on, when you're in the weird news business it pays to keep an open mind about these things.

I slipped on a pair of work gloves and hefted the cage holding the oversized toad. "We're taking a little road trip," I told her. "You'll be home soon."

It was irrationally anthropomorphic to assume the toad understood me. But she uttered a brief, throaty cluck-cluck song as I carried her out to my Explorer. She sounded happy. So, who knows?

I took a brief detour and stopped at the Skunk Ape Research Headquarters in Ochopee. I'd heard they had a new supply of tee-shirts in stock and mine was getting a little threadbare. I like to mix up the wardrobe from time to time—can't be too predictable wearing an obscure rock band shirt every single day, right? Nothing like a snarling swamp monster for a change of pace.

The rest of the trip to Everglades City was uneventful, and soon I found myself on the bank of the Barron River. I set the cage down in the grass and looked around to ensure I wasn't being observed.

Bufo toads aren't exactly welcomed with open arms, and this bad girl would be hard to miss with her gigantic size. I wanted her to at least have a fair chance at getting back into the wild before some crazed frog hunter spotted her.

Which, I knew, was stupid sentimentality. Bufos are an invasive species and toxic, and if one had killed my dog, I wouldn't be feeling so charitable. But who in Florida isn't invasive? The state is overrun with transplants. The numbers of humans who can trace their ancestry to the indigenous tribes who once populated the peninsula are fractional. Likewise for all of Florida's famous palm trees—most imported from somewhere else. Even the Florida panther is a Texas crossbreed.

Bufos were dragged against their will into the state's sugar cane plantations to eat bugs that threatened the crops, hence the nickname "cane" toads. To their credit, they *are* voracious insect eaters. But they're also prolific breeders, and soon they spread throughout the state. Not their fault that they're toxic. And, honestly, the greater threat to inhabitants hereabouts has nothing to do with toads—or gators or pythons or panthers, for that matter. It's our fellow *homo sapiens*.

This toad might be ugly and poisonous, but she couldn't possibly be as crazy and dangerous to the population as lunatics like Aggie LaFrance and his deranged conspiracy theories. How stupid did you have to be to believe Democrats secretly ate children in pizza parlor basements, or that Jewish financiers were firing lasers from outer space to start forest fires, or that school shootings and the coronavirus were hoaxes? Not even a toad was that stupid.

Of course, a lot of conspiracy theories were harmless. Lester's girlfriend Silver McFadden—if they were still an item, I'd lost track—was a nut about some things. She was a lunar landing denier, believed the government really had space aliens imprisoned underground at Wright Patterson Air Force Base, thought vampires were real, that sort of ridiculous stuff.

But LaFrance, QAnon, and the rest were fomenting a brand of dangerous absurdity that more closely resembled the religious fervor that led to the Jonestown massacre in Guyana. More than 900 followers of the messianic Rev. Jim Jones downed cyanide or were murdered there. It's where the expression "drinking the Kool-Aid" came from and represented the largest one-day loss of American civilian lives until September 11, 2001.

Abe Lincoln said it best: "You can fool some of the people all of the time." Well, historians now claim that's not exactly what he said, but point taken. Con men never have a shortage of marks. And Aggie LaFrance was just one of many shysters preying on the gullible.

Which reminded me of Mister Manners and his grand finale. What did he have planned? Obviously, it had something to do with the massive Trump flotilla LaFrance was organizing. Was Mister Manners going to commandeer the *Jose Gasparilla* and sail down from Tampa with a crew of pirates, canons blazing? I guess I'd have to wait until high noon tomorrow to find out.

And would the mob enforcer show up? Maybe we could save Terrell and bag the bad guy at the same time. Again, nothing to do but wait and see.

I opened the cage. "Here you go, froggy, plunk your magic twanger." She didn't budge.

Okay, toads aren't exactly racehorses. I rattled the cage. "Go on now. Time to leave the nest. Get on with your little green life."

Nothing.

Finally, I grasped the cage from the rear and tilted it forward, and she slid to the opening. "Don't make me dump you out," I said.

And she didn't. After a moment's hesitation, she took a small step into the grass, and I slid the cage away.

"*Adios camino.*"

I'd looked that up just for the occasion. Translated from the *español,* it means: "Get lost frog and don't come back."

CHAPTER 70

On the Jolley Bridge, Marco Island

THE MARCO ISLAND POLICE Department was restricting vehicle traffic on the Jolley Bridge to one lane on each of the bridge's two spans, and barricades cordoned off a space for the massive throng of pedestrians crowding the deck to view the Trumptilla that would soon pass below.

The boats were approaching on Marco Bay en masse, having squeezed their way past Keewaydin Island and the mainland, then ballooning outward into what, in all fairness, was an astonishing fleet of watercraft, most flying blue Trump flags, red Make America Great Again banners, and sporting signs that read: "No Mask Mandates!" and "Masks are for Villains" and "Don't Muzzle Me!"

Through my telephoto lens, I could see Aggie LaFrance standing on the bow of the lead vessel, a twenty-five-foot pontoon boat with twin Mercury outboards hanging off the back. A bright blue canvas Bimini top shaded the back half of the boat, which was filled with men and women, all maskless in swimsuits, drinking beer in carefree disregard of the superspreader event they were creating.

LaFrance had a holster on his belt and was gripping a megaphone. His voice boomed across the bay.

"Stop the Steal," he shouted. "Ban the masks. Stop the Steal. Ban the masks."

"Stop what steal?" Lester asked.

"The election," I replied.

"We haven't even voted yet."

"Right. And if Trump loses, then the election has to be rigged, right? Because he's Trump. He never loses."

Lester pondered that for a moment then said: "You follow baseball, right?"

I had no idea where he was going with that, but Lester usually had a point, so I nodded.

"There are thirty teams in Major League Baseball. They each play 162 games in a normal season. Then there's the playoffs. Thousands of games altogether. And guess what? Every single team loses its last game except one. And no team has ever not lost its last game most of the time."

"Your point being…"

"Losing is part of the game. You can't handle it, you don't have what it takes to play."

I nodded toward the armada nearing the bridge. "Tell that to them."

"These people worry me. They're divorced from reality."

"You think they're crazy now. Wait till the election."

It was raucous on the bridge, too, and Lester and I had to practically shout to hear one another. I let my camera dangle from the strap around my neck and checked my iPhone. No way I would hear it if it rang, so I had it on vibrate. No calls. No messages. No way of knowing if the juicer would show up.

Then a text message popped up. It was Linda Henderson.

"Got Ur 6"

I glanced behind me, but with all the people milling about I didn't see her. Nor had I run across Maryanne Mulligan.

"What's that?" Lester was pointing at an aircraft on a low approach from the Gulf. As it grew nearer, we could see it was a single-engine plane, but something was odd about its configuration.

"What are those orange things under the wings?" I asked.

"They look like pontoons," Lester said.

The plane dipped lower and buzzed the flotilla. People on the boats began waving and cheering as the airplane screamed overhead, skimming the tops of the largest yachts by mere feet, then climbing steeply to clear the bridge.

We could feel the prop blast as the airplane soared overhead, and the roar of the engine was deafening. Some people on the bridge were cheering, thinking it was part of the show. Others were screaming in fear. The herd began moving. People started pushing and shoving, either to get closer to the edge of the bridge or to get the hell out of there. It was devolving into chaos.

The plane made a broad circle overhead and headed back out toward the Gulf, becoming just a speck on the horizon. Then it banked and began another sortie. It was coming in hot and low. The flotilla's lead boats were now only a few hundred yards from the bridge and closing fast. The plane descended like a dive bomber, then one of the orange pods under its wings suddenly popped open and a shower of metallic objects plummeted down, pelting the first few dozen watercraft.

The boat people panicked. Several jumped out of their vessels into the roiling water, and those uncontrolled craft began colliding with other boats. A thirty-foot yacht slammed into a Jon boat, which flipped and capsized. Two skiffs banged into one another and then were smacked by a cabin cruiser. Boat captains began trying to speed their way out of the pandemonium, kicking up massive wakes, leading to at least two more runabouts taking on water. And as the larger watercraft turned away, many ended up colliding with oncoming traffic. All the while, passengers covered their heads and threw themselves on the decks to avoid the bombardment.

I was firing away with my camera, and as the plane once again roared overhead, I tried to capture a picture of the pilot, but he whizzed by much too fast. But there was no question about who he was.

"What the fuck was that ordnance?" Lester was yelling.

I aimed my camera back toward the boats and spotted Aggie LaFrance holding something metallic in his hand. I zoomed in with my telephoto lens and could see him unpeeling it—the bomblet appeared to be made of aluminum foil wrapping something inside. Then he extracted the contents. It was a KN95 surgical mask.

"He's bombarding them with face masks," I said.

Lester began cackling. "That's our boy!"

Mister Manners' plane repeated its wide turn and came barreling in for another run. Now the boats were only a hundred yards away from the bridge, but many had cut back their throttles and what had once been an orderly procession was now utter bedlam as trailing boats jammed up against the leaders of the flotilla.

Aggie LaFrance stood on the bow of his boat, still drifting toward the bridge, screaming at the approaching aircraft. He reached for the holster on his hip, and a gunshot echoed across the bay. Through my camera lens, I could see LaFrance collapse on the deck, a plume of blood erupting from his right foot.

"Holy fuck," I yelled. "He shot himself."

Lester was howling. "I warned him! You remember. I warned him about that trigger."

Two more pontoons of Mister Manners' attack plane sprang open, spraying more tin foil bomblets on the Trumptilla below. Now people on the bridge were scattering, screaming, no doubt fearful they would be the next targets, not realizing that the tin foil snowballs were harmless. The boaters once again were covering themselves and hiding under their hardtops to avoid being bombarded. Several boats accelerated and sped under the cover of the bridge, and in their churning wakes at least two smaller craft capsized flinging their hysterical passengers into the roiling bay.

The plane made a hard left, its wingtip nearly slicing the water, as it roared away from the bridge. Then it began climbing steeply, and the final pontoon under the aircraft's wings popped open and a banner furled out. It read:

WEAR A DAMNED MASK

The plane headed north toward Naples, up the Gordon River, then veered east and began its descent, dipping below the tree line and finally disappearing from sight.

It finally dawned on me: That airpark subdivision where I had picked up Mister Manners in the rain. He must have been preparing this assault all along in the hangar attached to that house. And then I recalled the story about the airplane that had been stolen, how police were puzzled how the thief could have gotten away unnoticed. Now I knew the answer: Because the thief never left. Not until today.

Below the bridge, the flotilla had stalled, Aggie LaFrance's lead boat was idling in a desultory circle as the pilot abandoned the wheelhouse to tend to LaFrance's injury. Police sirens were wailing. People surrounding us on the bridge and below in the water were screaming. And somebody was tapping me on my shoulder.

"Hi. Remember me?"

CHAPTER 71

On the Jolley Bridge, Marco Island

I TURNED TO FACE THE MOB ENFORCER. He was sporting a new scar
on his face, a jagged cut on his forehead vaguely shaped like Harry
Potter's bolt of lightning.

"Where's the kid?" I asked.

He dangled a green motel key fob at me, and I snatched it out of
his hand.

"What have you done to him?"

"He's unharmed. Sedated. I'm a professional, not a monster."

"Could have fooled Rennie Bhatia."

He scrunched his eyebrows in puzzlement, which crinkled his
lightning bolt, and he winced. "What are you talking about?"

"The way you pistol-whipped her. You really should lay off the
juice. Roid rage and all."

"Look, I don't have time for this. For the record, I never touched
her. She was drunk and tripped over her own feet. Not my doing."

I realized I believed him.

"All I wanna do is get out of this crazy hellhole of a state. Hand it
over and you'll never see me again."

"He's got it." I gestured toward Lester.

As he reached out to Lester, Linda Henderson slipped up behind him and with one hand snapped a handcuff on his right wrist and with the other yanked a small semi-automatic out of the back of his pants.

"You're under arrest," Linda shouted to be heard over the crowd.

He was fast. He whirled his elbow around, smashing it into the side of Linda's jaw, and she flew into me and we both tumbled to the bridge deck. Lester was fast, too, pivoting and then striking out with a spinning wheel kick aimed at the mobster's head.

But the mob enforcer blocked the kick with his forearm and grabbed Lester's leg in both hands, pivoting like a hammer thrower to hurl Lester over the guardrail. He was big enough and strong enough to do it. But he must have pressed the release button at the base of Lester's prothesis, and the artificial limb slipped free from Lester's leg. The enforcer, spinning and utterly off-balance, slammed his back into the railing, grasping the prosthesis over his head as he tipped backward, dangling over the bay below.

He balanced atop the rail for a heartbeat, half of him hanging over the water, one foot in the air, the other struggling to retain a grip on the pavement. Then a woman ran up and kicked that foot out from under him.

It was Maryanne Mulligan.

With monumental effort, he lurched his upper body forward even as the backs of his legs slid off the rail, his hands grasping thin air, hoping to grab anything to stop his fall. He still held Lester's prosthesis in his right hand, and I snagged it just as he let it go, bellowing in fear and anger as he tumbled backward, flipping head over heels toward the water fifty-five feet below.

A drop into Marco Bay at that height ordinarily is survivable, the water cushioning the impact. Unfortunately for the mobster, between his downward trajectory and the bay's surface was a colorfully decorated watercraft, specifically Aggie LaFrance's twenty-five-foot pontoon boat festooned with Trump flags—on poles—at each corner.

For the briefest of moments, it seemed as if he would impale himself upon one of the flagpoles as he hurtled toward the bay. But the boat was drifting and he missed the pole and, instead, slammed into the bright blue canvas Bimini top. The canvas sagged under the ferocious impact, crushing the erstwhile partygoers beneath it, then partially sprang back, tumbling the gangster to the deck—atop the bleeding Aggie LaFrance.

LaFrance screeched like a wounded animal as the enforcer struggled to his feet, slipped on the bloody deck, and landed with his knee right on LaFrance's groin. He staggered back up, lurched to the gunwale, then toppled into the water, sinking immediately.

I stood at the railing mesmerized by the spectacle playing out beneath me, wondering if the hitman would resurface or if this was his final act.

Since he'd arrived in the Sunshine State, this unwelcome visitor from Up East had been shot in the head, infected with a deadly virus, chased into the jaws of a raging hurricane, smashed in the face with a scotch glass, and now, tossed off a bridge atop a hate-crazed lunatic while a flotilla erupted in chaos after being strafed by a vigilante in a dive bomber.

"Welcome to Florida, dude. This is how we roll."

I tore myself away to check on Linda Henderson. She had been knocked senseless by the enforcer's elbow, and I knelt beside her as her eyes fluttered open.

"What the fuuck?"

She sounded odd, not just groggy. I touched the side of her face as gently as possible, but she flinched.

"You may have a broken jaw," I said. "My uncle had one. They wire you up for six weeks and you're good as new. You'll be drinking lots of milkshakes."

Lester hopped over on his good leg, and I handed him the prosthesis. He squatted down to reattach it—yes, a one-legged squat. Impressive. He sat beside Linda and tried to comfort her.

"Good news," he said. "He sank and hasn't come back up. So there should be less paperwork."

"Yeth," she replied through clenched teeth. "But I lotht my cuffs."

I noticed Maryanne Mulligan still leaning out over the railing and walked over to her. She seemed transfixed by the turmoil below.

I put my arm around her shoulders. "Good news," I said. "Terrell is safe. He's at a motel. Lester's already phoned it in to the Sheriff's Office, and they're on the way."

She looked up at me and nodded. Then stared back down at the water.

"Think I killed him?"

"Hard to say. He's a pretty good swimmer. But look, if you hadn't stepped in when you did, no telling what harm he might have done."

I was trying to console her, but I completely misread the situation. She turned to me and smiled.

"I think Pops would be proud."

CHAPTER 72

Naples

I WAS LEANING AGAINST my Explorer in the Naples Community Hospital parking lot on the phone with former sheriff's Detective Jim Henderson, Linda's grandfather, filling him in on her injury.

"Her jaw, it's broken?" he asked.

"I'm concerned it might be, but I haven't heard yet. She took a hell of a blow. You know everybody in this town, maybe you can find out. I sure can't. Not from here. They won't let me inside."

Fifteen minutes later, he called back. "Not broken," he said. "But she may have a mild concussion and some serious whiplash. They're going to keep her for a while, make sure she's alright."

I had just hung up when Mayweather stepped out of the ER. He spotted me and walked over.

"How is she?" I asked.

"Got her bell rung, but she'll be okay. Said her memory's a little woozy, but maybe you pushed that fuckhead off the bridge?"

"Love to take credit, but he did it to himself, slipped while wrestling with Lester Rivers and fell off, right on top of Aggie LaFrance's boat." I saw no reason to mention he may have gotten an assist from Maryanne Mulligan. I knew she wouldn't welcome the attention from the police.

"On top of LaFrance, himself, from what I heard. Damn, that must have been something to see."

We were both quiet for a moment, not quite sure what to say next, then he broke the ice.

"You know who he is, don't you?"

"Mister Manners?"

"Who else?"

"If you'd asked that question a few days ago, I would have dodged it rather than lie to you. Now I don't have to. The answer is no, I really don't."

"Could you identify him in a lineup?"

"Yes. But I won't."

I was expecting the standard-issue cop death stare, but he nodded and what could have been a smile briefly escaped the edge of his mask.

"He's wrapped it up," I said. "That stunt at the bridge, it was his grand finale. You'll never have to worry about him again."

"He told you that?"

"Yes."

"Too bad."

That surprised me. "Too bad?"

He shrugged. "I might have to arrest him. Doesn't mean I don't get what he was doing. Damn, I wish I had seen LaFrance's face when that thug landed on him."

"You guys find the body yet?" I asked.

He shook his head. "Not yet."

"How's LaFrance?"

He nodded back toward the hospital. "Got a hole in his foot and a ruptured testicle. He'll live, but his days as a baritone may be over."

Twenty minutes later, I met Lester and Naomi Jackson in The Third Eye offices.

"Let me run this past you," I said. "Right before he took a swan dive off the bridge, the mob enforcer said something that caught me by surprise."

"I heard it, too," Lester said. "That he never hit Rennie."

"Right. And I have to tell you, I can't think of a single reason he would say that other than my accusation caught him by surprise. I believed him."

Naomi said, "So she made that up. But why?"

I nodded. "He said she was drunk and tripped over her own feet. Maybe she was embarrassed about that. Or could it be something else?"

I chewed on my own question for a moment, then asked, "She was your client. You guys run a background check on her when she hired you? You do that sort of thing routinely?"

Naomi rose from her desk and walked over to a bank of wooden filing cabinets on the far wall and opened a drawer. She walked back with a folder and opened it. "We didn't pull a comp on her," she said, then looked up from the file. "That's a comprehensive background check using a propriety database, for you civilians." She read through the file a bit more. "Not too much here. Copy of her check. Name, address, occupation listed as an accountant. Moved here six months ago from New York. Next of kin her mother. Nothing remarkable. Most important piece of data in the file: Her check didn't bounce."

"Just out of curiosity, when do you, what did you call it, pull a comp?"

Lester said, "If we smell anything fishy, if we're being asked to do something that's particularly unusual, or if it's a job that looks like it will involve a long-term relationship. In this case, it was a straight-forward request—go to this address, bring back the memory card, fee paid in advance. She did advise me that Horace Sniffen had a screw loose, but I hadn't anticipated gunplay."

"Didn't hurt the way she batted her eyes at you either," Naomi said.

"That's perpetuating a stereotype. I'm not that kind of gumshoe."

"Whatever you say, boss."

"But back up a sec," I said. "She's from New York. And she's an accountant? Who else do we know who was a New York accountant?"

I answered my own question: "Milton Throckmorton, that's who."

Lester was fiddling with his cell phone. "Know how many CPAs there are in New York?"

"You're going to tell me, aren't you?"

"Over forty thousand."

"And how many have mob connections?"

"Two hundred and twelve."

"You just made that up."

"Prove it."

CHAPTER 73

Naples

NAOMI PRESSED THE buzzer to Rennie's condo. I asked her to take the point on the off-chance Rennie might not welcome seeing either Lester or me at her door.

"And you think I look less threatening than you?" she asked. Naomi was six feet tall, and her muscles had muscles. She had been a daunting presence in the courthouse during her years as a bailiff.

"She sees you through the peephole and she'll be too intimidated not to open up."

But it didn't matter.

Naomi rang three times, and there was no answer and no sounds from inside the condo. The window blinds were closed and we couldn't peek inside. Was she not home? Or was she avoiding us?

"Now what?" I asked.

"Avert your eyes," Naomi said. She crouched in front of the door handle, and I could hear clicking sounds, metal on metal, as she manipulated a set of small tools in the lock. The movies make picking locks seem effortless, but after a few minutes sweat began beading on Naomi's wrinkled forehead.

I thought I'd offer some encouragement. "I read *Lock Picking for Idiots* if you need some help."

"Bite me."

"I get that from my boss all the time."

"Your boss is a woman, right?"

"She is."

"Respect."

"Thank you."

"Not you, dildo. Her. For having to put up with you."

"Love you, too, Naomi."

Suddenly, there was an audible click, and the handle turned. She rose and gave us two thumbs up. "Piece of cake." Then she punched me in the shoulder.

Naomi stepped back, and Lester pulled the door open. I had feared the worst. Maybe the stench of dead bodies or all the furniture ransacked again. But no, an utterly vacant apartment yawned at us. The place had been stripped bare. No furniture, no pictures on the walls, and after doing a room-by-room search, no food in the pantry either.

I opened the refrigerator, assuming it would be deserted like everything else, but I was wrong.

Sitting on the top shelf, the only thing in the fridge, was an unopened bottle of New Zealand sauvignon blanc. A sticky note was stuck to the bottle. It read:

"Enjoy."

We all stared at the bottle for a few beats, dumbstruck, until Naomi broke the silence.

"Bitch is taunting us."

"I wonder if Rennie's mom is back at that memory care place," I said. "Maybe she can tell us where Rennie's off to."

As we stepped outside, another tenant was locking the door to his condo across the open-air hallway.

"Hey, there," Naomi greeted the man. "We're here to pick up some rental furniture, but this place has been cleaned out. You know anything about that?"

The guy was middle-aged, with thinning hair and a paunch. He studied us for a moment, then said, "You looking for Rennie Bhatia?"

"Just her furniture," Naomi replied.

"Right. Well, you're too late. She moved out yesterday. Big unmarked moving van showed up, and a half dozen guys were packing and carrying her things out all afternoon."

"You talk to her?" I asked.

He shook his head. "No, but I saw her right after the movers started carting stuff out. She and her mom left in a big black SUV. It was weird."

"What was weird about it?" I asked.

He pointed to the parking lot. "That's her car there. She left it. And there's something else."

Lester prodded him: "Yes?"

"That SUV, it was a big Suburban, and the windows were so dark you couldn't see anyone inside."

"I don't suppose you noticed the plate, did you?" I asked.

The guy frowned. "You're not here for the furniture, are you." It was a statement, not a question. No flies on this guy.

"No, we're not," I said. "But I we can't tell you why we're really here."

The man rubbed his chin for a moment. He was two days overdue for a shave and he was maskless. "I know cops when I see them. So, yeah, I did notice the plate, but I didn't get the number."

"What did you notice about it?" Naomi asked.

"It wasn't a Florida tag. It said U.S. Government."

Half an hour later, we were at the reception desk at the Collier County Memory Care Center where a very polite and very elderly woman in a blue polka dot dress sitting behind a Plexiglas shield informed us that Mrs. Margaret Bhatia was no longer residing in the facility, confirming what we already suspected.

Lester badged her and asked to speak to someone in charge, and in short order, a gray-haired man wearing a white lab coat emerged from a door in the back. His brass nametag said R. A. Bellamy.

"Mr. Bellamy," Lester said, "we are inquiring after a Mrs. Margaret Bhatia who has been a resident here. It now appears she no longer is?"

He fussed a bit, insisting on looking more closely at Lester's ID. Lester explained that Mrs. Bhatia's daughter had retained him. That he had been here with her when Mrs. Bhatia had gone missing a few days earlier. He once again asked about her status.

"Her status? Well, she has no status here. Her daughter called yesterday and said she wouldn't be returning."

We had caravanned to the assisted living facility, me in my Explorer, Lester in his Tahoe, and Naomi in a sporty red Miata. Not environmentally sound. taking three separate cars, but pandemically wise. We'd parked next to one another near where I had staked out the place just a few days earlier.

"I think they've been WITSECed," I said, referring to the federal Witness Security Program. "The Marshals have whisked them away to Never-Never Land."

"What makes you think so?" Naomi asked. "Besides the mysterious unmarked moving vans and blacked-out SUVs with federal tags?"

"The day Lester took a chunk of concrete to the head, I came straight here to make sure she was okay. When I arrived, an FBI agent I recognized had already been questioning Rennie and her mom. The Feds may be slow, but they're thorough, and they finally traced all this back to the memory card she had in her possession. That's my guess, anyway."

"Okay," Lester said. "But that was just a line of code, an encryption key. Not worth much without the actual document, right?"

I nodded. "Right. But what if Rennie found the document? Maybe her mother had a moment of clarity and recalled where she hid the file. Or something."

"Or something." That was Naomi.

"What do you think?" I asked her.

She shrugged. "You thinking WITSEC, that does fit. If so, be my guess we'll never know."

"That's not very satisfying."

"Like taking a pretty girl on a date and not scoring."

"That happen very often to you?"

She smiled. "Happens to the best of us, Alexander. Even me."

CHAPTER 74

Naples

AFTER NAOMI AND LESTER pulled out of the parking lot, I sat in my SUV harboring a gloomy sense of dissatisfaction about how all this had ended. There were still so many unresolved questions. No story should conclude like this.

To borrow from Bill Shakespeare, if all the world's a stage, then all of what we know is part of a story. And I hated stories that left me hanging. But we were, as often happens, on the outside looking in, and odds were long we would never know all the details that led to Rennie and her mother's mysterious disappearance. The Feds certainly wouldn't tell us. I could try reaching out to Linda Henderson and see if I could pry some details from her, but I wasn't hopeful.

When I'd asked her if the cops were going to provide protection for Rennie and her mom, I recalled her hesitancy before she answered. What was it she said? Oh, yeah: "That's being taken care of." Or something like that. I guess this is what she meant.

When Lester and I visited Rennie and her mother that first time, I had scribbled down her cell phone number. I reached into my back pocket and yanked out my notebook. What the heck? I thought. The odds were minuscule, akin to winning the lottery, but you can't bring home the jackpot if you don't play. I punched the number into my keypad.

She answered on the first ring.

"You owe me," I said.

The line was quiet for a moment, then she whispered. "I can't talk."

"Are you in the witness protection program?" I asked.

"Not yet. Look, Alex, I'm sorry."

"Are you and your mom okay?"

"Yes." I heard a toilet flushing nearby.

"You're in the bathroom. I'm surprised they let you keep your phone."

"I gave them mom's, but I hung onto mine, just for a little bit, but I'm going to have to surrender it soon."

"Rennie, what the heck's going on?"

"You can't print this, not until we're settled into the program. Mom will have to testify. It's about her, not me so much."

I took a wild guess. "It's about Horace Sniffen, isn't it?"

"Mostly Milton Throckmorton."

"He had records the FBI was after, didn't he?"

"Yes. And that's what the encryption key was about."

"And they found the records?"

"Mom remembered something. It was the most obscure thing, an electronic file disguised in some travel records. There was a list of names."

Again another wild guess: "Bent DEA agents?"

I could hear her suck in her breath. "How did you know?"

"Hugo. He was keeping those records for Milton, right?"

"Look, I have to go. This call never happened. I'm sorry, okay? Goodbye."

And she hung up.

CHAPTER 75

Naples

GWENN'S FLIGHT FROM Europe landed on the day of the Trumptilla boat parade, but she couldn't get out of the two-week quarantine at Joint Base Andrews. I had been counting down the hours until I could bring her home.

We spent three leisurely days driving from D.C. back to Florida, armed with Handi Wipes and facemasks for our two overnighters along the way. We took our time and stayed off the interstate highways as much as possible, meandering through small towns. We spent the first night in Hendersonville, N.C., where we ate takeout from Daddy D's Suber Soulfood, and the next evening in St. Augustine, where we chowed down on St. Louis smoked ribs from the Prohibition Kitchen.

She told me about her research on behalf of her Florida client who was claiming some gold Portugal had received in payment from the Nazis during World War II. The drift of her legal brief was that the Nazi war machine operated like a gigantic Ponzi scheme, rolling over countries and gobbling up their resources and using those resources to fuel their next conquest.

But Germany was desperate for precious metals such as tungsten, which it needed for steel production to make all those tanks and bombs and rockets that kept their criminal enterprise rolling.

Portugal had tungsten. It also had a wily leader who refused to take anything but gold in payment, gold stolen by the Nazis from banks and government treasuries, museums and stores, and even the teeth of their victims.

Now some people with claims to that loot wanted their money back. That was her case. She would have to return to Portugal as soon as normal international travel resumed, which we hoped would be by the middle of the year. The first of the coronavirus vaccines had passed their tests, and inoculations were rolling out. Joe Biden had promised that a hundred million people would get the shots in his first 100 days as president.

"I want you to come with me, will you?" she asked.

I readily agreed. I'd never been to Europe. It would be the first real vacation Gwenn and I had ever taken together.

Two weeks after the election, FBI agents executed warrants at Drug Enforcement Administration offices in New York, Philadelphia, and Miami. Fifteen DEA agents were arrested in a "major corruption crackdown" within the agency.

The FBI also announced it had a seized assets from the recently deceased mob accountant Milton Throckmorton. And *The New York Times* reported that a special grand jury had been empaneled in Manhattan as part of an investigation of three Brooklyn-based organizations believed to be engaged in "drugs, prostitution, and public corruption."

I hoped that Rennie and her mom were well protected. The mob enforcer was still on the prowl. Sheriff's divers searched all around the Jolley Bridge but never found his body. And it never surfaced elsewhere. He was an able swimmer—he proved that when he fled my boat with the leg lamp. So maybe he got away.

Police tried to pull prints from the .44 Magnum he dropped

outside Maryanne Mulligan's apartment, but it was clean. And there were no fingerprints on the bullets I had removed from the gun on my boat—except my own. So, his identity remained a mystery.

After the Trumptilla fiasco, I returned to Collier Wings Estates on the off chance either Mister Manners or Maryanne might still be there, but when I rang the doorbell, a stranger answered.

"Um, sorry to intrude," I said. "But a friend of mine was housesitting here. Last name Mulligan. Is he still around?"

The man was in his late fifties, crewcut, tanned, and fit, maybe five-nine with a military bearing. He looked me up and down as if he were inspecting a side of beef, then shook his head.

"No idea what you're talking about," he said, then shut the door in my face.

Since the Jolley Bridge incident, which received international media attention, there have been no further Mister Manners attacks. He told me during our interview that it would be his final act and that once his "mission" was completed, he would vanish.

I never heard again from Mister Manners nor his daughter. There were still the occasional copycat attacks, but they usually lacked Mister Manners' wit and imagination, and police were quick to call them out as imposters.

FLORIDA POLICE AGENCIES weren't exactly burning the midnight oil trying to find Mister Manners, but there were active warrants out for his arrest, not only for his acts of vandalism but for the theft of the airplane he used as a dive bomber on the Trumptilla.

They were all ghosts now—Mister Manners, Maryanne, Rennie, and her mother. Here one day, gone the next, as if they had never walked among us.

Disappearing like that isn't easy. Lester's a professional skip tracer. It's his job to track down people who go missing—spouses running out of their marriages, employees embezzling their firms, bail jumpers.

People usually leave bread comes in their wake, and with a little perseverance they almost always can be found.

But somehow they were beating the odds. And I was happy for them.

The Mister Manners Interview

By Alexander Strange

Tropic Press

For more than a year, a self-appointed vigilante known as Mister Manners has been terrorizing rude, inconsiderate, and annoying people in the Sunshine State. It's Florida, so he's had plenty of potential targets.

Who is this man of mystery who leaves his infamous calling cards when he punishes his victims, declaring, police have said, "your discourtesy has been avenged" and signed with the initials M.M.?

Before he was Mister Manners, he was a sniper in Afghanistan and elsewhere overseas, although it is unknown whether he served in the military or was employed by another American government agency. A personal tragedy in his life drove him to the acts of retaliation that have made him infamous. That and a gnawing sense of frustration that our civil order is being eroded by greed, disregard, and, of course, ill-mannered behavior.

He says he's done with all that now. His grand finale: The aerial bombardment of the recent Trumptilla boat parade in Naples that ended in chaos when he pelted the water-borne parade-goers with facemasks wrapped in tin foil.

What drove him to do all this? Was the nickname Mister Manners his idea? What did he hope to accomplish? He agreed to sit down for an exclusive interview with Tropic Press to answer these and a handful of other questions. He limited the number of questions he would respond to. And he refused to be photographed or video or audio recorded. And he requested that he be allowed to make a final statement, which is included here in full.

Let's start with the one thing most people want to know: Why are you doing this?

It started as a onetime thing. I never imagined it would turn into this. I was buying groceries in Panama City, and I noticed all the shopping carts scattered about the parking lot where people had abandoned them, sometimes literally within inches of the cart corrals. And I wondered, who does this?

I was imagining entitled jerks who left their socks on the floor expecting the little woman to pick up after them, just like their mommy did.

Then an older guy, probably in his sixties, comes out of the store, unloads his groceries into the backseat of a beautiful new Mercedes convertible, and leaves his empty cart sitting in the vacant slot next to him.

It infuriated me, so I walked over and said to him: "Don't you see those cart corrals over there?" And he looks at me like I'm some kind of crazy and says, "Not my job."

Now, I'd just returned from Afghanistan where I believed I was doing my duty to protect and defend the rights of people like him, and his attitude infuriated me. Where was his sense of responsibility to his fellow citizens? So, I grabbed the cart, raised it over my head, and jammed it into his passenger seat and told him: "There, mind your manners," and stormed off.

I knew I was suffering from P.T.S.D., trying to get my life back together, but I couldn't let it go. I kept noticing all the little insults, people talking loudly on their phones, drivers making turns without signaling, red-light runners, and then as the pandemic worsened, morons walking around without masks as if they were somehow entitled to their own rules and screw everyone else's safety.

It became an obsession. And even as it was happening, I knew my behavior was abnormal, but I couldn't help myself.

You referred to trying to get your life back together. I understand you had a personal tragedy. Was that part of what you were referring to?

I don't like talking about this, but I figured you'd ask. Yeah, while I was overseas, my wife was in an automobile accident. She suffered internal injuries, and before the ambulance could get her to the hospital, she died.

(At this point, Mister Manners stopped talking, and I had to prompt him.) But there's more to that story, isn't there?

When I got back to the States, I talked to the attending physician at the E.R. and, later, to the ambulance crew. The doc told me that if she had made it to the hospital sooner, they probably could have stopped the internal bleeding, given her a transfusion, saved her life. The medics in the ambulance—there were two of them, and I talked to them individually—both said the same thing: They couldn't get to the hospital any faster than they did because of traffic. And that people ignored their lights and sirens and wouldn't pull over.

There was a woman in that ambulance—my wife—dying, and people couldn't be bothered to be inconvenienced. They killed her.

That's when I started noticing all the rudeness, the callous disregard, just how self-centered so many people are, how oblivious they act toward their neighbors.

So, you've been trying to even the score, get back at people like those drivers who didn't make way for your wife's ambulance.

What they did was criminal. Literally. Most of the transgressions I've reacted to are minor in comparison, but they're part of a larger problem.

Which is?

I'm not unself-aware. I know what I've done is a bit unhinged, and, for that matter, hypocritical. After all, I'm acting out against people who break the rules and what do I do in response? I break the rules.

Fighting fire with fire?

Here's the thing. Like I said, I try not to kid myself, but we all tell ourselves stories about who we are. While I was in the sandbox, the story I told myself was that I was fighting to preserve an America that I'm afraid doesn't really exist anymore. Kind of a Norman Rockwell version of life, where neighbors help one another, where people take personal responsibility for their actions, where we know the difference between right and wrong and behave accordingly.

Well, that isn't the real world. In the real America, too many people are selfish, greedy, looking out for Number One, and screw the other guy.

I saw a movie about the founder of McDonald's. In one scene, he says that if he saw a competitor drowning, you know what he would do? He'd walk over and shove a hose down his throat and turn on the water. I killed people for a living in the name of our country. But I would never do that.

Your nickname is Mister Manners. It became popularized on social media because of the signature you left on your calling cards, M.M. Are those your actual initials? And how do you feel about this handle the media has given you?

That's two questions. And, no, those are not my initials. They were my wife's. I guess in my head, I've been doing all this for her. I signed those notes M.M. in her memory.

As for how I feel about being called Mister Manners, that was never my idea, but it fits, so I have no problem with it.

You've become an internet meme. A lot of people think what you've been doing is long overdue. How do you feel about this popularity you're enjoying?

That was never my intent. And I've been surprised by that. But I have to say that if it helps bring attention to people's need to be more thoughtful to one another, then I'd say it's a good thing.

Police sources have told me that there have been numerous copycat attacks around the state, people imitating Mister Manners. How do you feel about that?

I get why that would happen, but, no, you don't fight fire with fire.

I have to tell you, what you've been doing, it's forced me, on occasion, to pay more attention to my own behavior. I ask myself, what would Mister Manners do if he saw me doing this? Do you think you might have that kind of lasting impact?

Honestly, no. I think that would be wishful thinking. But wouldn't it be nice if I was wrong?

The punishment's you've meted out—grocery carts on car roofs, Super Gluing windows shut, pythons in motel rooms. Where did you come up with those ideas? And you seem to use a lot of Super Glue. You own stock?

Multiple questions again. No, I don't own stock. But I do have a lot of glue. It's very useful. And I guess sometimes it's just whatever's handy. The python? There was an exotic pet store down the street. If it hadn't been there, I would have thought of something else.

Have you shared your real name with anyone?

No. I can't have my identity known. And not just because of my Mister Manners gig. Some people who know me. Well, they don't. Not really.

And that was your last question. I'd like to make my final statement.

Go ahead.

Life is short. Don't wait for a tragedy in your life to appreciate what a gift it is. Nobody gets through life by themselves. We all need one another. When we work together, we can do great things. Greed, selfishness, rudeness, discourtesy, disrespect—all these things undercut what we would like to believe is our civilization. Don't be afraid to call out bad behavior. But promote civility through example. I am not that example.

Keep up with weirdness at *www.TheStrangeFiles.com*. Contact Alexander Strange at *Alex@TheStrangeFiles.com*.

EPILOGUE

SHORTLY BEFORE THIS book went to press, a U.S. Marshal named Ada Couzins paid a surprise visit to Alexander Strange aboard the *Miss Demeanor*.

"We know you were in touch with Rennie Bhatia. We have the record from her cell phone," she told him.

"And?"

"And we want to know if you've had any further contact."

"Go ask her," he replied. "She's in the program, isn't she?"

"She tell you that?"

"I certainly inferred it from the context of our conversation."

"Tell me about that conversation, then," the marshal said.

In the history of the Witness Security Program, the marshals have never lost anyone in their care who followed the program's rules. Or so they claim. Alexander knew this. Therefore, the marshal's question was revelatory in itself.

"You guys have lost them, haven't you?" he said.

She shook her head. "No. We don't lose people."

"Rennie turned over some documents to the FBI, and I'm guessing the Feds relied on them to make those DEA cases I've been reading about."

"I can't comment on that. Not my area."

"I wonder if she gave up everything. If she didn't hold back a little something for herself. That's how she's slipped the leash, isn't it? What was it? Offshore bank accounts? Probably from that mob accountant, Milton Throckmorton, right? I'll be damned."

The Marshal's Service ultimately issued a warrant for Alexander's phone records. Gwenn Giroux offered to fight it, but he declined. "Sooner they realize I haven't talked to her, the sooner they'll leave me alone," he said.

Since then, he has had no further contact with the Marshals nor Rennie Bhatia.

In other developments:

Alexander handed Kitty Karlucci a ninety-thousand-word manuscript exactly three months after receiving his down payment and Kitty's outline for the romantic mystery, *The Bad Mannered Girl*. He'll receive the balance of the commission when it's accepted by the publisher—assuming it is. As Kitty explained, "even I gotta jump through hoops with this sort of thing." The fine print on the contract—which Gwenn had pointed out—stipulated the final payment was contingent upon publication.

"Never again," Alexander swore, once it was done. "That was way too much like work." He approached the project like a factory job, he said—one thousand words a day, every day, until it was done. This from a millennial who pretends he's allergic to labor.

Through the writing process, Alexander and Kitty maintained regular contact, and said they got along with little, if any, friction. So much so, that he and Gwenn received an invitation to attend a seaside wedding reception at Karlucci's mansion celebrating her union with the Phoenix inventor Omar Franken, the inventor of Stealth Car Wax.

As a wedding present, Alexander and Gwenn gave the newlyweds a bottle of Dom Perignon. They attached a note that simply said:

Killer Champagne

Franken is still among the living, and Hector Morales is still employed as Karlucci's housekeeper.

Also among the living is Tropic Press Publisher Edwina Mahoney's mother who, while hospitalized a second time for complications resulting from her coronavirus infection, ultimately recovered after nearly a month of convalescence. She has completed the relocation of Tropic Press LLC to Florida.

Detective Linda Henderson finally confided to her boss, Mark Mayweather, that Alexander had accompanied her when they broke into Milton Throckmorton's house. And she dropped Alexander a text message that read simply.

"I confessed. No worries."

Which he took as permission to include those details in his notes that resulted in this narrative.

Henderson also finally acknowledged the big secret she withheld from Alexander. It wasn't the autopsy report, as he suspected, but, rather, an analysis of the filmy substance that they had swabbed from the broken glass in Milton Throckmorton's kitchen. It was milk.

Because of the pandemic, Jeff Probst suspended filming of *Survivor*, and even as this was being written it was unknown when the series would resume. Will "Boston Two," Maryanne's adopted handle, make the cut? We'll have to stay tuned, but don't hold your breath. Not because she wouldn't do well, but because we now know the name she gave Alexander (and the police) was fictitious as was much of the background story she shared with Alexander when they first met. Odds are the last thing she would want now is to have any attention directed her way and, consequently, shining unwanted light on her fugitive father.

Gwenn received a call from Silver McFadden shortly after the United States Capitol was stormed by insurrectionists on January 6,

2021, while Congress was certifying Joe Biden's victory over Donald Trump.

Silver and Lester had been an item for a while, and she told Gwenn that she had called him and was hoping they could rekindle their relationship. She also wanted to defend herself against any possible accusation that she was a "total loon" just because she had written that the moonwalk was staged on a Hollywood set and that vampires are real.

"Not all conspiracy theories are created equal," she said. "The goddamned election was not rigged. Anybody who says otherwise is insane and they can go to hell."

Speaking of hell, a location Phoenix is sometimes confused with when the temperatures soar into the triple digits, Sarah Strano, the wife of His Honor Leonardo D. Strano, was nearing term as this was being published.

Alexander and Gwenn were bombarding the couple with baby gifts and counting down the days until they could safely travel to visit.

Leo and Sarah had Zoomed Alexander and Gwenn to share two more pieces of important baby news. "We'd like you to be her godfather," Sarah said.

Leo added, "And we've settled on a name."

"What's that?"

"We're naming her after your mother," Sarah said.

"Alice."

ACKNOWLEDGEMENTS

I owe a deep debt of gratitude to many people in the creation of this book. Foremost to my friend and colleague at Tropic Press, Alexander Strange, for allowing me to tell this story and for his comprehensive notes that made it possible.

Many of the details in this story flow from the audio recordings Alex gave me. He is a meticulous notetaker and relies heavily on contemporaneous audio recordings as part of his record-keeping regimen. Despite the image he seeks to project as a laid-back nonworkaholic millennial, he's actually one of the more diligent journalists I know.

Other information sources include police reports, various news articles, and interviews with Gwenn Giroux, Lester Rivers, Linda Henderson, Kitty Karlucci, and Edwina Mahoney. I made every reasonable effort to reach out to Mister Manners, himself, but struck out.

While creating this narrative, I did from time to time fill in gaps not covered in interviews and notes, particularly when trying to relate Alexander's and others' internal dialogues. He's reviewed all this, of course. When I asked him if he saw anything that troubled him in my extrapolations, he offered his standard reply: "Close enough for non-government work."

These extrapolations extend to Señorita Bufo, of course, who was unavailable for consultation. As of this writing, there have been no reports of a gigantic toad having been captured in Everglades City, so I am assuming she is still out there somewhere entertaining her fellow night creatures with her toad song.

If I have introduced any errors in the writing process, I blame it on the internet.

The names of several characters in the book and some locations and names of businesses have been changed to honor confidentiality requests and to avoid pesky litigation. My lawyer tells me it is important to note that it is pure coincidence if any characters, places, or businesses included in this narrative bear any relationship with actual events that have transpired in this astral plane.

For instance, if your name is Aggie LaFrance, the only way this is about you is if you happen to have led a boat parade under the Jolley Bridge where, after shooting yourself in the foot, an enormous hitman fell out of the sky and landed on top of you. That happen? Then, yeah, this is about you. Otherwise, the name's just a coincidence, like other names in the book.

Thanks to all who assisted me in preparing this for publication, especially my family members, Sandy Bruce, Logan Bruce, and Kacey Bruce, to whom this book is dedicated. Sandy is my first reader, Logan is my copyeditor, and Kacey is my designer. Also, a shout-out to Eric Strachan for his invaluable expertise on the operations of private investigative procedures. A thank you to Anne Daley for her help with aviation questions, and to my former *Dayton Daily News* pals Brad Tillson and Ron Rollins for their critiques. Tip of the hat to ex-pats Beth and Marv Thordsen for their research assistance on all things Portugal. Kudos to my International Thriller Writers coaches J.D. Barker, Gayle Lynds, Meg Gardiner, Donald Maass, and F. Paul Wilson for their continuing inspiration and priceless guidance. And to the many fellow writers in several critique groups who have made invaluable contributions to my writing efforts. You know who you are.

This book is available in multiple formats—paperback, hardcover, e-book, and audiobook. A big shout out to Nathan Agin for his superb narration on the audio version, and a special thanks to narrator and author Tanya Eby for getting it through my thick skull that audiobooks are essential. (You can hear more of Nathan's work at *audionathan. com*).

Alexander also asked me to pass along his gratitude to the growing number of his contributors who constitute the Army of the Strange, with a special thanks to Patricia Freydberg and Ken Marks, among many others.

You, too, can become a member of the army. Just send a weird-news tip to Alexander, and if he uses it, you're in. Write to him at: *Alex@TheStrangeFiles.com*. Shortly thereafter, you will receive a secret decoder ring in the mail. The ring is invisible and comes in an invisible package, so look carefully. And whatever you do, don't take it off. They are easily lost. I know.

If you enjoyed this book, you could do me the biggest favor and write a brief review on Amazon and/or Goodreads. As an independent author and publisher, word of mouth is crucial. In fact, some people might think it rude if you didn't. And Mister Manners is still out there. Just saying…

Lightning Source UK Ltd.
Milton Keynes UK
UKHW011833130921
390533UK00006B/329/J

9 781734 784886